Building Alternatives

Building Alternatives

The Story of India's Oldest Construction Workers' Cooperative

T.M. Thomas Isaac and Michelle Williams

LeftWord

Offest edition first published in November 2017.
Reprinted April 2018.
Digital print edition, January 2020.

LeftWord Books
2254/2A Shadi Khampur
New Ranjit Nagar
New Delhi 110008
INDIA

LeftWord Books is the publishing division of
Naya Rasta Publishers Pvt. Ltd.

leftword.com

ISBN 978-93-80118-46-8

CONTENTS

LIST OF TABLES

TABLES

Vijay Prashad

PREFACE

POSSIBLE COMMUNISM

Misery greets the planet. Social inequality has reached unbelievable levels – where five individuals hold as much wealth as the bottom half of society. Climate change – driven by capitalist expansionism – threatens the vitality of our world. War of grotesque proportions comes amidst human-driven famine. It is as if the five horsemen of the apocalypse are no longer sufficient – untold horsemen ride around the planet, suffocating the possibilities of human life.

One of the great downsides of our current inflation of atrocities is the sense that nothing other than this nightmare is possible. Alternatives cannot be imagined. Mockery pushes aside thinking about a different future. When these are attempted, as they always are by resilient humans, those in power strive to snuff them out. It is better for the powerful and the propertied to see that no model of an alternative is allowed to flourish. It would call into question the claim that what governs the world now is eternal, that History has ended.

T.M. Thomas Isaac and Michelle Williams have provided

a detailed account of an alternative to the ghastly humanity diminishing system that dominates the world. This is a story of one cooperative – the Uralungal Labour Contract Cooperative Society (ULCCS) – in northern Kerala, which has thrived for the past nine decades to build a worker-driven enterprise for economic and social activity. An honest appraisal of a heroic venture, this book tells us that such cooperatives are not only able to survive in a small niche, but are able to grow into substantial institutions of the social life of a region. There are problems in the experience, and these are discussed with clarity. No sense in exaggerating the possibility of a cooperative that has to struggle to survive in a world where the capitalist law of value is the law of the land. But nonetheless, there is no sense in minimising the quite important contributions made by this Cooperative Society to the people who live in its area – in material and spiritual terms. Now, thanks to Isaac and Williams, the story of this Cooperative Society is available not merely as an inspiration to the world, but as a guidebook to the resilience of cooperatives as alternatives within capitalism.

The ULCCS is most likely India's oldest cooperative, which emerged – importantly – as part of the anti-caste movement in Kerala. The founders of this cooperative were workers – the first president, Chappayil Kunjyekku Gurukkal was a mason. Till now, only workers can be directors of the ULCCS. The cooperative emerged in the construction sector, with a pledge – as enshrined in its bylaws – that the purpose of the ULCCS is to 'promote the economic interests of the labourers of the Society'. Despite ups and downs, the ULCCS is a highly profitable cooperative and has been so even as the neoliberal policy slate has suffocated so much economic activity that is not harnessed for monopoly capitalism. The work of the cooperative has enhanced the lives of hundreds of families of the workers. The workers who manage the cooperative take their tasks seriously, meeting each evening – as an example – at 9 p.m. to fulfil their duties as directors. The rigour of this cooperative comes off on the pages of this book. It shows how seriously this enterprise is for the people, and how efficiently it competes against hierarchical firms.

In the ULCCS, the Left has an important alternative model of social growth to that championed by the neoliberal consensus in India. No need in this model to cannibalize the aspirations of people and to throw their hard-work to the mercy of the bottom-line. A close reading of this book shows how effective the ULCCS is in promoting a social form of economic activity against the pressures from dog-eat-dog competitive capitalism. In that regressive form of economic competition, the livelihood of the worker is the first to be dismissed as profit is enshrined as a god. The model of the ULCCS is in direct opposition to that approach.

People who are critical of the capitalist system often eschew books about alternatives that are being built within the parameters of the system because they argue that such institutions are captive to the system's logic. But this is a flawed assessment of cooperatives, which are – in fact – incubators of different logics of life and work and inspirations for what humans are capable of once the fetters of the capitalist law of value is transcended. In his third volume of *Capital*, Marx wrote,

> The cooperative factories of the labourers themselves represent within the old form the first sprouts of the new, although they naturally reproduce, and must reproduce, everywhere in their

> actual organization all the shortcomings of the prevailing system. But the antithesis between capital and labour is overcome within them, if at first only by way of making the associated labourers into their own capitalist, i.e., by enabling them to use the means of production for the employment of their own labour. They show how a new mode of production naturally grows out of an old one, when the development of the material forces of production and of the corresponding forms of social production have reached a particular stage.[1]

Marx's insight here is crucial. The cooperatives are not either inherently mired in the capitalist law of value or easily able to transcend it. They are 'sprouts', he writes, of an alternative, where the working-class is able to experiment with the annulment of capitalist management. Marx looked with great pride at the workers' utopia being built in the Paris Commune of 1871. He saw the workers develop – in the jubilation of setting aside the Second Empire of Louis Napoleon – workers' cooperatives and other means of building a new society. In his book on the *Civil War in France*, written during the Commune that lasted from March to May 1871, Marx wrote that the Commune was the 'form at last discovered' for the future workers' state. It was in this text that Marx wrote of the insights of the cooperatives,

> If cooperative production is not to remain a sham and a snare; if it is to supersede the capitalist system; if the united cooperative societies are to regulate national production upon a common plan, thus taking it under their control, and putting an end to the constant anarchy and periodical convulsions which are the

[1] Karl Marx, *Capital. A Critique of Political Economy*, New Delhi: LeftWord Books, 2010, Vol. 3, p. 440.

fatality of Capitalist production – what else, gentlemen, would it be but Communism, 'possible' Communism.[2]

This book, then, is about *possible Communism*, the possibilities in our time of a future society.

[2] Karl Marx, *The Civil War in France*, Collected Works, Moscow: Progress Publishers, Vol. 22, p. 335.

CHAPTER 1

CONTEXTUALIZING WORKER COOPERATIVES

Cooperatives have figured prominently in the left imagination for nearly two centuries. They have been viewed as important defensive struggles in the battle against capitalism's pernicious effects,[1] as utopian alternatives creating new economic and social relations,[2] and, still further, as pre-figurative moments (working in a strategic relation to the state and other organizations) that lay the basis for a future egalitarian society based on a democratic logic

[1] Karl Marx, *Capital,* Vol. I and III, Moscow: Progress Publishers, 1996; Frederick Engels 'The Condition of the Working Class in England' in *Marx and Engels on Britain*, Moscow: Progress Publishers, [1842] 1953; V.I. Lenin, 'On Cooperation' in *Collected Works*, 4th English edition, Moscow: Progress Publishers, 1966, vol. 33, pp. 467-75.

[2] Robert Owen was a utopian socialist and was instrumental in the development of modern cooperatives in England. He started the failed experiment of New Harmony in Indiana, USA, and was instrumental in founding Rochdale Society of Equitable Pioneers, which established the famous Rochdale principles for cooperatives. Fancoise-Marie Charles Fourier was also a utopian socialist who influenced the 'intentional communities'. William Thompson, also a utopian socialist, published *Practical Directions for the Establishment of Communities* in 1830.

of social organization.[3] In this book, we tell the story of a remarkable cooperative in northern Kerala – the Uralungal Labour Contract Cooperative Society (ULCCS) – that imbibes elements of all three of these positions, but most importantly has simply busied itself with helping change the lives of its members and their families as well as their communities. In this process, it has pioneered creative responses to questions of labour process, membership categories, ownership, modernization, and diversification. Ironically, one of its primary goals – to help uplift the lives of its members – has meant that the next generation have successfully moved upward out of construction, leading to a labour shortage for the Cooperative and a crisis of identity. What was the purpose of the Cooperative given these new changes? Over time the Cooperative realized that it needed to modernize and diversify not simply to stay alive, but more importantly, to create new types of jobs for the highly skilled generation coming to the fore. Our story tells the history of this 90-year journey from a construction cooperative to a diversified complex cooperative system – that includes property development, IT infrastructure development, residential housing, and public works – in which the Cooperative has maintained its values and principles.

Uralungal Labour Contract Cooperative Society is not

[3] For example, the solidarity economy forums and participatory budgeting in Brazil, the democratic decentralization in Kerala, and Hugo Chávez's 'twenty-first century socialism' all have an important role for cooperative forms of production. Marx and Lenin also saw the potential for cooperatives working together in laying the basis for socialism. See Humberto Miranda Lorenzo, 'Cooperativism and Self-Management in Marx, Engels, and Lenin' in *Cooperatives and Socialism: a view from Cuba*, edited by Camila Pineiro Harnecker, London: Palgrave, 2013, pp. 63-89. See also Vishwas Satgar (ed.) *The Solidarity Economy Alternative: emerging theory and practice*, Pietermaritzburg: University of KwaZulu Natal Press, 2014.

alone in pioneering alternatives to the status quo. There is a long tradition of cooperation that harks back to almost the beginning of social relations. People often find collective solutions to common problems. The modern cooperative movement finds its roots in the first quarter of the nineteenth century. In February 1819 'English tobacco workers who had been on strike for 11 days organized production',[4] which was the first time factory workers took over production themselves. In recent times, however, the number of worker-controlled workplaces and producer, consumer and financial cooperatives have increased across the globe in order of magnitudes. Many of these experiences have moved beyond isolated incidents of alternative production, consumption and finance relations to form networks and linkages across cooperatives. These linkages have expanded to such an extent that we now speak of solidarity economies, cooperative market economies, the human economy and civil economies.

The United Nations Department for Economic and Social Affairs undertook a global census of Cooperatives in 2013-14, which is today the most comprehensive survey ever undertaken. There are 2.5 million cooperatives with a membership/client base of nearly one billion. However, a substantial proportion of these memberships are multiple memberships. For example, in France with a population of 66 million, cooperative client/membership comes to around 147 million, over double the size of the national population. Therefore it may be more meaningful to look at employment. The 2.5 million cooperatives employ 15.6 million employees, 10.8 million worker-members and 223.7 million producer-members (and their employees), i.e., a total workforce of

[4] Humberto Miranda Lorenzo, 'Cooperativism and Self-Management in Marx, Engels, and Lenin,' p. 68.

250.1 million.[5] The agricultural sector accounts for nearly half the number of cooperatives (1.22 million) followed by banking and credit cooperatives (0.21 million). Consumer cooperatives, workers cooperatives, education and social cooperatives constitute the other important sectors with more than 80,000 units. While cooperatives exist in all sectors, the banking and credit cooperatives account for more than 703 million of the total 1 billion membership/clients followed by 122 million in agriculture.[6] Clearly, cooperatives are vital economic actors, existing across a range of sectors in the economy and in nearly all regions of the world. The data also demonstrates that cooperatives are present in developed and developing counties alike. For example, G-20 countries representing 85 per cent of the global GDP and 64 per cent of the world population account for 86 per cent of the global cooperative employment. The 234 million persons employed by cooperatives in G-20 countries constitutes 11.65 per cent of their total employed population. This ratio is in the highest proportion in China at 21.2 per cent followed by South Korea, Italy, India, and Turkey with the ratio about 10 per cent. In UK and US it's only 1.3 per cent each, but in continental Europe the ratio is comparatively higher at 7.6 per cent.[7]

Cooperatives are also increasingly playing a vital role in the global economy with an asset base of $ 19.67 trillion and gross revenue of $ 2.96 trillion. The latter constitutes 4.3 per cent of the global GDP.[8] At the national level, the

---

[5] United Nations, Department of Economic & Social Affairs, 'Measuring the Size and Scope of the Cooperative Economy: Results of the 2014 Global Census on Co-operatives', Madison 2014, pp. 1, 2.

[6] Ibid. p. 5.

[7] Hyungsik Roelants and Terrasi, *Cooperatives and Employment: A Global Report*, CICOPA, Quebec City 2014, pp. 30, 31.

[8] United Nations, Department of Economic & Social Affairs, 'Measuring the Size and Scope of the Cooperative Economy', p. 6.

cooperative economy comprises over 10 per cent of the GDP in four countries in the world (New Zealand 20 per cent, Netherlands 18 per cent, France 18 per cent and Finland 14 per cent). However, a word of caution is in order given that GDP is measured in value added terms while the cooperative economy is in gross revenue terms and therefore the actual significance in terms of share of national income may be much lower. Taking this distinction into account, the share of the cooperative sector in the national income of New Zealand would be around 3 per cent. Nevertheless, the data suggests cooperatives play an important, if under-acknowledged, role in national economies.

As regards the regional spread of cooperatives, Asia leads with 1.9 million units and 484 million members, followed by Europe with 0.36 million cooperatives and 368 million members. The cooperatives in Asia (India and China) are largely agricultural cooperatives while the European cooperatives are primarily non-agricultural in nature, which might account for the much higher density of members per cooperative in Europe. With their concentration in the agricultural sector the annual gross revenue of Asian cooperatives is only 3.25 per cent of GDP, while that of Europe is 7.08 per cent.[9] The leading cooperatives with annual turnovers of over US$100 million are largely located in the global north (e.g., the US, France, Japan, Germany, Netherlands, Italy, and Spain).

While these statistics are impressive, the focus on quantitative indicators of turnovers, revenues, and number of members/clients elides the actual practices, values, and characteristics of cooperatives. Indeed, are all these genuine cooperatives that promote the values, visions, and commitments to democracy and egalitarianism? What led

[9] Ibid. p. 6.

to the creation of the cooperatives and what are their core mandates? What are the relations to markets and to the state? These are some of the questions animating our analysis in this book. Through a detailed look at ULCCS's 90-year journey, we look at its formative years of cooperative formation, relations to markets and the state, autonomy, and core vision in order to develop a fuller picture of the possibilities for alternative production relations to exist within the neoliberal times we live in today.

DEFINING WORKER COOPERATIVES

With the impressive growth of cooperatives around the globe it is important to draw a few important definitional guidelines. What is a worker cooperative and why is it distinct from other cooperative forms? The International Cooperative Alliance (ICA) defines a cooperative as 'an autonomous association of persons united voluntarily to meet their common economic, social and cultural needs and aspirations through a jointly-owned and democratically-controlled enterprise' and which upholds the values of 'self-help, self-responsibility, democracy, equality, equity, and solidarity'.[10] In 1996 the ICA established seven guiding principles of cooperatives, which all cooperatives must adhere to: voluntary and open membership, democratic member control, member economic participation, autonomy and independence from outside influence, continuous education, training and information for members, and cooperation among cooperatives and concern for their communities.[11] These guiding principles clearly place economic activity within social relations and break capitalism's separation of the economy from society.

[10] http://ica.coop/en/whats-co-op/co-operative-identity-values-principles.
[11] Ibid.

Perhaps the best example of the guiding principles is a worker cooperative. Worker cooperatives account for 3.4 per cent of the total number, 0.41 per cent of the members, 9.6 per cent of the employees and 4.1 per cent of the gross revenue.[12]

A worker cooperative is the unique organizational structure in which workers democratically control production and self-manage organization.[13] Most often it also requires workers to own the means of production, but there are some examples in which the state (or communities) owns the means of production and either leases them to workers or gives them the right to use the factory or equipment free of charge. Thus, a worker cooperative is a worker-owned and -managed economic enterprise. Worker-owners work in the 'enterprise under conditions determined by them collectively'[14] and share in the benefits and losses jointly. Internal democratic practices are central for worker cooperatives, which means workers must make all decisions about production, distribution, and redistribution of surplus. This democratic organization of production stands in stark contrast to hierarchical organizational forms of capitalist enterprises. Some of the central principles of worker cooperatives are one member, one vote (rather than voting linked to ownership shares like in a capitalist enterprise) as well as the commitment to member

12 United Nations, Department of Economic & Social Affairs, 'Measuring the Size and Scope of the Cooperative Economy', p. 5.

13 International Organization of Industrial, Artisanal and Service Producers' Cooperatives (CICOPA), 'World Declaration on Worker Cooperatives', Approved by the International Cooperative Alliance (ICA) General Assembly in Cartagena, Colombia, on 23 September 2005. http://www.cicopa.coop/IMG/pdf/Declaration_approved_by_ICA_EN-2.pdf

14 Vishwas Satgar and Michelle Williams, 'Cooperatives and Worker Ownership in South Africa' in *New South African Review 2*, edited by John Daniel, Prishani Naidoo, Devan Pillay and Roger Southall, Johannesburg: Wits University Press, 2011.

control over strategic decisions of the cooperative and the principle of equality. As a result, worker-members develop a range of skills that facilitate democratic practices in other arenas. Indeed, cooperatives are schools of democracy, which has additional benefits for society as they help prepare workers with the democratic skills necessary for democratizing society.

The uniqueness of worker cooperatives is seen when we compare them to other cooperative forms such as service or consumer cooperatives. Consumer cooperatives, for example, have as their members, consumers of goods and services who have membership through their consumption activities. They do not work in the organization[15] and the decisions they make do not affect their own role in the production process or the labour process in general. Unlike a worker cooperative that democratizes the labour process, a consumer cooperative focuses its collective decisions on the procurement and consumption side.

EMERGENCE OF COOPERATIVES: INVITED VERSUS INVENTED

Over the nineteenth and twentieth centuries, cooperatives primarily emerged through two pathways: (1) cooperatives 'invented' themselves through member initiated bottom-up processes and (2) cooperatives were 'invited' to form through government initiated top-down processes. The implications of this distinction between member driven and state initiated cooperatives are far-reaching for the characteristics of the cooperative as well as for the broader structural conditions under which the cooperative operates. The two different

[15] There are exceptions to this. For example, a small number of consumer cooperatives have an additional requirement that consumer members work a nominal number of hours per year in the cooperative.

pathways to formation are also linked to the different understandings of the role of cooperatives in social and economic relations.

For bottom-up cooperatives, they have often been formed out of defensive struggles against capitalism's pernicious effects (such as poverty, joblessness, precarity) as seen in Argentina and Mondragon or utopian moments of creating an egalitarian society as seen in many UK and US worker cooperatives and communes worldwide.[16] While in the nineteenth and twentieth centuries these two visions were often embroiled in polarizing ideological debates, they ultimately sought to create similar practices, visions, and principles. Both are driven by values and visions of egalitarianism, meeting social needs, human dignity, and democracy. The polarizing ideological debate has tended to fade and many cooperatives today recognize that the challenges are vast and the need for solidarity across worker

[16] For Argentina, see John Restakis, *Humanizing the Economy: cooperatives in the age of capital*, Gabriola Island, Canada: New Society Publishers, 2010, pp. 191-218; Andres Ruggeri, 'Worker Self-Management in Argentina: problems and potentials of self-managed labour in the context of the neoliberal post-crisis' in *Cooperatives and Socialism*, pp. 235-258. For Mondragon, see Joseba Azkarraga Etxagibel, George Cheney and Ainara Udaondo, 'Workers' participation in a Globalized Market: Reflections on and from Mondragon' in *Alternative Work Organizations*, edited by Maurizio Atzeni, London: Palgrave, 2012; Larraitz Altuna Gabilondo, Aitzol Loyola Idiakez, and Eneritz Pagalday Tricio, 'Mondragon: The Dilemmas of a Mature Cooperativism' in *Cooperatives and Socialism*, pp. 167-189. For the utopian aspect in many UK and US cooperatives, see Robert Owen, *A New View of Society and Other Writings*, ed. G. Claeys, London: Penguin Books, [1813] 1991, and *The Selected Works of Robert Owen*, ed. G. Claeys, 4 vols., London, Pickering and Chatto, 1993. Anthony Webster et al. (eds.) *Hidden Alternatives*, Manchester: University Manchester Press, 2011; Ana Margarida Esteves, 'The emergence of the United States Solidarity Economy Network' in *The Solidarity Economy Alternative*, 2014, pp. 129-149. An example of a commune is the Nieder Kaufungen Intentional Kommune in Germany.

cooperatives is pressing.[17] Cooperatives that emerge through bottom-up initiatives have the distinct advantage that comes with the commitment, practices, and experience borne out of the struggle to form the cooperative. Formation requires a great deal of commitment from the founding members, often through fierce struggles with the private sector, government institutions, and the generally hostile market environment. The practices that individuals and the collective glean from the process of formation leave an indelible mark on the cooperative for many years to come. For many cooperatives such as Mondragon cooperatives[18] and ULCCS, the story of their founding is deeply encoded in their identity and stands as a constant measure against which the members self-evaluate their present experience. Another major advantage of worker-initiated cooperatives is that the process of forming the cooperative imbibes democratic practices both in the institutional framework as well as in the members themselves. Thus, cooperatives that form through bottom-up processes have a deep sense of their identity, firm commitment by members, and learned experience in practicing democracy, collective deliberation, and self-management.

State initiated cooperatives, on the other hand, have often been formed as defensive struggles to help meet people's needs (and quell potential resistance to the state) or prefigurative institutions for various economic activities. For states, however, the prefigurative moment can be either for creating

[17] The growth of the solidarity economy in many places such as Brazil, Germany, and Italy is evidence of cooperatives overcoming difference and working to find networks of solidarity.

[18] Joseba Azkarraga Etxagibel, George Cheney and Ainara Udaondo, 'Workers' participation in a Globalized Market: Reflections on and from Mondragon' in *Alternative Work Organizations*, edited by Maurizio Atzeni, London: Palgrave, 2012, pp.83-4.

alternatives to capitalism (e.g. Venezuela[19]) or for providing stepping stones into capitalist entrepreneurial activities (e.g. South Africa[20]) or as part of the planning process in a mixed economy (India[21]). Here, the state forms cooperatives to address social and economic needs, but states often see cooperatives as means to an end (e.g., reduce poverty, provide jobs, deliver services) rather than ends in themselves (e.g., democratic economic spaces that have value in their own right). In the current climate of globalized neoliberal capitalism the utilitarian approach has been strengthened through global institutions such as the World Bank and International Labour Organization, which promote cooperatives and the 'social economy'. In South Africa, for example, this has led the state to see cooperatives as stepping stones to micro-enterprises and skills development for entry into competitive market as capitalist firms. The major problem with state-initiated cooperatives is that they are often controlled through government bodies, instrumentalized for government targets, and empty of genuine bottom-up support. For example, unlike bottom-up initiated cooperatives where members drive the cooperative, in state-initiated cooperatives members are 'beneficiaries', often selected by the state (either government officials or political representatives) with the criteria for selection tied to the state's goals of delivery and development

[19] Harnecker, *Cooperatives and Socialism*. See also Camila Pineiro Harnecker, 'Democracy and Solidarity: a study of Venezuelan cooperatives' in *Alternative Work Organizations*, pp. 103-128; Dario Azzellini, 'From Cooperatives to Enterprises of Direct Social Property in the Venezuelan Process' in *Cooperatives and Socialism*, 2013, pp. 259-277.

[20] Vishwas Satgar and Michelle Williams, 'Cooperatives and Nation Building in Post-Apartheid South Africa: Contradictions and Challenges' in *Hidden Alternatives*, 2011, pp. 177-202.

[21] Planning Commission on Cooperatives.

rather than community initiated goals. As a result, many state initiated cooperatives do not see the same level of commitment from members, especially in hard times, and do not have the same legitimacy among communities.

Paradoxically, while states' experiences in cooperative development have been chequered, government support is vital for cooperatives to survive and thrive in the fiercely competitive market conditions of a globalized economy. The type of support cooperatives need is for the state to provide such things as enabling conditions, access to alternative markets, and favourable access to state tenders for public works and finance. Many states, however, limit their role to regulating, controlling, and instrumentalizing cooperatives.

Under Hugo Chávez's presidency, the Venezuelan state spent a great deal of energy and resources in trying to roll out massive cooperative programmes as part of its socialist strategy. Venezuelan cooperatives started through massive state programmes, which created the space, training, finance, and work contracts for cooperatives.[22] With the generous state support many cooperatives survived, but the degree to which deliberative participation over a wide range of decision making areas is maintained varies as well as the depth to which members imbibe the alternative principles. For a number of cooperatives the record is mixed with many cooperatives struggling to survive without non-competitive state contracts. Despite these challenges, many cooperatives took root and demonstrated their survival and commitment to creating socialist alternatives to capitalism through self-managed production.[23]

[22] Harnecker, 'Democracy and Solidarity', pp. 103-128.

[23] This information about their fragility and struggles is from interviews that Michelle Williams and Vishwas Satgar did with government

Unlike some of the positive experiences of state initiated cooperatives in an effort to lay the foundations for socialist production in Venezuela, in Tanzania and South Africa the states' involvement in cooperative development has been much more chequered. In post-apartheid South Africa, the number of cooperatives jumped from 1,300 in 1994 to 31,898 in 2010 as a result of massive state support for starting up cooperatives. Wanting to show quantitative growth, government support emphasized legal registration and fast-track incubation through financial incentives, which has not resulted in genuine empowerment based on cooperative principles and values. Rather, government support has resulted in cooperatives becoming stepping stones to small and medium sized capitalist businesses for poor people.[24] The emphasis on numbers hides the fact that many of these cooperatives do not function according to cooperative principles and that a significant number of these cooperatives only exist on paper with an 88 per cent failure rate.[25] The top-down and heavy handed manner in which the post-apartheid state has financially invested in cooperatives has 'polarized cooperatives, prevented the emergence of a racially unified and integrated cooperative movement, and have created patronage dependencies'.[26]

officials and cooperatives in Venezuela in 2008.

24 Vishwas Satgar and Michelle Williams, 'Cooperatives and Nation Building in Post-Apartheid South Africa: Contradictions and Challenges' in *Hidden Alternatives*, pp. 177-202; Vishwas Satgar and Michelle Williams, 'Cooperatives and Worker Ownership in South Africa' in *New South African Review 2*.

25 Department of Trade and Industry (DTI). Baseline Study of Cooperatives in South Africa, Pretoria: Research Report, 2009. http://www.dti.gov.za/

26 Michelle Williams, '**Alternative production and consumption relations: fair trade, the state, and cooperatives in the global South**' in *Journal of Contemporary African Studies*, 31, 1, 2013.

In Tanzania cooperatives originally emerged as an organic member-driven response to colonial control of the economy and were deeply rooted in local communities. At independence in the 1960s, Tanzanian cooperatives accounted for 82 per cent of total exports (the only other countries that cooperatives accounted for larger percentages of exports was Denmark and Israel), largely made up of cashew, cotton, coffee, and tobacco. Many food producing areas were also organized as cooperatives. At its peak in the late 1960s, approximately 25 per cent of the population were involved in cooperatives. But government control of cooperatives in the 1970s and 1980s led to a severe decline and by 2007 this number had dropped to under 1 million people (out of approximately 42 million inhabitants). The Tanzanian State controlled cooperatives and used them for patronage forms of control of communities, which eventually de-linked cooperatives from their communities and devastated production. For example, coffee production dropped from 70,000 tons a year in the early 1970s to 15,000 tons a year in the 1980s and nut production dropped from 190,000 tons a year to 30,000 tons a year in the same period. In the 1980s, the government reversed its policy of state control and decreed a return to independent cooperatives.[27] While cooperatives have recovered some and production has increased, the organic people-driven process of cooperative development has not re-emerged and the cooperative movement is a shadow of its former self.

This distinction between bottom-up and top-down cooperatives is brought into sharp relief when we compare member-driven cooperatives such as Argentina, Mondragon, Trentino, and ULCCS's experiences to the state-led cooperative movements in Venezuela, South Africa and Tanzania. To

[27] Ibid.

take one example, the Mondragon Cooperative Group is a federation of worker (as well as finance, education, and consumer) cooperatives that has its origins in struggles in the Basque country in the northern region of Spain. Mondragon was formed in 1956 with a group of young engineers working together with a catholic priest, Jose Maria Arizmendiarrieta, who had spent years working in the community and popularizing humanist values of solidarity and participation. The ideas of solidarity, egalitarianism, collective ownership, democratic authority, distribution of profits among members are deeply engrained in the cooperative institutions as well as the members. For Mondragon this has always meant that self-management of the cooperative has to extend to the larger society and include community development and social justice.[28] Over the past six decades, Mondragon has grown into a complex network of cooperatives, that include banking, social welfare, consumer and worker cooperatives with over 83,000 worker members, 15 technology centres, and a total revenue of €14,081 million in 2013. It is the seventh largest business group in Spain and the largest in the Basque country. Like ULCCS, Mondragon's growth and survival have required modernization and diversification while attempting to maintain its commitment to its cooperative principles and values. This has not been an easy mix with the degeneration of some of its principles leading cooperative members to raise concerns over the loss of their values and principles in the early 2000s.[29] Members' commitment and the constant self-reflexive process of re-evaluating the cooperative in terms

[28] Joseba Azkarraga Etxagibel, George Cheney and Ainara Udaondo, 'Workers' Participation in a Globalized Market: Reflections on and from Mondragon' in *Alternative Work Organizations*, p. 78.

[29] Camila Pineiro Harnecker, 'Introduction' in *Cooperatives and Socialism*, pp. 1-24.

of its values and principles has been an important strength of Mondragon. As a result, in 2007 Mondragon initiated a massive programme to look at enhancing and deepening democratic structures, member participation, and deliberation processes.[30] Mondragon is self-consciously trying to ensure that its values and principles that place people before profits are not lost in the complex globalizing market economy in which it operates. What is particularly noteworthy is that members themselves are raising concerns about the direction the Mondragon group has taken and are insisting on deepening and extending democracy as part of the revival of its values and principles. However, without a broader movement and alternative markets, experiences like Mondragon will be the norm for cooperatives trying to create alternatives to capitalist relations.

The distinction between bottom-up versus top-down approaches to cooperative formation translates into varying degrees of member commitment, levels of democracy, and capacity to survive without direct state support.

VISION AND MANDATE: EFFICIENT BUSINESS MODEL OR ALTERNATIVE TO CAPITALISM?

Another important faultline coursing through the global cooperative movement is the differing views on the core vision or mandate of cooperatives. Again, there are two primary strands: (1) cooperatives are simply an efficient business model within capitalism and (2) cooperatives are based on alternative

[30] Etxagibel, Cheney and Udaondo, 'Workers' Participation in a Globalized Market', pp. 76-102; Larraitz Altuna Gabilondo, Aitzol Loyola Idiakez, and Eneritz Pagalday Tricio, 'Mondragon: The Dilemmas of a Mature Cooperativism' in *Cooperatives and Socialism*, pp. 167-189.

values, principles, and vision that challenge capitalism.

One of the best examples of the business model strand is the mainstream German cooperative movement headed by the Deutscher Genossenschafts Raiffeisen Verband (DGRV) which has 18 million members[31] and is strongest in banking and agricultural sectors.[32] The DGRV cooperatives do not see themselves as social enterprises with an alternative vision or mandate, but rather as an efficient organizational form representing their members' interests in the competitive and globalized market economy. For the DGRV, the democratic dimension of the cooperatives increases efficiency and allows them to compete more effectively in the global economy. They do not see democratic decision-making as a value in its own right, but rather as an efficient business model. The DGRV sees its job as representing its members' interests within capitalism largely by assisting members with access to markets, and it does not see the cooperatives' practices as challenging capitalism or creating an alternative system of production. Unlike other cooperatives in Europe, the DGRV is adamant that its cooperative members do not need nor want any special status or particular assistance from government. They diverge from the rest of Europe in this way as other cooperative movements are pushing the European Union (EU) to provide special assistance to and conditions for cooperatives. The DGRV strongly lobbies government (it even moved office from Bonn to Berlin when the government moved) and is one of the strongest lobby groups for agricultural subsidies including subsidies for green technology for its farmers. While

[31] The actual number is likely to be less as some of these are double membership. For example, members of agricultural cooperatives are also members of banking cooperatives and Raiffeisen.

[32] This information is based on research and interviews with the DGRV by Michelle Williams and Vishwas Satgar in July 2008 for a book they are writing on the solidarity economy.

it is aware that such positions undermine farmers in the global south, its responsibility is to its members and thus it does not have a commitment to solidarity and social justice that extends beyond its members.[33] For the DGRV, its social contribution comes through taxes (its members paid €3 billion in taxes in 2008). The primary way in which democracy is practiced is through the Annual General Meeting of the DGRV and its affiliated cooperatives. For our purposes, we do not see cooperatives like the DGRV as genuine cooperatives as they are driven by market forces and their goals are tied to profits rather than social commitments.

Cooperatives with a transformative vision are worker-owned and self-managed enterprises that operate on principles and values of collective ownership, one member one vote, deliberative and democratic decision making, and an ethics of cooperation and solidarity. In contrast to capitalist enterprises that place profits at the centre, genuine cooperatives place human needs at the centre of their activities, even if they still have to ensure profits in order to survive. The point is that profit making is not the primary goal, but rather is the means to the end. Mondragon's insistence that capital is in the service of labour, rather than the capitalist formula of labour in the service of capital, is an example of a cooperative system placing human needs at the centre of the organization. The *sine qua non* for genuine cooperatives that seek to create an alternative to the status quo is deliberative and democratic decision making and collective self-management. There are degrees to which democracy is internalized within an organization. Drawing on Pateman's distinction between different degrees of participation (pseudo, partial, and real), we argue that real participation in which members are part

[33] Interestingly, the DGRV supports cooperative development in various countries of the global south and has offices in a number of countries.

of the deliberation over a range of decisions and have the power to make decisions and ensure they are implemented is vital for cooperatives.[34] There are additional dimensions that indicate whether democratic participation is meaningfully incorporated into the cooperative through the range of issues deliberated on, the 'extent of control' over decisions, and levels within the organization that control is exercised.[35]

This focus on meaningful participation does not negate the necessity for delegation of decision making at certain times for practical functioning of the cooperative. It does, however, indicate that members should be part of the regular decision making process and involved in the vital strategic decisions that affect the cooperative. For meaningful participation, members must have regular access to information and the capacity to understand the information, and transparency among the leadership is essential. Thus, the transformative vision that challenges capitalism is through a democratic, pluralist process of worker and popular control of the means of production, distribution, and consumption. Implicit in this vision is an understanding of class struggle that requires shifting power to workers and popular forces such that they increasingly make decisions about the way goods are produced, what goods need to be produced (e.g., what do people *want and need* to consume), as well as how the surplus should be distributed.

The vision of the cooperative – good business or alternative to capitalism – has far-reaching implications for the internal democracy within the organization as well as the transformative potential of the cooperative. For cooperatives

[34] Carol Pateman, *Participation and Democratic Theory*, Cambridge: Cambridge University Press, [1970] 1999.

[35] Etxagibel, Cheney and Udaondo, 'Workers' Participation in a Globalized Market', p. 86.

to become a challenge to capitalism they must develop the practices in their daily functioning, create the culture of solidarity, and empower members to meaningfully participate in the life of the cooperative.

THE KERALA CONTEXT

India's cooperative movement is a model of a state-sponsored programme whose vision is not in any sense a transition to a post-capitalist society. The colonial government promoted cooperatives as an instrument to protect the peasantry from the machinations of usurious moneylenders who took advantage of the hardships created by frequent famines. During this period, the legal framework for setting up cooperatives was established, but the colonial government provided very little actual support. After Independence, the situation changed and cooperatives became a key pillar of the state's development planning. The new Constitution enshrined cooperation as a Directive Principle and the state officially adopted cooperation as an important component of the so-called mixed economy. The most important focal point of cooperative intervention was the extension of credit to the unorganized rural sector as the formal financial institutions provided virtually no services to rural areas and confined their activities to the urban organized sector. The second major area of state intervention was in the traditional and cottage industries, which provided employment to vast numbers of people in the countryside but faced serious adverse pressures from the raw material and product markets resulting in abysmally low income for the producers and workers. The government's cooperative framework not only provided a channel for government financial support, but also got rid of the parasitic middleman in the sector. In addition to traditional and cottage industries, cooperatives were promoted in a variety of sectors such as consumer outlets, marketing, housing, dairying, fisheries and provision of services. Locating cooperatives within the planned development of the Indian economy translated into the rapid and expansive growth of the cooperative movement into a network of 0.6 million cooperatives with a membership of 250 million covering 98 per cent of villages.

It is in this context that Kerala stands out as one of the states in India with a relatively more developed cooperative structure. Lying on the southwest tip of the Indian subcontinent, Kerala is a relatively small state with its population share registering at 2.76 per cent of the national share, but its cooperative membership share accounts for 17 per cent and 7 per cent of share capital.[36] The growth of cooperatives in Kerala is the result of national initiatives and, very importantly, the local traditions of public action and the high density of grassroots social organizations. The pressures from below for fashioning state-level policies promoting civil rights, social equality, collective bargaining, land reforms and public provisioning of education, health care and social security was the prime mover in Kerala's achievements in the social sectors for which the state is famous. Despite its relatively low level of economic development, the state has succeeded in ensuring basic needs to its citizens and a quality of life much higher than other states in India. Kerala has a human development index of 0.625 while the Indian average is 0.504.[37] The relatively higher

[36] National Co-operative Union of India, *Indian Co-operative Movement: A Statistical Profile*, 2012, p. 126.

[37] M.H. Suryanarayana, Ankush Agrawal and K. Seeta Prabhu, *Inequality-adjusted Human Development Index for India's States*, United Nations Development Programme New Delhi, 2011.

Table 1.1: Selected developmental indicators, Kerala and India, 1951 and 2001

Indicator	Kerala	India
(a) Literacy rate, 1951 (%)	40.7	16.6
(b) Literacy rate, 2011 (%)	93.9	74.0
(c) Expectation of life at birth (in years)		
Men, 1951-60	46.2	41.9
Men, 2011	70.0	62.6
Women, 1951-60	50.0	40.6
Women, 2011	76.0	64.0
(d) Birth rate per 1000, 1951–60	38.9	41.7
(e) Birth rate per 1000, 2011	14.6	22.1
(h) Infant mortality rate, per 1000 live births, 1951–60	120	140
(j) Females per 1000 males in the population, 1961	1022	941
(k) Females per 1000 males in the population, 2011	1084	940

Source: AKG Centre for Research & Studies, *Development Report*, International Congress on Kerala Studies, Vol. I.

achievement of social development has a history extending over a century, starting with the social reform movements in the late nineteenth century. Kerala's social advance continued to gain momentum in the post-Independence period (Table 1.1).

The Kerala state was formed in 1956 combining the erstwhile princely states of Cochin and Travancore and the district of Malabar of Madras Province, at which time the per capita income of Kerala was estimated to be nearly 20 per cent lower than the national average. While social indicators in Kerala were better than the Indian average, they were also abysmally poor in absolute terms. Even in the 1950s, the average life expectancy at birth for men in Kerala was only four years higher than that of India (see Table 1.1). In the 1950s, the infant mortality rate of Kerala was 120, very close to the infant mortality rate for India that stood at 140. During the next five decades, the social indicators in Kerala made rapid advances and at a faster rate than the rest of

India. Besides the tailwind of the pre-Independence legacy, the redistributive strategy of development initiated by the periodic Left governments have contributed in large measure to this outcome.[38] These included land reforms, protection to collective bargaining, much higher investment in education, health care, social security and basic needs such as housing, drinking water, and village roads. However, the initial advance in social indicators was not accompanied by a comparable improvement in economic growth, which remained below the national average until the late 1980s. This spawned a robust literature from the latter half of the 1970s, when there was absolute stagnation in economic growth, underlining a possible trade-off between equity and growth and the limits to social sector led growth.[39] These fears were obviated as growth picked up from the late 1980s and has been sustained through the subsequent decades, ultimately raising Kerala's growth rate to above the national average.[40]

[38] Centre for Development Studies, Poverty, Unemployment and Development Policy, *A Case Study of Selected Issues with Reference to Kerala*, Thiruvananthapuram, 1975; Jean Drèze and Amartya Sen, *Uncertain Glory: India and its Contradictions*, Princeton University Press, 2013; Richard W. Frankie and Barbara H. Chasin, 'Kerala State, India: Radical Reform as Development', in *Monthly Review*, 42, 8, January 1991; Patrick Heller, 'Problematizing the Kerala Model', in *Bulletin of Concerned Asian Scholars*, 30, 3, 1998; V.K. Ramachandran, 'On Kerala's Development Achievement', in J. Drèze and A. Sen (eds.), *Indian Development: Selected Regional Perspectives*, Oxford University Press, Delhi 1996, pp. 205-225.

[39] K.K. George, *Limits to Kerala Model of Development: An Analysis of Fiscal Crisis and Its Implications*, Centre for Development Studies, Thiruvananthapuram; K.P. Kannan, 'Kerala Economy at Cross Roads' in *Economic and Political Weekly*, September 8, 1990; Tharamangalam Joseph, 'The Perils of social Development Without Economic Growth: The Development Debacle of Kerala', in *Bulletin of Concerned Asian Scholars*, 30, 1, 1998 and 'A Rejoinder' in 30, 4.

[40] K.P. Kannan, 'Kerala's Turnaround in Growth, Role of Social Development, Remittances and Reform' and Achin Chakraborty, Kerala's Changing Development Narratives, *Economic and Political*

There were three factors that led this revival of economic growth. First, the agricultural sector in the state was responding to the stimulus of land redistribution of 1970s, though with a lag. Secondly, advances in education and health between the 1960s and 1980s were having a virtuous and endogenous impact on economic growth. Thirdly, there was a strong inflow of remittances into the state after the two oil shocks of 1973 and 1979 and the mass migration of job-seekers from Kerala to West Asia.

Though the growth rate accelerated into the 2000s, there appeared two disquieting trends.[41] First, the growth of agriculture subsided primarily due to the sharp fall in agricultural prices after 1997-98. From 1997-98, soon after India signed the WTO agreement, agricultural commodity prices in Kerala sharply fell for a prolonged period. As a result, agriculture and industry did not participate in this period of rapid growth seen in other sectors of the economy. The annual rate of growth in agriculture between 1997-98 and 2013-14 was just 0.4 per cent and the annual rate of growth in manufacturing fell between 1997-98 and 2008-09 to 4.31 per cent per annum. During this period, growth came to be dependent primarily on the services sector. The share of services in Net State Domestic Product (NSDP) rose from 60 per cent in 2004-05 to 71 per cent in 2013-14. Secondly, inequality rose sharply during the 2000s. In 2004-05, Kerala's Gini co-efficient for consumption expenditure was 0.34 in rural areas and 0.40 in urban areas. In 2009-10, the Gini co-efficient was 0.42 in rural areas and 0.50 in urban areas. In other words, the rapid growth of the 2000s had deeply un-equalizing impacts in the society across classes and castes. Worse still the overall growth has also begun to decelerate in

Weekly, 40, 06, 5 Feb. 2005.

[41] AKG Centre for Research and Studies, Vol. I, Ch. 1.

recent years.[42]

Is it possible to have a regional progressive alternative development strategy in these circumstances given the neoliberal policy environment? The neoliberal policies that are being pursued by the central government have further undermined the federal autonomy of the states and makes it harder to pursue an alternative development strategy. Nevertheless, the Left that constitutes the dominant political combination in Kerala has to address the immediate needs of the people as well as provide an alternative development strategy to ensure rapid growth of productive forces while reversing the trend of growing inequality.

The new strategy envisions walking solidly on two feet. One foot is comprehensive social security and welfare measures for the people, protection of the traditional livelihoods, public health and education and special programmes for the marginalized, including mainstreaming of gender. Except perhaps for increasing concern about gender, Kerala's development focus has always been heavily biased towards these social concerns. But a number of new, second generation problems, particularly in the health and education sectors, have emerged and need to be newly addressed within this framework.

But one cannot hop around on one foot alone for long. The second foot of rapid growth of productive sectors so that quality jobs, in accordance with the expectations of the educated young generations, have to be created. Industrial growth based on labour intensive traditional industries or

[42] A.P. Sreeraj and Vamsi Vakulabharanam, *High Growth and Rising Inequality in Kerala Since the 1980s*, Oxford Development Studies, Nov. 12, 2015; K.K. Subramanian, and S. Prasad, *Rising Inequality with High Growth: Isn't this trend worrisome? Analysis of Kerala Experience*, Working Paper No 401, Centre for Development Studies, Thiruvananthapuram, 2008.

energy intensive, chemical industries, upon which Kerala has thus far been dependent, has reached a dead-end. Kerala needs to urgently shift to new sunrise sectors such as knowledge industries, service industries and skill-based industries, which are more appropriate to its resource endowments.[43] This transition cannot be achieved without attracting significant amounts of private capital into these sectors. For this purpose, the Left government cannot agree to renounce labour laws, dilute environmental laws or abolish land utilization laws. Nor does the present budgetary situation permit any competitive tax concessions. So why should capital come to Kerala? The solution lies in building world class infrastructure in connectivity and industrial common facilities as well as a major upgrading of social infrastructure in education and health care. Given the fiscal crises of the state and the three per cent limit for public borrowing imposed by the FRBM Act, what is the Left's fiscal alternative? The answer lies in systematizing and expanding the present practice of centre and state governments to set up special purpose vehicles to mobilize resources and implement major infrastructure projects.

What is the role of cooperatives in such an alternative development strategy? Cooperatives have three important roles to play.[44] First, the social security strategy includes not only insurance and direct ameliorative measures but also employment guarantee and modernization of agriculture and traditional industries where the majority of the poor are located. Cooperatives will be the basic social framework for such reorganization. Second, it is proposed that the three-

[43] Jayan Thomas, 'Kerala's Industrial Backwardness: A Case of Path Dependence in Industrialization?' *World Development*, May 2005, 33, 5, pp. 763-783.

[44] For details on KIIFB, visit www.kiifb.kerala.gov.in and Left Democratic Front, Kerala State Election Manifesto, 2016 and Budget Speech by Thomas Isaac in the Kerala Legislative Assembly, July 2016.

tier credit cooperatives that account for 70 per cent of the total cooperative deposits in the country is restructured into a two-tier structure so that the apex body will emerge as the largest bank in the state. Such a financial institution can play a very important role in mobilizing resources for development. Three, with a huge injection in infrastructure investment appropriate contracting agencies are required for efficient and time-bound implementation. It is here that the experience of the ULCCS becomes instructive as one of the largest infrastructure contractors in Kerala and a model for cooperative egalitarian and democratic ethics.

STRUCTURE OF THE BOOK

In this chapter, we have contextualized ULCCS in the broad theoretical arena of the international cooperative movement. In terms of number of workers and also in terms of revenue, the cooperative movement plays a significant role in the world economy. Despite the well-known resilience of cooperatives, their experiences vary widely. One important factor that influences a cooperative's experience is the extent to which bottom-up processes (as opposed to state-initiated) formed the cooperative and continue to influence its functioning. The ULCCS provides an example of a cooperative that 'invented' itself rather than 'invited' by government. A second distinction we highlighted was the varying visions of cooperatives – whether envisaged as an efficient business model or as a part of an alternative socio-economic order. From its beginning, ULCCS envisioned a democratic and egalitarian social world in which the Cooperative plays a key role. We also highlighted that Kerala's development experience underlines the importance of public action in designing a redistributive strategy of development, which would ensure that at least the basic needs of people are met. Having succeeded in this democratic endeavour, Kerala has embarked upon an experiment which would improve the social security of the ordinary citizens and the public character of the social infrastructure and at the same time ensure major investment in infrastructure so that private investment is attracted to new sectors of growth that are more appropriate to the resource endowments of Kerala. ULCCS, and other cooperatives, has an important role to play in this growth strategy.

In Chapter 2, 'Historical Legacy of Renaissance and Birth of the Cooperative', we examine the socio-cultural milieu of Karakkad, near the town of Vatakara in Malabar, which gave birth to the 'The Mutual-help Society of Wage Workers of Uralungal'. We underline the importance of teachings of Vagbhatananda, one of the most important social reformers in Malabar, Basel Mission and the New Work Ethic, the progressive stirrings in the Muslim community and the national movement. We also provide a comparative analysis of Vagbhatananda's philosophy and social intervention with that of Sree Narayana Guru from Southern Kerala whose influence on Kerala was more pronounced and sustained. We argue that ULCCS was born out of local initiatives of a group of young people motivated by the winds of radical change that were sweeping through Malabar during the first decades of the twentieth century.

Chapter 3, 'The Challenges of the Early Years', discusses the evolution of the Cooperative during its formative years. It is only from the 1930s that the Cooperative started to function regularly and stabilize. Two key issues that we examine in this chapter are how the initial contracts were won and how the activities of the Society were financed. We look at the fluctuations and expansion of memberships and the related organizational issues. We focus our analysis on the gradual strengthening of internal democracy and participation, which is the most important and enduring feature of ULCCS. During this period, the national movement in the region radicalized and the group of young nationalists moved into communism through Congress socialism. After setting this context, we examine the nature of ULCCS's embededness in the radical social milieu of the region.

Chapter 4, 'Post Independence Expansion of ULCCS', discusses the remarkable expansion of the Cooperative, particularly from the latter half of the 1990s in terms of membership, share capital, assets, turnover and gross profits. We focus on four main questions: (a) How did the Cooperative face the challenge of having to rapidly expand the workforce and rely on casual non-member workers without, in the long run, compromising cooperative principles? (b) In what ways has government support facilitated the rapid expansion of the Cooperative, and how did it succeed in preserving its autonomy? (c) How was the rapid expansion of the physical asset acquisition and modernization financed? What were the strategies employed? (d) What was the incentive for accumulation? In answering these questions, we discuss the creative and innovative solutions the Society adopted to each of these questions.

Chapter 5, 'Labour Contract Societies in Participatory Development', examines the way in which ULCCS was a role model to be emulated in the People's Plan Campaign for empowering local governments and ushering in participatory planning processes in Kerala. The campaign attempted to bypass the contractors and undertake public works through beneficiary committees of the people. Initially labour contract societies on the model of ULCCS were encouraged to be formed in order to assist the beneficiary committees and also to undertake local works independently. The chapter assesses the success of the programme and its impact upon the prestige and scope of activities of ULCCS. We argue that the People's Plan Campaign was a turning point in the expansion of the Cooperative.

Chapter 6, 'The Diversification of ULCCS', deals with successful transition of ULCCS from a contractor to a developer that provides not only constructed space but also related services as a package to clients and diversification to other sectors in information technology, tourism, farming and skills development. The most significant achievement was construction of UL Cyber Park, which, when completed, will have a built-up area of 31.10 lakh sq. ft for IT processing activities apart from the related residential and commercial complexes. This transformation raises a number of questions. If there is need for diversification, why did it choose the IT sector? How can an IT facility be constructed and maintained efficiently without compromising on its cooperative character? Are there threats to ULCCS's cooperative principles in such diversification? What other options are available for diversification?

Chapter 7, 'Technology, Labour Process and Labour Regulation', discusses how changes in technology impact upon the labour process and its organization. We discuss the transformations that have occurred in the way in which roads are built and the implications this has on the labour process. We then discuss the construction of buildings and in particular the construction of ULCC Cyber Park. Our major concern is to understand how these changes impact work ethics and the egalitarian spirit within the Cooperative and the consequent threat of degeneration. Heavy capital investment in new technologies poses many threats such as widening the earnings' inequality within the firm, greater employment of outside specialists, subcontracting to outsiders, and impersonal labour regulations. We ask whether the Cooperative addresses these challenges and whether it can withstand the tendencies to degeneration into a capitalist firm. We examine the nature of labour regulations and disciplinary actions in an effort to shed light on whether it is successfully sustaining feelings of ownership and involvement among the worker-members.

In Chapter 8, 'Socio-Economic Status and Working Conditions of Workers', we discuss the socio-economic background of the worker-members, their working conditions, their level of satisfaction, and their aspirations. We begin with the social origins of the workers. Construction workers come from socially backward, economically poor and relatively uneducated backgrounds. Second, we discuss how the wage and other benefits from working in the Cooperative have significantly contributed to improving their status and contributed to their increased well-being and satisfaction. We link this to the deep sense of commitment and bond they have with the institution. Finally, we undertake a brief discussion on the status of migrant workers in the Cooperative and examine their attitude towards the Cooperative.

Chapter 9, 'Lessons from the Experiences of ULCCS', concludes the book by drawing out broader lessons from the detailed history of ULCCS. Here we challenge mainstream economic thought, which does not accept that a non-capitalist firm like a cooperative can succeed and not degenerate into a capitalist firm. We situate the experience of ULCCS to show that this is patently untrue and cooperatives can flourish under the right conditions. We conclude by highlighting the factors behind this rather rare phenomenon.

CHAPTER 2

HISTORICAL LEGACY OF RENAISSANCE AND BIRTH OF THE COOPERATIVES

In Malabar cooperatives have not yet been formed in every village. Only 1817 cooperatives so far have been founded. When considering the area of the district, they can cover only a small part. [. . .]

There are three sets of factors that indeed block the growth of cooperatives. One, the caste and pollution norms. Two, Hindu-Muslim rivalry. Three, landlord-tenant crisis.

Social pollution is an all India problem, but nowhere else in India you can see such an obscene form as in Kerala. It is for this reason that Vivekananda Swami described Kerala to be a 'lunatic asylum'. The system that prevents the depressed castes among Hindus to go near high castes is not at all suited in any way to human nature and prosperity of society. The principal ideal of a cooperative society is that everyone should work unitedly. [. . .]

There is a close relationship between the cooperative movement and matters related to livelihood. Malabar is a

> district spread over 5792 sq. km and 80,98,871 people live here. Of them 19,05,182 are agriculturists. Among them only five out of 100 have their own land. The number also includes landowners who are also actually cultivating the land. This situation underlines the importance of the permanency of tenure on the land for the peasants in Malabar. Unless the land is equally divided among all there will not be prosperity and welfare among the tenants.
>
> Ambattu Sivarama Menon[1]

Ambattu Sivarama Menon, a leading co-operator and nationalist, addressed the Second Malabar District Conference of Cooperative Societies at Ottappalam in April 1924. The audience numbered nearly 800, including 600 delegates from cooperative societies across Malabar. His message reached far beyond the conference delegates to distant villages through a detailed report in *Mathrubhumi*, the organ of the national anti-colonial movement. In the village of Karakkad – part of the present day Onchiyam panchayat which is adjacent to the town of Vadakara – about 100 miles to the north of Ottappalam, a small group of people sat around in a teashop, sipping tea and listening to the speech that was being read out from the newspaper. The teashop and a few other sundry shops had recently sprouted up near the newly established railway station. The teashop had become the public space for an animated discussion group who were mostly inspired by

[1] Ambattu Sivarama Menon, 'Malabar District Cooperative Societies Conference', *Mathrubhumi*, April 19, 1924, Kozhikode, p. 2. Sivarama Menon was a brilliant lawyer from Madras, and a pioneer co-operator who founded the first consumer society in the country, Triplicane Urban Cooperative and leader of the Justice Party. He later joined Cochin Congress and was elected to the legislature and afterwards became a minister in the state of Cochin. (http://en.wikipedia.org/wiki/Ambat_Sivarama_Menon)

Vagbhatananda, the leading social reformer of north Malabar. Some of the participants in the discussion later recalled that it was Menon's speech that inspired them to establish the Uralungal Labourers' Cooperative Society.[2]

The incident at Karakkad was neither isolated nor accidental; it was part of a larger journey that was taking place in Malabar society, paving the way for the emergence of a 'public sphere' of the type popularized by Jürgen Habermas.[3] Within Malabar traditional society, where all social discourse was vertically structured and stifled by caste hierarchies and landlord domination, the teashops, libraries and market centres emerged as spaces of horizontal democratic communication. By the time of Independence in 1947, the teashops – where the agricultural labourers squatted around newspaper readers before the day's labour began – and the *beedi-pan* shops – where the newspaper reader and the *beedi* roller entered into eloquent dialogue with listeners and customers – had become the stereotyped image of inquisitive Malayalam speaking people.

The history of the printing press in Kerala dates back to the first half of the nineteenth century and is crucial to understanding the history of social and political mobilization.

2 Interviews with Punneri Nanu, who was a close aide to Chappayil Kunjyekku Gurukkal, the first member and President of Uralungal Labourers Cooperative Society during 1940s and 1950s, dt. 12.03.2012. This incident has also been independently corroborated by Karakkattil Kumaran, who belonged to the second generation of co-operators, closely connected to the pioneers dt. 04.01.2013. These testimonies prompted us to search the back volumes of *Mathrubhumi* newspaper for 1924. To our great surprise we stumbled upon a fairly lengthy report on the Second Malabar District Conference of Cooperatives, referred to in the interview and quoted at length at the beginning of the present chapter.

3 Robin Jeffrey, 'Testing Concepts about Print, Newspapers, and Politics: Kerala, India, 1800-2009', *The Journal of Asian Studies*, 68, 2 (May) 2009, pp. 465-489.

Herman Gundert, the pioneer missionary from Basel Evangelical Mission (hereafter Basel Mission) founded the first press in 1838 in Thalassery. In addition to Missionary tracts, the press published grammar books, lexicons and secular books. In 1847, *Rajayasamacharam*, the first newspaper in Malabar, started publication, but it was only during the twentieth century that newspapers began to flourish. Many of them such as *Mithavadi* (which means 'The Moderate') founded by Moorkottu Kumaran in Thalassery in 1907, *Nayar Samudaya Pariskhari* (1916), and *Samudaya Deepika* (1916) from Kannur were largely concerned with social reforms in their communities. The nationalist upsurge in the 1920s also witnessed the emergence of a large number of periodicals and newspapers popularising social reforms and nationalism. Among the most important was *Mathrubhumi* (1923), which was considered the mouthpiece of the Kerala Pradesh Congress Committee (KPCC). In 1924 *Al-Ameen* from Kozhikode was founded by Mohammed Abdurahiman and *Kerala Kesari* from Vadakara (near Karakkad) by Moyarath Sankaran. Both became prominent nationalist newspapers in Malabar.

The dramatic increase in the number of periodicals, journals, and newspapers was vital to the spread of social reform and nationalist ideas. While the circulation of these publications was limited, each copy was read and reread by multiple people and subjected to discussions and oral dispersal to the mass of people. Malabar was waking up to broader social issues through the circulation of ideas in newspapers and journals.[4]

[4] Puthuppally Raghavan, *Kerala Pathrapravarthana Charithram*, Kerala Sahithya Academy, Thrissur, 1985, and G. Priyadarshan, *Malayala Pathrapravarthanam Prarambhaswaroopam*, Kerala Sahithya Academy, Thrissur 1982.

TRADITIONAL SOCIETY IN MALABAR

The significance of the great awakening, popularly known as the Kerala renaissance, can be appreciated only if one understands centuries of social stagnation and eclipse of innovation and enterprise, even of scholarship, that resulted from the stranglehold of the caste and *jenmi* (landlord) systems. Menon's speech to the 1924 cooperative conference (presented in the opening paragraphs of the chapter), lucidly captures the social and economic bondages of traditional society. Caste norms and practices permeated every aspect of public and private life, deeply entrenching a system of domination and control.

The caste system in Kerala had been extended to its most absurd limit in the code determining the mandatory 'pollution' distance between different castes. The pollution distance of nairs to brahmins was 16 feet; that of intermediate caste such as ezhavas or thiyyas was 32 feet; that of the serf castes such as cherumas or pulayas was 64 feet. Even just the sight of the lowest of the outcastes, such as the adivasis, would defile the brahmins. Temple entry as well as the right to travel on public roads was denied to the lower castes. There were also elaborate systems of caste rituals, norms of public behaviour, strict dress codes, and even appropriate speech that each caste was meant to follow. It is little wonder that Swami Vivekananda described Kerala as a lunatic asylum. The rigid and extreme caste system became totally untenable and irrational with the growing commercialization of the economy, the rise of modern classes, and the spread of education.

With the advent of Western powers in the sixteenth century and the concomitant growth of commerce, a process of political centralization took root in the north, south and central regions of Kerala.[5] In Travancore in the south, a centralized monarchy emerged by demolishing the traditional chieftains and taking over their landed property. The new centralized monarchical state eventually gave property rights to tenants and cultivators in the wastelands creating a new class of rich cultivators who further prospered by utilizing the opportunities created by the commercialized economy. By the late nineteenth century Travancore had developed a complex class structure with modern classes of traders, small-scale industrialists, middle class, and wage labourers. Cochin state in the central region of Kerala had a similar, though much weaker, process of monarchical rule and class formation.

In contrast to Travancore and Cochin, the centralization of state power in Malabar was slower and interrupted by the Mysorean invasions. The victory of Tipu Sultan was a devastating loss to the traditional chieftains and *jenmis* of Malabar, most of whom fled to the southern regions for safety. Inadvertently, Tipu Sultan's victory liberated tenants from the burden of the *jenmi* system, and many converted to Islam. The defeat of Tipu by the British brought yet another major shock: Malabar was brought under direct British rule, initially as a part of the Bombay Presidency and after a brief period under a district of the Madras Presidency. Under British rule, the traditional chieftains were pensioned off, but allowed to keep large tracts of lands. The *jenmis*, who had fled to the south, were reinstated with absolute property rights under customary British law. As a result, *jenmis*' power increased to the detriment of tenants, who could now be evicted from their

[5] P.K. Michael Tharakan, 'History as Development Experience: Disaggregated and Deconstructed Analysis of Kerala', Ph.D. Thesis, School of Social Sciences, Mahathma Gandhi University, 1997, and 'Development of Colonial Economy in Kerala, 1850-1947', in 'Perspectives on Kerala History. The second Millennium', State Editor, Kerala Gazetteers Department, 1999.

lands or have their rents increased at the will of the landlord. Thus, under British rule, tenants lost even the little rights they enjoyed under the traditional caste system.

The traditional social system in Kerala was characterized by three pillars of domination: the upper castes (i.e. brahmins) in social relations, the landlords or *jenmis* in economic relations, and feudal chieftains in political relations.[6] These three pillars of domination in the social, economic, and political spheres mutually reinforced each other through the alliance of class-caste hierarchical identities. British colonial rule grafted onto this traditional social structure making the system extremely oppressive for the lower castes, the landless, and the subjugated.

The colonial administration in Malabar did not challenge the vicious caste domination of the Malabar region, but rather adopted a neutral stance to the denial of civil rights of the majority of people, justifying their position on the grounds that caste domination was intertwined with religious beliefs. In this way, colonial rule was superimposed on traditional social and economic relations. Indeed, colonial subjugation was reinforced by the traditional *jenmi* system. The system of governance undertaken by the British in Malabar identified the *jenmis* as their 'faithful associates' elevating them into social and economic prominence by conferring the *jenmis* absolute land rights. The rulers of Travancore Kingdom in the south, by contrast, were under indirect British rule and adopted a firmer line against caste domination. Under pressure from missionaries and protest movements from below, the princely rulers were forced to modify caste norms and practices. Thus, in the princely states of Travancore and Cochin, caste norms

[6] E.M.S. Namboodiripad, *Keralam: Malayalikalude Mathrubhumi*, Trivandrum: Chintha Publishers, and *Kerala Yesterday, Today, Tomorrow*, Calcutta: National Book Agency.

and practices softened relative to colonial-ruled Malabar.

The new land tenure system introduced by the British in Malabar deepened social cleavages and increased the power of the elite. The traditional *jenmis*, who were mostly Namboodiris, and chieftains monopolized the land. Under them came a stratum of superior tenants (also known as *kanam* tenants) under different types of tenures who leased the land from landlords for an annual lump sum payment. The third tier of the agrarian system was the stratum of tenants-at-will (*orverum pattakkar*) who subleased land from the *kanam* tenants. This lower stratum of tenants enjoyed no rights whatsoever and the heavy surplus extraction left them with miserable subsistence. The fourth and lowest stratum was the class of agricultural labourers, who squatted on the lands of landlords and tenants, and worked under varying degrees of servitude.[7]

From the settlement reports and population census data, we have collated the distribution of land by caste for two *desams*[8] of Vellikulangara and Rayarangoth, which constitute the immediate area surrounding our cooperative society. As we can see from Table 2.1 the upper castes constitute hardly 15 per cent of the population but controlled 82 per cent of the land. In contrast, lower castes, the majority of whom are thiyyas, constitute 70 per cent of the population but controlled only 4.6 per cent of the land.

Of the 96 upper caste landholders who held 868 acres of land, Vellikulangara Devaswam Uraima alone accounted for 388 acres or 37 per cent of the total land. The second largest landlord was Kadathanattu Valiya Raja who owned 220 acres or 21 per cent of the total land. Throughout the region,

[7] T.C. Varghese, *Agrarian Change and Economic Consequences*, New Delhi: Allied Publishers, 1970.

[8] *Desams* are minor administrative units.

Table 2.1: Distribution of population and cultivable land by caste of two Desoms in Malabar

Caste/ Community	No. of people	Percent	No. of land holders	Area of land (Acres)	Percent share of land
Upper castes	348	15.0	96	868	82.43
Lower castes	1628	70.2	22	49	4.64
Muslim	344	14.8	52	136	12.93
Christian	0	0	0	0	0
Total	2320	100.0	10	1052	100

Source: Descriptive Memoir of Rayarangoth Desam No. 12 of the Kurumbranad Taluk, Surveyand settlement register of Vellikulangara Desam No. 10 of the Kurumbranad Taluk and Census of India 1901, Regional Archives, Kozhikode.

devaswams were very often the largest landowners. *Devaswam* land was administered by hereditary *uralars* who for practical purpose were the landlords. There were many instances where *devaswam* land was transformed into *brahmaswam* land and later into *jenmam* land. The etymology of Uralungal – which the cooperative is named after – is related to the hereditary *uralars*[9] who dominated the area.

The sharp contrast between the agrarian structure and class formation in Travancore and Malabar is very important in explaining the divergent economic and social trajectories of the two regions. The pace of commercialization of agriculture and the emergence of modern classes was much faster in Travancore compared to Malabar. The new, modern social strata of small traders, professionals, and the middle class formed the backbone of the powerful social reform movements in Travancore. In other words, class formation translated into struggles for social reform. In the absence of relatively powerful modern classes, the social reform movements in Malabar were relatively weaker and often subsumed under the pan-Kerala social reform movements that emanated from

[9] *Uralars* were hereditary custodians of temples.

the south. The peasant and national anti-colonial movements played a more direct role in carrying forward the social reforms in Malabar. Our brief discussion below of the life and ideology of Vagbhatananda Guru, the source of inspiration for establishment of the first labour cooperative at Uralungal, and the comparison to Sree Narayana Guru illustrates this difference between the way social reform struggles manifested in north and south Kerala.[10]

SREE NARAYANA GURU AND KERALA'S RENAISSANCE

A close examination of the socio-religious movements in Kerala reveals a large number of regional and localized protest movements. This is particularly true of the ezhava social reform movement. In Travancore the ezhava reform movement was subsumed under the broad umbrella of Sree Narayana Dharma Paripalana Yogam (SNDP) during the initial decades of the twentieth century. As its name implies, SNDP was founded to propagate the *dharma*[11] of Sree Narayana, the most powerful personality of the Kerala renaissance. Philosophically Sree Narayana believed in *advaita's* oneness of self and god, or *brahma*. *Brahma* is the ultimate truth and the phenomenal world is maya or illusion. The traditional interpretation of *advaita* sees social reality as only an illusion, and therefore something that could be ignored. However, Sree Narayana Guru born into the ezhava lower caste, could not ignore the reality of caste oppression simply as an illusion.

[10] See Divya Kannan, 'Social Reform in Twentieth Century Malabar: Vagbhatananda and the Atma Vidya Sangham', unpublished M. Phil. Dissertation submitted to Centre for Historical Studies, School of Social Sciences, Jawaharlal Nehru University, New Delhi, 2012, for a detailed discussion of Vagbhatananda from a comparative perspective.

[11] *Dharma* is a complex term, but here it is used to refer to the message of 'responsibility' or 'duty' propagated by Sree Narayana Guru.

On the contrary, he used his philosophical understanding to justify resisting and transforming the caste system. Since caste oppression was part of the maya and not the ultimate truth, it could be changed. Sree Narayana Guru argued that it was the *dharma* of the oppressed to change caste oppression, which would enable individual victims of caste oppression to realize the ultimate bliss. Through this reinterpretation of *advaita* he converted it in to a powerful liberation philosophy in the struggle against caste oppression.[12]

Though an exponent of *advaita* philosophy and a traveller along the ultimate path of *jnana-marga* (path of knowledge) Sree Narayana Guru was willing to advise ordinary mortals on the path of *bhakthi-marga* (path of piety). For the travellers of the *bhakthi-marga* he consecrated temples and transformed ceremonies and rituals from forms of caste domination into spiritual practices open to everyone. Though these programmes were ostensibly conservative in form, they also challenged the caste hierarchy of enshrined practices. For example, Sree Narayana Guru challenged the exclusive right of upper castes to consecrate idols when he consecrated the Siva idol in Aruvippuram temple. He wittily defended the right of the lower castes to consecrate an idol of Siva, instead of traditional folk gods, by arguing that he consecrated an ezhava Siva. This event marked his initiation into socio-religious reforms and the end of his solitary ascetic pursuit of salvation. In a powerful statement that undermines caste domination he wrote the following inscription on the walls of the Aruvippuram temple:

[12] T.M. Thomas Isaac and P.K. Michael Tharakan, *Sree Narayana Movement in Travancore, 1888-1939: A Study of Social Basis and Ideological Reproduction*, Working Paper 214, Centre For Development Studies, Trivandrum, 1986.

Here is a model abode
Where men live like brothers
Bereft of the prejudice of caste
Or rancour of religious difference

Sree Narayana Guru's deep scholarship in the scriptures gave him legitimacy among the various strands of ezhavas social movements, many of which also sought to strengthen their own legitimacy through proximity to Sree Narayana Guru. Perhaps his most famous dictum was 'One caste, one religion, one god for all,' which underlined his universalistic approach that went beyond narrow ezhava caste boundaries. Sahodaran Ayyappan, one of his most beloved disciples, paraphrased it into a new dictum 'No caste, no religion, no god for man.' Sree Narayana Guru responded to those who came to complain about Ayyappan's sacrilegious dictum by asking 'What is Ayyappan's karma?' He, thus, implied that Ayyappan was not to be judged by what he professed but by what he practised. Ayyappan's pursuit was the same as that of the Sree Narayana Guru: that is, the creation of a casteless society and spiritualism beyond the bounds of any one particular religion.

Sree Narayana Guru's teachings were, thus, a broad envelope that could encompass varied trends such as reformers who were lukewarm to the nationalist movement like Kumaranasan (the harbinger bard of the renaissance), to ardent nationalists like T.K. Madhavan (the organizer of Vaikom Satyagraha for the right to walk on temple roads), to radical agitators like Sahodaran Ayyappan (who made the first poetic reference to the Soviet Revolution in Malayalam literature). Despite the fact that he was a deeply religious ascetic within the Hindu philosophical tradition, Sree Narayana Guru also attracted allegiance from a whole range of ezhava religious and non-religious proponents, some of whom rejected Hinduism altogether. For example, in protest against caste injustice in Hindu society, many reformers argued for conversion to other religions such as Buddhism (Mithavadi C. Krishnan), Christianity (C.V. Kunjiraman), Islam (Kamal Pasha) and Sikhism (K.C. Kuttan). E. Madhavan argued that the ezhavas should constitute themselves as an independent community, while Sahodaran Ayyappan was one of the founders of the rationalist movement. Despite the vast array of responses, they all laid direct claim to the legacy of anti-casteism and universalism preached by Sree Narayana Guru.[13]

VAGBHATANANDA: THE RENAISSANCE LEADER OF MALABAR

Vagbhatananda was the greatest socio-religious leader of the Kerala renaissance in Malabar.[14] Like Sree Narayana Guru in Travancore, Vagbhatananda was born into the ezhava community in 1884 in the village of Patyam near Thalassery. His initiation into Sanskrit studies was under his father Koran Gurukkal who was a well-known scholar with outspoken ideas. After in-depth study of grammar, logic and philosophy under different Gurukkals, Vagbhatananda moved to Kozhikode to set up his own Sanskrit school in 1906. He was also involved in activities of Brahmo Samaj, a pan-Indian Hindu social reform movement, in Kozhikode

[13] T.M. Thomas Isaac, *Elements of Casteism and Radicalism in Ezhava Social Reform Movement*, Malayalam, *Alappuzhayude Samarapaatha*, Chintha Publishers, Thiruvananthapuram, 1990.

[14] Vaghbhadanan, *Vaghbadanandate Sampoorna Krithikal*, Mathrubhoomi Printing and Publishing Company 1998; K.K. Pavithran, *Vaghbhadanandan Athmeeya Himalayathil*, Imprint Books, 1995; Dr. M.S. Nair, *Vaghabhadanada Guruvum Samoohika Navodhanavum*, 1988.

when he heard a lecture by Brahmananda Swamy Siva Yogi. Siva Yogi expounded a philosophy that jettisoned idolatry and organized religion, and severely differed with Sree Narayana Guru's temple consecration programme. Until around 1917 Vagbhatananda was the most powerful propagandist for Siva Yogi, travelling throughout Malabar and parts of Travancore delivering oratories in religious and social meetings. He also launched a magazine, *Siva Yogi Vilasam*, to propagate the ideas of Siva Yogi. However he began to distance himself from his mentor when Siva Yogi's critique of religion began to border on atheism.

Like Sree Narayana Guru, philosophically Vagbhatananda was also an *advaitin* and emphasized the need for awakening the self in order to realize the ultimate truth. *Atmavidya* means self-knowledge/consciousness, which requires individual mental discipline in the search for knowledge and discarding unhealthy habits and negative behaviour. This self-improvement and spiritual transformation would also lead to social change as it would usher in a society based upon harmony and peace. Unlike Sree Narayana Guru, Vagbhatananda considered that everyone including ordinary people could pursue the path of *jnana-marga* (path of knowledge). He argued that

> It is utter foolishness to believe those who argued that *jnana-marga* is not open for sinners and unintelligent people. The pandits claimed it as their prerogative. But such belief is stupid [. . .]. It is like believing that only the rich brahmins have the right to receive relief from the heat by stepping into cold water [. . .]. If anybody claims there is a hierarchy among those who follow *jnana-marga*, understand that it simply emanates from irrationality.[15]

[15] Quoted in Divya Kannan, 'Social Reform in Twentieth Century Malabar', p. 58.

In addition, Vagbhatananda was opposed to building temples and consecrating deities. On Sree Narayana Guru's visit to Malabar, he consecrated many temples, including the important Jagannath Temple in Thalassery. To the dismay of Sree Narayana Guru the temple was soon converted into an exclusive ezhava temple, a development far removed from his universal humanism. In the last decade of his life, Sree Narayana Guru began to discourage the establishment of new temples. In a famous dialogue between them at Advaitda Asramam in Aluva, Vagbhatananda personally interrogated Sree Narayana Guru regarding the establishment of brahmanic model temples. Vagbhatananda seems to have appreciated the position of Sree Narayana Guru and drastically toned down his criticism in the next issue of *Sivayogivilasini*. Sree Narayana Guru, in his turn, renounced not only membership of any caste but also of the Hindu religion. This declaration of no caste and no religion in 1916, 11 years before his death, continues to be an issue of deeply divisive interpretations but provides inspiration for those who seek legitimacy in the Guru for the secular standpoint.[16]

By this time Vagbhatananda was charting his own path in which he clearly distinguished himself from both the *bhakthi-marga* of Sree Narayana Guru and the atheism of Siva Yogi. He argued that idol worship and the attendant rituals were antithetical to *advaita* philosophy. His philosophy of *atmavidya* gained an organizational form in Atmavidya Sangham in 1917. The venue was Karakkad, the village referred to in the opening paragraph of this chapter. A group of radical youth headed by Karappayil Kanaran Master invited Vagbhatananda to deliver a lecture at Karakkad. A large

[16] Sunil P. Elayadom, 'Guruvinte Matham', in N.R. Grama Prakash (ed.), *Sree Narayana Guruvum Mathanirapekshathayum*, Maithri Books, Thiruvananthapuram, 2016.

gathering of people listened spellbound to Vagbhatananda's eloquent discourse ridiculing idol worship, rituals and outdated customs. Atmavidya Sangham – a forum for study and propagation of *atmavidya* – was born in this meeting. Even though Vagbhatananda eschewed violence and never called for the desecration of temples, according to popular narratives some of the participants of the founding meeting of Atmavidya Sangham in Karakkad removed the deities from their local family temples. They declared the deities to be scarecrows of caste domination and superstitious customs and took them in procession and immersed them into the sea. A new phase of uncompromising struggle for social reforms was inaugurated. The salutation of the new organization was a clarion call for struggle against caste injustice in the name of the creator: 'Awake, remember the Creator, arise and fight against injustice.' In 1925 Vagbhatananda published his *Atmavidya* which became akin to the manifesto of the movement.

The ideals of justice and equality resonated across a wide range of social groups beyond his native thiyya community spanning from the fishing community to some people in upper caste communities. Within a short period of time, branches of Atmavidya Sangham sprang up in villages across north Malabar. Besides religious discourses, the activities of these groups included protest actions against degrading customs related to death and puberty, and meaningless and wasteful rituals related to marriage, caste discrimination and idol worship. Vagbhatananda participated in the campaign against the traditional pilgrimage to Kottiyur in northern Malabar.[17] While the movement addressed caste issues such as inter-dining and inter-marriages across caste boundaries, it also

[17] For a discussion of Kottiyoor Pilgrimage, see Dilip M. Menon, *Caste, Nationalism and Communism in South India: Malabar 1900-1948*, Cambridge: Cambridge University Press, 1994.

included other social issues such as the temperance movement as Vagbhatananda believed that alcoholism was a major impediment to mental discipline and thus self-realisation.

Given Atmavidya Sangham's universalistic messages and widespread appeal across caste lines, the question arises as to why it failed to develop a mass movement like Sree Narayana's movement in the southern Kerala, which even came to dominate the thiyyas in Malabar. There is no simple answer, but a few key factors stand out. First, after Vagbhatananda's death Atmavidya Sangham began to organizationally disintegrate. Vagbhatananda never took interest in building an organization similar to SNDP Yogam, but rather preferred a loose and decentralized organizational structure. Atmavidya Sangham units sprang up spontaneously as a broad platform for dialogue and debate. Second, the economic and social strength of the Malabar thiyya elite was much weaker than the ezhava elite in Travancore. The Travancore ezhava elite found in SNDP Yogam an ideal organizational instrument to pursue their sectarian interests, which often diverged from the universalism that Sree Narayana Guru preached. Dr. Palpu, one of the earliest organizers of SNDP Yogam and leading light of Sree Narayana movement, stated in the inaugural meeting, 'What we must try to do through this organization is to try for the prosperity of our caste by every means. [. . .] This organization is in reality nearly the great congress of ezhavas in Kerala, but it is true that its name does not reveal this meaning. That has its use. No community in India is honoured by its material prosperity alone. [. . .] It is rare for us to have such a competent and prominent person as our president. If we do not make use of this opportunity properly, this will one day without doubt become an irreparable loss and cause of heavy sorrow.'[18] Ironically, the Sree Narayana *dharma* that Dr. Palpu wanted to protect had little to do with the essential religious teachings of Sree Narayana Guru. While the ezhava elite's participation helped ensure the organization's long-term survival, it also compromised the radical values of inclusion, justice, and equality that Sree Narayana Guru advocated.

Third, Vagbhatananda's uncompromising stand against idol worship and temples alienated the thiyya elite whose programme centred around the establishment of exclusive temples for thiyyas, like the famous temple of Jagannath in Thalassery, to reinforce caste pride and identity.[19] This turn to exclusive temples for thiyya and ezhavas concerned Sree Narayana Guru to the point that in 1917 he declared:

> Temple consecration must not be further encouraged. People's faith in temple worship is declining. There is a chance that they shall grieve about the money spent on building temples. But people will not pay heed to my exhortation. If need be let small temples be founded but the main place of worship must be schools. I thought temples would bring together people cutting across caste differences. But experience has shown otherwise. Temples have perpetuated caste distinctions. We must now attempt to build more schools for people. Let there be knowledge.[20]

Finally, unlike Sree Narayana Guru's teachings,

[18] Quoted in Thayattu Sankaran, *Asan: Navodhanathinte Kavi*, Kottayam: NBS, 1978, p. 66.

[19] Dilip Menon, *Caste, Nationalism and Communism in South India*.

[20] E. Madhavan, *Swathanthra Samudayam*, Trivandrum: Prabhath Book House, p. 109. The final years of Sree Narayana Guru's life were enmeshed in tragic overtones and the estrangement of Guru from the ezhava elite, which almost reached a breaking point. But it was too late for him to stop the trend and the agenda of the elites prevailed.

Vagbhatananda did not provide a broad platform for convergence of the divergent socio-political trends dominant among the thiyya elite in Malabar. We have already referred to the conservative religious trends, but there were also conservative political trends emerging. The most prominent intellectuals among thiyyas were Moorkkothu Kunjappa, the editor of *Gaja Kesari*, and C. Krishnan, the editor of *Mithavadi*. While both were in the forefront of reforms against outmoded customs and practices and supported the struggle for civil rights, they also represented politically conservative strands in the renaissance movement that sought accommodation with British rule in order to undermine the domination of the upper castes and win equal civil rights. Thus, the thiyya elite were socially more progressive but religiously and politically conservative. Vagbhatananda's radical teachings did not resonate with the thiyya elite, but rather found widespread appeal among the young radicals of the nationalist movement that was emerging in Malabar. Thus, even though Atmavidya Sangham did not develop into a mass movement, Vagbhatananda's contribution to rendering Malabar more secular and non-casteist compared to southern Kerala can not be understated. His ideas percolated into Malabar society in myriad and unexpected ways.

THE BASEL MISSION AND THE NEW WORK ETHIC

The emergence of an enlightened public sphere in the village of Karakkad and the adjacent Vadakara town was the background for the invitation to Vagbhatananda's public lecture in Karakkad and the subsequent founding of Atmavidya Sangham. While the social reform movement largely in the Hindu community was finding strong roots, there were also important developments among the Christian and Muslim minorities. This climate of rethinking and change formed the background for the emergence of the secular and radical nationalist movement (discussed in the next chapter) and deeply influenced the labour cooperative.

The ethics of a feudal caste-based society differs significantly from a capitalist work culture. The feudal caste society is characterized by petty production and services whose hierarchy of social status is determined by the caste of the worker or the service provider. The freedom of choice of occupation is denied to the vast majority of people as they are bound by birth to their caste vocations. Norms of purity and pollution fragment the workforce and prevent labour from collectively organising. Manual labour is looked down upon and there is no social or personal pride in such occupations. In a feudal caste-based system one's place in the economic and social hierarchy is determined by birth, experienced in lonely isolation, and degraded by social norms.

In contrast, capitalism depersonalizes economic relations and 'frees' labour to pursue any occupation that it can secure.[21] Every labourer in the factory is a wage worker of equal worth in terms of exchange value and subject to the same discipline of hierarchical factory organization, irrespective of caste or social status.[22] In order for such an impersonal system to function efficiently a new work ethic is required. In Europe and the United States Calvinism provided the basis for a capitalist work ethic that married personal salvation to hard work and economic success.[23] Success in economic endeavours

[21] Karl Marx and Frederick Engels, *Manifesto of the Communist Party*, 1848, p. 3.

[22] Of course social cleavages have also been used by capitalism. For example, apartheid South Africa grafted systemic and institutional racism onto capitalism.

[23] Max Weber, *The Protestant Ethics and the Spirit of Capitalism*,

is an indication of salvation, turning work into a form of worship. Thus, the spirit of capitalism sees hard work in the economic realm and the accumulation of wealth as spiritual pursuits rather than simply material rewards. Interestingly, both caste-based feudalism and capitalism draw on religion to justify exploitation and oppression.

It was in the factories established by the Basel Mission that for the first time labourers in Malabar experienced the 'capitalist spirit.' The Basel Mission was a Swiss based Calvinist Mission that came to Malabar for the propagation of Christianity in 1834 and within six years Herman Gundert laid the foundation for a mission branch at Chombala adjacent to Karakkad. The mission station at Chombala had 549 congregants out of the 7,595 in Malabar as a whole. Like other Anglican Missions such as the Church Missionary Society (CMS) and the London Missionary Society (LMS) that came to Travancore in the early nineteenth century, the Basel Mission did not undertake mass conversions and opposed the caste system to varying degrees. This led to a difficult position for the individual converts of the new missions, who faced severe hostility and social ostracism from their caste communities. As a result, the missions were forced to confront the caste order and adopt special measures to protect their converts. In the case of LMS in southern Travancore these special measures took the form of social struggles against discrimination and for equal rights. The Basel Mission in the north of Kerala organized factories and other avenues of alternative employment for their converts, and looked to education as an important element in the struggle. For the Basel Mission, running factories and providing modern education were as important as proselytising itself. As Raghaviah noted,

London: Routledge, 2013 [1905].

given the Calvinist theology of the Basel Mission, 'Economic activity of the mission was not a support of the mission but was considered to be the mission itself. [. . .] The idea of pray and work gave way to the notion that praying is working and working is praying.'[24]

Around 1860, the mission set up its fifth factory, a weaving factory at Chombala. In subsequent years, the mission set up two other weaving factories and a dye house in Malabar as well as seven tile factories. At the outbreak of the First World War the factories employed 3,633 workers. While more than a quarter of the workers in all the factories were non-Christians, all of the 88 workers at Chombala were members of the mission. The factory at Chombala was an important modernizing influence on the area with its new fly shuttle technology, modern dyes and factory organization.

The Manacaudu theru was a small traditional weaving community of 65 workers (in 1901) in Karakkad. 'Theru' was the name given for a traditional weavers' street on both sides of which weaving sheds and the weavers' houses were located in a ribbon format. The weavers at Karakkad used traditional pit looms, but learning from the Chombala factory they modernized their looms into fly shuttle looms. During the second quarter of the twentieth century, some of the master weavers set up small-scale factories employing as many as 40 looms. The cloth produced from these small-scale factories was exported via Kannur to the rest of India and overseas.

In addition to setting up factories, the Basel Mission also invested in educational institutions. In 1888 the mission started a primary school at Chombala, which continues to exist today

[24] Jayaprakash Raghaviah, *Basel Mission Industries in Malabar and South Canara (1804 - 1914): A Story of its Social and Economic Impact*, New Delhi: Gian Publishing House, 1990, p. 10. Our subsequent discussion on Basel Mission in based on this study.

as Karakkad Government LP School. The primary reason for setting up a network of schools and a non-formal educational system was to ensure that every Christian could read the bible. By the second decade of the twentieth century there were eight primary schools in and around Karakkad, including one established by Atmavidya Sangham. In the nearby town of Thalassery, the mission also set up an institution of higher education which eventually became the premier educational institution in Malabar. Many young activists, like Moyarath Sankaran who played a leading role in moulding the first generation of nationalist and radical activists, were educated at the mission school. Thus, the Basel Mission's investment in factories and education inadvertently played an important role in shaping the economic and social contours of Malabar society.

KARAKKADU THANGAL AND THE MUSLIM COMMUNITY

Vadakara was a minor port town and an important commercial centre for coconut and fishery products. It had a significant Muslim population. The Muslim elites were traders, many of whom had trade links with countries in the Middle East. Vadakara was an important gateway for the goods and products produced in the interior villages and towns such as Karakkad. In Karakkad, one of the most prominent families was 'Tharammel *tharavad*.' The Tharammel family was extremely wealthy and also had a hoary past of Sufism, magic, witchcraft, jinns, and maliks, the fables of which have been handed down by word of mouth from generation to generation, and immortalized in the novel of Punathil Kunjabdulla *The Tombstones*. In the magical realism of the novel, Pookkoya Thangal – who petitioned and influenced the authorities in establishing a railway station in Karakkad – is transformed into a great magician who mesmerized the train to stop on the tracks in front of a crowd of head-load workers carrying his baggage and awestruck onlookers.[25] The Tharammel family inspired such fables because of the important role it played in the economic development of Karakkad as well as the communal amity it promoted that came to characterize the social life of the region.[26]

The first generation of Tharammel tharavad, Salim bin Hussain, was a Yemeni believed to be a descendent of the Prophet Mohammed, who came to Malabar in the beginning of the nineteenth century in the company of one of the men who went on a Haj pilgrimage from Karakkad. Salim bin Hussain was a scholar and Sufi and never returned to Karakkad from one of his long distance wanderings. He left behind at Karakkad a family of three sons, a daughter, and a wife. One of his sons, Syed Sayn Koya, was a poet and Sufi scholar not interested in worldly pursuits, while his brother Syed Hydros Koya specialized in material pursuits. The latter accumulated wealth through trade and acquired substantial landed property by successfully bidding for Kadathanattu Raja's mortgaged land when they were auctioned by the courts.

Muthu Koya Thangal, the elder son of Syed Hydros Koya, was a close friend of Vagbhatananda and a progressive thinker who supported the social reform movement. He played an important role in protecting the pioneering members of Atmavidya Sangham who were threatened with physical assault by the tradition bound caste leaders. It was

25 Punathil Kunjabdulla, *Smaraka Silakal*, Kottayam: DC Books, 1977, p. 32.

26 Rajendran Edathumkara, Jineesh P.S., Soman T.K., *Munnettam: Uralungal Labour Contract Co-operative Society*, Vijayagadha, 2013, p. 44.

Muthu Koya Thangal's mediation on a number of occasions that avoided violent confrontations. His house was the seat of informal adjudication for many local disputes not only among the Muslim community but also among non-Muslims. Swamy Brahma Vrithan recalls that at the annual conference to celebrate the success of the campaign against the outmoded customs in the thiyya community, 'Muthu Koya Thangal, who always extended a strong helping hand for the social reform efforts of Gurudevan, was invited as a special guest.'[27] The conference was also a venue for open confrontation between Vagbhatananda and the chairman of the conference Krishnan Vakil who was an ardent follower of Sree Narayana Guru. The conference report of the activities included a narrative of the successful eradication of certain community customs. The chair objected that some of the actions may not have the sanction of Sree Narayana Guru. Clearly showing his disregard for Sree Narayana Guru's sanction, Vagbhatananda responded:

> Why should we need the permission of Sree Narayana Guru Swamy? Without seeking anybody's permission Atmavidya Sangham has been able to wipe out these customs from many parts of Malabar. Here in Kunnothu Parambu itself upright and self-respecting members of more than 400 families have been freed from the madness of these customs. The chairman misunderstood that the report was speaking about things to be done. No. They are things which have already occurred. Even if they are about future actions why should we need the permission of Sree Narayana Guru Swamy? Sree Narayana Guru Swamy was born into a community suffering from caste discrimination.

[27] Swami Brahma Vrithan, *Maharshi Vagbhatananda Gurudevan*, Institute of Vagbhatananda Memorial Research, Thottappally, 1971, p. 138.

> [. . .] Atmavidya Sangham is also opposed to all idol worship including those in the temples consecrated by Sree Narayana Guru Swamy. What is the meaning of those who have never learned anything from Swamykal calling him as their Guru?[28]

In support of Vagbhatananda, Muthu Koya Thangal publicly endorsed lower caste women's right to cover their breast and actively supported their processions organized by Atmavidya Sangham. He even invited the ire of the conservative Muslims by hosting Hindu circus artists from Thalassery to perform for the women in his family. Thangal passed away while on a business trip to Singapore, where he was a prominent businessman, and the Atmavidya Sangham organized three days of prayer for their departed friend. Even after his passing, the legacy of communal tolerance that he helped to create in the area continued and was an important factor in preventing communal tensions in Vadakara in the aftermath of the Mappila Rebellion of 1921 (discussed below). In addition to the stimulus from the social reform movement, the nationalist movement would also come to play a role in shaping the region.

THE FIRST WINDS OF THE NATIONALIST MOVEMENT

The first winds of the nationalist movement had started blowing through Karakkad around the same time that the labour cooperative was formed. The *Mathrubhumi* (Motherland) newspaper started publication in Kozhikode in 1923 as the mouthpiece of the fledging Indian National Congress, and unintentionally had a role in the labour cooperative's formation. *Mathrubhumi* reported on the

[28] Ibid., p. 69-93.

Malabar District Cooperative Conference, which prompted a number of key people to decide to form the labour cooperative. At the same time, the newspaper regularly reported on the nationalist movement, making almost certain that the avid newspaper readers in Karakkad had also become aware of the nationalist movement sweeping the rest of India.

Until the second decade of the twentieth century, the nationalist movement had bypassed the Malabar District. Malayali professionals settled in Madras and other areas outside of Kerala participated in the annual conferences of the Indian National Congress. But these individual involvements hardly had any impact in Malabar. It was with Annie Besant's home rule movement that political activities started in Malabar. With the arrival of K.P. Kesava Menon from England, the founder of *Mathrubhumi*, a core group of politically active people emerged in Kozhikode. District committees of Congress and the Home Rule League were formed. Meanwhile at the all-India level three trends emerged in opposition to the Home Rule League's moderate programme: the armed groups in Bengal and Punjab, Muslim leaders such as Ali Brothers and Abul Kalam Azad resolutely opposing British rule, and Gandhiji's radical satyagraha struggle. By 1919 Gandhiji dominated the Congress scene at the national level and was also gradually finding resonance in Malabar. In Malabar, on the other hand, the intellectual leaders of thiyyas, such as Moorkottu Kumaran and C. Krishnan adopted a moderate position, which they espoused through C. Krishnan's journal, *Mithavadi* (The Moderate). Their moderate approach largely permeated the thiyya community.

The struggle between the moderates and the Gandhians reached fever pitch at the Indian National Congress's Manjeri district conference in 1920. While Gandhiji prepared for the 'Non Co-operation struggle,' the Muslims started their Khilafat movement in response to the way the British treated Khalifa of Turkey. The collaboration between the Congress and Khilafat brought Hindus and Muslims together on an anti-imperialist platform, and they jointly rejected the administrative reforms proposed by the British. Annie Besant and her loyal followers attended the conference. Unlike the previous conferences in which only rajas, *jenmis* and professionals attended, this conference included a large number of delegates from tenants and the middle class. The combination of a wider spectrum of social classes and a range of contentious issues meant that the conference erupted in serious and heated debate, especially around the resolutions on Khilafat, administrative reforms, and the tenancy problem. The moderates were defeated on each of these issues by a large majority. The Manjeri Conference was followed by a Kerala-wide political conference with delegates from the three regions of Kerala: Malabar, Cochin and Travancore. Threatened by the growing nationalist movement, the Malabar local police arrested and jailed some key leaders attending the conference and beat up volunteers at the venue of the conference. At the conclusion of the Manjeri conference, Malabar was plunged into the Non-Cooperation movement led by Gandhiji, and the moderates lost support within the thiyya community.

The climax of the Non-Cooperation–Khilafat movement was the Malabar uprising by Muslim peasants in and around present day Malappuram. In a sense, the Malabar uprising was a continuation of the numerous agrarian uprisings since the nineteenth century that had characterized the ascendancy of British rule.[29] Even the British collector, William Logan,

[29] M.B.D. Namboodiripad, *Khilafath Smaranakal*, Mathrubhoomi Printing and Publishing 1965.

underlined the agrarian causes of the Mappila rebellions. The repression unleashed by the British authorities against the Non-Cooperation–Khilafat movement provoked the Muslim peasants into armed resistance initially against the *jenmis* – who were mostly among the Hindus – but soon it degenerated into communal violence in some pockets. The Hindu-Muslim unity that was being forged by the Non-Cooperation–Khilafat struggle was virtually destroyed. The British brutally repressed the uprising, killing hundreds of people and arresting and deporting to jails outside of Malabar thousands more. The goods wagons were filled with hundreds of rebels and were closed without ventilation, turning them into suffocation chambers. In the infamous 'wagon tragedy' 90 people were despatched in a freight wagon from Tirur to Coimbatore and 67 of them died by the time the train reached Coimbatore.

Moyarath Sankaran recounted in his memoir that there were rumours in Vadakara that similar 'wagon tragedies' were a common occurrence. He narrates an incident when a passenger train compartment was forced open, there were 160 rebels in the compartment of whom 22 had died and 45 lay unconscious, on the verge of death. The inhuman sight of packed railway wagons and cries for help coming from within the trains enraged the Muslim community. A platoon of reserve police came to camp at Vadakara, which further exacerbated the situation. Every day a group of Congress activists led by Moyarath had to go to mosques and Muslim neighbourhoods to try to pacify the situation. It was with much effort by Congress and Muslim leaders in Vadakara that a riot was prevented.[30]

The communal overtones into which the uprising

[30] Moyarath Sankaran, *Aathmakatha*, in Janardhanan Moyarath ed., *Athmakathayum Charithra Smaranakalum*, Trivandrum: Chintha Publishers, 2012, pp. 45-46.

degenerated had its impact on sections of the Hindu community. Moyarath recalls that when Madhava Menon, who was active in the Non-Cooperation–Khilafat movement, came to meet him a crowd trailed him showering abuses on him.[31] The communal tensions strengthened the moderate editorial line of *Gaja Kesari* and *Mithavadi*. Moyarath Sankaran's *Kerala Kesari* took up the cudgels against the moderate journals and vigorously supported radical social reforms, exposed government corruption, and criticized the high handedness of officials, who were mostly upper caste. Moyarath humorously later recalled that nairs criticized the journal for being anti-nair and pro-thiyya, while some sections of the thiyyas criticized the paper for having Moyarath, a nair, as editor.[32]

The political activities of the Congress dropped dramatically as a result of the degeneration into communal violence. Instead, the Congress focused its attention on the temperance movement, picketing toddy shops, finding constructive work for 'Harijan' upliftment, and relief work as well as sporadic petitioning and protest by tenants. The boycott of the Simon Commission in 1928 was the only notable moment of protest. While lawyers and other professionals withdrew into the confines of their occupations, a group of activists like Moyarath Sankaran remained committed to the nationalist movement, and kept it alive in the Malabar area.

THE FORMATION OF URALUNGAL LABOURERS' MUTUAL AID AND COOPERATIVE SOCIETY

The most important moment in the birth of the first labour cooperative in Kerala was the formation of Atmavidya Sangham at Karakkad in 1917. The struggle against upper

[31] Ibid. p. 45.
[32] Ibid. p. 49.

caste discrimination as well as against thiyya superstitions and customs brought Atmavidya Sangham activists into conflict with the upper castes and thiyya elites. The conditions of the social reformers were extremely precarious as they were denied work, security of tenure, customary services of barbers, washermen, marriage alliances, and, importantly, admission to schools for their children. In a meeting attended by Vagbhatananda, an appeal was made to Kadathanadu Raja for protecting tenants against eviction. As part of the resistance, Atmavidya Sangham decided to establish the Atmavidya Sangham Lower Primary School in 1922. Two years later a credit cooperative society 'Aikya Nanaya Sangham' (United Credit Cooperative) was formed to break the financial boycott of banks and meet the needs of local community residents. And in 1925, 'Uralungal Koolivelakkarude Paraspara Sahaya Sangham,' the labour contract cooperative, came into existence.

There are four common features of the 14 original members of the cooperative: (1) they all belonged to the thiyya community, (2) they were all labourers except for three of them, (3) most of them were also founding members of the cooperative credit society, and (4) they were all members of the Atmavidya Sangham and ardent followers of Vagbhatananda. Thus, they all shared community background, spiritual inclinations, social reform commitments, and political histories that were characterized by radical visions of a social commitment, idealism, and the possibility of a just and egalitarian world.

To give a sense of the deep commitments to social reform of the founding cooperative members, we give a brief description of three of the leaders. The first president of the labour cooperative, Chappayil Kunjyekku Gurukkal, was a skilled mason and the most prominent follower of Vagbhatananda in Karakkad.[33] He led the team who went to Mahe to invite Vagbhatananda to Karakkad for the first time in 1917, and organized the inter-dining feast that included the outcaste communities at Karakkad. Paleri Chandaman, another pioneer of the labour cooperative, belonged to a relatively economically well off family in Karakkad.[34] Chandaman made his mark when he threw the idols from the family temple into the well, shocking the entire village. He also organized the daring procession of thiyya women wearing blouses for the first time and the irreverent and innovative polluting of the temple and public ponds by bathing in them. Once they formed the cooperative, Chandaman donated the land and the basement of his own house to the cooperative to build an office. Finally, Kayyala Chekku began the reforms within his own family by digging a well for dalits on his own land as he considered lower castes equals not only in public places, but also in his own house.[35]

The pioneers of the labour cooperative belonged to a stream in the social reform movement that exemplified the ideals of Vagbhatananda. Though they focused on the reforms within their own community, they were secular in outlook and maintained an amicable relationship with the Muslim community. They were willing to adapt the work discipline of the missionary factories, learned from the practices of missionary schools, and importantly for their future, had political links with *Kerala Kesari* of Moyarath Sankaran (and not with *Gaja Kesari* or *Mithavadi*).

[33] Rajendran Edathumkara, P.S. Jineesh, T.K. Soman, *Munnettam: Uralungal Labour Contract Co-operative Society*, Vijayagadha, 2013, p. 136.

[34] Ibid., p. 137.

[35] Ibid., p. 139.

CHAPTER 3

THE CHALLENGES OF THE EARLY YEARS

The Uralungal Labourers' Cooperative Society in north Malabar is the only one of its kind in Kerala: the poor labourers through their mutual cooperation take up public works and share the profits among themselves. In the western countries there are many such societies. There are many contractors in Kerala and worldwide who have become millionaires through contract works. In our times it is possible for contractors to engage labourers for arduous work at low wages. Contractors are interested only in fattening their profits by squeezing the wages of workers to the lowest level possible. Therefore it is not possible for the wage labourers to get a fair remuneration for their labour. However if the labourers cooperate they can get liberated from the clutches of the contractors and ensure fair remuneration for their labour.

Not many may be aware of Uralungal Society. It is not surprising that their fame has not spread around because the president and secretary of the Society are ordinary poor people [. . .] If a society succeeds and prospers in one place, similar societies will come up in other places also. Workers will gain

> the capability of directly managing their work. Their slavery will end. If only the workers realise that their problems can be solved through mutual cooperation and organize themselves can their poverty be eradicated.[1]

This quote is taken from a *Mathrubhumi* editorial. A decade earlier, the same newspaper reported on the cooperative movement in Malabar that had inspired Atmavidya Sangham activists to setup the first labour contract cooperative society in Kerala, the Uralungal Labour Contract Cooperative Society (ULCCS).[2] The Cooperative Act had been passed in British India in 1912 and 380 cooperative societies formed in Malabar, most of which were credit societies, consumer cooperative societies, and agricultural societies. At the time ULCCS was formed in 1924 there were no official bylaws governing a labour contract society, which meant that the Cooperative had to create its own bylaws by modifying the bylaws of credit cooperatives. The absence of existing models to emulate also afforded the pioneers a great deal of space to fashion a labour contract society in their own image. Thus, the founders clearly defined the Cooperative's objectives in the following manner:

> The object of the Society shall be: to promote the economic interests of the labourers of the Society and to find suitable and profitable employment for them by obtaining contracts in government, public and private bodies or individuals, and by executing those contracts through or with the help of the members and to encourage thrift, self-help and co-operation among the members. The society may also act as agent for the

[1] Editorial, *Mathrubhumi*, December 12, 1934.

[2] We use ULCCS, the Cooperative, and the Society interchangeably to refer to the Uralungal Labour Contract Cooperative Society.

joint purchase of the domestic and other requirements of its members.[3]

The bylaws are very clear that the primary objective of the Cooperative is to service the interest of its members, the labourers of the Cooperative, through securing and rewarding, well remunerated works. It was thus striving to bypass the intermediary profit-seeking contractors in public works projects. In this chapter we focus on the initial challenges that the Cooperative faced in securing contracts, raising the required finance, and ensuring better wages and service conditions for the worker-members.

ULCCS's origins are linked to the social renaissance and nationalist struggles of the early twentieth century. Within the first decades of its founding, the areas in and around Uralungal were at the vortex of the political turbulence of the 1930s and 1940s when powerful peasant and workers' movements sprang up in Malabar. At the same time, the nationalist movement took a radical turn and the Communist Party emerged as a hegemonic force in Malabar. In this chapter we also discuss the ways in which the radicalization of Malabar in the 1930s and 1940s influenced the formative years of the cooperative.

THE FALTERING 1920s AND THE STABILIZING 1930s

After its official formation, it took the Society more than a year before it secured its first contract for road maintenance. The work was successfully completed in 1927-1928 for an amount of Rs 925. Despite its timely completion of the road maintenance project, the Society struggled to secure additional contracts and little seemed to be working in its

[3] Bylaws 1924, p. 1, Record of ULCCS.

favour. For example, the auditor expressed serious doubts about the viability of the Society and the Cooperative Department expressed its reservations through a formal letter. The general body meeting of the cooperative on 22 January 1928 responded by making clear that the members believed in their Cooperative and would make every effort to find further work:

> The Society started functioning in 1925. Yet it did not get any contract work till May 1926. Then it received a contract for Rs 925. It was completed to the satisfaction of the authorities. From this work, not only there was no loss but we also made a small profit. We have no previous experiences in this type of work. We firmly believe that as we gain experience, the Society will achieve larger profit. If you cancel the registration it will cause severe disappointment for us. Therefore it is resolved to seek the help of the Deputy Registrar to sustain our society by helping us to get work orders from the District Board.[4]

With only one of its members being a contractor, the cooperative had limited experience and capability in managing road and building construction projects. In addition to the challenges of site management, the members also found the paperwork and tendering process extremely onerous. In 1928-29 the turnover was only Rs 350 and the subsequent two years, 1929-30 and 1930-31, were dry years, throwing up serious doubts about the future of the fledgling workers' cooperative. It received a thin lifeline in 1931-32, when the Cooperative secured a small contract of Rs 167. The Cooperative thus faced both internal (i.e., limited capacities of its members) and external (i.e., lack of support from authorities) challenges

[4] Minutes of ULCCS, Board of Directors meeting, January 22, 1928, Vol. I, p. 25.

Table 3.1: Turnover and gross profit / loss and net profit / loss 1927-28 to 1949-50 (Rs)

Year	Turnover	Gross profit/loss (-)	Reserves and provisions	Net profit/loss (-)
1927-28	925	20	0	12
1928-29	315	23	0	18
1929-30	0	0	0	0
1930-31	0	0	0	0
1931-32	167	16	9	(-14)
1932-33	1135	149	29	93
1933-34	1875	184	21	111
1934-35	1349	6	61	(-164)
1935-36	2971	36	177	(-158)
1936-37	6923	204	164	(-67)
1937-38	8500	162	74	(-84)
1938-39	13152	336	92	159
1939-40	12917	218	6	275
1940-41	12969	167	9	22
1941-42	21933	228	9	358
1942-43	30031	673	10	450
1943-44	20493	40	25	(-326)
1944-45	8069	(-3675)	351	(-4370)
1945-46	18055	3000	4395	(-1712)
1946-47	15661	1671	1730	(-305)
1947-48	3373	0	322	(-354)
1948-49	29576	3514	1177	2052
1949-50	34353	3541	766	2375

Source: Collated from the Yearend Audit Report for the relevant years, Records of ULCCS.

and was barely surviving. The general body meeting on 15 November, 1931 once again recorded the lack of support from the authorities and the imminent crisis the Cooperative faced: 'It is six years since the Society started functioning. Within this period after petitioning the Local Board a number of times we received one contract and from the Fisheries Department seven contracts. We record the dire situation of the Society in the absence of any other contract.'[5]

[5] Minutes of ULCCS, General Body Meeting, November 15, 1931, Vol. I, p. 29.

In order to break the monopoly of the private contractors, the Society began aggressively under quoting its tenders. This was a conscious strategy by the board of directors as the minutes account numerous instances in which they under quoted tenders. For example, in 1939 the contract for a fish curing yard was awarded at 27.5 per cent below the estimated rate.[6] While under quoting tenders meant they were not operating at a profit, the implementation of these contracts provided invaluable experience and helped earn the Cooperative a strong reputation for their capacity and efficiency. Nevertheless, the Cooperative had to start earning a profit if it was to survive in the long term.

Table 3.1 provides the annual turnover of the Society between 1925-26 and 1946-47. During the first years, the annual turnover of the Cooperative was low, but after 1932 there was a steady growth in turnover peaking in 1942-43 at Rs 30,031. After 1942-43 the turnover fluctuated markedly. While the turnover fluctuated, the Cooperative enjoyed a positive gross profit every year except for 1944-45. The accounting practices of the Cooperative system added miscellaneous income to the gross profit, while the establishment charges and the reserves and provisions were subtracted to identify the net profit or loss. When this formula is applied the Cooperative's record is more mixed. The year 1944-45 was an exceptional year with a gross loss of Rs 3,675 and net loss of Rs 4,370. One of the main reasons for this negative outcome in 1944-45 was the unrealistic increase in the wages to 10 annas, which eventually had to be cut by one anna to recover losses. If the entire period up to 1949-50 is considered, the Society suffered a net loss of Rs 1,339. However, if we take away 'the reserves and provisions,' which include provisions

[6] Minutes of ULCCS, Board of Directors meeting, November 5, 1939, Vol. I, p. 104.

for employee retirement benefits and provisions for bad debts, the gross profit totalled Rs 4,247.

The Cooperative received most of its contracts from local authorities including District and Taluk Boards. The main contracts from the local authorities were for the construction and maintenance of small and medium sized roads and school buildings. As the Cooperative continued to demonstrate its capacity to deliver on these projects, the relationship to local authorities strengthened over time, leading to further contracts and more government departments using its services. For example, the Fisheries Department also became an important source of work with contracts for constructing fishery schools, temporary fish curing yards, and fences. The Public Works Department also entrusted the Society to build and maintain some of the major roads in the area. The Society was also contracted to dig public wells and ponds as well as the extremely complex deepening and widening of the Connolly Canal in 1944. Thus, by the end of the 1940s the Cooperative had a major foothold into government projects.

The widening of Connolly canal proved to be very tough not only because of technical complexities but also because the Cooperative had underestimated the amount quoted. The board of the Cooperative decided to petition the Public Works Department requesting an adjustment to the contract. The petition was discussed in detail in the Cooperative's board of director's meeting on March 27, 1944.

> The mud excavation in widening of one furlong long portion of Connolly Canal between 17-03-1944 and 23-03-1944 was examined. It involved a quantity of 24118 Cu Ft. It would require hard labour of 395 workers. Therefore for further continuation of the work, a petition may be submitted to the Department of

> Public Works (DPW) for sanctioning the following wage rates.
>
> Rs 18 per 1000 cu. ft. for mud excavation above the water level; (2) Rs 25 for excavation of mud from below the water level; (3) if there is rock or stone at the bottom of the water proportionately higher rate and; (4) the main cross bund should be constructed by DPW.
>
> The labourers are coming from far and staying at the worksite. Therefore, every worker should be provided with 1 ser[7] of rice and kerosene. They must also be provided with temporary shed.
>
> The present work may be continued till 30-3-1944. If the above rates are not accepted, it will not be possible to continue the work. This may be intimated to the Department.[8]

The records do not tell us the outcome of these negotiations, but the tone of the minutes suggest a new confidence of the board members in bargaining over the terms and conditions of contracts with the authorities. The confidence in which the board was negotiating shows the distance the Cooperative had travelled from the initial years of constantly petitioning for special consideration and under quoting in order to win contracts. The Cooperative faced very real challenges from private contractors who were able to out-compete Cooperative due to their lower wage rates, petty thieving and corruption (e.g., bribing officials). Over time, however, the Society had gained such a reputation for efficient and quality work that it more than made up for these disadvantages and continued to win contracts despite the cheaper bids by private contractors. The Cooperative was thus breaking capitalism's inherent link between competition and squeezing labour, demonstrating that

[7] 1 Ser = .87 kg

[8] Minutes of ULCCS, Board of Directors meeting, March 27, 1944, Vol. IA, p. 8.

poor wages do not necessarily translate into more competitive enterprises. The Cooperative was forging a new approach to labour that placed the value of human labour at the centre of economic activity.

FROM INFORMAL FINANCE TO INSTITUTIONAL FINANCE

From the very beginning, the Society was handicapped by inadequate finance, which was made worse by the fact that government only paid contractors after the work was completed. Not only would government departments not give advances on projects, but they required 'an earnest money deposit' by contractors submitting proposals. In addition, government often had inordinate delays in making payments all of which put severe strain on the Society's finances. For instance, the following quote from a board meeting in 1942 highlights the difficulties the Cooperative and its members faced due to the government's delayed payment on a high school project.

> For this work the Society has already spent Rs 4,249 and 14 annas. The members who were entrusted with the work have spent an additional Rs 700. However the District Board has released only Rs 2,768. The rest of the money has to be released after check measurement.
>
> The Society is one of poor labourers and therefore does not have much capital. In order to provide work to the labourers the Society has to borrow money from individuals and keep payment to workers in arrears. If we do not receive money in time the poor labourers would be put into serious difficulties and it would be difficult to the Society to continue functioning.
>
> Therefore, this meeting requests the Deputy Registrar

to write to the engineer of the District Board to take steps to immediately release the remaining balance of Kadirur School.[9]

Due to the nature of the work, the construction industry requires substantial working capital, which always posed a challenge to the Cooperative. The paid-up share capital of the Cooperative (i.e. its primary source of capital) was not sufficient for the substantial operating funds required. When the Cooperative formally registered its authorized capital was Rs 12,500, made up of 500 shares each worth Rs 25. Members could pay in one lump-sum or instalments (the amount and frequency of the instalments could be decided by the board of directors).

The general understanding was that 4 annas would be collected per week for the instalments for the shares whenever there was work. In 1931-32 there were 102 members but their combined share capital was only Rs 77. Therefore in August 1932, a formal decision was made to strictly enforce the collection of share capital by instalments. This decision immediately paid off as the share capital increased to Rs 163 within one year (1932-33) and continued to steadily improve thereafter. In addition, the Society's authorized capital and the limit to the number of shares a member could hold were increased on two occasions in order to mobilize more share capital from economically better off members. These financial changes paid off and by 1949-50 the share capital had increased to Rs 2,965. During the period between 1931-32 and 1949-50, the value of paid up share capital per member increased from Rs 2 to Rs 24 (Table 3.3). Despite these changes, the share capital was still not enough to meet the Cooperative's needs and only met a small proportion of the

[9] Minutes of ULCCS, Board of Directors meeting, February 16, 1942, Vol. I, p. 150.

fund requirement. For example, in 1932-33, it constituted 32.9 per cent of the total liabilities and the ratio steadily declined as business expanded. In 1949-50, it was only 11.27 per cent of the total liabilities. The rest of the liabilities consisted of institutional credit, various sources of informal credit, and reserves and provisions.

As a primary cooperative, ULCCS was entitled to receive financial support from the district apex cooperative bank, the Malabar Central Cooperative Bank (MCCB). The board of directors' meeting on March 21, 1926 resolved to take shares in MCCB, which allowed it to apply for a Rs 500 loan. Despite this early loan application, MCCB only extended support to the Society in 1937-38. For two years, however, MCCB released limited finance to the Cooperative: the first was a term loan of Rs 1,500 for the Cooperative's working capital requirements and the following year it released another term loan of Rs 907. It was only from 1939-40 that cash credit was made available to the Cooperative. Over the years, as a ratio to the total liabilities, the credit fund by MCCB fluctuated between 13 to 55 per cent of the total liabilities. Thus, ULCCS was dependent on informal sources and sundry creditors for a substantial portion of its fund requirement. For example, between 1948-49 and 1949-50 'miscellaneous liability' constituted approximately 53 per cent of the total liability (Table 3.2).

Short-term borrowings and repayments claimed a substantial portion of the transactions.[10] From the records, we can identify three distinct sources of funds in its first two decades of operation. The first and most important source was short term loans from relatively better off members of the Cooperative. For example, the records show instances

[10] This is recorded regularly in the minutes of the board of directors' meetings throughout this period.

where the Cooperative asked certain members to pledge their personal landed property and take personal loans from money lenders. Moreover, the cooperative laws did not facilitate solidarity across primary cooperatives. For example, even though Uralungal Cooperative Credit Society was a sister cooperative society, the cooperative laws prohibited primary societies from giving credit to each other. This left ULCCS with limited options such as asking its members to take personal loans to provide credit to the Cooperative.[11]

The second source of loan finance was short term loans from non-members. Given the fact that the majority of members were from the working class with limited resources, it became inevitable that the Society sought loans from wealthier and sympathetic community members. At this time, fixed deposits from the public were rare, but would later become an important source of financing for the Cooperative in the post-Independence period.

Third, the Cooperative's financial situation was often so severe that the board of directors were forced to take short term loans from the traditional micro-finance system. The most popular traditional micro-finance system in the region were 'panam payattu' (money gathering game) and 'kuri kallyanam' (notice for marriage). In this system, a villager who required credit for social or economic purposes would extend an invitation to his friends and relatives for an evening gathering for tea. Those who accepted the invitation would come to the gathering and hand over a sum of money according to their financial status. When all the money was put together, the total collection would be substantial. In return, the obligation of the host was that whenever someone who had contributed to his 'panam payattu' or 'kuri kallyanam'

[11] Minutes of ULCCS, Board of Directors meeting, March 16, 1934, Vol. I, p. 43.

extended a similar invitation, he was honour-bound to return more than the amount he was originally given. In this way, the informal money chain constantly incorporated more and more village households. Despite the fact that there were no formal records kept and no security taken for the credit, the system functioned through community pressure and honour. One would rather commit suicide or leave the village than renegade the obligation. In our personal discussions with long-time members of the Cooperative, they explained how members of the board of directors would go to the house of the host of the 'panam payattu' and borrow the money for a few days. The Cooperative was able to roll over a substantial amount of money through this method.

Together these three sources of finance were crucial to the Cooperative's survival during its first twenty years. During the 1940s fixed deposits from the public and credit from MCCB became more reliable sources of funding, though neither were enough to meet the needs of the Cooperative (Table 3.2).

THE EXPANSION OF MEMBERSHIP: NEW ADMISSIONS AND EXPULSIONS

At the first general body meeting of ULCCS, on March 24, 1925, the membership consisted of ten founding members each with a single share. The first decision they made was to extend the membership to an additional six people, which meant that when ULCCS started functioning it had 16 members. Since its founding in 1925, the membership has steadily grown (except for 1948-49 when there was a drop in membership, which we discuss later). What is especially interesting is that within the first ten years, the Cooperative nearly doubled its membership on two occasions – first in 1926-27 it added 14

Table 3.2: Composition of total liabilities of ULCCS 1931–32 to 1949–50 (Rs)

Year	Credit from MCCB	Fixed deposit	Reserves and provisions	Miscellaneous liabilities	Total liabilities
1931–32	–	–	90	–	167
1932–33	–	–	182	150	495
1933–34	–	–	263	31	476
1934–35	–	–	230	563	993
1935–36	–	–	235	1047	1491
1936–37	–	–	234	2117	2613
1937–38	1500	–	234	3999	6064
1938–39	907	–	415	2696	4446
1939–40	1267	–	737	3730	6234
1940–41	1784	500	981	2049	6207
1941–42	2863	–	989	1537	6451
1942–43	2299	500	1447	1610	7147
1943–44	4383	950	1444	1413	9750
1944–45	4000	2460	1376	1906	11048
1945–46	2754	1500	1376	1396	8503
1946–47	–	700	1376	53	3636
1947–48	5000	850	1376	165	8843
1948–49	3603	300	4229	11976	22764
1949–50	5090	–	4247	14004	26306

Source: Collated from the Yearend Audit Report for the relevant years, Records of ULCCS.

members to the existing 16 members and in 1931-32 it added 72 members to the existing 30 members – while the rest of the time it saw steady, moderate growth. Despite the expansion in membership, the values underpinning the Cooperative were maintained and even strengthened. Table 3.3 presents the number of new members admitted each year, the number of members removed each year, and the final yearend membership for the years 1925-26 to 1949-50.

As per the original bylaws of ULCCS, any labourer above 18 years of age and a resident within the area of the Cooperative's operation (that is, Uralungal and Mattungal Amsams adjacent to the town of Vadakara all of which lies

Table 3.3: Membership and share capital of ULCCS 1925–26 to 1949–50

Year	Opening membership	New admissions	Removals	Yearend membership	Share capital (Rs)
1925–26	16	–	–	16	–
1926–27	16	14	–	30	–
1927–28	30	–	–	30	–
1928–29	30	–	–	30	59.80
1929–30	30	–	–	30	59.80
1930–31	30	–	–	30	59.80
1931–32	30	72	–	102	77.12
1932–33	102	12	–	114	163.40
1933–34	114	–	1	113	181.11
1934–35	113	–	–	113	200.00
1935–36	113	–	4	109	208.80
1936–37	109	13	–	122	262.12
1937–38	122	6	1	127	331.12
1938–39	127	59	2	184	428.30
1939–40	184	5	2	187	500.15
1940–41	187	18	3	202	892.70
1941–42	202	9	–	211	1061.20
1942–43	211	3	2	212	1291.10
1943–44	212	5	–	217	1326.10
1944–45	217	–	1	216	1306.10
1945–46	216	–	1	215	1476.10
1946–47	215	–	–	215	1506.10
1947–48	215	–	12	203	1452.00
1948–49	203	4	81	126	2655.14
1949–50	126	19	3	142	2965.10

Source: Collated from the Yearend Audit Report for the relevant years, Records of ULCCS.

within the Vadakara *taluk*) was eligible to become a member. The bylaws further stipulate that 'Any other person other than [a] worker may also be admitted as member provided that the total number of such persons shall not exceed 1/10th of the total number of members in the list at any time. But no person can claim admission as a matter of right.'[12] In 1931 the area of operation of the Society was extended to cover the entire Vadakara area, in 1938 it was again extended to North

[12] Bylaws of ULCCS 1967, p. 3.

Table 3.4: Geographical distribution of membership of ULCCS 1924–25 to 1949–50

Year	Number of members admitted	From Uralungal Amsam	From outside Uralungal but inside Vadakara *taluk*
1924–25	16	14	2
1925–26 to 1930–31	14	13	1
1931–32	73	14	59
1932–33 to 1939–40	90	42	48
1940–41 to 1949–50	39	18	21

Source: Collated from Membership Register of ULCCS, Records of ULCCS.

Malabar, and again in 1942 it was further extended to the whole of the Malabar district. While the Cooperative's area of operation grew, the catchment area of the membership was kept confined to Vadakara *taluk*. As can be seen from Table 3.4, out of the initial 16 members 14 were from Uralungal Amsam itself. However, of the 73 members admitted in 1931-32, 59 were from outside Uralungal, but no members were recruited from outside Vadakara *taluk*.

Though the bylaws did not specify gender or religious criteria for membership, there were no female members during the entire period from 1924-25 to 1950. This is largely due to the fact that construction work was almost entirely the preserve of males. Similarly, while the Cooperative was open to all labourers regardless of religious faith, the membership was almost entirely Hindu, and particularly the thiyya caste. Even with the large expansion in membership in 1931-32, only one Muslim and three Christians became members. Table 3.5 presents the age of members when they joined and their previous occupation. An important development for the Cooperative's internal make-up was the fact that more and more young members were joining the Cooperative over the

Table 3.5: Distribution of members by period of entry into the cooperative

Age/occupation	1920s	1930s	1940s	Total
18-30	13	103	16	132
31-40	7	39	5	51
41-60	9	20	0	29
above 60	0	0	0	0
Coolie	17	130	18	165
Agriculture	2	6	0	8
Business	6	2	0	8
Others	5	7	0	12

Source: Collated from Membership Register of ULCCS, Records of ULCCS.
Note The details were not available for the entire membership and that accounts for the difference in the total number of members in the previous tables.

years. During the 1920s only 44 per cent of the new members were below the age 30, the ratio rose to 61 per cent during the 1930s and 77 per cent in the 1940s. In contrast, the proportion of those above the age of 40 steadily declined from 31 per cent in the 1920s to 12 per cent in the 1930s and 8 per cent in the 1940s. Table 3.5 clearly shows that the age of entry tended to come down over the decades. For 87 per cent of the members the occupation at the time of entry into the Cooperative was 'coolie work' (wage work). Interestingly, during the initial decades six out of the 30 members (20 per cent) were business people, and some of them were engaged in small-scale construction work. Their experience and skills turned out to be vital for the effective functioning of the Cooperative. Over time, however, their influence diminished and by the 1940s all the new entrants were wage workers.

Between 1926-27 and 1949-50, the Cooperative experienced growth with 216 new members admitted. During the same period 113 members were removed from the rolls, more than 80 per cent of whom were between 1947 and 1950. Only the general body meetings had the power to remove a member from the roll. During the initial years members were taken off the Cooperative's roll for one of three reasons: 1) the death of the member or his incapacity to do manual works, 2) voluntary withdrawal of the membership by the member, and 3) due to disciplinary action. At the end of the 1930s, the first President of the Society and a member of the board of directors voluntarily withdrew from membership due to differences of opinion with the rest of the members. The mass removal of 113 members at the end of 1940s was due to disciplinary action. The issue of dismissals is an issue that requires elaboration.

The first recorded instance of a removal from membership was in 1939 when a member was dismissed by the general body for deliberately causing losses to the Society. His share contribution of Rs 25 was impounded as compensation to the Society.[13] In 1940 another member was suspended for six months for violating the sub-contract agreement with the Society. One of the requirements of membership in the Cooperative is that members only work for the Cooperative and do not work for private contractors on the side. The Society took this issue extremely seriously and would discipline members in the sternest manner for violating this rule. In 1941 one of the erstwhile members started a private contract business and a few members went to work for him; they were subsequently removed from the Cooperative's rolls. In 1945 two other members were expelled for similar reasons.[14]

The other contentious issue was the issue of share capital payments, which the Society took very seriously. The general body meeting held in December 1939 resolved that members

[13] Minutes of ULCCS, General Body meeting, 11 March 1939, Vol. I, pp. 92-93.

[14] Minutes of ULCCS, Board of Directors meeting, 24 June 1945, Vol. IA, p. 21.

who had paid only 4 annas entry fee and had not paid their share capital within three years of their entry into the Cooperative, had one year to pay the deficit. If they failed to pay their deficit within one year, they would be removed from the membership. The attempt to implement the decision created much furore, and a public statement by a number of members was issued protesting against the decision. The general body meeting in January 1941 proved to be stormy with a number of members submitting written questions to the board of directors. After detailed discussions, 70 members who continued to refuse to pay any additional amount other than the entry fee were removed from the roll. This was a difficult decision, but the Cooperative's ability to make firm decisions like this was crucial to its long term viability.

THE ORGANIZATIONAL STRUCTURE AND INTERNAL DEMOCRACY

All members were entitled to attend the general body meetings where all important strategic decisions were made. In addition, the general body meetings elected the five members of the board of directors, which was often called the panchayat.[15] Members' democratic right was not confined to the formal function of voting for elected leaders, but extended to workplace participation and in the decision making process of the Cooperative.

The board of directors was responsible for carefully considering the tenders to be submitted both in terms of their profitability and viability and with regard to working conditions, and making the final decision as to whether the

[15] Panchayat literally means a five member body. It later came to refer to rural local government because they initially consisted of five member leadership.

Cooperative would participate in the tender. Once a tender agreement was signed the project would be implemented either directly by the Society or sub-contracted to a group of workers. The bylaws of the Society had clearly provided for such flexibility in operation:

> The board of directors shall be competent to enter into contract for the execution of the public or private works or to undertake piece or job work on behalf of the Society. These works shall be executed through or with the help of members. Works may be executed either by giving subcontracts to groups of members or by employing them on daily wages or on piece work. When sufficient members are not available, the board of directors may employ persons other than the members to such extent as may be necessary to do any work which the Society has in hand and may pay them such remuneration as may be reasonable. The board of directors can enter into agreements with members for the due performance of work or works entrusted to them or of the work allotted to them from day to day. They may also take steps to enforce the fulfilment of such agreement in accordance with the provisions of the workman's Breach of Contract Act III of 1859.[16]

If the work was sub-contracted to a group of workers a formal agreement would be signed with the Society. Like all its other projects in which the Society did the work directly, the Society would allocate one of its board members supervisory oversight to manage the project and ensure the Society's standards are maintained. One of the conditions for such agreements was that a certain amount of the net profit would go to the Society. The way in which the Cooperative organized

[16] Bylaws of ULCCS, 1925, p. 3.

the labour process distinguishes it from a normal capitalist enterprise. At the end of every working day the workers would review the day's work and collectively decide on the next day's tasks and division of labour. Every night, the site leaders (who were members of the board of directors) returned to the head office from the worksites and would collectively review the day's works at all the sites. This allowed them to problem solve and ensure efficiency across sites. For instance, if one site was short of building material, through these evening meetings with all site leaders they would quickly know if another site could send some of their material to fill the shortfall. The site leader would then report on the evening meeting to the worker-members at the site the next morning. An additional benefit of this system was that it meant that all board members were on construction sites every day and had regular and close relations with the members. Overtime this organizational structure became a key feature of the functioning of the Society and site leaders were either board members or as the number of projects grew the site leaders were also selected from among the worker-members. The structure not only ensured quick and efficient decision making (which is often the critique of democratic workplaces), but also maintained democratic processes and constant communication from the various levels of the Cooperative and across the different construction sites.

While the Cooperative faced many challenges in meeting its members' needs, it creatively addressed many issues through collective solutions. For example, because of their financial difficulties wages often fell into arrears. The Society, therefore, began to provide meals and refreshments to workers at the worksites or make arrangements with nearby teashops to provide meals. The Society also made arrangements to provide groceries on credit with various shops. These various arrangements demonstrated the Society's structural power in the local economy, and also showed its members that it was doing everything it could to ensure members' immediate needs were met. Similarly, if the worksite was far from Uralungal, the Society provided temporary accommodation at or near the site. Wages were also relatively better than the private sector and in 1948 the wages were substantially increased to Rs 2.50 for male workers and Rs 1.0 for women workers.[17] The discrepancy in male and female wages is problematic and it is a shortcoming of the Society that it did not take on gender inequality at this time, but it also must be placed within the patriarchal context and historical time in which the Cooperative came of age as well as the nature of the industry. Construction work has traditionally been largely a male profession, and the women who joined the Cooperative usually did so in other capacities and low-skilled jobs such as office assistance, cooking, and cleaning. Eighty years later, the Cooperative would show itself to be more gender sensitive and consciously recruit women to positions once dominated by men such as engineering and architecture.

The Cooperative's democratic internal functioning is also demonstrated in the robustness of the annual general body meetings, which were not formalities but rather occasions for serious discussions. In the latter half of the 1930s, the Cooperative failed to convene annual general body meetings for consecutive years for various reasons. This sparked widespread criticism from the members who insisted that a general body meeting be convened. The self-styled union president of ULCCS workers, Maniyoth Choyi, served notice for the meeting as union president. The president of the

[17] Minutes of ULCCS, Board of Directors meeting, 3rd March 1948, Vol. IA, p. 45.

meeting, however, ruled that Mr. Choyi could not address the general body as union president – the Society never had a union – but could raise questions as an ordinary member of the Society. Maniyoth Choyi's attempt to parachute himself and his union into Cooperative's leadership was, thus, resisted and he withdrew his claim to be the union president and raised the following pertinent questions. Secretary C. Kunjyekku Gurukkal replied for the board of directors.

> Question 1: Have all the members read the bylaws of the Society? If not will it [*sic*] be read aloud before this gathering?
> Answer 1: All members have read or heard and agreed to the bylaws before they joined the Society. If anybody so desires it [*sic*] can be read to them.
> Question 2: (a)What is the reason for not convening the general body for last five years? (b) What is the term for the Panchayat?
> Answer 2: (a) Because no member demanded a general body meeting. (b) Until the next election.
> Question 3: Is there provision for the audit report or inspection note by higher authorities to be presented in the general body? If yes, why was not general body convened?
> Answer 3: There is provision for placing the audit report and inspection note in the general body. They have also been placed. The query why the general body is not convened has already been raised in the second question and answered.
> Question 4: Is there any bylaw provision for sub-contracting to the members the contract received by the Society? If yes, has it been given to anyone? If yes, would you place the accounts related to them on the table?
> Answer 4: There is no legal provision. No sub-contract has been given. There is no need to place the accounts of an action not yet undertaken. It is also not the customary practice.

Question 5: What is the capital of the Society? What is the profit for each year?
Answer 5: The registered capital is Rs 17,500. The profit for each year can be seen from the audit report. Audit report is placed on the table.
Question 6: Has the notice been given to all the members and signed by them for the general body meeting being convened on 4-12-1938? If not, why?
Answer 6: Notices have been delivered to the houses of all members. It has been signed by everyone who could be directly contacted.[18]

This exchange reflects the vitality of Cooperative's internal structure as members demanded accountability from the elected leadership. Unfortunately, we do not have further records of the discussions surrounding the above exchange between Choyi and Gurukkal. From the records, it is unclear as to why the provisions in the bylaw to sub-contract the orders were denied. This is especially curious as sub-contracting was not to individuals but to a group of members who would function as a democratic unit. Nevertheless, the first sub-contract was given in October 1939, nearly a year after the general body meeting referred to above. The issue of the Union does not re-appear in any records of the Cooperative. The criticism, however, had long standing effect. On December 16, 1938, another general body meeting was convened and the board of directors was re-organized. Since then the Cooperative has convened at least one annual general body meeting every year.

One important factor that shaped the democratic character of the Cooperative is that both the members and the elected leaders in the board of directors were all workers –

[18] Minutes of ULCCS, General Body meeting, 4th December 1938, Vol. I, pp. 82-83.

the only exception was the first secretary who was a coconut trader. This gave the board of director's legitimacy among the membership and prevented them from being alienated from the members even when the board had to take strong decisions to enforce discipline and financial propriety from the members. A perusal of the records throughout this period shows that all the members of the board of directors were construction workers except the first secretary mentioned above and two school teachers who were among the initial promoters of the Cooperative. Membership on the board of directors was a full-time activity because it also included the supervisory roles at the construction sites. In fact, the members of the board had extra obligations as it also met every evening to share information about the different sites. Yet board members were not paid an additional monthly honorarium, but received the same daily wages as worker members. The Cooperative statute allows for an additional payment to the secretary, which the Society only made if there was net profit.

For most of the board members, their engagement in the Society was more a social commitment than simply a source of livelihood. The deep commitment to egalitarianism is reflected in the system of remuneration and the relationship between the board members and worker members. The cooperative spirit and commitment to egalitarian values and democratic participation of the original members, which continue to define the Cooperative, cannot be understood independent of their embededness in the social milieu of the region. The radical social reform movement engendered a social awakening that also led to the formation of the Cooperative. In the next section we discuss the socio-political evolution during the later decades that left deep imprints on the ethos of the Cooperative.

FROM SOCIAL REFORM TO RADICAL NATIONAL MOVEMENT

The Civil Disobedience Movement of 1930 finally broke the lull in the national movement of Malabar after the fiasco of Non-Cooperation and Khilafat movement. The campaign to boycott the Simon Commission – the team of British parliamentarians examining the possibilities of constitutional reforms in India – created ripples in Malabar. Influenced by the disastrous experience of 1921, a large section of Congress men thought that it was too dangerous to launch the Civil Disobedience Movement in Malabar. Moyarath Sankaran, one of the Congress leaders, took the initiative to break the stalemate. A special meeting of KPCC was held in Vadakara and he introduced a resolution proclaiming Payyannur as the satyagraha site for breaking the salt law in Malabar. After heated debate the resolution was adopted with near unanimous support and the large crowd that had gathered to observe the meeting applauded approvingly.[19]

The salt satyagraha started with Gandhiji and his fellow satyagrahis taking a long trek from his ashram to the beach at Dandi in Gujarat. Payyannur was the Dandi of Malabar and a week long journey from Kozhikode similar to the Dandi Yatra by Gandhiji was re-enacted under the leadership of Kelappan. Moyarath Sankaran, the pilot of the Jatha, recalls that one of the largest receptions was at Vattoli, a village near Vadakara.[20] The satyagraha at Payyannur was peaceful but the repressive arm of the government came down heavily on the participants at Kozhikode beach. One of the most famous accounts of

[19] Janardhanan Moyarath (ed.), *Moyarath Sankaran: Athmakathayum Charithra Smaranakalum*, Trivandrum: Chintha Publishers, 2012, pp. 53-55.

[20] Ibid., p. 56.

heroism in the face of the government's violence was how P. Krishna Pillai defied the lathis until he lost consciousness in order to protect the national flag that he carried. In response, there was widespread picketing of toddy shops and shops selling foreign cloths as well as convening large public meetings and demonstrations that rocked the towns and villages.

The Movement drew a new crop of young political activists, like P. Krishna Pillai, E.M.S. Namboodiripad and A.K. Gopalan, into the forefront of the national movement. The heroic and enthusiastic participation of young people aroused mass appeal. The withdrawal of the Civil Disobedience Movement following the Gandhi-Irwin Pact and diversion of the political movement into nation-building and constructive work and the 'Harijan' welfare programme deeply disappointed this new generation of young activists. The Fifth All Kerala Political Conference was held in Vadakara which put forward the programme of satyagraha at the Guruvayur temple for the right of avarnas to enter the temple. The Guruvayur Satyagraha also had a disappointing and subdued outcome. The disenchantment of the youth with Gandhi's compromises was evident in the relative failure to organize the second campaign of the Civil Disobedience Movement in 1932.

However, these disappointments with the moderate turn by nationalist leaders did not lead the youth to become inactive. Rather the disillusioned young activists turned their attention to more radical positions. The search for an alternative attracted them to the Congress Socialist Party (CSP), which was emerging at the national level as a left pressure group within Congress. The CSP unit of Malabar was formed at Kozhikode in May 1934.[21] The most important contribution

[21] For a comprehensive narrative of the history of Communist Party in Kozhikode district, see T.P. Ramakrishnan, et al (eds.), *Kozhikode Jilla, Communist Party Charithram*, Kozhikode: Keluettan Padana

of the CSP was mobilizing the poorer strata of the peasantry, particularly the tenants at will, focusing on rent reduction, security of tenure and debt relief. It was in northern Malabar, including the region of our labour Cooperative, that the peasant upsurge was most widespread and militant. Starting with campaigns against illegal land evictions and oppressive social customs the peasant movement in the region developed into a 'no rent' campaign. In addition to local conditions, the sharp fall in the agricultural prices due to the Great Depression also contributed to the agrarian unrest. In this climate of mass unrest, trade unions also rapidly advanced and took root in various factories. For example, Vadakara was the arena of a prolonged struggle of *beedi*[22] workers.

The CSP activists in Malabar tended to gravitate towards the Communist Party and Marxist Leninist ideology. In 1937 the first communist group was formed with E.M.S. Namboodiripad, N.C. Sekhar, K. Damodaran and P. Krishna Pillai. Forming the communist group sharpened the conflict between the right and left factions within Congress. The CSP was ousted from the leadership of KPCC in 1934, but regained it in 1938 in alliance with the faction of Muslim nationalists under the leadership of Abdur Rahman Sahib. In the same year, a secret conclave of some CSP members – including the newly formed communist group – was held and at this meeting the decision was made to convert CSP into the Communist Party. The September 1939 anti-imperialist mass mobilization called by the left in the KPCC and the violent confrontations that resulted led to the purge of CSP leaders from the leadership of Congress. But by this time, almost all the CSP units in Malabar had shifted their allegiance to the Communist Party and they controlled the grassroots level of Congress. Thus, the

Gaveshana Kendram, 2011.

[22] Beedis are hand rolled cigarettes with tendu leaves.

Communist Party planted firm roots in Malabar.

The transformation that occurred in the national movement is a ubiquitous theme seen in every autobiography and biography of communist leaders in Malabar. To take one example, Moyarath Sankaran was the secretary of Congress in Kurumbanadu *taluk* for 13 years, a member of Malabar district committee and a member of the KPCC. Born into a lower middle class nair house, Moyarath was a rebellious child from his school days. As a keen school debater and budding poet, young Moyarath was attracted by Vagbhatananda's challenge to temple worship and traditional customs. He was often an attendee in the gatherings of devotees and admirers of Sree Narayana Guru and Kumaranasan when they visited Thalassery. He recalls how the Sree Narayana Guru responded to Kumaranasan who was trying to advocate his new-found enthusiasm for conversion to Buddhism, 'Does it matter what the religion is? Is it not enough that people are upright?' Moyarath, reflecting his mission school education, loudly commented 'But Buddha was an atheist.' Sree Narayana Guru smiled and asked, 'How many ahimsa atheist incarnations of Buddha do we have?' Such exchanges left a deep imprint on the young Moyarath.

Moyarath went to study medicine in Calcutta where he was introduced to the different trends in national politics from Bengal terrorists to Bengali renaissance leaders. Frightened by his alleged proximity to radical politics, his family made him return to Malabar where he drifted into the national movement. He was a participant in the Manjeri district conference of the Congress in 1921 and argued for Congress taking up the cause of tenants-at-will rather than the superior tenants alone, highlighting the severe oppression of tenants-at-will by the *jenmis*. The Manjeri Conference marked a major shift in Congress, which went from a forum of moderate upper caste elites to a movement espousing the cause of tenants and open struggle against British rule. Moyarath's main area of activities was Kurumbanadu *taluk* – which consists of present-day Koyilandi and Vadakara *taluks*, and is where Onchiyam panchayat and Uralungal are situated – and returned to live in his maternal house in Onchiyam. Like other young activists, he was deeply disappointed with Gandhian tactics and got into an angry argument with Kelappan, the unquestioned Gandhian leader in Malabar, on the second day of his incarceration in Kannur jail. He was annoyed at the inedible food that was being accepted by the satyagrahis without protest and on the first day he led a chorus of slogan shouters protesting against jail conditions. The next day Kelappan admonished him. Moyarath replied that there should not be different grades for political prisoners, better food must be served and political prisoners will not do heavy labour. Kelappan's position was that as Gandhians, they must obey the jail rules. Moyarath retorted that he was in jail for breaking laws and therefore it made no sense why he would follow them once he was in jail. As this exchange shows, the conservative Congress leaders were being challenged by a new generation of activists. Like many other young people of his generation, it is this course of events of disappointment with the Congress's moderate positions that took Moyarath initially to CSP and then later to the Communist Party.[23]

In the subsequent years, Moyarath played an important role in building the left movement in the Vadakara area and gained a respected reputation for his self-sacrifice, endurance, heroism and organizational skills. His first contribution was the tenancy conference held in 1924 near Vadakara which sent

[23] Janardhanan Moyarath, *Moyarath Sankaran*, pp. 29, 43.

a delegation of a hundred poor tenants to Madras.[24] Over the years, he became a mentor to a large number of left activists in the region such as P.R. Nambiar (who played a signal role in building up the teachers movement), K. Kelu (who organized the peasants along the hilly tracks of the *taluk* and would later become the most important leader of the Communist Party in Kozhikode), and U. Kunjhiraman (who played the leading role in organising the workers particularly the *beedi* workers in Vadakara).

The intense political activity during the Second World War brought the Vadakara region into the vortex of radical politics. The anti-Japp mela[25] at Onchiyam was one of the largest in Malabar. Communist activists were at the forefront of activities that brought relief to people distressed by the hardships caused by war such as famine, scarcity of cloth and kerosene, and the general deterioration of health conditions causing outbreaks of epidemics. Those who could afford to hoard goods such as food, cloth, kerosene exacerbated the shortages. As a result, hoarders and landlords were the targets of the food campaigns. It was campaigns like these that fought causes for the most vulnerable segments of society that helped communists shore up support of a disciplined mass base in the region. Slowly Onchiyam and its surroundings became such a stronghold of communist influence that it became a favourite underground shelter area for the communist leaders.

The pinnacle of Onchiyam's radicalization was in 1948, a year after India's Independence. The Communist Party's mobilization of peasants came to a head in violent

[24] P.P. Shaju, *Onchiyathinte Viplava Porattangalude Charithram*, Kozhikode: Chintha Publishers, 2011, p. 66.

[25] After the entry of the Soviet Union into the war, the Communist Party adopted a slogan of people's war and undertook preparations and propaganda to resist a possible Japanese invasion of India.

confrontation between the police and peasants in various parts of Malabar. A team of Malabar Special Police, a paramilitary force organized in the wake of Malabar rebellion of 1921, came in search of the Communist Party *taluk* leadership, who were holding a clandestine meeting in Onchiyam. The Special Police failed in the search, but apprehended two villagers who they brutally assaulted and locked up in the police station. A large crowd quickly gathered, pointing out that no one can be arrested without warrant and that the two villagers must be set free. The police opened fire on the unarmed crowd, killing eight people and injuring dozens more. Acting with impunity, the police issued arrest warrants for a large number of cadres and over the next few weeks search and assault operations continued. Tales of heroic resistance and sacrifices by large numbers of people have become folklore and part of the identity of the region. For example, Mandodi Kannan drew the party symbol on the wall of his cell with his own blood before he was tortured to death. By the time the repression ended, there was hardly a house that was not raided or a member of one's family beaten up. Onchiyam became one of the 'Communist villages,' where the vast majority of residents are communists or sympathizers and the party's hegemony is total.

A month after the Onchiyam tragedy, Moyarath was captured by a group of Congress volunteers and police while he was on the way to his wife's house in Edakkad. He was declared a communist terrorist, beaten up by the Congress goons and again later by the police while in lock up. He was moved to Kannur Central Prison badly beaten and died of his injuries at Kannur Central Prison.

While all this turmoil was happening in Onchiyam and the surrounding areas, the daily work in the labour Cooperative in Uralungal also experienced inevitable disruptions. The turnover in 1947-48 shows a sharp decline, but returned to normal levels soon after. The Cooperative was not directly involved in the political unrest though many of the workers were active in the movement. For example, Kattil Andi Master, the school teacher involved in setting up the Cooperative as well as the credit society, housing society, milk society, carpenter society, and jaggery society, was arrested and kept in police lock up for his involvement in the struggle, which included providing shelter and food to party leaders. He later became the panchayat president of Onchiyam.

There is an interesting, and surprising, feature of the ULCCS in comparison to other leading cooperatives in Malabar such as Kerala Dinesh Beedi Cooperative. Unlike other leading cooperatives, there are no well-known senior leaders of the Communist Party at the helm of the ULCCS. While most of the members of the board had clear leftist orientations, none were party activists. The reason for this is due to the Society's decision to constitute the board only from worker members (except for the few exceptional cases of original promoters). All board members were workers, and were expected to be involved in the day-to-day activities of the Society, including the evening site review meetings. An unintended outcome of only having worker leaders managing the Cooperative was that it facilitated the functional autonomy of the Cooperative. It also suggests that the political environment of the area allowed and facilitated autonomous activities like the Cooperative. Indeed, the egalitarianism and grassroots democracy that the left was inculcating had a very strong influence on the evolution of the Cooperative. Thus, while the Cooperative was only tangentially involved in the unrest, it was integrally linked to the larger political environment of its region.

CHAPTER 4

POST-INDEPENDENCE EXPANSION OF ULCCS

One of the standing committees of Second Five Year Plan has recently drawn the attention of the State Governments to the importance of entrusting the public works to the labour contract societies in the respective areas. [. . .] It is a painful fact that even though the first half of the Plan is over, labour contract societies have not been formed in most of the States. This reality has prompted the Standing Committee to issue a warning to the States.

In Kerala State, during 1957-59 government took initiative to form one labour contract society in every block for implementing the public works. [. . .] Since it was a new programme, the societies were not able to effectively move forward. Can we blame the activists of the cooperatives for this failure? The experience shows that we cannot. They had to face numerous problems. [. . .]

Normally our cooperatives require 4 or 5 years of work before they can hold their heads straight. Therefore there is no need to despair that the labour contract societies have not been successful within one and half years. But there is one point on which there can be no compromise. If there has been any

> corruption in any society there must not be any delay in taking stringent action.
>
> Since our state has already taken one step forward in forming labour contract societies it would be highly improper to go back now, particularly after the position taken by the standing committee of Five Year Plan. There is much to be gained by avoiding middle men and entrusting the public works directly to the workers in the locality. Workers will get better remuneration. Local development activities would be taken up with greater sincerity. Labour contract societies can also be utilized to mobilize volunteer work for development programmes.
>
> Joseph Mundassery[1]

The advent of planning in post-Independence India heralded a new era in the history of cooperatives in India. During the colonial period, cooperatives were encouraged by the state but the nature of state intervention was largely regulatory. In contrast, the planners in the post-Independence period considered cooperatives an important instrument for providing rural credit, processing and marketing of agriculture and agricultural-allied sector products, reorganizing the handicraft traditional industries as well as for other objectives such as intervention in consumer markets and housing. The second Five Year Plan mooted the idea of labour contract societies and emphasized the state's role to actively support cooperative societies.

The first elected government of the newly formed State of Kerala (1957-59) drew up a programme to actively

[1] Joseph Mundassery was a co-operator and former Education Minister in the state government, 1957-59; Joseph Mundassery, 'The Future of Labour Contract Societies,' *Sahakarana Prabhodhini*, 31, 11, May 1960, pp. 3, 4, 19-20.

promote labour contract societies. The programme continued in the subsequent decades with varied degrees of success. Because it was already well developed with over thirty years of experience, ULCCS was able to effectively utilize the new opportunities and steadily expand its membership and turnover. There are two important moments of state support for labour contract societies in Kerala: (1) the Communist Ministry of 1957-59 and (2) the People's Plan Campaign for Democratic Decentralization initiated by the Left Government in 1996-2001. In this chapter, we focus on the first moment of state support (we cover the second moment in chapter 5).

THE COMMUNIST MINISTRY OF 1957-59 AND LABOUR CONTRACT SOCIETIES

In November 1956, United Kerala was formed integrating the Malabar district of the Madras Presidency and the erstwhile princely states of Travancore and Cochin, a long cherished dream of Malayalam speaking people. Surprising both India and the rest of the world, the Communist Party won majority by a slender margin in the first election to the State legislature in 1957.[2] Forming one of the first elected communist governments in the world, the Communist Party had only 31 per cent of the votes but still earned the majority in the Assembly because of the split among the non-communist parties. Given the intense political contestation, it is a remarkable achievement that the Communist Party emerged as the largest political formation in the state. The peasant struggles in north Malabar and the working class uprising of Punnapra Vayalar in the south firmly established the Kerala communists in the leadership of the national

[2] G.K. Leiten, *The First Communist Ministry in Kerala, 1957-59*, K.P. Bagchi, Calcutta, 1982.

movement, which was a determining factor in the meteoric rise of communist influence during 1946-1956.[3]

The Communist Party's experience in government came with serious challenges. The new communist government tried to implement a modest programme consisting mostly of progressive pronouncements made by the nationalist movement (i.e., Congress) with regards to agrarian reforms, cooperatives, civil rights, and universal education, all of which were also proclaimed principles of the national Five Year Plans. However, the actual implementation of the programme triggered intense resistance, paving way to the deeply undemocratic 'Anti-Communist Liberation Struggle of 1959,' which culminated in the dismissal of the Communist Ministry by the central government.[4] Within the short duration of its time in government, the Communist Ministry left an indelible mark on Kerala's socioeconomic life. The programme to support labour contract societies is only one minor example of the Party's achievements in government.

In 1957, ULCCS was the only labour contract society in the State. When discussions about the formation of new labour contract societies were initiated in ULCCS, one concern that arose was whether a multiplicity of societies in the same locality would result in unhealthy competition. ULCCS's general body meeting on December 28, 1957 adopted a resolution requesting government to limit the number of new labour contract societies to one society per *taluk*. The resolution also stated that ULCCS was willing to accommodate all construction workers in Vadakara *taluk*

---

[3] George K.C., *Immortal Punnapra Vayalar*, Communist Party of India, New Delhi, 1975.

[4] Thomas Isaac, *Vimochanasamarathinte Kaanappurangal*, Chintha Publishers, Thiruvananthapuram, 2009.

who wanted to join the Cooperative as members.[5]

The government eventually decided to limit the number of labour contract societies to one per block, perhaps as a response to ULCCS's resolution. A model bylaw was prepared by the Public Works Department incorporating provisions that government thought were necessary to address certain problems that the labour contract societies would face. There were three primary threats that they feared: (1) It would be difficult for labour contract societies to raise sufficient capital to undertake public works; (2) Ordinary workers were unlikely to have sufficient managerial ability to supervise the large public works; and (3) Given the above conditions, there was the danger of middlemen and contractors capturing the cooperatives. The model bylaws developed special features to address these particular challenges.[6]

First, only workers including skilled workers such as carpenters, iron-smiths, and masons were allowed to be members of the labour contract societies. It was understood that a few persons who may not be workers might be required in-order to properly supervise the work and keep the accounts. Yet the model bylaws were insistent that their numbers must be kept to a minimum and workers autonomy and initiative should not be compromised. The characteristic feature of ULCCS was thus being mainstreamed. Second, the president of the labour contract society should be the Block Officer or another equivalent government officer. Third, the representative of Cooperative Department and PWD should be given representation in the working committee of the cooperative. Fourth, a government officer who is a member of the working committee should be responsible for all the

[5] Minutes of ULCCS, General Body meeting, 28th December 1957, Vol. III, p. 77.

[6] Joseph Mundassery, 'The Future of Labour Contract Societies,' p. 4.

materials and equipment provided by the PWD.

Clauses two to four were alien to the character of ULCCS. There was no representation of government on its board and there was no day-to-day intervention by government in the activities of ULCCS. The Society deeply cherished its autonomy and did not want it compromised. However, the Department of Public Works insisted that societies would not function effectively without official members from government given the complex nature of their work. A compromise position emerged: once the cooperatives gained experience, the number of officials may be reduced or removed.

And fifth, all bills issued by government departments must be cashed through an account in the District Cooperative Bank (DCB). This clause was included to ensure timely repayment of loans provided by the credit cooperatives. There were two options for the government to provide finance to the labour contract societies. The first option was for government to contribute to the share capital. The second option was to provide credit for a minimum percentage of the estimated cost of the work. The government chose the second option, but it was felt that there must be a special mechanism to ensure repayment. ULCCS operated an account with the Malabar District Cooperative Bank (MDCB), which often provided cash credit after pledging the future payment drafts and cheques from the PWD. Rigid implementation of this procedure often created severe working capital constraints for the Society and on a number of occasions the Society had to formally request greater flexibility from the MDCB.[7]

Finally, in the general body meeting on 28 December 1958, ULCCS resolved that it would make the necessary

[7] Minutes of ULCCS, Board of Directors meeting, 8th March 1954, Vol. II, pp. 115-116.

amendments to its bylaws so that the Society would be included in the scheme of the National Extension Service (NES) block labour contract societies. However, the entire programme of labour contract societies never took off as it became the centre of controversy with the anti-communist opposition alleging that the new labour contract societies were a nefarious effort to siphon off public funds by party cadres. The private contractors also came out against the new societies arguing that they were subverting a well-established system of executing public works.[8] Fortunately for ULCCS the amendments to its bylaws were never made.

In 1961, the Deputy Chief Minister of the new Congress-led government that came to power after dismissing the Communist government reported in the legislative assembly that there were 45 labour contract societies in the NES Block Scheme and 17 societies outside the scheme. Fifty-six societies had formed in the short period of the Communist-led government and the new government had formed six additional labour contract societies. However, out of the 62 societies only 20 were active. The government launched an enquiry in to the 12 non-functioning societies and reported that it recommended dissolving two societies.[9] The experience of the first five years of a united Kerala, thus, yielded mixed results for the cooperative societies in the state.

LABOUR CONTRACT SOCIETIES IN KERALA

From 1967 to 1980 the growth in societies and the concomitant growth in members was relatively slow, growing

[8] Proceedings of Kerala Legislative Assembly, 3rd session 1958, 6th December 1958, Vol. 6, No. 12, p. 816.

[9] Proceedings of Kerala Legislative Assembly, 28th December 1961, p. 1348.

from 58 to 75 societies with a membership of 7,844 and 10,718 respectively. Table 4.1 summarizes the trend in the number of labour contract societies, their membership, paid-up capital and turnover from 1967 onwards. The number of societies continued to rise slowly until the latter half of the 1980s after which time it has tended to rise rapidly, particularly in the latter half of 1990s when the People's Plan Campaign (PPC) was launched (discussed in the next chapter). The steady (and rapid) expansion in the number of labour contract societies did not reflect a healthy trend for three reasons. (1) A significant proportion of labour contract societies were dormant. During the early 1960s the proportion of dormant societies was around 50 per cent, during the 1970s it dropped to 25 per cent, and, during the latter half of 1990s it rose to more than one third. (2) Only a small and declining proportion of the societies were earning profits. The majority – though it should be noted that this figure includes the dormant societies – were in the category 'not on profit or loss.' (3) ULCCS was one of the few successful societies and thus skewed the overall data. Even though the proportion of ULCCS in the total membership declined from 2.16 per cent in the latter half of 1960s to 0.52 per cent in the end of 1990s, the share of ULCCS in the paid-up capital and turnover steadily increased. At the end of 1990s ULCCS accounted for 66 per cent of the overall turnover of all labour contract societies of Kerala.

Some of the labour contract societies tried to emulate the experience of ULCCS and were efficient and profitable ventures, though on a much smaller scale (discussed further in the next chapter). Nevertheless, the majority of the societies were well-meaning attempts that ultimately failed to take off in the generally hostile environment created by private contractors. Former minister and co-operator

Table 4.1: The growth of labour contract societies in Kerala and the relative share of ULCCS

Year	No. of societies	Dormant societies	Members	Paid-up capital	Profit making societies	ULCCS Membership	ULCCS Paid-up capital	ULCCS Turnover
	Nos	Nos	Nos	Rs	Nos	%	%	%
1967-70	58	-	7,844	333	NA	2.16	12.97	24.18
1971-75	64	17	8,431	512	NA	1.29	13.04	26.58
1976-80	75	24	10,718	794	NA	1.87	18.15	27.36
1981-85	87	17	18,775	1,345	NA	1.11	29.39	16.86
1986-90	97	14	12,642	1,855	28	1.04	31.07	NA
1991-95	231	58	28,074	5,559	56	0.77	21.64	13.11
1997-03	424	152	50,497	15,536	92	0.52	37.16	66.57

Source: Collated from the Department of Co-operation, Statistical Abstract from 1966-67 to 2009–10, GOK, Thiruvananthapuram.

Joseph Mundassery explained, 'They had to face numerous problems such as not receiving credit from the bank in time, not receiving the cooperation of block officers who are the presidents, non-friendly attitudes of the officials of the PWD, and the inefficiency of supervisors and so on. It should also be remembered that the cooperatives do not have the freedom of the private contractors for manipulation. Some of the cooperatives got into trouble by taking up more responsibilities than they can shoulder.'[10]

A significant proportion of the cooperatives were also *benami* organizations of private contractors trying to take advantage of the preferences given to labour contract societies in the awarding of public works. Given the widespread prevalence of this practice, it is surprising that the turnover of the vast majority of societies is still meagre. The private contractors use the name of the society to secure contracts and then carry them out independently so that the work executed does not ever enter the accounts of the society. Through a power of attorney issued by the society the payment is directly made to the private contractor's account. This capture of the societies by private contractors brought disrepute to the entire sector. It is in this rather gloomy context that the performance of ULCCS becomes inspirational and extraordinary.

THE EXPANSION OF MEMBERSHIP AND SHARE CAPITAL OF ULCCS

As we have seen in the last chapter, the membership in ULCCS dropped to 126 in 1948-49 as a result of the removal of a large number of members due to arrears in the payment of the share amount. During the first two decades

[10] Joseph Mundassery, 'The Future of Labour Contract Societies,' p. 90.

of the post-Independence period the membership fluctuated between 140 and 180, and dropped to 89 in 1971-72 and only began to revive in 1975-76 when it sharply jumped to above 200 (Table 4.2). This increase was primarily due to a special membership drive to retain the 'A class' classification for the Society. Membership of 200 was a necessary condition for a cooperative to be classified as A class. The increase in membership put severe strain on the capacity of the Society to provide full-time work for all members. The tradition in ULCCS was to provide members full-time work in exchange for members' commitment to not seek work under private contractors. Going to work under private contractors was considered a serious breach of discipline. The bylaws stipulate that members cannot work for any private contractor, which had periodically posed a problem and was one of the reasons for occasional expulsions from membership.[11] In addition, unauthorized absenteeism was also severely sanctioned and could be cause for expulsion.[12] Thus, the society took its responsibility of providing full-time work to its members very seriously as it also demanded discipline and commitment from its members in return.

One of the most important features of ULCCS is that membership is restricted to actual workers. In the 1969 bylaws, the number of non-workers was restricted to a total of seven members, which was later revised in the 2008 bylaws, removing the clause entirely and formally restricting all membership to actual workers. Another challenge the Society faced was the geographical restriction on membership

[11] Minutes of ULCCS, General Body meeting, 4 June 1954, Vol. II, p. 108. The expulsion of four members in the general body meeting after debate. See also Vol. XVII, 16 June 1968, p. 128.

[12] Minutes of ULCCS, General Body meeting, 16 June 1968, Vol. VII, for reference to the expulsion for absenteeism.

to the *taluk* of Vadakara, which created problems when the Society increasingly took work projects in other *taluks* and districts. On the one hand, some members were unwilling to travel outside their locality for work. On the other hand, local workers in the different *taluks* demanded employment in the contracts taken by the Society. The matter came to a head at Meppayyur – in the adjacent *taluk* of Quilandy – where local workers demanded employment at the worksite of ULCCS. The Society's position was that being a workers' cooperative its main objective was to provide work to its members and therefore it was against the Society's principles to employ outside wage labourers as the main body of workers. This principle was so dear to the Society that it relinquished the contract in order to resolve the issue.[13]

Because of the regular employment and relatively better labour conditions that the Society guaranteed, the demand for membership was high. The society had a system of recruitment where an aspirant member would have to work in the quarry site for two to three years. As he – they were all men at this time – became a skilled stone crusher his sense of discipline, temperament and commitment to work were assessed by the team leaders and board of directors before membership was given.

This situation, however, changed with the rapid expansion of turnover from the 1970s. Three new developments occurred at this time. (1) The nature of work became more and more technical and complex requiring skilled workers who were in short supply in the membership. (2) As the area of operation of the Society extended to the rest of Malabar and later throughout Kerala, it became impractical to transport

[13] Minutes of ULCCS, Board of Directors meeting, 22 September 1974, Vol. XXXIII, pp. 312-313.

Table 4.2: Membership and share capital of ULCCS, 1950–51 to 2015-16

Year	Opening membership	Admission	Removal	Closing membership	Members share amount Rs	Govt share amount Rs	Total share amount Rs
1951-55	142	42	34	150	40087	0	40087
1956-60	150	49	41	158	52837	0	52837
1961-65	158	19	40	137	107367	4000	111367
1966-70	137	42	10	169	185901	10000	195901
1971-75	169	17	104	82	313476	10000	323476
1976-80	82	170	41	211	698265	16000	714265
1981-85	211	32	26	217	1954280	50000	2004280
1986-90	217	43	58	202	4154870	90000	4244870
1991-95	202	43	37	208	5925195	75000	6000195
1996-00	208	53	23	238	9861920	12012000	21873920
2001-05	238	191	21	408	20862370	13200000	34062370
2006-10	408	649	64	993	58318507	357300000	415618507
2011-13	993	1153	106	2040	85459715	883430000	968889715
2014-16	2040	118	18	2140	52362555	216630000	268992555

Source: Collated from Auditor's Final Report, relevant years, Records of ULCCS.

the entire workforce from Vadakara to these distant places. (3) Bunching of works and commitment to complete every work project on time created occasional labour shortages. All three of these issues necessitated hiring temporary workers from outside the membership and in the subsequent decades, the relative importance of non-member workers increased. Another new dimension to the problem of labour supply arose when the traditional recruitment source of construction workers began to dry up. The new generation of educated youth increasingly withdrew from construction work, an unintended consequence of the progressive and successful state government programmes to expand access to education. Similar to the other construction worksites in Kerala, ULCCS was also compelled to employ migrant workers from North India. In 2003-04, an estimated average number of non-member workers were 829 with about 724 working in any given month. The membership at the time was only around 300.[14]

Having such a large number of non-members in relation to actual members was an embarrassing situation for the Cooperative. The Society decided to recruit hard-working workers in the non-member category as members. A major issue was that most of the migrant workers did not plan to remain in Kerala long-term and therefore were not interested in membership and the labour turnover among them was very high. The Cooperative responded to the problem with an innovative solution: a new class of membership, 'C class,' was created to provide membership to non-regular workers. Any non-member workers who had been employed by the Cooperative for around one year, could request C class

[14] Rajinder Chaudhary, 'ULCCS: An 80 Year Old Construction Labour Cooperative', *International Journal of Rural Management*, 1(2), 2005, 1, pp. 263-284.

membership. The value of C class share was Rs 5 until 2007, when it was raised to Rs 25. Such a 'nominal member' was entitled to receive all fringe benefits of A class members such as a bonus, leave with wages, medical allowances, Provident Funds (PF), Employment State Insurance (ESI), gratuity and holiday wages. They were not, however, entitled to receive a dividend or to participate in general body meetings. The creation of C class membership explains the sharp increase in the total number of membership to 636 during 2006-2010 and further to 1,951 during 2010-13.

Every year new admissions are given and retirees, absentees and those expelled for disciplinary reasons are removed from the rolls. There have been wide fluctuations from year to year in the number of new admissions and removals. Around 40 to 50 new members were admitted for most of the decades except for the 1970s when 170 members were admitted – this was a part of the targeted membership drive to ensure sufficient membership numbers to remain accredited as an 'A class' society – and the 2000s when there was a sharp increase in the number of new admissions due to the new 'C class' membership. Throughout the Society's history, most of the removals were due to retirement or prolonged absenteeism. Every year there would be one or two cases of expulsion for breach of discipline like working under private contractors, refusing to go to outside worksites, corruption, disorderly conduct at the worksite, etc. The relatively high drop-out rate during the 1970s was partly due to the Society's insistence on members' contribution to share capital, a decision taken in 1966, when the Society decided that those who do not pay full share value within five years would be removed from the rolls.[15]

[15] Minutes of ULCCS, General Body meeting, 25 December 1966, Vol. X, p. 59.

The way in which the Society innovated on different types of membership in order to meet its various needs shows both creativity and confidence in their model. The complex membership structure has not translated into the loss of worker control, but rather has allowed the Society to leverage resources in the interest of its worker-members. Currently, there are four categories of membership. 'A class' members are the full members with an original share value of Rs 25. Initially the ceiling for the number of shares per member was 20, which has subsequently been revised on a number of occasions: it was raised to 40 shares in 1954, through successive upward revisions to 800 shares in 1993, and in 1999 it was decided that an individual could have any number of shares as long as they do not exceed one-fifth of the total paid share capital of the Society. The value of the A class share was raised to Rs 100 in 2008. In 2012-13 there were 631 A class members with total share capital of Rs 3.47 crore.[16] Table 4.3 gives the frequency distribution of shareholders by the number of shares they hold.

The second category of membership is 'B class' for government shares. The share value of government investment in 2012-13 was Rs 27.09 crore. The third type of membership is 'C class' members of which there are 699 with a total share value of Rs 0.18 lakh. Initially the share value of C class members was Rs 5 and then increased to Rs 25. Only one share is issued to each C class member and therefore they have been excluded from Table 4.3. The fourth category of membership was created in the 2008 bylaws as 'D class' members with a share value of Rs 5 to accommodate depositors. D class members have no rights in the Cooperative other than depositing their savings for a fixed term with the Cooperative.

[16] One crore is equal to ten million. One lakh is equal to one hundred thousand.

Table 4.3: Frequency distribution of shareholders by number of shares

Number of shares of A class members (Face value of a Share is Rs.100/)	Number of shareholders	Percentage
1	22	3.49
2 -10	11	1.74
10-50	25	3.96
50-100	9	1.43
100-500	181	28.68
500-750	236	37.40
above 750	147	23.30
Total	631	100.00

Source: Collated from Share Capital Register, Records of ULCCS.

In 2012-13 there were 9,001 D class members with a share value of Rs 0.45 lakh. The A and C class members constitute the worker members and make up the total membership of the Cooperative.

The increase in share capital contribution over the years was due to a number of initiatives by the board of directors. All members had to take at least one 'A' class share of Rs 25 (later Rs 100). The Society monitored defaulters carefully and issued warnings that disciplinary action would be taken – and given the history of severe action taken in 1948-49 members knew this was not an empty threat. In 1954, compulsory thrift of one anna per rupee (6.25 per cent) was introduced. Whenever savings reached Rs 25, it was added to share capital and if the ceiling of the number of shares one may hold had been reached the thrift was paid into a recurring deposit account. The authorized capital of the Society was systematically enhanced from Rs 12,500 in 1925 to Rs 50,000 in 1965 and further to Rs 1 crore in 1969. As per the revised bylaw of 2008, the authorized share capital of the Cooperative is now Rs 100 crore.

GOVERNMENT SUPPORT FOR ULCCS

The state government provided two types of support to labour contract societies as per the scheme drawn up by the government in 1958: (1) direct financial support to cooperatives and (2) various concessions and preferences given to labour contract societies while awarding public works. The direct financial support was very meagre and consisted of share capital contribution subject to a ceiling and managerial subsidy for the first three years. During the 1970s the average annual expenditure for direct support for labour contract societies was only Rs 44,000 per annum for the whole state, and during the 1980s increased modestly to an average annual expenditure of only Rs 57,000.[17]

The financial support from the government may be as share capital contribution, loan or subsidy. Normally, all the share capital contribution and loans are to be repaid within a specified time-frame with the difference between the two being that a loan accrues interest that would have to be paid, while for share capital contribution only a dividend, if any, needed to be paid. In 1963-64, ULCCS received its first government capital contribution of Rs 2,000. The largest financial support that ULCCS ever received was 30 crore from National Cooperative Development Corporation (NCDC) towards share capital contribution in 2009-10. Table 4.4 summarizes the various types of financial support received by ULCCS from the Government of Kerala. An interesting feature of the devolution of funds is that all the major allotments since 1990-91 have been provided by successive left governments. The 2012-13 allocation was also a project approved by the

[17] Collated from Administrative Report of the Co-operation Department, Government of Kerala, 1971-72 to 1990-91.

Table 4.4: Financial support received by ULCCS from Government of Kerala 1963–64 to 2012–13 (Rs 000)

Year	Share capital	Loan	Subsidy	Total	Objective
1963-64	2			2	
1979-80	8			8	
1984-85	10			10	
1990-91		2,800		2,800	Setting up a stone crusher unit, purchase of vehicles and machinery.
1996-97	300	300	150	750	Towards Rs. 1.5 crore hollow bricks project.
2007-08	27,000	117,000		144,000	Expansion of the crusher unit. (NCDC Loan)
2009-10	300,000			300,000	NCDC contribution for modernization for the long term repayment schedule.
2010-11	900	900	400	2,200	Model cooperative society scheme
2012-13	28,000	35,000		63,000	Expansion of the crusher unit.

Source: Records of ULCCS.

previous left government. There has not been any instance of political discrimination against ULCCS, but a closer affinity by left governments is clear.

The special concession to labour contract societies in tendering for public works varied from time to time. For example, in 1957 there was permissive sanction for directly giving contract to the societies without public tender for works up to Rs 5,000. At the time, the ULCCS demanded that the ceiling be raised to Rs 10,000 and should be made mandatory.[18] The issue of concessions to labour contract societies in the public tendering process was an important and recurring theme in the general body meetings of ULCCS. On 26th May

[18] Minutes of ULCCS, General Body meeting, 1 January 1957, Vol. III, p. 30.

1957, ULCCS estimated that Rs 16,306 was locked up as Earnest Money Deposit (EMD). Accordingly a memorandum was submitted to government with the following demands: (1) EMD may be waived for the labour contract societies; (2) Works up to Rs 25,000 may be contracted to societies without public tender; (3) Five per cent price preference must be given to societies, and the works may be awarded to the labour contract societies if they are willing to accept the contract at the rate of the lowest bidder; and (4) Fifty per cent of the estimated cost may be given as an advance.[19] The exact concessions given to labour contract societies vary over time and were fully utilized by ULCCS to gain orders and expand.

Over the decades, all the main demands raised by ULCCS have been favourably considered by the successive governments, indicating that ULCCS has successfully garnered sufficient prestige and power in relating to government. The provisions of government orders are given in Table 4.5 (overleaf). Numerous government orders were issued successively raising the limit of the value of estimated work that ULCCS may submit to tender as well as increasing the ceiling of the tender value of a single contract that the Cooperative could take up as well as the overall ceiling of the value for all contracts that could be taken up at one time. Special government orders were issued to enable the Cooperative to take up specific major projects by different departments such as Rs 35 crore KSUDP Kozhikode Road Improvement Project and Rs 18 crore Nenmara-Nelliyampathi road in Palakkad. Some major projects (e.g., Punnapra Engineering College project) were directly entrusted to the Society without going through the tender process. Thus, it is clear that government support for the Society has been vital to its growth and success.

[19] Minutes of ULCCS, Board of Directors meeting, 1 July 1958, Vol. III, p. 107.

ACCELERATION OF THE GROWTH IN TURNOVER AND ASSETS

Both in terms of total assets and turnover, ULCCS has achieved a very impressive record of growth during the last six decades. We have summarized the information for this period in five-yearly averages in Table 4.6. The turnover increased from Rs 1.30 lakh per annum during the 1950s to Rs 150.5 crore during 2011-2013. Similarly, the average assets increased from Rs 0.65 lakh to Rs 349.2 crore during the same period.

While there have been significant year-to-year fluctuations, the five-yearly averages reveal a relatively steady growth of 10 to 15 per cent per annum. However, from the mid-1990s there has been a definite acceleration in the growth rate which catapulted ULCCS into a front ranking firm in the infrastructure sector in Kerala. The basis for the burst in expansion in the recent period was laid in the previous decades. During the first half of 1950s turnover increased by 11.5 per cent per annum followed by a phase of deceleration in the growth rate until the end of 1960s. The five-year annual growth rate declined to 6.24 per cent per annum during 1966-1970. From 1971-75 there was relatively more rapid growth, which was broken by a decline of 7.6 per cent per annum during 1986-90. This is an exceptional period where despite the relatively more supportive left government the turnover declined. According to Rajinder Chaudhary, this decline was due to a leadership crisis that the Society faced in the mid-1980s.[20]

In 1984 P. Kanaran, who had provided able leadership for three decades from 1952, passed away while on an official trip to Thiruvananthapuram. His demise was a shock to everyone

[20] Rajinder Chaudhary, 'ULCCS: An 80 Year Old Construction Labour Cooperative', pp. 263-265.

Table 4.5: Government Concessions Extended to Labour Contract Societies and ULCCS

No.	Government order no, date, dept	Government order provisions
1	792 ,13-03-1954, Dy Secretary to Agriculture and Co-operation Dept	Recommendation of the All India Co-op. Planning committee for entrustment of works to labour co-op societies. 1. The govt. and local bodies should give preference for contract to labour cooperative societies. 2. Contract for work need not be given by tenders but by offer to labour contract societies.
2	27-12-1954, Registrar of Cooperative Societies	1. Security deposit may be waived 2. Bills may be paid at shorter intervals. 3. The payment of fees for registration in the register of contractors may be exempted.
3	3967, 14-10-1955, PWD	Concessions to ULCCS, and Vanaramutti Labour Contract Coopearative society, Thirunalveli: 1. Works up to a limit of Rs. 5000 which do not require any special technical skill may be entrusted to the ULCCS and VLCCS at estimate rate without calling for tenders. 2. Deputing PWD officer for supervision of major contract works. 3. Exempting the ULCCS from payment of tender deposit
4	340,10-04-1958, PWD	1. The EMD to be deposited with tenders by labour contract co-op society for works in PWD may be fixed as 1% of the probable amount of contract of the work subject to a maximum of Rs.500/-. 2-the labour contract society may be given exemption from payment of registration fee
5	795/60/Agri,08-10-1960, Agriculture (Cooperation) Dept	Exemption from executing agreement in stamp paper.
6	978/61/Agri,12-06-1961, Agriculture (Cooperation) Dept	Exemption from Earnest Money Deposit (EMD).
7	3577/76/AD, 13-10-1976, Co-opeartive Dept.	Permission for ULCCS taking up of works for amounts excess of the ceiling prescribed for A class societies.
8	1031/78/AD, 06-04-1978, Co-operative Dept.	Enhancement of the advance drawn by ULCCS to Rs 10000.

9	135/97/co-op,13-11-1997, Co-operative Dept.	When a labour contract cooperative society participated in the tender, the work awarding authority is to ascertain the willingness of the labour contract co-op society in writing if the labour contract co-op society is willing to take the work, and if it is willing, the work may be awarded at 10% above the lowest tender.
11	1284/98,15-06-1998, KSEB	Labour societies entrustment of work on preferential terms and conditions revised orders–adoption in KSEB sanctioned.
12	162/2001/COP,22-03-2001, Co-opeartive Dept.	ULCCS is exempted for the payment of performance guarantee.
13	140/03/COP25-02-2003, Co-opeartive Dept.	Price preference for the work invited by NH to ULCCS
14	1011/2003/LSGD, 23-03-2003, LSGD	LSGD approves ULCCS as accredited agency for local government contract works
15	01/2008/LSGD, 01-01-2008, LSGD	Supply of Bitumen for works undertaken by local government permitted
16	10780/H3/07/PWD, 19-05-2008, PWD	10% Tender Preference
17	181/08/COP,02-08-2008, Cooperative dept.	Granting permission to ULCCS to take up and execute any work without the restriction of financial limit through tender process and restoring the priority benefits provided in the GO (Ms.) No 135/97/Cop dated 13-11-1997
18	5287/09/TSM,23-07-2009, Tourism Dept	Tourism Department–Appointment of ULCCS as an executing agency
19	(Ms) No 124/2010/TD,14-05-2010, Tax Dept	Exempting from excess liability over compounded sale tax
20	GO (P) No.339/2015/Fin dated 07.08.2015	Finance Department, Government of Kerala- Appointed as Accredited Agency viz. An agency to which work may be assigned without tender subject to a ceiling of Rs. 250 Crore

Source: File on Government Orders, Records of ULCCS

and created a leadership vacuum. In a period of one decade, there were three changes in the presidency of the Society. The third president was Paleri Ramasen, who agreed to stand for the position only after a great deal of persuasion and has continued to hold the position with unanimous support from members. His presidency introduced the beginning of a more professional style of management. While the Society was challenged by the loss of one of its top leaders, it was not a period of membership decline or withdrawal of fixed deposit, as Rajinder Chaudhary has suspected. The data presented in the present chapter demonstrates that these were not crisis years for the Society. More than fiscal crisis, the Society suffered from a lack of managerial confidence to compete in the market and secure contracts. As a result, turnover declined from Rs 81 lakh in 1984-85 to Rs 75 lakh in 1985-86, and finally to Rs 44 lakh in 1988-89. Slowly gaining confidence to compete in the market, orders steadily picked up in the first half of 1990s and continued to accelerate thereafter. By 2016, ULCCS has completed more than 6,000 projects, and an additional 130 projects worth more than Rs 1,300 crore are in various stages of completion.

The single most important factor that fuelled the expansion of turnover was the aggressiveness with which the Cooperative's management pursued every opportunity for contracts from different government departments. The Society's reputation for high quality work and reliability of on-time delivery earned it widespread official and social respect. The most important source for contracts was the Public Works Department, which qualified ULCCS with an A class contractor's license. The contribution of the PWD to the turnover of the Society has come down from the high of 77 per cent during 1980s, yet it continues to be the main contributor with a current share

Table 4.6: Expansion of assets and turnover of ULCCS 1950-51 to 2014-16 (5 year average)

Year	Turnover (Rs)	Turnover growth rate (%)	Turnover per member (Rs)
1950-55	60,292	11.51	385
1956-60	2,12,965	9.26	1,309
1961-65	5,31,976	8.70	3,739
1966-70	6,86,291	6.24	4,217
1971-75	12,67,373	12.53	13,831
1976-80	30,70,287	10.59	15,524
1981-85	58,39,631	15.80	28,244
1986-90	57,66,334	-7.63	28,291
1991-95	97,58,783	14.49	46,567
1996-00	4,68,94,077	28.15	2,03,380
2001-05	21,57,07,936	22.95	6,71,826
2006-10	58,88,19,986	14.46	9,54,485
2011-13	1,50,53,64,101	26.92	11,88,001
2014-16	2,62,28,10,321	42.60	11,72,992

Source: Collated from the Yearend Audit Reports for the relevant years, Records of ULCCS.

of 52 per cent. The Society does not undertake contracts from private individuals, and the growth in the number of projects from 'private institutions' during 2000 to 2010 was due to projects related to schools and other cooperatives. The category 'others' that became prominent during 2010-13 was mostly projects under centrally sponsored programmes such as Prime Minister's Grameen Sadak Yojana (PMGSY). From the mid-1990's local governments – ULCCS was recognized as an accredited agency by the Local Self Government Department (LSGD) – became an equally important source of contracts (Table 4.7). However, the LSGD contracts were relatively small in size and tended to become a drag on the exponential growth of the more recent years.

In terms of volume and turnover, large-scale projects have become the mainstay of the Cooperative. The growing

Table 4.7: Distribution of projects by agency (in Rs. lakhs)

Period	PWD		LSGD		Rural development		Other departments		NH		Private institutions		Others		Total	
	no.	amt.	no.	amt.	no.	amt.	no.	amt.	no.	amt.	no.	amt.	no.	amt.	no.	amt.
1981-90																
	186	378.17	49	32.16	0	0.00	25	60.40	0	0.00	11	22.81	0	0.00	271	493.54
%		76.62		6.52		0.00		12.24		0.00		4.62		0.00		100.00
1991-00																
	543	2506.03	321	794.08	0	0.00	83	296.57	0	0.00	7	19.17	0	0.00	954	3615.84
%		69.31		21.96		0.00		8.20		0.00		0.53		0.00		100.00
2001-10																
	853	17880.30	1274	6198.93	3	544.83	16	2410.90	3	72.20	148	10164.97	0	0.00	2297	37272.13
%		47.97		16.63		1.46		6.47		0.19		27.27		0.00		100.00
2011-13																
	114	27276.44	361	2090.62	17	2010.63	8	3321.89	1	22.22	44	3563.09	32	14486.06	577	52770.96
%		51.69		3.96		3.81		6.29		0.04		6.75		27.45		100.00
2014-16																
	171	95216.68	626	6241.00	20	2299.92	65	36707.62	7	28029.50	41	4906.13	44	3834.34	974	177235.17
%		53.72		3.52		1.30		20.71		15.81		2.77		2.16		100.00

Source: Collated from Contract Work Register, records of ULCCS.

capability to undertake large-scale projects has been an important factor in the expansion of turnover (Table 4.8). During the decade of 1980 to 1990 smaller works worth less than 5 lakh constituted 95 per cent of the contracts implemented and no large works worth more than Rs 1 crore was undertaken. During the subsequent decade, in contrast, the number of such large contracts increased to 54 and further to 60 during the three years from 2011-2013. Of the 60 projects completed 14 were for amounts larger than Rs 10 crore between 2011 and 2013.

Finally, over the course of its history the Cooperative's area of operation also expanded. At the time of establishment, the ULCCS was confined to Vadakara Cooperative Union only and was expanded to north Malabar and finally to the entire Malabar district by the time of Independence. It was only in 2005 that the bylaws were formally amended so that the area of operation covered the entire Kerala.[21]

ULCCS has also diversified the types of works it undertakes. Its main strength has always been the construction of roads. During the pre-Independence period the Society built country roads with gravel toppings and the transition to modern tarred roads occurred in the post-Independence period. During the 1950s the Society built its first bridges. Lacking adequate experience in bridge construction at the time, the Society hired skilled workers from Tamil Nadu to complete the first bridge.[22] Today the society has the capability of constructing major bridges such as the one across Chaliyar river. More recently, ULCCS has diversified into the construction of buildings with its most ambitious project being the Rs 44 crore Cyber Park

[21] Minutes of ULCCS, Genera Body meeting, 25 June 2006, Vol. II.

[22] Minutes of ULCCS, Board of Directors meeting, 6 May 1951, Vol. II, p. 21.

Table 4.8: Size distribution of contracts. Number and value of contracts of ULCCS from 1971 to 2016

Period	Less than 5 lakh 5 lakh	5-10 lakh	10-25 lakh	25-1 crore	1-10 crore	above 10 crore	Total number of works
1981-90	257	6	7	1	0	0	271
%	94.83	2.21	2.58	0.37	-	-	100
1991-2000	815	94	26	18	1	0	954
%	85.43	9.85	2.73	1.89	0.1	-	100
2001- 10	1789	199	172	83	49	5	2297
%	77.88	8.66	7.49	3.61	2.13	0.22	100
2011-13	390	37	45	45	46	14	.577
%	67.59	6.41	7.80	7.80	7.97	2.43	100
2014-16	477	157	116	104	97	23	974
%	48.97	16.12	11.91	10.68	9.96	2.36	100

Source: Collated from Contract Work Register, records of ULCCS.

at Kozhikode. Table 4.9 gives distribution of ULCCS projects by type of work.

As this accounting demonstrates, the period from the mid-1990s was marked by rapid expansion achieved through the diversification of activities into areas such as building bridges, shifting the focus to larger projects, and extending the area of operation to cover the entire State. This transformation was made possible by modernizing the construction process.

THE MODERNIZATION OF CONSTRUCTION

In the highly competitive construction industry, ULCCS has had to keep abreast with advances in technology, equipment, and management systems. An important feature of the expansion of ULCCS has been the rapid modernization of the plant and machinery for construction as well as the development of backward linkages to supply construction materials such as rocks and sand from its own quarries and bricks from its own brick-making units. In 1962 the Society purchased its first major equipment, a second-hand lorry.[23] Until 2000, the fixed investment consisted of lorries and auto-rickshaws for transport, one each of a concrete mixer, tar mixer and road roller at a cost of Rs 1.56 crore. During 2001-05 the focus remained as in the past only that activities expanded requiring that the Society purchase more of the equipment. Signs of change were emerging with the purchase of earth moving machinery and a road compressor for a total cost of Rs 3.60 crore. The real shift to modernizing its production process came during 2006-10 when the Society purchased a number of machinery for building and bridge construction, more earth moving machinery, and improved technology for

[23] Minutes of ULCCS, Board of Directors meeting, 25 June 1962, Vol. X, p. 50.

Table 4.9: Distribution of projects undertaken by ULCCS by type of work (in Rs. lakh)

Period	Rural roads		District roads		State highways		National highways		Bridges		Buildings		Others		Total	
	no.	amt.	no.	amt.	no.	amt.	no.	amt.	no.	amt.	no.	amt.	no.	amt.	no.	amt.
1981-90																
	76	34.49	0	0.00	151	359.76	0	0.00	0	0.00	23	38.90	21	60.40	271	493.54
%		6.99		0.00		72.89		0.00		0.00		7.88		12.24		100.00
1991-00																
	246	516.34	62	231.97	454	1834.20	13	514.42	4	36.51	97	328.90	78	153.51	941	3615.84
%		14.28		6.42		50.73		14.23		1.01		9.10		4.25		100.00
2001-10																
	780	10911.22	476	6953.93	533	3493.20	189	11553.87	15	2311.37	276	1980.14	28	68.42	2108	37272.13
%		29.27		18.66		9.37		31.00		6.20		5.31		0.18		100.00
2011-13																
	209	7371.27	151	1105.90	60	15032.37	6	7233.15	8	4178.45	136	17117.59	13	732.24	577	52770.96
%		13.97		2.10		28.49		13.71		7.92		32.44		1.39		100.00
2014-16																
	439	11761.89	52	1401.39	30	84568.90	9	16382.58	10	29074.87	212	27166.56	222	6878.97	974	177235.17
%		6.64		0.79		47.72		9.24		16.40		15.33		3.88		100.00

Source: Collated from Contract Work Register, Records of ULCCS.

road tarring. Consequently, the fixed investment rose to Rs 66.62 crore with the investment in new plant and machinery continuing to accelerate and during the last three years the purchases included state of the art technology such as a bitumen sprayer, cement silo, cement feeding machine and improved quarry machinery. See Table 4.10 for a detailed overview of the assets purchased.

In addition to equipment and technology, the Society also invested in land. Today the ULCCS owns 224 acres of land. The book value of land is Rs 47 crore but the market value is estimated to be above Rs 300 crore. Almost all the land is used for sourcing sand and soil for construction or for boulders and metals from quarries. The first purchase was four cents of land for the construction of the office and another 39 cents was purchased for sand mining during the 1960s.[24] The Society is well aware of the environmental impact of over-exploiting the land, and closely monitors land utilization and at a certain point stops mining and quarrying the land. The wasteland is converted into real estate space for creating infrastructure like the Cyber Park, agriculture farms for food production (the Society provides breakfast and lunch to all its members and sources much of the food from its own farms), or for setting up manufacturing units such as its hollow brick units. More than 80 per cent of the land acquisition occurred since 2000. The largest purchase was 71 acres for establishing a crusher unit in the eastern part of Kozhikode *taluk* costing around Rs 6 crore. The most expensive purchase was 25 acres near Calicut town at Rs 11 crore, which is now the site of the Cyber Park.

Overtime, the physical and financial assets of the Cooperative increased from less than Rs 10 lakh during 1991-

[24] Minutes of ULCCS, Board of Directors meeting, 14 June 1960, Vol. III, p. 234.

Table 4.10: Types of assets purchased by period

Purchase of vehicles, machinery and equipment						
Item	Before 2000	2001-2005	2006-2010	2011-2013	2014 2016	Total
Lorry & tipper	15	4	0	0	31	50
Auto rickshaw	7	11	17	7	9	51
Concrete equipments like miller & pumps	1	0	3	4	1	9
Cement feeding machines & silo etc.	0	0	3	5	2	10
Tarring equipments, drum mix, hot mix etc.	4	8	14	4	2	32
JCB, excavator, breakers etc.	0	1	7	7	6	21
Crusher Equipments	0	1	1	4	6	12
Jeep (including Scorpio, Economy, Innova, etc.)	0	5	2	4	5	16
Bobcat	0	0	5	1	7	13
Paver	0	0	2	1	1	4
Diesel generator	12	9	12	8	11	52
Tractor cum compressor	0	2	0	0	4	6
Batch plant setter	0	0	1	1	1	3
Bar loader	0	0	1	0	0	1
Motor grader	0	0	1	0	0	1
Bar bending machine	0	0	0	1	0	1
Bitumen sprayer	0	0	0	1	0	1
Computers	0	0	12	10	50	72
Others	6	6	10	2	23	47
Grand total	33	43	80	63	159	402

Source: Collated from Stock Register, records of ULCCS.

95 to Rs 150 crore during 2011-13. The growth of assets follows broadly the same trends as the growth in turnover. The decade following the mid-1960s and the latter half of the1980s were phases of deceleration in the growth of assets. Since the 1990s there is a tremendous acceleration in the acquisition of assets, led by the growth in fixed assets (Table 4.12).

Significantly the turnover to asset ratio tended to decline from an average of 2 between 1950 and 1980 to reach a low

Table 4.11: Purchase of land property by ULCCS

Year	In Vadakara *taluk* area (cents)	Outside Vadakara *taluk* but inside Kozhikode district area (cents)	Outside Kozhikode district area (cents)	Total area	Total amount (Rs)
1961-65	74.00	-	-	74.00	5,250
1966-70	-	-	-	-	-
1971-75	99.75	-	-	99.75	14,350
1976-80	61.00	-	-	61.00	16,000
1981-85	-	-	-	-	-
1986-90	-	-	-	-	-
1991-95	500.00	-	-	500.00	3,62,500
1996-00	1,255.56	-	-	1,255.56	56,85,865
2001-05	3,928.15	2,941.92	-	6,870.07	583,08,801
2006-10	9,157.57	1,304.43	-	10,462.00	1396,23,455
2011-13	1,746.38	122.41	-	1,868.79	1857,42,949
2014-16	560.97	122.91	311	1175.88	818,15,549
Total	17,383.38	4,491.67	311	22,367.05	4715,74,719

Source: Collated from the Land Register, records of ULCCS.

of 0.38 in 2014-16. This is partly a reflection of increasing the capital intensity of construction as a result of modernization. Fixed assets steadily increased from 1.46 per cent during 1950-55 to 11.81 per cent during 1976-80, but fell to 5.24 per cent during 1981-85. Since then it has steadily increased to peak at 17.99 per cent during 2011-13 (Table 4.12). Until around 1990, 80 to 90 per cent of fixed assets consisted of plant and machineries. Reflecting the growth and development of the Cooperative's activities, fixed assets declined and the share of land assets has increased since the 1990s. The sharp increase in 2004-05 is due to the revision in the valuation of the land assets and an increase in the assets themselves.

While ULCCS has successfully modernized its construction methods and developed important backward linkages that allow it to internally source more and more construction

Table 4.12: Expansion of assets of ULCCS 1950-51 to 2015-16

Year	Total assets (Rs)	Total asset growth (%)	Assets per member (Rs)	Turnover to asset ratio	Fixed assets % to total assets
1951-55	39,106	12.04	248	1.55	1.46
1956-60	90,597	12.11	557	2.35	2.77
1961-65	2,81,145	17.45	1,985	1.88	7.05
1966-70	3,72,187	7.36	2,287	2.12	6.43
1971-75	6,22,027	5.53	6,654	2.08	11.50
1976-80	14,73,361	18.50	7,476	2.07	11.81
1981-85	37,66,904	18.68	18,192	1.47	5.24
1986-90	61,29,895	4.03	30,148	0.94	6.51
1991-95	114,04,448	10.58	54,345	0.86	8.46
1996-00	475,30,495	31.09	2,06,303	0.99	16.40
2001-05	2858,92,950	27.59	8,84,023	0.77	19.41
2006-10	12614,19,601	28.52	18,39,409	0.51	16.27
2011-13	34920,40,571	10.87	27,67,791	0.42	17.99
2014-16	66794,98,617	21.20	29,87,253	0.38	24.79

Source: Collated from the Yearend Audit Report for the relevant years, records of ULCCS.

material, the costs of this modernization and development strategy have also burdened the financial resources of the Society. To stay competitive the Society had to modernize, but the very process of modernization has increased the Society's debt burden.

FINANCING THE EXPANSION OF BUSINESS

Financing the expansion has two components: long-term fixed capital investment and working capital. The major problem that ULCCS faces is working capital because of delays in government payments. The system is set up in such a way that it favours government's interest and poses serious hardship on capital poor cooperatives with limited financial resources. Government pays in instalments on work completed or, even worse, only pays after the completion of the project. To compound the difficult situation, the ubiquitous delays in payment due to bureaucratic inertia and red tape are now joined by a systemic problem that government does not have funds. The deterioration of the state government finance started in the 1980s and reached crisis proportions in the late 1990s. These conditions were rife for nepotism in the payment process. In early 2000s, in order to prevent nepotism in payments, the High Court intervened and a queue system was introduced, which helped reduce nepotism but did not speed up the payment process. By 2006 payments to contractors were delayed by around two years. Contractors suffered from heavy interest burdens due to the delays in payments and thus tried to compensate cutting corners on the work project (including squeezing labour) and reducing the quality. The cooperative principles of the ULCCS, on the other hand, did not allow for it to adopt such tactics, but the consequence was that it often found itself in severe financial crisis. The ULCCS submitted petitions to government after completion of every project seeking a special order for immediate payment, but because of the queue system even the left government could not assist.[25] It was only in 2007-08 that government made a systematic effort to clear the pending bills to contractors, which was completed by 2009-10.

The inefficient government payment system forced the Society to rely heavily on credit to meet its working capital requirements. Table 4.13 shows the fluctuations in the Society's liabilities and clearly demonstrates the significant variations in the percentage share of various components of liabilities over time. Loans from banks constitute the most important source of finance, but also came with a heavy interest burden. By

[25] Memorandum submitted to Government of Kerala on 8 Dec. 2005, 14 Nov. 2007, 11 June 2007.

statutory restrictions ULCCS could only borrow from DCB whose interest rate was relatively higher than commercial banks. A better option for the Society was fixed deposits from public, which had a much lower rate of interest (e.g., between 1995 and 2005 the interest differential was as high as two to three per cent). Since the Reserve Bank of India insists that cooperatives mobilize deposits only from their members a new class of members (i.e. D class for people who make fixed deposits in the Society) was created. This strategy paid off and during 2000-05 the share of fixed deposit went up to 72 per cent and the share of bank loans declined to four per cent. As we can see from Table 4.13 the fluctuation from the share of bank loans and fixed deposits are inversely related.

Another important form of credit is 'other liabilities.' During the early decades of its operation, the Society took a substantial proportion of sundry credit (also known as 'other liabilities') through short term loans from members and well-wishers. Similarly, in times of severe delays in payment from government, the Society would only pay a proportion of wages for subsistence (wage payment arrears also fall under 'other liabilities'). As the Society's financial situation became more secure, these practices declined and by 1980s 'other liabilities' primarily referred to payments due to sundry supplier creditors. The other two areas to source working capital were 'Reserves and Provisions' (the share of which declined from the 1980s) and share capital (the relative significance of which has sharply come down in the recent periods).

The heavy debt burden from large working capital requirements has become a drag on the profitability of the Society. However, the trend in gross profits is very impressive as accounting practices of cooperatives in Kerala do not include interest costs and establishment charges in determining

Table 4.13: Distribution of liabilities of ULCCS Ltd by share of components

Years	Total liabilities Rs	Share capital %	Bank loan %	Govt loan %	Fixed deposit %	Reserve & provisions %	Other liabilities %	Total liabilities %
1951-55	39,412	12	41	0	0	36	11	100
1956-60	90,597	12	34	0	16	22	17	100
1961-65	2,81,145	8	27	0	17	22	26	100
1966-70	3,72,187	11	34	0	13	27	15	100
1971-75	6,22,027	10	23	0	19	29	19	100
1976-80	14,73,361	10	18	0	26	20	26	100
1981-85	37,66,904	11	38	0	15	15	21	100
1986-90	63,47,269	14	44	0	15	18	9	100
1991-95	120,68,420	10	25	23	16	18	8	100
1996-2000	475,88,743	10	12	12	43	14	9	100
2001-05	2858,92,950	3	4	1	72	12	8	100
2006-10	12614,19,601	4	25	2	49	9	11	100
2011-13	34920,40,571	9	24	2	25	21	18	100
2014-16	6679498617	4.37	12.74	1	40.28	22.20	19.41	100

Source: Collated from the Yearend Audit Report for the relevant years, records of ULCCS.

Table 4.14: Gross profit ratios

Year	Gross profit Rs	Gross profit ratio %	Fixed assets % to total assets %	Interest cost to turnover %
1951-55	2,107	3.37	1.46	1.92
1956-60	6,571	3.18	2.77	1.41
1961-65	23,430	4.53	7.05	1.69
1966-70	37,735	5.60	6.43	2.40
1971-75	83,257	6.62	11.50	2.45
1976-80	2,32,443	7.52	11.81	3.43
1981-85	5,60,170	9.52	5.24	5.56
1986-90	7,57,968	13.36	6.51	11.03
1991-95	14,80,304	14.91	8.46	13.01
1996-2000	64,82,078	14.60	16.40	11.53
2001-05	337,24,527	15.33	19.41	14.34
2006-10	1353,50,393	21.86	16.27	16.36
2011-13	1908,76,692	12.72	17.99	10.94
2014-16	5307,64,996	20.23	26.13	18.16

Source: Collated from the Yearend Audit Report for the relevant years, Records of ULCCS.

gross profits, shown in Table 4.14. The Society's gross profits have grown consistently and steadily throughout its history, but registered a significant increase since 1995 when it went to Rs 6.4 crore and by 2011-13 it jumped to Rs 31.8 crore. Similarly, the gross profit to turnover ratio steadily increased from 3.37 per cent during 1950-55 to 20.23 per cent in 2014-16. Despite these positive trends, there has also been a steady increase in the ratio of interest cost to turnover from 1.92 per cent in 1950-55 to 18.16 per cent in 2014-16 and if the establishment charges are also considered the net profit of the Cooperative very sharply declines over time (Table 4.15).

Again, the distribution of gross profit and miscellaneous income show impressive growth, but net profit registers only a meagre increase. To calculate net profit, interest cost, establishment charges and reserves and provisions are

Table 4.15: Distribution of gross profit and miscellaneous income

Years	Gross plus misc. income	Interest cost	Establish-ment & contingencies	Reserves profit/loss	Net	Total
	RS	%	%	%	%	%
1951-55	2,452	36.54	12.35	43.41	7.70	100.00
1956-60	7,267	36.20	12.80	5.60	45.40	100.00
1961-65	28,708	22.20	26.80	18.80	32.20	100.00
1966-70	42,202	35.80	34.40	10.00	19.80	100.00
1971-75	96,500	28.00	43.00	16.60	12.40	100.00
1976-80	2,93,208	28.00	56.20	11.00	4.80	100.00
1981-85	6,99,390	36.60	48.40	13.20	1.80	100.00
1986-90	10,40,754	54.72	49.82	8.92	-13.47	100.00
1991-95	22,37,773	46.79	47.20	6.42	-0.41	100.00
1996-2000	95,55,455	37.20	47.40	12.00	3.40	100.00
2001-05	576,72,181	42.80	43.80	12.80	0.60	100.00
2006-10	1879,08,911	42.20	50.00	6.80	1.00	100.00
2011-13	3812,19,054	48.00	43.00	8.00	1.00	100.00
2014-16	5658,78,599	45.00	48.00	6.00	1.00	100.00

Source: Collated from the Yearend Audit Report for the relevant years, records of ULCCS.

deducted from the gross profit and miscellaneous income. Two out of three categories – interest costs and establishment charges – have steadily increased and place further burden on the Society. The interest charges are a massive burden and claimed up to 56 per cent of the gross profit during 1986-90. In the previous two decades from 1960 to 1980, the ratio of interest charges was relatively lower, but in the recent decades the interest charges have increased markedly. The causes for the increased interest debt are multifarious, but one of the crucial reasons is the Society's modernization strategy that requires significant investment in heavy equipment, land, and professional personnel. The heavy and rising burden of interest charges is clear when we examine the interest cost to turnover. The share of establishment charges also shows an upward trend from nearly 5 per cent during the 1960s to around 45-

50 per cent since the 1980s. The growth in establishment costs partly reflects the growing cost of professionalization that is taking place in the Society. Around 10 to 18 per cent of gross profit is set aside as reserves and for statutory provisions; the proportion of reserves has come down since 2006-07. When we look at the whole picture of gross profits and miscellaneous income together with the three types of expenditures, we find a steady decline in the net profit over the years and from the 1980s net profit has been meagre.

While a low net profit might sound alarm bells for mainstream business acumen, it is actually the outcome of a conscious decision by the Society. The Society's objective is not to pay the highest dividends – which are derived from net profits – possible to its shareholders, but rather to provide relatively high and growing real income to its worker-members through increasing the wage rate and fringe benefits as well as to continually expand the employment opportunities in the Cooperative (discussed further in chapter 7). The priority to increase the workers' share of the profits is clearly seen when we compare dividend payments and bonus payments (Table 4.16). The dividend given to the shareholders has hovered mostly below 20 per cent of the net profit, which is the current statutory limit. The bonus given to workers, on the other hand, has been around an impressive 35 per cent. The net profit bonus is distributed in proportion to the total wages received by the each worker and is in addition to the statutory bonus given to workers before gross profits are declared.

Given the low dividend to shareholders, the question arises as to why would members choose to buy shares rather than invest in an interest-bearing bank account. This is an especially pertinent issue as the Cooperative's policy has been to expand its share capital among its members by converting

Table 4.16: Allocation of net profit of ULCCS for selected years

Year	Reserve fund	Business loss	Education fund	Building fund	Dividend	Common good fund	Labour welfare fund	Secretary honararium	Bonus	Loss recoupment fund	Total
	%	%	%	%	%	%	%	%	%	%	%
1948-49	25.00	-	-	-	8.09	7.46	-	25.00	19.88	14.57	100.00
1956-57	25.00	25.00	-	-	17.46	7.50	-	15.00	10.04	-	100.00
1966-67	14.98	-	-	15.32	19.70	-	-	-	39.98	10.02	100.00
1975-76	15.00	-	1.82	10.10	21.87	2.00	-	-	34.21	15.00	100.00
1986-87	15.00	-	1.63	5.56	20.32	2.49	4.99	-	35.01	15.00	100.00
1997-98	15.00	-	5.00	5.04	17.46	2.50	5.00	-	35.00	15.00	100.00
1998-99	15.08	-	5.03	6.16	16.46	1.99	5.03	-	35.18	15.08	100.00
2005-06	15.00	-	4.10	5.00	18.40	2.50	5.00	-	35.00	15.00	100.00

Source: Collated from the Yearend Audit Report for the relevant years, records of ULCCS.

their thrift savings into shares. If shareholders are only paid a very low dividend, there would be no incentive for members to buy shares. To deal with this issue, the Society distributes 'production incentives' equal to 10 per cent of members' share capital before gross profits are calculated. Thus, the shareholders are guaranteed minimum interest rate return on their investment. The meagre net profit data reflects a radical distribution of profits among workers and shareholders. In this way, the Society not only provides a transformative alternative in terms of the organization of the labour process, but also in terms of the distribution of surplus.

One of the fundamental questions that arises for genuine labour cooperatives is 'what are the incentives for accumulation?' There are four main reasons that ULCCS accumulates. First, the Cooperative formed in order to meet the needs of local people through creating a democratic worker owned and managed construction cooperative. The radical influences of the early social reform and political movements continue to pulse through the veins of the Cooperative. For example, the values and principles of social justice, democracy, and dignity are deeply embedded in the Cooperative. Thus, there is moral, political, and economic mandate to prioritize distribution among workers rather than iniquitous distribution to shareholders. Second, workers are primarily concerned about their stability of employment and steady rise in real income, which ULCCS has been able to guarantee even before the gross profit is distributed. Relatedly, all shareholders are also workers, and therefore benefit from work security and real income increases. Third, workers strongly identify with their cooperative, which they have helped to build, and take pride in its modernization and expansion. Fourth, the Cooperative understands that it is the custodian of not only the present workers' interest, but also those of the future. In practical terms, the accounting practices give management the autonomy to set aside funds for investment through raising sufficient resources as reserves or as credit. The fixed asset expenditure does not appear in the profit and loss account, but is adjusted on the assets and liability side of the balance sheet. This accounting practice gives sufficient autonomy to management to plan their investment in the best long-term interest of the Cooperative.

The expansion and modernization of ULCCS has entailed many changes in terms of membership categories, share capital, finance, and relations with various government bodies. The Society continues to demonstrate creative and innovative solutions to each new phase of its development, but what stands out as one of its key aspects is its continued commitment to its principles and values.

CHAPTER 5

LABOUR CONTRACT SOCIETIES IN PARTICIPATORY DEVELOPMENT

As part of the People's Plan Campaign an effort is being made to give a new lease of life to the labour contract societies. Before the People's Planning Campaign all construction works related to the government were being carried out by contractors. People's Plan, instead, is attempting to undertake public works through beneficiary committees. If this is not possible the next desirable system would be institutions like labour contract societies. The labour contract societies can also support the beneficiary committees to undertake works which require modern machinery. [. . .]

In large construction works an organizer, middleman or contractor is inevitable. But the present practice is that even small scale works which we otherwise directly undertake by ourselves in our houses, when they are implemented as part of a government programme, is handed over to contractors. This contract system has degenerated and has become a whirlpool of corruption. It corrupts not only public property but also public life.

The People's Planning is attempting to change the situation by entrusting public works to beneficiary committees as far as possible. When beneficiaries themselves directly implement construction projects not only do we save on the profit of the contractor but also avoid corruption and leakages. Further, with better participation of the people it would be possible to mobilize additional resources locally through voluntary contributions and labour.

The beneficiary committees that have been formed as part of the People's Plan are facing severe challenges from the contractors and vested interests. If it is a contractor or his *benami* everything will proceed smoothly. Some are trying to create an impression that if the works are executed through a beneficiary committee everything will be in trouble. We have to arouse popular awareness and resistance.

It is in the above context that the labour contract societies become relevant. The labour contract societies would help to avoid the contractors. As already pointed out they can also work complementary to the beneficiary committees. This is a new opportunity provided to labour contract societies by People's Planning.[1]

I.S. Gulati

The latter half of 1990s was a turning point in the history of ULCCS, heralding in a new era of rapid expansion in the number of works, the turnover, the outreach and state wide social recognition. Its achievements become even more

[1] I.S. Gulati, 'Introduction', The Working of Labour Contracts Societies, State Level Workshop, State Planning Board, Government of Kerala, Onchiyam, 1999.

extraordinary when compared to other labour contract societies. Most of the first generation of labour contract societies had become dormant and the new societies that registered during the subsequent periods remained anaemic with little popular participation or support. The People's Plan Campaign for Democratic Decentralization (PPC) reinvigorated the growth in the number of labour contract societies from 173 during 1991-95 to 272 during 1997-2003.[2] Trying to overcome the usual departmental bureaucratic strings within which the societies get enmeshed, the new cooperative societies became part of a larger social movement. In this mobilized context, the ULCCS was recognized as a model to emulate across the state. From its side, ULCCS was able to utilize the opportunities provided by the increased devolution of funds to the local governments, expand its activities, and use its growth as a springboard for modernization and diversification.

In this chapter we outline the People's Plan Campaign between 1996 and 2001 and the left government's efforts to avoid middlemen in the implementation of local level public works through the promotion of beneficiary committees. Labour contract societies like the ULCCS were to be complimentary to the beneficiary committees. In the second half of the chapter we discuss why the attempt to replicate the ULCCS model did not succeed.

PEOPLE'S PLAN CAMPAIGN FOR DEMOCRATIC DECENTRALIZATION

According to the minutes of the Board of Directors of 1926, the first work taken up by the nascent ULCCS was

[2] Department of Cooperation, Administrative Reports, Relevant Years, Government of Kerala, Thiruvananthapuram.

from the local fund circle. Local fund circles had come into existence in the nineteenth century with a nominated local board with the district collector serving as president. By the time ULCCS was formed these institutions had been replaced by a three tier structure of village unions, *taluk* boards and district boards under the provision of the Madras Village Panchayat Act and Madras Local Boards Act of 1920. Thus the reference in the Society's minutes appears to be a misnomer as local fund circles no longer existed. However, the name of local fund circle may have remained a common nomenclature used for all types of local authorities. The relevant point for our purposes is that the Society received its first work contract through local authorities. The local authorities' obligatory functions included construction and maintenance of public roads, drainages and drinking water, while health and education were discretionary functions. Local authorities raised funds through their limited taxation powers and grants from the government. The local boards were the main source of contract work for the Society until the formation of the state of Kerala.

When united Kerala was formed there were three different systems of local authorities in Malabar in the north and Travancore and Cochin in the southern regions. The 1957-59 communist government began to draw up a comprehensive legislation for uniform structure of local governments across the new state of Kerala with substantial devolution of funds, functions and functionaries. Its efforts came to an abrupt halt with its dismissal from power. The proposed legislation's vision of local government sought to decentralize power to councils at the district level. District councils could eventually develop into a district government with supervisory control over the entire district administration. The radical decentralization envisioned in the original draft legislation was eventually watered down and passed into law in 1960, providing Kerala a uniform village panchayat and municipality system. As a result, Kerala never had – except for a brief period at the beginning of 1990s – a democratically elected district administration nor an intermediate tier of local government above the gram panchayats and municipalities. Indeed, until the mid-1990s Kerala had one of the weakest local government systems in the country, a fact that is surprising given the many factors conducive to democratic decentralization such as high literacy, land reform, weakened caste structures, and the density of associational structures prevalent in the state. This begs the question of what changed in the 1990s that turned the state's attention towards democratic decentralization.

In 1994 the parliament passed the 73rd and 74th Constitutional Amendments, and the Kerala state government quickly followed suit and amended the panchayat and municipality acts of Kerala. When the left government came to power in 1996, it turned its attention to meaningfully pursue the transformation of the local government system now that the new legislation provided more possibilities for radical decentralization. The left argued that genuine democratic decentralization had to be part of a larger social movement rather than mere top-down administrative reforms. The left government, then, launched the People's Plan Campaign in 1996, which proved to be the most radical attempt in India for realizing the ideal of democratic decentralization.[3]

The government declared that around 35 to 40 per cent of the state's 9th Five Year plan would be devolved to local

[3] Thomas Isaac and Richard Franke, *Local Democracy and Development: People's Campaign for Decentralized Planning in Kerala*, New Delhi: LeftWord Books, 2000. The discussion on People's Plan Campaign is based on this book unless otherwise indicated.

governments. Before the local governments could lay claim to the funds, they would have to prepare a comprehensive local plan demonstrating how the funds would be used. The state government laid down procedures to guide the preparation of the local government plans with the objectives of ensuring inclusiveness, transparency and scientific deliberation. As the left government's approach was through mobilizing a state-wide campaign, thousands of people participated in the various arenas of the decentralization process and plan formation. Hundreds of thousands of people participated in the Gram Sabhas (village assemblies) to discuss the plans; tens of thousands of delegates of the village assemblies participated in the local development seminars to draw up the priorities that would go into the plans; and around ten thousand officials and experts worked in the task forces to prepare the projects. In addition, thousands of volunteer technical experts worked in the Expert Committees to review and correct the projects and plan documents before they were adopted by the local governments and approved by the District Planning Committee. In a sense the process of planning was transformed into an instrument for social mobilization in support of decentralization. The People's Plan Campaign was also an informal mechanism to empower local governments by providing the support of volunteers and non-official experts, generating new values of administration more conducive to decentralization and, importantly, creating the political will to institutionalize the achievements of the movement.

The PPC was one of the largest non-formal education campaigns ever conducted in India. The planning process spread over a year through successive rounds of cascading training which facilitated the preparation of local plans by every panchayat and municipality in Kerala. Since the initiation of the People's Plan Campaign, every year, every local government in Kerala has been preparing their own plans in a participatory manner. This is an enormous achievement, especially when compared to the rest of India. Kerala is the only state in India where local governments prepare their own plans. Kerala's experience of decentralized planning has received a great deal of attention in the literature, and rather than covering well-trodden ground we focus on the effects of decentralization on labour contract cooperative societies.

A distinctive feature of the PPC when compared to participatory budgeting in Latin America[4] has been the PPC's attempt to extend the participatory and deliberative process to the implementation stage. The 'normal' practice at both the central and state level governance systems is that once a decision is made by the elected executive the implementation is left to the departmental bureaucracies. People's participation is at best confined to nominated advisory bodies. In contrast, the PPC idea was that democratic decentralization could facilitate a genuinely different form of government where people can not only participate directly in planning and decision making, but also in the execution of the projects. The idea is that people's participation contributes to the increased efficiency in implementation through better supervision, prevention of leakage and public monitoring.

Unlike the planning process which has uniform procedural guidelines, the implementation process requires flexibility and,

[4] Gianpaolo Baiocchi, *Militants and Citizens: The Politics of Participatory Democracy in Porto Alegre*, Palo Alto, CA: Stanford University Press, 2005. Ben Goldfrank, 'Making Participation Work in Porto Alegre', in *Radicals in Power: The Workers' Party (PT) and Experiments in Urban Democracy in Brazil*, edited by G. Baiocchi, New York: Zed Books, 2003, pp. 27-52. Gianpaolo Baiocchi, Patrick Heller, and Marcelo K. Silva, *Bootstrapping Democracy: Transforming Local Governance and Civil Society in Brazil*, Palo Alto, CA: Stanford University Press, 2011.

therefore, there is no single uniform procedure for popular participation in the execution of the plan. Every development sector – such as agriculture, industry, public works and so on – would have specific features requiring separate institutional structures to facilitate people's participation. The mandatory monitoring committees were the most popular form of participation and were constituted for nearly all the projects. Social audits were encouraged, but there was no blueprint for social audits as the procedures and methods of social auditing varied from sector to sector. In some sectors relevant popular agencies had powers to directly implement their projects. For example, the Parent Teacher Associations (PTA) in the education sector and the Hospital Development Committees (HDC) in the health sector were endowed with powers for direct implementation of the projects. The PPC also engendered a dynamic web of civic associations at the grassroots which was seen in the emergence of numerous popular agencies such as self-help groups, activity groups, watershed committees and farmers associations.

One of the major challenges the Campaign faced was with regard to implementing construction projects like roads, buildings, soil and water conservation measures, side walling, houses and latrines. As Kerala's settlement pattern has houses spatially distributed in individual plots of land, there are ubiquitous demands for road connectivity to every household. This accounts for Kerala's very high density of road networks. Nevertheless there continues to be a heavy local demand for new roads and upgrading the existing roads. The State-level planning authorities, therefore, considered it prudent to place a ceiling of 35 per cent on the proportion of plan funds that could be earmarked for roads. Besides the construction of roads, if the allocation for the construction of buildings for health, education and other development sectors as well as allocations for housing, sanitation, irrigation, soil conservation and water supply were also taken into consideration, construction activities would constitute more than 50 per cent of the plan outlay. With half the plan outlay going to construction, this posed serious challenges in terms of delivery as the construction sector was notorious for inefficient, exploitative, and often corrupt contractors. How were these projects to be implemented?

BENEFICIARY COMMITTEES AS ALTERNATIVES TO CONTRACTORS

Local governments had six options for undertaking construction activities. First, local government could take on the construction project directly, which many did for very simple and small works like repairs. However, few local governments took the risk of directly undertaking large public works as they were incapable of managing the labour required and had inadequate supervisory personnel available. Second, local government could engage piece work contracts, in which the overall project was implemented directly by the local government, but its different activities were sub-contracted out. Another variation on the piece work system is that local government would provide the materials but labour was sub-contracted at a piece rate. This was a more viable option than direct implementation. Third, construction contracts could be given to voluntary organizations that were accredited to undertake construction activities for local government such as Nirmithi – a state sponsored autonomous agency specializing in alternative building technologies – and Costford – a non-governmental agency with similar objectives to Nirmithi.

Fourth, a system known as deposit works could be used for projects related to existing water supply schemes or electricity distribution, which had to be implemented through the Kerala Water Authority and Kerala State Electricity Board, by depositing the cost in advance. The government departments and agencies were permitted to accept deposit works from local governments, but the danger with this system was that once the money was deposited, the local government could exercise little control over the execution of the project and nearly all projects under this system had significantly run over time. Fifth, local governments could use contractors, which was the norm for public works but was heavily criticized. The strong nexus between contractors, politicians and bureaucrats resulted in various forms of leakage through artificial cost-inflation, manipulation of tenders, and non-adherence to specifications for quality of the construction materials or technical specifications. Contractors made big profits, which were shared with politicians who connived to grant the work, engineers who gave technical sanction and monitored the work, as well as clerical staff who approved payments of the bills. The web of interests that underlay construction projects by private contractors made it very difficult to challenge the system. Operating in this kind of system made it extremely difficult for alternative popular organizations to intervene such as the ULCCS.

Finally, local governments could implement projects through committees formed from the beneficiaries. While this option was potentially a radical alternative to the private contractors, it was soon manipulated by contractors. Throughout Kerala, irrespective of political affiliation, contractors implemented the employment generating programmes in the name of fake (*benami*) beneficiary committees. In most places the contractor would form a committee with himself as the convenor. Nominating the convener became an opportunity for patronage for elected officials, which is commonly known as the 'nominee system'. In an effort to contain corruption, numerous checks and balances and ad hoc rules were introduced over time. The myriad rules and regulations, however, had the perverse effect of undermining genuine committees in a web of delays and the approvals that were required made it even more difficult for them to operate, while the private contractors were able to buy their way through the system.

For example, according to the guidelines for an important centrally sponsored employment generation programme, Jawahar Rosgar Yojana (JRY), implementation through beneficiary committees was compulsory. However, the central government's prescribed wages for labourers were often 50 per cent below the prevalent market rates in Kerala. While keeping accounts, false vouchers for employing two persons would have to be created for every person employed. It would be difficult for a beneficiary committee to fudge the accounts in this manner. Again, in works commissioned by the state government, the Department of Public Works had fixed the rates for labourers and for certain materials. These rates were revised infrequently and would become inconsistent with actual wages and prices. Contractors often colluded with each other and quoted their tenders in excess of the approved rates or save on materials or cheat outright. Such options were not available to beneficiary committees. Further, at every stage of execution of public works beneficiary committees had to interact with the corrupt bureaucracy who preferred to work in the system of contractors. While contractors and *benami* committee projects could afford to grease the palms of officials, almost all the genuine beneficiary committees complained that they faced undue delays. The delays would prove to be fatal because the beneficiary committees operated on borrowed funds and delays in payment would put them into severe financial hardship.

The public work rules for municipalities and for panchayats issued in 1997 anticipated these problems and specified that local governments could utilize the services of contractors only as a last resort (that is, if no beneficiary is willing to undertake the responsibility and the local government cannot directly execute the work). The People's Plan Campaign promoted the direct participation of people in plan implementation. The issues that needed to be addressed is how best to break the past system of contractors and how could conditions be created so that the beneficiaries themselves were empowered to implement the works by forming beneficiary committees? The decentralization adopted measures at every key stage of implementation of a public work and a structure for the smooth functioning of the beneficiary committees. We briefly survey the key changes in the rules and procedures in each of the five stages.

The first stage was the preparation of the estimate. Actual market rates were fixed for each district and local governments were permitted to prepare estimates only on the basis of these local rates, thereby eliminating the unrealistic rates that contractors sought. This approach proved to be cumbersome and was amended to allow local governments to prepare estimates on the basis of local rates that they declared which were subjected to a ceiling for over-estimates of the official PWD rates. The local governments that did not have their own engineers were permitted to utilize the services of private engineers to prepare the estimates. In some districts the departmental engineers were given the responsibility of preparing the estimates for the local governments.

The second stage was the technical sanction of the projects, which was a major problem area as officials had to be bribed for speedy and favourable decisions. The decentralization process put mechanisms into place to make technical sanctioning procedures transparent and simple. Instead of the traditional practice of senior departmental officials giving technical sanction, block-level Expert Committees were created with the departmental official as the convener and a technical expert as a chairperson. Formal technical sanction was signed by the convener who was a government engineer on the basis of the committee decision.

The third stage was the tendering process. Beneficiary committees were exempt from tender procedures and could be awarded work simply based on their existence. Thus, beneficiary committees were to be formed at a well-advertised general body meeting of beneficiaries. While the beneficiary committees could avoid tendering, there were clear rules regarding maintaining records and other procedures that they had to follow. The fourth stage was supervision of the project and measurement of quantity of work undertaken by the local governments. Gram panchayats without engineers were allowed to utilise the services of other government engineers or engineer members of the Expert Committees for supervision and measurements of work. The payment of remuneration up to 1.5 per cent of the cost was also permitted for private engineers who supervised and measured the work.

The final stage was the preparation of bills and payments. In a significant departure from the past, permission was granted to provide up to Rs 50,000 or 25 per cent of the cost, as a mobilization advance to the beneficiary committees and a provision also made for the payment of part-bills. Before a part-bill payment could be drawn, four steps were required: (1) the work done to date had to be measured by an engineer; (2) the measurement had to be checked and verified by a government engineer; (3) a bill had to be prepared on the basis of the work done; and (4) payment would be made from the treasury. A strict time-table was also drawn up for measurement, verification, preparation of bills and the final payment so that a part-bill payment should not take more than 21 days.[5]

In the first annual plan, the total number of road and bridge projects came to more than 24,000 and when added to other public works projects, local bodies implemented approximately 30,000 to 35,000 public works projects. Around 10 per cent of the projects were awarded to contractors, which means that around 27,000 to 30,000 beneficiary committees were involved in implementing the first annual plan. This is an extraordinary achievement and begs the question of how many were genuine beneficiary committees. Given the history of corrupt contractors, we can estimate that nearly one-fourth of beneficiary committees were fake, headed by contractors or their nominees.[6] Interestingly, the proportion of *benami* committees was relatively much lower in the northern districts than in the rest of Kerala.

A majority of the beneficiary committees started as genuine committees but over time many degenerated. Some of them, though not motivated by corruption, were forced

[5] Isaac and Franke, *Local Democracy and Development*, pp. 237-245.

[6] This is based on Thomas Isaac's personal involvement in the process and access to information in the State Planning Board. See also: Thomas Isaac, 'Gunabhoktra Samithikalude Anubhava Padangal', in *Gunabhoktra Samithikalum Janakeeyasoothranavum*, Kerala State Planning Board, Thiruvananthapuram. G.K. Leiten, *The First Communist Ministry in Kerala*.

to compromise with contractors or vested interests in order to overcome the general adverse environment and numerous obstacles that they continued to confront despite the best efforts of the Campaign. Many others were not controlled by professional contractors but failed to follow proper procedures or were controlled by particular individual beneficiaries who were motivated by personal profit or vested interests. Our judgment is that only a quarter of the beneficiary committees survived the tendencies for degeneration and functioned effectively as genuine participatory forums. That means of the estimated 30,000 to 35,000 public works projects, approximately 8,000 to 9,000 were at the behest of genuine beneficiary committees.

THE RELEVANCE OF LABOUR CONTRACT SOCIETIES IN THE PEOPLE'S PLAN CAMPAIGN

With such a large number of public works projects undertaken through the Campaign, it provides both tremendous opportunities for people's participation as well as avenues for vested interests to take root. In this context, the labour contract societies could potentially play a vital role in bridging the gap and supporting the beneficiary committees. To understand the contribution labour contract societies could play, we must first understand the key problems that the beneficiary committees faced. Based on a survey of 503 successful cases, we have identified a number of problems ranging from bureaucratic apathy to overly long delays in payment. The survey was conducted in 1999 with the participants nominated by their local governments as the 'best beneficiary committee.' Questionnaires were sent to 750 beneficiary committees and 503 provided complete information. In Table 5.1 we summarize some of the major problems identified by the survey.

One of the major problems identified is that the local government bureaucrats were not familiar with local rates and the new procedures for preparing the estimates, creating a great deal of confusion. For example, during the first year, the estimates neglected to contain any provision for sales tax, income tax, or contribution to the Construction Workers Welfare Fund. When the final bill payment was made all these items were deducted resulting in a major loss to the beneficiary committees. Another problem was linked to the beneficiary contribution that was meant to be raised as a portion of the estimates. The beneficiary contribution was fixed at the time of project preparation, often at an unrealistic level. As a result, nearly half the committees faced problems in collecting the beneficiary contributions (Table 5.1). The elected representatives generally took a hard line arguing that once the agreement was signed it was the duty of the beneficiary committee to collect the contributions.

Another problem with local government is that in many areas, even though technical sanction was officially given by committees, ultimately the government engineer – functioning as committee convener – had a decisive say. This posed a major problem for the campaign as engineering departments had a general hostility to the Campaign as it challenged their once-absolute power. Given this general hostility towards the Campaign, getting technical sanction continued to be a tortuous exercise if the works were to be carried out by a beneficiary committee.

There were also internal problems to the beneficiary committees. Even though the work was awarded to beneficiary committees without going through the tender procedures,

Table 5.1: Self-assessment of problems faced by 503 better-performing beneficiary committees

	No problem	Slight problem	Moderate problem	Serious problem	Very serious	Total
Formation of the beneficiary committee	82.3	10.7	4.0	1.2	1.8	100
Signing the contract	77.8	13.7	8.0	3.0	0.8	110
Cooperation by engineers	60.4	21.7	7.2	5.0	6.2	100
Preparation of estimate	66.2	16.9	9.7	4.0	3.2	100
Technical support	60.2	19.9	8.2	5.8	6.0	100
Supervision of work	67.2	19.5	7.2	4.2	2.0	100
Measurement	54.3	21.1	13.1	7.2	4.4	100
Check measurement	52.1	17.9	15.9	6.8	7.4	100
Getting the equipment	49.1	22.1	13.9	8.2	6.8	100
Getting the material	47.1	21.3	17.1	8.9	5.6	100
Getting the advance	63.8	19.9	8.9	4.2	3.2	100
Part bill payment	51.1	17.1	12.9	7.8	9.1	100
Final bill payment	55.5	10.9	8.7	7.8	17.1	100
Collection of beneficiary contribution	51.3	10.9	10.5	5.6	21.7	100

Source: Survey of Beneficiary Committees, State Planning Board, Government of Kerala,1999.

twenty-five per cent of the committees took more than one month after formation to sign an agreement with the local government (Table 5.1). Committees were supposed to form only after the estimate was prepared and technical sanction received, in many instances committees formed before the procedures were completed, which exposed them to pressures from engineers and vested interests. There were different ways in which engineers, officials and vested interests undermined the process. For example, in many cases, beneficiary committees found themselves working with grossly undervalued estimates done purposefully by engineers hostile to the new system. In some instances, officials openly discouraged the committees from undertaking the work. In other cases, signing the contract itself proved to be cumbersome; in many places officials insisted on three separate revenue stamped documents, each costing Rs 50. For many cases, the estimates were purposely prepared in overly technical language that most committee members could not understand, and thus committees often did not realize what they were committing themselves to at the time of signing.

For those committees that managed to get through the laborious process of estimates and technical sanction, they faced a new set of challenges once the work began. Committee members found it difficult to do day-to-day supervision not only because of the time requirements, but also because of their lack of technical know-how. The estimates often did not contain provisions for a paid supervisor. Another challenge they faced was in procuring material and equipment. Twenty-five per cent of the committees reported that they had to rely on contractors for the necessary construction equipment. With a mini-construction boom taking place in Kerala when the public works projects were undertaken, there was a scarcity of building materials, particularly sand, tar and cement. This caused serious delays in project implementation.

In addition to problems with the construction process, beneficiary committees also faced serious financial constraints. Thirty-seven per cent of the committees had problems getting the initial project advance money on time and 77 per cent considered the advance insufficient to carry out the work. The Work Rule had limited the advance to 25 per cent of the estimate with a ceiling of Rs 50,000, which was insufficient even for medium-sized works. There were also serious limitations with the part-bill payment procedure. A portion of the advance was to be deducted from every part-bill payment, which caused financial shortages toward the end of the work when committees had no money on hand. A surprisingly large number (45 per cent) faced problems during the final bill settlement, with 17 per cent of them reporting the problem to be very serious.

In numerous instances, the work done was under-measured by government engineers. Each of the three steps (i.e., measurement check, bill preparation, and payment) was meant to take a *maximum* of seven days, but the maximum very often turned into a minimum. In addition, there were always delays in drawing money from the treasury. The shortage of funds caused by the part-bill payment delays led to frequent work stoppages. Only committees whose members had personal funds to advance to the project were able to keep their projects underway, which made them very vulnerable to capture by vested interests. Indeed, it was at this juncture that many committees began to degenerate into the hands of a few who could advance the funds.

Needless to say, some local elected representatives were not immune to contractor influence and found in the new arrangements an easy means for rent seeking, which could only be curbed through making the procedures more transparent. Numerous allegations were made that committees were formed without the knowledge of some of the beneficiaries in the area, the details of the work were not exhibited at the site, proper minutes and documents of the committee were not maintained and so on. The survey of 503 genuine beneficiary committees showed that 55 per cent of them did not keep stock registers, 20 per cent did not keep work diaries, and 14 per cent did not present the accounts in the committee meetings. Clearly, the conditions were rife for corruption and abuse of the process, which could best be countered through proper records that were transparently and openly presented.

Despite all the drawbacks and limitations, beneficiary committees during the People's Plan Campaign of 1996-2001 made a major contribution to ensure transparency and reduce corruption in public works. Even if one quarter of the beneficiary committees might have been *benami* committees of contractors and a significant number degenerated in the course of implementation and were forced to compromise their principles, the heightened public scrutiny and monitoring significantly reduced corruption. Therefore the general feeling among the PPC organizers was that the beneficiary committee experiment should be carried forward.

As noted above, one of the major problems was that the beneficiary committees did not have the equipment or expertise to undertake building works, not even a relatively simple road tarring project. As a result, beneficiary committees were forced to engage contractors or subcontract the work. It was this challenge that raised the potential of labour contract societies to serve as support organizations for the beneficiary committees. Once the idea of labour contract societies came to the fore, it also became clear that they could be another alternative option for the implementation of public works by local government. Thus, labour contract societies could play two roles: (1) they could support beneficiary committees and (2) they could undertake the work directly from local government.

In the third year of PPC a state level convention of nearly

1,000 beneficiary committees was convened at Thiruvananthapuram and case studies of 200 model beneficiary committees were presented. Out of this process, the critical review of beneficiary committee experiences underlined the importance of restructuring labour contract societies so that they could supplement the beneficiary committees. It was in this process that the gaze turned to the ULCCS as a model to emulate.

ULCCS AS A MODEL FOR KERALA

Labour contract societies were given special recognition from the beginning of the People's Plan Campaign. Some of the local governments even included projects for setting up labour contract societies in the annual plan of 1997-98, the first year of the Campaign. In 1998-99, local governments proposed 56 labour contract societies as part of their annual plan, 22 were by block panchayats, 22 were by gram panchayats, and nine by municipalities.[7] The total outlay of these projects was Rs 1.35 crore with plan support of Rs 0.75 crore and the rest had to be sourced from financial institutions and own contribution of members.

We do not have similar detailed data for subsequent years, but the number of labour contract societies including the dormant societies increased from 308 in 1996-97 to 375 in 1997-98, and in 1998-99 the number increased to 392 and further to 431 in 2000-01 (of these 161 were dormant). Many of these societies were sponsored by the contractors in order to take advantage of the various concessions that were offered to labour contract societies, especially after the launch of the

[7] Thomas Isaac, 'People's Planning and Beneficiary Committees' (Malayalam), in Sivaramakrishnan et al., *Gunabhoktra Samithikalude Anubhavapadangal*, State Planning Board, Government of Kerala, 1999, Thiruvananthapuram, p. 45.

PPC which further enhanced the concessions to societies. This led to the serious challenge of distinguishing between a *benami* labour contract society and a genuine labour contract society.

In order to address this issue, a consensus emerged that only labour contract societies by local governments should be considered for concessions. Local government sponsored labour contract societies were required to follow a certain uniformity in their structure, mode of functioning and transparency norms. A general approach of the PPC was to identify successful model projects and best practices experimented by non-governmental organizations, cooperatives and also government agencies and departments at the local level, and project them as model programmes that could be scaled up to state level.[8] The search for a model labour contract society led to ULCCS which at the time was known only in and around Vadakara *taluk*. There were four key features of ULCCS that endeared it to the organizers of PPC.

First, the worker ownership, worker management and worksite level worker participation were a rare exhibition of industrial workplace democracy. The membership was confined to workers, and the board of directors were workers themselves – except for the three cases in its early history – and each worker was involved in the decision making process at the worksite. Second, the board of directors visited the sites every day and met every night to review the work of the day and plan the next day's work. Each board member was in charge of a worksite and thus board members were also involved in the project execution. These procedures not only enhanced the democratic process and transparent communication, but also created impressive harmony and comradeship in the Society.

Third, the Society had evolved home-grown methods

[8] Ibid., pp. 52-77.

of organization to keep track of its multifarious activities, ensure transparency and achieve efficiency. Each contract was considered as an independent profit/loss line of activity with clearly identified norms for material use and work efficiency, while still assuring maximum autonomy to the actual worksites. The efficiency and success of the Society was proven by its consistent profits and expanding turnover. Finally, the hoary history of ULCCS which harks back to Vagbhatananda, the Kerala renaissance, and the radical socio-political movements of the first half of the twentieth century had an evocative appeal to the People's Plan Campaign. Moreover, the Society's strong local level links and stellar reputation in Malabar made it a symbol of local pride. It was an ideal model for the PPC to champion.

The best way to popularize the ULCCS model was through an information sharing workshop hosted by the panchayat. By the third year of the PPC, the mass campaign training programmes were institutionalized through selected institutes and a new stream of training activities – that is, experience sharing workshops hosted by model panchayats and municipalities – were also initiated. The workshop themes were to showcase and learn from a programme in which the local government host excelled. Even though the main presentation would be related to the host, there would be opportunities for other participating local governments to present their experience also.[9] In October 1999, a two-day workshop on labour contract societies was organized by Onchiyam panchayat in partnership with ULCCS. A brief history of the society and a model bylaw for labour contract societies based upon the experience of ULCCS was printed and distributed to the over 100 local governments participating

[9] Ibid., p. 331.

in the workshop. ULCCS officially became the model labour contract society for the Campaign.

NEW EXPERIMENTS IN LABOUR CONTRACT SOCIETIES

ULCCS inspired many similar labour contract society experiments in other parts of Kerala. Unfortunately we do not have aggregate data to assess the expansion of labour contract societies since the PPC. In 2009-10, there were 528 labour contract societies of which 228 were dormant, and *benami* societies continue to exist as well. Given the data we do have, it is reasonable to assume that many of the new labour contract societies sponsored by local governments experienced the same process of degeneration as beneficiary societies as they faced the same challenges.

By way of illustration, we present the experiences of three selected cases of the different types of labour societies. The first case is the Udayapuram Labour Contract Cooperative Society in Kasargod (hereafter Udayapuram LCCS),[10] which was inspired by the ULCCS and follows its model. We focus on Udayapuram LCCS for two reasons. First, its brief history is a saga of continuous struggle against contractors and vested interests. Second, Udayapuram LCCS has close fraternal ties to ULCCS, which extends technical and logistical advice and assistance, including short-term financial assistance when Udayapuram LCCS needs it.

Udayapuram LCCS is located in Kodom-Belur panchayat in Kasargod district, where the corruption of contractors

[10] There are similar success stories such as Kunhithanni Labour Contract Cooperative Society (in Idukky) and Thaliparambu Labour Contract Cooperative Society (in Kannur) that were inspired by ULCCS. Discussion with A.C. Mathew, President Udayapuram Labour Contract Co-op society.

in local public works projects was challenged by a group concerned citizens even before the People's Plan Campaign started. When the PPC started, the group of concerned citizens quickly took the initiative to form beneficiary committees, but eventually incurred heavy losses for the reasons discussed above. After this experience, popular enthusiasm waned. It was at this time that the panchayat standing committee chairman took initiative to form a labour contract cooperative society, which formally registered in January 1997. The initial source of finance came from loans by well-wishers and the Society was able to take up contract work of Rs 11 lakh in the first year. The turnover steadily increased to nearly Rs 1 crore by 2001-02. While the growth of the Society was celebrated by many, it also created panic among local contractors who had always monopolized public works projects in the area. The usual practice of contractors was to divide the works among themselves by mutual agreement and ensure that contracts were awarded at excessively high tenders. The surplus was divided among the contractors who had collaborated in the tender. The entry of Udayapuram LCCS in the public works construction scene made such tender fixing impossible.

In response, the nexus of contractors and engineers clandestinely worked together to undermine the Society. Within a couple years, the Society's turnover dropped to Rs 25-50 lakh, it slipped into losses, and its membership declined from 260 in 2001-02 to 155 in 2004-05. When the Society was on the brink of collapse, the new government that came to power in 2006 pro-actively supported genuine labour cooperatives. The Udayapuram LCCS was declared an accredited agency for local government in 2007-08, reversing its decline. That year the Cooperative became the sole contractor of public works for Kodom-Belur panchayat, which deposited its entire public works budget worth around Rs 80 lakh with the Cooperative. However, under the pressure from contractors, the panchayat had to go back to the tender system the following year.

The Society was given A Class registration which enabled it to enter the contract market for roads under the Department of Public Works, which triggered open hostility from the engineer-contractor lobby. Whenever the Society quoted for a public works project the private contractors would under quote the job, forcing the Society to negotiate for 10 per cent higher than the lowest quote and still incur loss. Additionally, the Society faced difficulties in terms of shortages in measurement and delays in the payment of bills. The engineer-contractor lobby was even able to disrupt the cash credit from the DCB, bringing the Society almost to a standstill. The Society was only saved in these moments of financial crisis by the loans from the well-wishers and members' mortgages of gold and land. In a few instances, the Society's representatives were physically prevented from tendering. For example, the Society's President was physically assaulted and narrowly escaped a murder attempt.

The intense conflict with the contractors' lobby had an unexpected consequence. In search of allies, Udayapuram LCCS supported the formation of four more labour contract cooperative societies on the model of ULCCS in Kasargod District. The idea was that they could form a negotiating group of labour contract societies in order to collectively engage the authorities and improve their bargaining power.[11] The Society's quality work in prompt time earned it respect and prestige and enabled it to steadily expand its turnover

[11] Discussion with A.C. Mathew, President, Udayapuram Labour Contract Co-op Society, 5 November 2013.

to 4.4 crore in 2009-10 and Rs 16.3 crore in 2012-13. The government raised the permissible limit for participating in tenders to Rs 15 crore, and the overall limit for all projects happening simultaneously to Rs 50 crore. The membership increased again from its low in 2004-05 to 225 in 2012-13 with a member share capital of Rs 11 lakh and the total share capital – inclusive of the government share – is more than Rs 1 crore. Thus, through perseverance, commitment and strategic government support, Udayapuram LCCS has overcome a number of challenges and is poised to consolidate its gains.

The second case of a labour contract society is Kunnathukal Labour Bank, which was one of the most innovative projects of the entire People's Plan Campaign, combining the concepts of labour contract, employment guarantee, agrarian reforms and banking. The labour bank formed in Kunnathukal panchayat in the southernmost part of Kerala and was registered under the Charitable Societies Act (rather than under the Cooperative Act). The labour bank's innovation is found at every level. The capital of the labour bank consisted of the labour committed by the members, which could be loaned to the farmers or customers. Any farmer could enter into a contract with the labour bank for a specified agricultural operation or cropping cycle in which the labour bank agreed to undertake the specified operations in a time-bound manner for a mutually agreed price, which would be paid only when the crop is harvested. The farmers also had the option of handing-over their land for cultivation to the Society. The member-workers were guaranteed 20 days employment per month. If sufficient agricultural work was not available, the Labour Bank would arrange for implementation of public works for the panchayat, which had agreed to appoint the Labour Bank as its implementation agency. These arrangements were granted special approval by government. The initial success of the Labour Bank led to some of the neighbouring local governments to also entrust the Labour Bank with some of their public works.

The Labour Bank developed a holistic programme in which all the labourers underwent special orientation training in the Agricultural University and were provided modern equipment. Salaries were dispersed at the end of the month, but during the course of the month the labourers could receive advances in the form of coupons with which they could buy daily essentials from the local shops. Thus, the Labour Bank had also integrated the local shops into the overall programme and the local shops were encouraged to stock products from the women's self-help groups promoted by the panchayat. The local government was, in a sense, experimenting with its own local currency and trying to maximize the multiplier impact of expenditure in its locality. The programme was an enormous success and won widespread attention across the state. In 2000, a participatory training programme, similar to the one held at Onchiyam showcasing ULCCS, was organized in Kunnathukal to showcase the Labour Bank's model.[12] The far-reaching influence of the Labour Bank is seen in the guidelines of the national Employment Guarantee Programme and the land army experiment sponsored by the Agricultural University.

The third case we highlight is Pinarayi Engineering and Construction Cooperative (PECC), which is located in Pinarayi

[12] Thomas Isaac, 'The Relevance of Kunnathukal Labour Bank' (Malayalam) in *Bhooparishkaranam eni enthu*, Trivandrum: Chintha Publishers, 2008, pp. 169-184. Lijo Thomas and Siddayya, 'Labour Bank Experiment in Kerala–SWOT Analysis', *Agricultural Economics Research Review*, Vol. 24, 2011, pp. 511-516.

panchayat, famous for the high density of various cooperatives (there are approximately 35 cooperatives in the panchayat). Some industrial cooperatives, like PECC, have successfully extended and diversified their activities to contract work and construction activities. PECC is an important supplier of concrete posts to the Kerala State Electricity Board (KSEB) and manufacturer of floor tiles with a turnover of Rs 6 crore. The opportunities provided by the public works projects of the local governments and the yearning of many elected representatives to avoid contractors attracted PECC to expand its activities and undertake public works contracts. During 2011-12, its turnover in construction was Rs 4 crore, it had 208 individual members with a share capital of Rs 1.8 lakh and a government share capital contribution of Rs 2.16 crore. In this particular case an existing cooperative successfully diversified into labour contract work. The relative ease with which PECC entered the public works construction scene highlights the important role supportive local government institutions can make as well as the relative advantage an existing cooperative has, especially if it supplies crucial inputs for the construction process.

As these examples illustrate, the effort to spread the ULCCS model resonated across Kerala. However, many labour contract societies have not survived the degeneration tendencies prevalent in local spaces across the state. The situation has been exacerbated by the disruption in PPC when the new government came to power in 2001. While the new government continued the devolution process and left the structure of decentralized planning largely untouched, they discontinued the People's Plan Campaign and dismissed the volunteers and experts who were seen as extra-constitutional intrusions into the local government system. With the withering of the Campaign and popular participation, bureaucratic tendencies came to the fore once again and the corruption nexus re-emerged. The first casualties were the beneficiary committees and then the labour contract societies.

ULCCS, however, managed to survive these changes. The ULCCS was initially given the right to directly undertake local government projects in Vadakara block panchayat and later was recognized as an accredited agency for the whole state, which meant that any local government could reach an agreement with ULCCS without it having to go through the tender process and could deposit project funds with the Society. Since every local government was obliged to spend at least 75 per cent of their annual allocation before the end of the financial year – or risk losing the unspent funds – local governments were under severe pressure to implement projects before the end of the financial year. Thus, some local governments found it convenient to deposit the amount for public works with ULCCS and then claim the expenditure, knowing that the ULCCS would deliver on the projects. This explains the rapid rise in ULCCS's turnover from the late 1990s. The deposits also unintentionally helped resolve ULCCS's working capital scarcity that it regularly faced. Equally significant, the deposits demonstrated the high credibility and respect that ULCCS had earned among people and government officials throughout Kerala and helps to explain the widespread support it received in its efforts for modernization and diversification.

Labour contract societies similar to ULCCS clearly played a significant role in the decentralized planning of the PPC. The democratic participation of worker-members together with the high quality timely construction projects resonated with the twin goals of the PPC – enhanced democratic participation in local government institutions and increased quality of infrastructure and service delivery. While ULCCS clearly played an important role in the PPC, its participation in the process also shaped the future of ULCCS.

CHAPTER 6

THE DIVERSIFICATION OF ULCCS

A priest who was defeated by Vagbhatananda in a debate on re-birth angrily responded: I shall vigorously prepare and defeat you when I meet you next year. Vagbhatananda replied 'It is very good you have decided to study. But don't study to vanquish me. Even after one year, the difference between us would continue to be there. I am not going to sleep while you are studying. I shall also continue my studies.'

On this historic moment I want to say with pride that we have also not slept. The present function is the proof. It is from the words of Vagbhatananda that we have drawn the confidence to make the claim that if you show us a model of the heaven and we shall construct it here.

Uralungal Labour Society was started in 1925 taking up a contract for Rs 950. Today we have the courage and strength to enter the IT world with an investment of Rs 600 crore. This was made possible by a band of workers who carried in their heart of hearts, without losing a drop, the confidence that overflowed from the words of Vagbhatananda. The source of all that you see around is the strength of their muscles and the will of their

> mind. [. . .] The formation of the society of wage labourers of Uralungal by 14 pioneers was a bold response to the caste discrimination and monopoly of land and wealth by the *jenmis*. [. . .] Today we are more than 1700 workers and 750 members in whom agencies of centre, state and local governments have reposed full confidence.
>
> Today on 20th January 2012 we are commencing the first phase of realization of a new dream, an IT Park owned by the construction workers.[1]
>
> Paleri Ramesan

The establishment of UL Cyber Park at Kozhikode marks a fundamentally new phase in the history of ULCCS. The Society has diversified from a contractor for construction of infrastructure to a provider of infrastructure services. It is the first IT Park in the Malabar region and the first of its kind owned by a labour cooperative in India. The preparations and discussions for the establishment of the IT Park started in 2009, a formal Memorandum of Understanding was signed with the Government of Kerala in 2010, Special Economic Zone (SEZ) status granted in 2011 and the formal foundation stone for the main building laid in 2012. A five lakh square foot IT facility, the first of the series which when completed would total 31 lakh square feet, was ready for customers by the end of 2014.

While this is a remarkable achievement, it raises a number of questions. Given the success record of ULCCS in construction what is the need for diversification? If there is need for diversification, why did it choose the IT sector? How can

[1] Welcome speech by P. Rameshan, President, Uralungal Labour Contract Co-operative Society Ltd, in connection with the foundation stone laying ceremony of UL Cyber Park, 20 January 2012.

the facility be constructed and maintained efficiently without compromising on its cooperative character? Are there threats to ULCCS's cooperative principles in such diversification? What other options are available for diversification? In this chapter we explore the above questions.

WHY DIVERSIFY?

While the rapid expansion of ULCCS into a Society with a Rs 200 crore turnover parachuted it into a front-ranking construction firm in Kerala, it still only registers as a medium level construction firm at the national scale and a small player internationally. To become a leader on the national scale, ULCCS would have to make a number of changes that would allow it to take advantage of the enormous opportunities emerging in infrastructure development. For example, the country has entered an infrastructure boom with investment in road infrastructure expanding from 3.3 per cent of the GDP in 2003 to more than 8 per cent in 2011-12.[2] In addition, an ambitious programme of 50,000 kilometres of six to eight lane super highways, widening and modernizing the network of national highways by the National Highway Authority of India (NHAI), and developing a 60,000 kilometre network of quality all weather rural roads connected to road arteries under Pradhan Mantri Gram Sadak Yojana (PMGSY) are being undertaken. The rapid expansion of railways, seaports, and airports are also planned. As a result, the scale of operation of construction firms and the innovation in construction technology are undergoing a sea-change necessitating a significant increase in investment. In this context of rapid

[2] Saji Gopinath, IIM Kozhikode, Project Report submitted to UNDP through National Labour Co-operative Federation 2007, p. 13.

expansion of the construction industry what is the rationale for diversification of ULCCS's activities?

One of the reasons according to the board of directors is the changing labour market in Kerala. When the ULCCS started in 1925 construction labourers were in ample supply and members were recruited through a selective process of apprenticeship, but, as we noted previously, with the increased access to education in the state the younger generation were not interested in construction work, leading to serious labour scarcity for the Society. While supply has dried up in Kerala, demand for construction workers has increased, often leaving the Society with serious shortage of sufficient hands for work. This has been a problem for the Society since the mid 2000s and necessitated the recruitment of migrant labour from northern India (Table 6.1).

Two factors are responsible for the phenomenal increase in the demand for construction workers. The first is large scale migration to the Gulf countries both by skilled and unskilled construction workers from the mid-1970s. The escalation of petroleum prices initiated a construction boom in the Gulf countries and Kerala was one of the important catchment areas for migrant workers. The state was able to take advantage of the new job opportunities abroad because of the plentiful availability of educated people and also the traditional trade links between the Malabar coast and the Gulf countries. There are approximately two million Malayali migrant workers in the Gulf countries around half of whom are construction workers. This has translated into a serious shortage of construction workers in Kerala.

The second factor leading to an increase in the demand for construction workers has to do with boom in the construction

Table 6.1: Composition of workforce in ULCCS

Year	Members	Non-members			Total workers	% of non-workers	% of migrant workers
		Keralites	Migrant	Total			
2000-01	275	1191	0	1191	1466	81.24	0.00
2001-02	273	1220	0	1220	1493	81.71	0.00
2002-03	301	1134	0	1134	1435	79.02	0.00
2003-04	317	1160	0	1160	1477	78.54	0.00
2004-05	275	1056	12	1068	1343	79.52	0.89
2005-06	416	990	14	1004	1420	70.70	0.99
2006-07	495	845	22	867	1362	63.66	1.62
2007-08	568	803	26	829	1397	59.34	1.86
2008-09	708	782	88	870	1578	55.13	5.58
2009-10	993	721	120	841	1834	45.86	6.54
2010-11	1212	681	198	879	2091	42.04	9.47
2011-12	1235	578	252	830	2065	40.19	12.20
2012-13	1330	475	380	855	2185	39.13	17.39
2013-14	1401	480	907	1387	2788	49.75	32.53
2014-15	1527	514	1082	1596	3123	51.10	34.64
2015-16	1616	814	1546	2360	3976	59.10	38.88

Source: From the workers register of ULCCS.

sector in Kerala due to remittances inflow. The remittances from the migrant workers in Gulf steadily increased to Rs 60,000 crore in 2012, and constituted nearly 25 to 30 per cent of the State Domestic Product (SDP). The first impact of the remittance inflow was on the consumption level in the state which is one of the highest in the country. The remittances that have gone into savings have taken the form of investment in financial assets such as bank deposits and in durable assets such as land and buildings. As a result, the construction industry experienced growth due to remittances and the contribution of the construction sector to the SDP has increased from 2.9 per cent in 1970-71 to over 12 per cent during the recent years. There has also been a significant increase of the share of construction in the workforce from 1.7

per cent in 1971 to 9.4 per cent in 2001. Thus there has also been a remarkable increase of the demand for construction workers in the domestic market.

In contrast, the supply of construction workers has been shrinking as a result of the spread of education and rising job expectations of youth. The educated young generation is not interested in the traditional occupations of their parents or grandparents and, instead, aspire for secure quality jobs that are more in consonance with their higher educational status. In addition, the lingering subterranean elite caste value system discounts manual labour and is yet another subsidiary factor in the withdrawal of educated people from the traditional occupations. The labour scarcity resulted in the escalation of construction wage rates relative to other skilled and unskilled wage rates in the rural areas, a process that has been strengthened by the unionization of construction workers. In 2013-14 the wage rates of male construction workers varied between Rs 500 to Rs 750 per day. However, the reserve price (i.e., minimum wages that workers accept) has also tended to rise and is usually set with an eye on the nominal wage rate in the Gulf countries.

The above situation accounts for the paradox of high levels of unemployment and growing shortages of labour for manual jobs. In 2004-05, the unemployment rate of women in Kerala was 20.1 per cent in rural areas and 33.4 per cent in urban areas in contrast to the national rates of 1.8 per cent and 6.9 per cent respectively. As for men, the unemployment rate in Kerala is 5.1 per cent in rural areas and 6.2 per cent in urban areas in contrast to the national rates of 1.6 per cent and 3.8 per cent respectively. The high unemployment and simultaneous shortage of manual labourers is a direct result of the spread of education, the rise in job expectations, and the escalation of the reserve price for manual labour. The educated unemployed, in their long waiting period for jobs, pursue additional qualifications or engage in service activities in the informal sector that are of lower payment than construction but more in consonance with their perceived status.[3]

The scarcity of domestic labour in construction activities has given rise to inter-state migration into Kerala. During the 1980s skilled Tamil workers from Kanyakumari District migrated to areas along the coast and Central Travancore to work on construction sites. During the 1990s, this became a generalized pattern of migrants from Tamil Nadu in search of work not only in construction sites but also for work in the agricultural lands in districts adjacent to Tamil Nadu and also service sectors such as restaurants.[4] More recently, there has been a sharp decline in migration from Tamil Nadu, which has been replaced with migration from North and Northeast India. While the main area of employment is the construction sector, migrant workers are also employed in agricultural fieldwork, industries such as plywood and brick making, and service sectors that involve manual work such as restaurants. There is no comprehensive database either regarding the number of migrants, their labour conditions or social and welfare situation. The Gulati Institute of Finance and Taxation (GIFT) has estimated the number of the migrant workers to be around 25 lakh,[5] which is generally considered to be an overestimate. Nevertheless, even if we take half this estimate,

[3] C. Mukherjee and Thomas Isaac, *Survey of Educated Unemployed in Kerala*, Centre for Development Studies, Thiruvananthapuram, 1991. AKG Centre for Research Studies, Vol. I.

[4] S. Anand, 'Migrant Construction Workers: A Case Study of Tamil Workers in Kerala', M.Phil. Dissertation, Centre for Development Studies, Thiruvananthapuram, 1986.

[5] D. Narayana et al., *Domestic Migrant Workers in Kerala*, Gulati Institute of Finance and Taxation, Thiruvananthapuram, 2013.

migrant workers today would still constitute a significant proportion (one tenth) of the workforce in the State.

The above developments have had a significant impact on ULCCS's workforce. For one, the number of members as a proportion of the total workforce tended to decline from the 1970s so that by 2000-01 members were less than 20 per cent of the total workers. The decline in worker-members is linked to the fact that the local supply of workers from Vadakara *taluk* began to dry up, necessitating the hiring of migrant workers from other parts of Kerala as well as northern India. This led to a growing proportion of migrant workers in the total workforce of the Cooperative; in 2012-13 migrants constituted 13.4 per cent of the total workers (Table 6.1). This situation raises the possibility of degeneration of the Cooperative into a capitalist firm where a few hundred elite members own the Cooperative and employ non-members as wage labourers, mostly migrant workers on a large scale. Thus, the accumulation process in the Cooperative has been constrained by the traditional line of production and changes in the labour market. To deal with this situation required a fresh organizational and technological response. It is in the context that the strategy of diversification assumes significance.

What is particularly interesting is that even the current members do not want their children to enter into their parents' occupation in construction unless it is modernized thoroughly through technological upgrading. Nearly all the children of both members and non-members attend school or college, which reflects the fact that education is seen as a social ladder for upward mobility. Few of the parents want their children to be even skilled construction workers, and clearly none want them to be unskilled wage labourers either. Table 6.2 gives the distribution of parents' job expectations of the children after

Table 6.2: Job expectations of parents for their children

Distribution of workers by job expectation for children and category (only non students)

Category	Skilled worker	Factory job	Job in pvt sector	Teachers and govt employees	Engineers and profes-sionals	Job abroad	Others	Total
A class member	3	12	1	107	29	3	8	163
C class member	1	2	3	105	34	1	4	150
Non-Member Keralite	1	2	8	53	29	1	2	96
Migrant Worker	20	15	10	29	10	0	23	107
Total Workers	25	31	22	294	102	5	37	516
	4.84	6.01	4.26	56.98	19.77	0.97	7.17	100.00

Source: Survey of workers in ULCCS, 2014.

their education. The most coveted job is the secure government white collar employment accounting for 57 per cent, and surprisingly, 20 per cent of parents want their children to achieve technical or professional jobs. These aspirations already reflect in the Cooperative's membership. Ten years back more than half of the members of the Cooperative membership were the children of erstwhile members while today they constitute hardly 10 per cent. The contrast with the expectations of the migrant workers is interesting as 50 per cent want their children to become skilled workers or factory workers and 20 per cent want different types of self-employment jobs for their children (Table 6.2).

The original objective of ULCCS was to provide employment to its members in the Vadakara area. With all the changes discussed above (labour market, migration, aspirational goals of youth and parents, increased skills, education, and status), this objective is becoming increasingly difficult to achieve through construction activities alone. P. Ramesan explained the dilemma that ULCCS faced as follows: 'The primary objective of ULCCS was to provide employment to its members. However we are not getting sufficient members from our area to undertake construction activities. Nowadays more and more young people with professional qualifications are coming to us seeking technical jobs. How do we provide employment to them?' He went on to explain that 'The solution lies in diversifying into sectors such as IT and tourism where quality jobs that young people aspire to can be created. It however does not mean that we are going to shift away from construction. It will continue to be the main activity of ULCCS.'[6] Thus, unlike capitalist firms that diversify to expand production and shore up profits, the ULCCS's desire to diversify stems from its continued commitment to meet members' needs and provide quality jobs, and hence livelihoods to the next generation.

WHY DIVERSIFICATION INTO INFORMATION TECHNOLOGY?

With current assets worth around Rs 350 crore, proposing the creation of a facility worth Rs 600 crore took many by surprise. In a sense, the entry of ULCCS as an important player in IT infrastructure in Kerala was accidental. Construction of the Kozhikode bypass road was a major contract work undertaken by ULCCS in 2003, which cost an estimated Rs 10 crore. The road runs through marshy low lying areas and required substantial land filling. ULCCS sought a suitable barren hill for soil excavation in the neighbourhood of the road project, and identified 14 acres of top land on Kachilat

[6] Interview with P. Rameshan, President ULCCS, 6 September 2013.

hill in Nellikode village. The land was purchased at Rs 26 lakh per acre. The soil excavation removed the crest of the hill and created a flat top, which was ideal for an urban housing project.

It was at this juncture that the Government of Kerala declared a project for establishing an IT park in Kozhikode through acquiring around 68 acres of land including the 14 acres that ULCCS owned. The Society was suddenly facing the danger of losing the land whose price had escalated to Rs 3 to 4 crore per acre. At the same time there was also an opportunity for collaborating with the government in establishing the IT Park. The Government of Kerala appreciated the concerns of ULCCS and decided that a 25 acre Special Economic Zone (SEZ) IT park would be set up jointly by government and ULCCS, adjacent to the wholly government owned IT park. The SEZ programme has been controversial as labour laws and environmental standards are normally relaxed in these zones. After prolonged debates, the left government concluded that a complete rejection of this national programme would not be in the state's interest. Therefore, it was decided to allow small-scale SEZs that would not require large land acquisition and had strict norms requiring land use for industrial purposes, and very importantly there is no relaxation of environmental or labour laws in the SEZs in Kerala.[7]

In a meeting convened by the IT secretary in 2008, the following decisions were made: (1) A Special Purpose Vehicle (SPV) to be formed with 26 per cent share for government and 74 per cent share for ULCCS. (2) The 14 acres of land owned by ULCCS would be exempted from the acquisition notification and would remain the property of ULCCS. In addition, government would acquire another 11 acres of land

[7] Interview with Shaju S., Secretary ULCCS, 7 September 2013.

to create a joint park of 25 acres, which was the minimum area required for recognition of SEZ status from the central government. This land would be the share of the state government in the joint venture. (3) The state government would recommend SEZ status for the joint venture. (4) The state government would also ensure technical support to provide a single window clearance and would also include it in the master plan for Kozhikode Technopark. (5) The rest of the funds required for the SPV would have to be made available by ULCCS. And (6) the SEZ norms would be strictly followed and the construction activities should be started within a year. Failure to do so would result in the government IT Company automatically taking over the land acquired by the state government.[8]

Delays in the land acquisition upset the time schedule and it was only in June 2009 that the cabinet formally approved the above conditions for the joint venture. Meanwhile, ULCCS under its bylaw, clause 4.14, formed a corporate company under the name ULCCS IT Infrastructure Pvt. Ltd. As per the articles of association of the company, ULCCS would always hold majority of shares and the right to appoint the Chairperson and the Managing Director (MD). Kerala State Industrial Development Corporation (KSIDC), the official industrial promotion agency of government of Kerala was allotted 5 per cent shares for Rs 9.24 crore. The Board of Directors included one representative of KSIDC and also technical and managerial experts selected by ULCCS. The president of ULCCS was the Chairperson and Managing Director of the new company.

[8] Minutes of the meeting before the Secretary Information Technology Department, Government of Kerala, 7 September 2013, records of ULCCS.

After the formation of the company, ULCCS decided to directly negotiate and purchase 11 acres of land from 21 owners without further waiting for land to be acquired by the government. The land was purchased for about Rs 10 crore using a loan made available by the District Cooperative Bank. Those who sold their house sites were given alternative house sites down the hill with houses built by ULCCS. Finally, in February 2010, on the recommendation of the state government, SEZ notification was issued by the central government and the new company was formally launched in May 2010.

An expression of interest was sent out to develop the architectural plan, and a Japanese company, M/s Nikken Sekkei, was selected to prepare the master plan and Chennai based M/s CRN was appointed as architects while Bangalore based M/s Diligent was entrusted with the overall project management. A team of professionals with hands-on experience in construction and marketing of IT space was positioned as the project team. ULCCS was given the contract for constructing the park.[9]

Thus, with its deft manoeuvring, ULCCS was making its entry into the IT world through infrastructure construction, the core area of its competence. In addition to the IT infrastructure project, ULCCS still plans to develop housing projects in order to make the best use of land that it acquires for material sourcing. The Society chose to move beyond being merely a construction contractor to becoming an independent developer, constructing and selling commercial space and residential flats. It is hoped that the social prestige of the Society will prove to be an asset in marketing the newly

[9] Detailed Project Report for UL Cyber Park Project 2008.

built spaces. Moreover, ULCCS's decisions were in tune with major policy shifts taking place in the construction sector.

Instead of the conventional government funded project where the contractor's role is limited to construction, the new model envisages a contractor who is also able to be a developer and raise the major part of the financial resources as well as operate the infrastructure under different models of partnership with the government such as Build-Operate-Transfer (BOT), Build-Own-Lease-Transfer (BOLT) and Build-Own-Operate-Transfer (BOOT).[10] If the Society was to continue with its extraordinary growth, it would have to take a proactive attitude in redefining its role in infrastructure development. The original residential housing project was the first major initiative in this direction. A fortuitous coincidence of events led it to deviate from residential infrastructure to IT infrastructure, which produced UL Cyber Park. ULCCS has not set up a software or hardware company, but has created the infrastructure to house such companies, both private and public.

The process was challenging as ULCCS was handicapped by its lack of expertise in the creation of IT infrastructure, marketing of the infrastructure products, raising resources on a large scale and even the construction of mega building projects. It overcame these shortcomings by sourcing in the right forms of support such as selecting appropriate consulting agencies and consultants. The prestige of the Society and goodwill it enjoyed from many experts and leading IT firms enabled it to successfully seek advice and support from experts and also from some of the foremost software companies in India on a voluntary basis.

[10] Scheme and Guidelines India Infrastructure Project Development Fund by Ministry of Finance 2007, Records of ULCCS.

INFORMATION TECHNOLOGY IN KERALA'S DEVELOPMENT STRATEGY

The entry of ULCCS into IT coincided with critical changes in the evolution of development policy in Kerala. We have already discussed in the introductory chapter, Kerala's growth strategy emphasising redistribution that ensured relatively high quality of life in terms of education, health care, social security, housing and other basic needs for ordinary citizens. These achievements are especially noteworthy in relation to the relatively low level of economic growth. This paradigm has been celebrated as the Kerala Model. There was a general concern that the economic growth would come at the cost of equity, resulting in a near stagnation of the economy during the 1970s and early 1980s. The investment in human resources eventually paid off through increased remittances from educated migrant workers and the economy gained momentum from the late 1980s. The acceleration in economic growth has raised Kerala's per capita income significantly above the national average and Kerala today is one of the fast growing regional economies.

However, the current remittance-led growth focused on consumption services is unsustainable unless the growth is linked to industry and agriculture and generates quality jobs for the educated unemployed. Moreover, Kerala's model faces other threats as the egalitarianism for which Kerala is famous is under threat from neoliberal reforms happening at the central government level and the sustainability of development is threatened from the growing crisis in the state. This situation has strengthened the search for a new development paradigm. Kerala's industrialization started with the development of agro-processing industries, but the resource-based industrialization never advanced beyond a proto-industrialization and primary processing of agriculture-forest-fishery products. The upper end of the value chain in these primary commodities always lay outside Kerala. The government did provide sufficient policy intervention to enhance value addition in agro-processing within Kerala. With the erosion of the cheap labour-assisted competitive base of these industries, the situation reached a crisis point.

For historical reasons, state intervention in industrial development was focused on the promotion of investment in energy-intensive chemical industries. An important factor was the ostensible availability of cheap hydroelectric power, which proved to be a mirage. There were also constraints with respect to the marketing of chemicals and allied industrial goods produced in Kerala as downstream industries consuming chemicals or other intermediate goods never emerged on a large-scale. There have also been popular protests against the pollution of air and water by chemicals-producing units. All these factors limited the expansion of the chemicals-dominated, modern industrial sector of Kerala.

To overcome the historical trajectory, an acceleration of future industrial growth in Kerala involves a conscious reorientation of its industrial policy towards promoting sectors in which Kerala has clear comparative advantage. The availability of skilled and educated, but not cheaper, labour, an ecological system characterized by inter-linked water systems and a dense population that is sensitive to pollution concerns are some of the basic considerations to be borne in mind in any policy formulation. The focus also has to be on industries where investment would have greater linkage effects with small-scale capital in the domestic economy. It is in this context that the 'knowledge-based' industries (such as information and communication technology (ICT) and biotechnology) skill-intensive industries (such as light engineering), and service industries (such as tourism) become vital for the future industrialization prospects of Kerala. Evidence from various countries clearly indicates that effective state intervention is crucial for a region's success in knowledge-based industries.[11]

Information Communication Technologies can contribute to the acceleration of economic growth in many ways: (a) creating ICT industries, such as hardware, software, telecommunications and entertainment; (b) providing new and more efficient methods of production for the existing industries; and (c) improving the delivery of government services and increasing access to basic social goods and services. The ICT sector could thus open up a number of opportunities in the state towards bringing in better technology, attracting investments and generating employment for educated work seekers.

The current status of the ICT industry in Kerala relative to India is relatively under developed.[12] Even though Kerala was the first State in India to take definitive steps towards building an electronics industry its sales revenue in the ICT industry as a share of total revenue in the ICT industry in India was only 2 per cent and share in IT exports was approximately 1 per cent. The IT sector in India is poised to expand and in order to exploit these emerging opportunities Kerala is seeking to develop a pro-active policy. Given these conditions, Kerala's growth strategy for the ICT industry will focus on a number of areas simultaneously: building up substantial strengths

[11] Peter Evans, 'The Developmental State: Divergent Responses to Modern Economic Theory and the Twenty-first Century Economy' in Michelle Williams (ed.), *The End of the Developmental State?*, London and New York: Routledge, 2014.

[12] Report of the Working Group on IT, State Planning Board, Government of Kerala, Thiruvananthapuram, 2016.

in service segments, capitalizing on existing strengths in the manufacturing segment, improving the performance and quality of the micro and small industry base, accelerating the incorporation of ICT technologies in the production and delivery systems, and moving more rapidly towards universal e-literacy. The state's role will also have to shift from being directly involved in the economy through investment and planning to more of a role of facilitator and regulator. Such a growth strategy will have to be driven by private sector investment.

The left government's (2006-11) Information Technology Policy emphasized aggressive promotion of private investment in IT infrastructure, promotion of human resource development and facilitation of knowledge creation on the one hand, while drawing out clear strategies to disseminate the benefits of ICT services to the common person. In order to ensure that ICT services are not captured by large corporations and the elite, the IT policy expressly opposes the monopolization of knowledge and intellectual property regimes in the software sector, and, thus, supports the use of free and open software in all government funded ICT projects.[13]

Few States in India have Kerala's advantages to exploit the possibilities offered by ICT. Kerala's advantages include high quality human resource development, availability of low-cost professionals at the entry level, excellent connectivity (as shown by the highest telephone density and international gateway presence at Kochi) and significantly lower operational costs compared to other cities. Despite these important advantages, it also has disadvantages that must be overcome in order to successfully engage the ICT sector opportunities. For example, the disadvantages include a shortage of middle-

[13] The IT Policy, Department of Information Technology, Government of Kerala, Thiruvananthapuram, 2009.

and senior-level professionals, inadequate power supply, insufficient industrial park area and facilities, and the poor image of the State as an investment destination. In an effort to try to overcome the insufficient industrial park area and IT facilities, the government took the initiative to build one of the first IT Parks in India, namely Technopark in Thiruvananthapuram. Technopark is not only expanding its base in Thiruvananthapuram, but is also erecting a satellite centre in Kundara, Kollam district. A second IT park, Info Park, was developed in Kochi and the growth of smaller centres is being facilitated in Cherthala in Alappuzha district and Koratty in Thrissur district. With Info parks in the south and central parts of the state and no IT hub in the Malabar region, there was an opportunity for establishing a similar park in northern Kerala which has a number of advantages even within Kerala. The ULCCS saw this opportunity and vigorously pushed for the establishment of the Cyber Park in Kozhikode. The first phase of ULCCS's portion of the venture is complete, while the government-owned park is still being constructed.

UL CYBER PARK

The ULCCS's IT Park, officially named UL Cyber Park, sits on the top of a picturesque hill and is ideally located adjacent to the national highway bypass of Kozhikode with convenient hubs for rail, bus and air transport nearby. According to the master plan, the completed park will include a built up area of 31.1 lakh square feet, including 21.4 lakh square feet for IT processing activities, and will have two construction phases with clear timelines. The distribution of the building areas is divided into various activities; 1.5 lakh square feet for domestic market oriented companies, 2 lakh square feet for

Table 6.3: Distribution of cumulative built-up area by purpose as per master plan (lakh sq. ft.)

Purpose	On completion of first phase	On completion of second phase
IT Building	13.05	21.4
Multi-level car parking	0.4	1.15
I T domestic	1.5	1.5
Commercial	1.0	2.0
Residential	1.5	5.05
Total	17.45	31.1

Source: Detailed Project Report for UL Cyber park project 2008.

commercial activities, and 5.05 lakh square feet for service apartments and residential apartments (Table 6.3).

The design philosophy emphasized integration of space for residential, commercial and entertainment activities without intruding into each other. Eco-friendly building materials and construction techniques, waste processing and energy use are important features of the development. The contemporary style of the buildings was consciously chosen to stand apart from the traditional style as well as take advantage of the spectacular views given its location on the top of the hill, which looks over a thickly wooded valley.

Getting the exact location right was a major architectural challenge as the 25 acre campus is planned to sit as a horseshoe on the top of two hills connected by a corridor. The park area is planned to be divided into two distinct zones, the north wing and south wing. The larger north wing of the horseshoe is for the five buildings designed for IT processing units and the smaller south wing for residential and commercial purposes. The commercial building is located in the western mouth of the southern wing followed by the residential apartments and then service apartments. High volume traffic has been minimized to the processing area and the entry road to the processing zone is restricted, while the road to the non-processing zone is open to the public and shared with the proposed government-owned park.

As per the master plan the total estimated cost of the project is Rs 600 crore, and the cost of the first phase is Rs 386 crore, which was planned to be financed through equity contributions of Rs 200 crore from promoters and a loan of Rs 400 crore from financial institutions. By the time the master plan was ready, the world economic recession had set in, casting a shadow over immediate prospects of IT industry investments. For example, some of the prestigious investment programmes like the Smart City in Kochi by a Dubai-based firm were postponed. ULCCS decided to continue with their schedule but on a smaller scale than initially envisaged. The logic was that the Society would be ready to take advantage of the inevitable up swing that was bound to come sooner or later.

The first phase of investment was reduced from Rs 386 crore to Rs 210 crore. The main changes made from the master plan for the first phase were in the reduction of IT building area from 13.05 lakh square feet to 4.8 lakh square feet, which is the signature building located at the entrance of the processing zone. The second major change eliminated the IT building for non-export domestic units, the multi-level car-park, and commercial building. The rationale for these decisions was that the demand for commercial space would only pick up in the last phase of the park. The residential apartment area in the southern wing, on the other hand, was doubled to 3 lakh square feet. The revised calculations at lower rentals and occupancy rates indicated that there would be a cash-flow crunch during the initial years which could only be neutralized by selling residential apartments.[14]

[14] Minutes of the Board of Directors Meeting of UL Cyber Park, 28 December 2013.

With the economic recession financial institutions were reluctant to provide finance, making it extremely difficult to raise Rs 210 crore for the revised first phase. In the end, a consortium of banks led by Punjab National Bank provided a loan of Rs 126 crore. In order to secure the loan, additional capital had to be raised through share contribution. The paid-up capital of ULCCS is Rs 65 crore, which includes Rs 21 crore for the value of the land utilized for the first phase. In addition, ULCCS is trying to secure funds from the Kerala State Industrial Development Corporation (KSIDC), which has contributed capital of Rs 3 crore and efforts are being made to get support from other successful cooperatives in the state and NRIs for capital contribution.

The building design integrates various services as well as green principles such as use of grey water and water harvesting. For example, Building no. 1 has three basement floors, a ground floor and six upper floors. The basements levels are for car parking, an underground sump and water treatment, and sewage treatment plants. Water recovered from tertiary sewage treatment plant is recycled for toilet flushing, for the air conditioning cooling tower, and for external irrigation. The building also integrates various services on the ground floor such as a food court, banks, travel agencies, and convenience stores. The double height entrance lobbies of the ground make for a dramatic entrance and bring in extra light. The IT processing companies will be located on the first to sixth floors. The utility building in phase one houses equipment for building services and maintenance such as diesel generators, transformers, chillers, solar panels, and cooling towers.

All the services planned for the building adhere to international standards and the building has been pre-certified for LEED-GOLD standard by Indian Green

Building Council.[15] The benefits offered by a LEED-certified building include lower operating costs, waste reduction, water conservation, greenhouse gas emission reduction, and healthy and safe buildings. There are 10 passenger lifts with the capacity to carry 17 persons and two service lifts. As for fire and safety, all the requirements are met with stipulations as per the National Building Code 2005. The construction of residential flats will commence once the facility is ready for customers. The Society's vision not only tries to meet local labour needs and take advantage of Kerala's engagement in the IT sector, but is doing so through ecologically and socially sensitive ways.

DIVERSIFICATION INTO OTHER SECTORS

ULCCS has broadly outlined its future development strategy in a document submitted to United Nations Development Programme (UNDP)[16] in 2013 in which it confirms that its main operations will continue to be construction, but with major modifications to the present system. The goal is to move up to higher levels in the value chain by undertaking the development work of modern highways and long-span bridges, which requires a number of strategic interventions. First, the Society will only be able to move up the value chain by augmenting its technology capabilities. While some of the new equipment replaces obsolete equipment, some of the existing technologies themselves need to be upgraded and new ones acquired. Second, backward linkages have to

[15] Indian Green Building Council: New Building Rating System 2012, ULCCS Records.

[16] ULCCS, 'A Proposal for Development: The Uralungal Labour Contract Society Limited, a Unique Cooperative Success Story', 2013 by IIM Kozhikode.

be strengthened in order to ensure consistent supply of raw materials. For example, ULCCS already has its own crusher unit and brick unit, but the production capacities of the stone crusher and hollow brick unit have to be expanded. Another new line of modernization in the construction process is the prefabrication of walls and bridge spans, which ULCCS plans to explore.

Third, ULCCS's major competitive asset is its skilled labourers with commitment to high quality construction work. The Society is also working to enhance the technical capabilities of its members so that there is upward mobility for them (discussed in the next chapter). Given the limitations of the current formal technical training institutes in the State, it is considering establishing the Uralungal Institute of Bridge and Highway Engineering (UBHE) to provide high quality training that incorporates both theory and practice. UBHE would be open to outside students and also provide refresher courses and training for the worker members. Fourth, ULCCS is currently entirely dependent on outside consultants for major design planning, which is an area that it would like to be able to eventually do in-house. One option would be for it to start a subsidiary entirely devoted to design and architecture consultancy. How it does this will have to be carefully considered, but its goal is to be able to do as much as possible in-house and thus create quality jobs for a greater number of skilled workers.

Fifth, the ULCCS model of direct involvement of worker-directors in the management will have to be supplemented with professionals as the Cooperative enters into complex high-end product areas. This poses a potentially serious challenge as it will have to develop an appropriate organizational mix of cooperative spirit and member participation with professional and technical management. The project management methodology may have to be modified to accommodate the enhanced scale of operations without losing the Cooperative's main goals and spirit. The ULCCS has already acknowledged the need for organizational redesign by launching a private limited company under its control to set up the UL Cyber Park. ULCCS will continue to operate in its traditional manner, but the subsidiary IT company will operate under new management methods. A large number of professionals including financial experts would have to be recruited to augment the HR capabilities. Thus, as it moves into this new area of activities, it will have to pioneer new organizational structures that combine the uniquely cooperative ethos with the professional capabilities of specialized expertise.

Finally, costly finance is the Achilles heel of ULCCS's ambitious expansion programme. The 'Vision' document estimated their financial requirement for fixed and working capital to be Rs 2,000 crore to achieve a turnover of Rs 2,000 crore per annum. Formation of a financial subsidiary to mobilize and manage the required finance has also been suggested. The steady shift in the government policy towards PPP models with viability gap funding still requires that the cash credit limit of the society be enhanced and interest rates reduced. For example, the consortium interest rate for UL Cyber Park finance was 13.5 per cent (now reduced to 11.5 per cent). In fact, high interest rates are an important factor adversely affecting the viability of the entire project. While the diversification process is both challenging and exciting, the Society continues to insist on the primacy of members' needs.

Indeed, the Society's commitment to its members lies at the centre of the diversification project. For example, while the Society commercially focuses on high-end value products, it remains committed to providing low cost housing for the poor (and old age houses receive special mention in the new bylaws[17]) and the production of the necessary building material for sale.[18] In addition to the usual social security measures adopted in the Society for its members, short and medium term loans to the members 'to purchase motor vehicles and household articles, to construct houses and for other purposes under hire purchase and hypothecation schemes' have been introduced.[19]

The ULCCS has already diversified into a couple of non-construction projects such as a software company titled UL Technology Solutions and tourism project named Sargalaya, Kerala Arts and Crafts Village. UL Technology Solutions was started under the initiative of four young postgraduates with specialization in Geographic Information System (GIS) in November 2011 at Thiruvananthapuram. The domain of the new company is IT based remote sensing, GIS, photogrammetric, geography and geology. At present the major clients include transport authorities who use the services of the company for identification of highway and railway alignment and local governments who are utilising its services for resource mapping, property tax mapping and river mapping. Currently 42 persons are employed at the company facility at Technopark.[20]

The Sargalaya craft village was a project of the tourism department spread over 20 acres at Iringal near Vadakara with adequate space for around 200 people making handicraft items to exhibit and demonstrate their products and skills.

[17] ULCCS Bylaws, Clause 4.29, 2008.

[18] ULCCS Bylaws, Clauses 4.21 to 4.27, 2008.

[19] ULCCS Bylaws, Clause 4.29, 2008.

[20] ULCCS Bylaws, Clause 4.50, 2008, Agreement with Director Tourism, 20 April 2011.

ULCCS undertook the construction of the building and landscaping, and was later entrusted with the management of the village for a period of ten years through a public tender. Lacking adequate experience in the handicraft sector, the new venture has been undertaken in collaboration with Dakshin Chitra, Chennai. The agreement is that during the first three years, government will provide a viability gap funding and during the next four years, a rental will have to be paid to the government. More than 40 workers are employed for management and maintenance at this facility. Situated at a scenic backwater location, the first tourism-related venture of ULCCS has attracted widespread positive attention.

ULCCS has also embarked on a Charitable Foundation.[21] The Cooperative statutes state that a specified proportion of its profits have to be set apart for a 'common good fund.' The fund has been used to support local reading rooms, schools as well deserving persons for medical, marriage or educational expenses. In November 2011, under the Company's Act Section 25, a wholly owned subsidiary of ULCCS was established for charitable and social activities. It manages Vagbhatananda Edu Fund for the advancement of bright but economically backward students who are selected from schools through competitive exams. The scholarships provide special classes and support by experts to help the students in the national talent scholarship tests and attain excellence in their academic achievements. The programme is now being extended throughout Kozhikode district.

The amendments to the bylaws of ULCCS also reflect the changing vision of the Cooperative. The original bylaws were revised in 1952 and 1967, and except for certain technical issues the objectives of the Society as enshrined in the bylaws

[21] ULCCS Bylaws, Clause 4.49, 2008.

remained the same. The four objectives were the following.

1. Spreading the cooperative principles: To find solutions for betterment of employment prospects among members, to encourage savings, cooperation and self-independence among members, to propagate principles of cooperation and to implement them. (Clause 1.1)
2. Undertaking contract work: To take up labour contracts and to carry it out by providing employment opportunity to its members. (Clause 1.2)
3. Undertaking transport contracts: To carry out works of transportation by labourers who are members of the Society under the supervision of the Society. (Clause 1.6)
4. Providing tools and machineries: To provide tools and machineries for labour to the members procuring either for rent or price. (Clause 1.3) If necessary tools may also be manufactured. (Clause 1.5)

In the latest bylaws passed in 2008 all the above clauses regarding contract work and tooling reappear with almost no change (Clauses 4.1 to 4.8), but unlike the earlier bylaws the objectives now have expanded to 57, mostly reflecting the changed and changing vision towards diversification from the traditional labour contract work.[22] The main activity remains labour contract, but it will concentrate on the high-end value areas. The clause 4.1 of the objectives state: 'To undertake and execute major skilled works such as construction of major roads, bridges, multi-storied buildings canals, harbours, runways, railways and drinking water supply so as to provide more employment opportunities to the highly educated, technically expert and trained or untrained labourers of the

[22] ULCCS Bylaws, Clauses 4.1 to 4.8, 2008.

Society.'[23] In order to achieve this objective the bylaws provide for collaboration with agencies in India and outside of India as well as establishing autonomous subsidiaries to the Society (Clause 4.13).

The Society is in the process of transitioning from a mere building contractor to a service provider who builds and leases out or sells buildings to customers. Operating housing projects, commercial malls and warehouses are some of the future activities envisioned for the Cooperative (Clause 4.28). The focus, however, is on the IT sector as Clause 4.14 states: 'To establish IT park in Special Economic Zones (SEZ) or others, with the participation of the government in the basic IT development field, for the diversification of business in accordance with changing situation, with the objective of the betterment of the labourers and families. To organize and form institutions as per Company Act to establish IT park, enter into contract with individuals and institutions within the area of operation and outside, even in the foreign countries, and conduct business.'[24]

The backward linkages of sourcing its own raw material for production have long been a competitive asset of ULCCS. The new bylaws, however, permit not only manufacturing raw materials and tools for its own use, but also for their commercial sale (Clause 4.12). Factories for agricultural products such as manure and machinery have also been included in the scope of the activities (Clause 4.48). Tourism and specifically handicraft promotion are also specially identified as an area for diversification and an area 'to provide more employment opportunities and economic improvement of members.'[25] The new bylaws envisage the Society to start

[23] ULCCS Bylaws, Clause 4.1, 2008.

[24] ULCCS Bylaws, Clause 4.14, 2008.

[25] ULCCS Bylaws, Clauses 4.50, 4.51 to 4.55, 2008.

educational institutions (Clause 4.32) and also training institutions for the employees and the apprentices of the Society or outside agencies (Clause 4.46). These shifts in the Society's activities require certain reforms in the organization which also necessitate changes in the bylaws. For example, new ventures may be formed under the Company Act or Charitable Societies Act and the Society may acquire and hold shares in other companies and may take over other business ventures in its domain. Technological collaboration and expert consultancy from the country and outside are also permitted.

In short, the bylaws reflect ULCCS's new vision that includes its traditional line of construction contracts but will increasingly focus on high value products strengthening the backward linkages of raw material production as well as services in the design and planning. At the same time, it will further diversify into modern IT and tourism related projects. While it envisions expansion and diversification into wholly new areas, it remains committed to its social values and principles reflected in the priority given to the large number of social and welfare objectives. The new bylaws also recognize the need for creation of new subsidiaries not only as cooperatives but also as private limited company subsidiaries. While these might be considered controversial decisions by some, the Cooperative is unanimous that it needs to be able to have such mechanisms in place in order to survive in the complex market conditions. These changes clearly have potential implications for ULCCS's industrial democracy and cooperative ideals. How will the Society remain true to its values and principles while pursuing diversification? These are some of the issues we turn to in the next chapter.

CHAPTER 7

TECHNOLOGY, LABOUR PROCESS AND LABOUR REGULATION

Have no doubt, it was hard work. The workday would start early in the morning and would end only at dusk. There was no fixed time for work in those days. It was flexible and could be shifted through mutual consensus. But nobody would shirk or cheat work. We took pride in the quality of work and its timely completion. It was our cooperative. There was even a funny incident when we were constructing a road in Kannur. As usual the work had started early in the morning and continued to late evening. Some of the local trade union activists intervened against overtime work and protested against exploitation. Our workers replied, 'There is no Boss here, we work for ourselves, it is our cooperative.'

In a sense, we were a band of travelling workers. We, the members of the Cooperative were all from Vadakara and camped at the worksites, which were often in distant towns and villages. A travelling kitchen also accompanied the team so that there was always good food. After bath in the evening we would gather around under some tree or shed and have fun. There would be songs, jokes and laughter. These evening gatherings were also inevitable because in those days we could not go to sleep before the shops closed. We would spread our mattresses on the shop verandas and go to sleep.

The evening gatherings were remarkable for their informal review of the day's work and planning of next day's work. The team leader and the director in charge would also participate in these discussions before the latter left for Vadakara to attend the daily meeting of the directors at the headquarters. The team leader co-coordinated the activities at the worksite. But he was one among us and often, one of the best. He would also have to do his daily work as all of us.

Now things have changed, there are machines for crushing the stones, excavating soil, mixing and spreading tar and compacting. In the past everyone could do any work but now some of the work can be done only by specialists. But more work gets done. Now there are fixed timings, better food and accommodation and, of course, high remuneration. We take pride when the public admire the quality of work; still there is no boss at our worksite.

M.K. Damu[1]

The formation of ULCCS in the early twentieth century provided an alternative to the system of contractors in the construction of public works in Malabar. The emergence of government contractors in the construction of railways, roads, bridges and public buildings introduced profit-motivated intermediaries in the construction industry heralding the era of capitalist transition. Because of the specific features in the construction industry – such as customer involvement

[1] Interview with M.K. Damu, Director, ULCCS, 5 January 2013.

in production decisions, the nature of the end product, and its limited commoditization – a capitalist class who directly employ wage labourers and sell construction products were slow to emerge in the early stages. Capital could only intervene in the construction process in the form of contractors who operated between customers and workers. This type of contract system is a specific feature of capitalist development in the construction sector.[2] Over the course of the twentieth century, contractors became the norm first in public works during the pre-Independence era and then for the construction of private buildings in the second half the century.

For private domestic construction, customers directly employ artisans and other workers, paying them wages directly. The objective of the customer is not to make profit but to construct a useful structure. A contractor, by contrast, works out the specifications for the structure to be built with the customer and determines the estimated cost with the objective of making a profit. One of the ways profit is made is through employing wage workers. In contrast, a cooperative is not motivated by maximising profit, but rather an entirely different set of principles and objectives. What are the implications of this difference in the labour process and its regulation under a private contractor and a workers' cooperative? To answer this question we have to understand the evolution of technology and labour conditions in the construction industry of Malabar.

Traditional Malabar society has very few public monuments except a few palaces and temples, which are a

[2] K.N. Harilal, 'Kerala's Building Industry in Transition: A Study of the Organization of Production and Labour Process', M.Phil. Thesis, Centre for Development Studies, Trivandrum, 1986, pp. 14-20. Our discussion on the labour process and transformation of the construction industry in Kerala in general largely follows this study.

mere shadow of the grandiose monumental constructions in the rest of India. The principal mode of transport was the waterways and footpaths for head loaders, and thus there were hardly any cartable roads before the invasion of Tipu Sultan during the early eighteenth century.[3] Tipu built an extensive network of gun roads for the movement of his troops and artillery throughout Malabar. After Tipu's defeat and the British annexation of Malabar, these roads were largely abandoned and fell into disuse. The British focused more on railway linkages, which was a major enterprise because of the numerous bridges that had to be built over the myriad rivers in Malabar. Road development was largely neglected until the Mappila unrest, which prompted a new strategy of road connectivity for troop movements into the interior areas. The old gun roads of Tipu, particularly those across the Ghats, were widened and hardened for cart traffic.

The traditional source of labour for public works, even under Tipu, was forced labour of lower caste and slaves. However, after the banning of slavery in the latter half of nineteenth century, this ceased to be an option. This raised a problem of how to execute public works projects. Employment of large numbers of artisans and casual workers directly by the state was not efficient and was prone to corruption. Contractors in the construction of public works emerged in this context with major bridge or rail works handled by British firms and road works by local contractors.

The entry of contractors had far reaching consequences for the organization of labour. A contractor was not merely a coordinator of the vast aggregation of artisans and unskilled labourers, but his profit was crucially dependent on his ability to extend the duration of work, intensify the work, and

[3] William Logan, *Malabar District Manual*, pp. 60-68.

reduce wages. The intensification of exploitation inevitably resulted in various forms of passive and active resistance from workers. As a result, the need for regulation of the workplace emerged and assumed an equal importance to coordination of the labour process. The ideals that inspired ULCCS were far removed from such exploitative practices and instead were centred on the need to create decent jobs and job security for workers.

The above discussion refers to the social framework of the labour process in construction but equally important is its material content. For a long period, traditional artisanal technology and manual labour remained the technological base for road construction. In the initial phase of capitalist development in any industry, capitalists merely take over the existing artisan or manual labour process. It is only at a later stage that the technological basis in the labour process is transformed by the introduction of machinery. This is clearly seen in the industrial evolution from petty production and manufacturing – which were based on handicraft technology – to modern factories which are based on power-driven machinery. The technological changes are often a response to resistance from workers to exploitation (i.e., class struggle) or may also be responses to changes in market demand.

For example, in the case of the history of construction in Kerala, the initial introduction of road construction machinery during the 1980s was in response to growing labour scarcity, militant trade unionism among workers and escalation of wages, while in contrast, further mechanization during the 2000s was in response to the new road building standards adopted by the Public Works Department. These changes have serious implications for the labour process and labour regulations. The material content and the social form of the labour process can be separated only at a conceptual level as they coexist and continually interact with each other in practice.[4] There are five distinct phases in the evolution of road making in Malabar, which have a bearing on the labour process and labour regulations: traditional earthen roads, metalled macadam roads, black-topped macadam roads, mechanized black-topped macadam roads, and bituminous macadam and bituminous concrete roads. We discuss each phase below.

TRADITIONAL EARTHEN ROADS

The initial roads built by the British were earthen roads formed by widening and strengthening the village pathways and gun roads of Tipu in order to facilitate smoother traffic of bullock carts and other carriages. Their construction involved a general level that is fixed and the valleys filled and summits cut. The cutting and filling works are labour intensive and the exact number of labourers would depend on the terrain of the land. The summits were cut using pick axes, shovels and hoes and mud carried using simple bamboo, cane, or palm-leaf baskets. The filling process was also tedious with small layers of earth rolled over by hand rollers, which was a single wheel made up of stone weighing around two to three tons and pulled by three or four workers using a handle or chain. Once brought to the same level, the road was ready for traffic. Given the heavy monsoon rains, the earthen roads required annual maintenance for strengthening the base and cutting vegetation overgrowth. Given the simple implements used, the labour process did not involve any artisanal skill. The levels were checked purely based on observation without

[4] Harilal, 'Kerala's Building Industry in Transition'.

using any instruments. The work involved large number of labourers and a rough sequencing of cutting summits, filling valleys, and flattening the road.

METALLED MACADAM ROADS

The growth of urban centres and the advent of motor vehicles necessitated better roads which were less dusty and able to withstand vehicular traffic. From the 1930s many of the important earthen roads were converted to metalled macadam roads, which was the new material introduced into road making. Using metals of various sizes complexified the process and required a preparatory stage of collecting boulders and breaking them into specified sizes. Before a road work starts a quarry for mining metals would have to be identified in a nearby neighbourhood.

From the beginning, the Society always operated its own quarries and most of the workers started their careers breaking boulders into required sizes in the quarries or the worksites. M.K. Damu, one of the directors recalls:

> I started working at the age of 14, in a quarry at Thalaayi. Unlike the normal quarries, here the granite was mined from below the ground. But most of the other quarries were granite hills from which boulders were collected through blasting or manually driving in the wedges. Only blue granite was used then for the works. The boulders were to be broken into metals of different sizes like ½", 1", and 1½", etc., using simple hammers. The wages were given as piece rate. Stones which were not of the appropriate size would not be measured for wages and the quarry leaders were very strict about it, therefore one learnt the hard way. After a few months anyone can become an expert

> and prepare stones of appropriate size habitually. These were transported to the site and stacked for measurement. . . I have worked in a number of other quarries. At times the big boulders had to be brought to the worksite in hand pulled carts and broken into pieces. My efficiency as a head load worker was appreciated and qualified me for membership in the Society.[5]

The roads were to consist of three layers: sub-grade, sub-base, and base. While the earthen roads required only earthwork and hand-rolling for compacting, the metal roads required a large number of workers for breaking the granite, stacking, metal laying, red earth spreading, watering, and hand-rolling. The 70 year-old Andy Karikkandy, a retired worker, recalls:

> I joined Society at age of 16 as a water carrier from the river to the worksite. The road laying at that time was a long drawn out process. Unlike the earthen roads, the new roads consisted of three layers prepared with metal of three different sizes. The first step was to mark the boundaries of the road with lime. The area was levelled using pick axes and hoes. 6" stones were laid over the levelled ground and strengthened by spreading wet red earth over it. This was the foundation of the road.
>
> Over this, three inch metal stones were spread. Once again, red earth is spread with profuse pouring of water and rolled with hand roller. The road was allowed to lie in this condition for six months. Meanwhile this work team moved to other sites.
>
> After six months 1 ½" sized metal is laid on top. Over this red earth is spread and as a binding material, rolled over with hand roller for compacting. A worker walked along the roller profusely pouring water over the roller to the stones. This helps

[5] Interview with M.K. Damu, Director, ULCCS, 5 January 2013.

> to fill up the voids between the metal with the cream mix of water and red earth. It is made sure that the earth has worked into all crevices and only a slurry remains on top. Many workers were employed to carry water from the river to the site and this was my main job. When water is being poured, polishing of the road top is done by using wire brush which helps in smoothing the road surface.[6]

The above was a description of traditional metal road-laying. Over time road construction has been compressed into a much shorter duration.

BLACK-TOPPED MACADAM ROADS

During the early 1950s only certain roads in the towns were tarred and even the National Highway to Mangalapuram was a metalled road. With the rapid expansion of motorized vehicles black-topped roads became the norm. Andy Karikkandy continues his description:

> Normally a metalled road is tarred after one or two years only. The mud from the top would be removed using pick axes, wire brush, and brooms. The dust would be blown away by experts by swinging jute bags. After this, tar will be sprayed manually using a holed tin. After this ½" metal mixed with tar is spread. There were hand mixers for the mixing but to my knowledge this was not being used by society, instead ½" metal is mixed with bitumen on a metal sheet over open hearth.
>
> The departments used to provide steam powered rollers to level the tar metal mix. This machine was a novelty and attraction at that time. On top of this layer, yet another mix of

[6] Interview with Andy Karikkandy, 5 January 2013.

> sand and tar is laid and once more rolled. The tarred road was ready. In the society, there was one more step, a tradition which is continued to date i.e. the road edges were cut and smoothened to a straight line. The sides of the road would also be cleared.[7]

The above is an account of the process entailed in black topping roads. Now that most roads are tarred, re-tarring and upgrading roads is a major activity. The following is a graphic description of a day's work at a re-tarring site by M.K. Damu:

> Work started at around 5 a.m. in the morning when two persons from the team would burn firewood for the boiler, heating up the tar required for work. This would be followed by other people who would move to the site with their tools in hand-drawn carts. People at the site are allotted various tasks based on their skills and experience. Beginners usually do cleaning work only.
>
> Work could begin in the early morning because the whole team normally camped near the worksite (many times on shop verandas) during weekdays. We returned home only during the weekends. Food was served from the field kitchen – rice gruel and tapioca for breakfast, fishy meal for lunch, tea in the evening and once again rice meal in the night.
>
> Since there is road traffic, work is planned on one half of the road covering a distance of 100 meters. There would be four teams of two persons each for cleaning with equipment such as pickaxe, broom, sack and various kinds of wire brushes etc. Once the required portion is cleaned, an experienced worker along with an assistant would mark the width and side lines of the road using lime. [Good line and level is one of the most

[7] Ibid. A major difference with the current practice is that in the finishing stage nowadays, 6 mm metal is used instead of sand giving the required finish on the road.

important features of roads worked by ULCC Society.] A team of 11 persons [seven men and four women] work on eliminating holes and bumps in the road and prepare it for tarring. This is done by filling the holes with six inch metal after spraying tar and then locking the same with ½" metal.

Including the two people who started work at the tar boiler in early morning at 5 a.m., eight persons are placed for lifting the heated tar to the work area – four people at boiler and four people for lifting. Tar boiler is set at a maximum of 100 metres at the site according to the convenience of work. One person is placed for applying tin spray on the cleaned, patched and locked road surface.

There are four teams comprising four people each for mixing tar and metal. This is done by placing an iron sheet of 8x4 feet with three empty barrels each on both sides. Firewood is placed beneath the sheet. [Firewood is regularly collected at the Society's office and then brought to each of the worksites.] Once the sheet is heated up by lighting firewood, 16 buckets of ½" metal is poured and after heating up, two iron buckets of tar is poured into the mixture. This is then mixed using shovels by the teams. The mixture is taken to the sprayed road surface in four hand-carts drawn by three people each. The mixture is then spread evenly over the surface by a group of four experienced people. Two women also assist in this process using special shovels. The levelled area is then pressed and flattened using road roller.

A mixture of sand and tar is then applied on top. It is smoothened by two women using wooden boards. This is then hardened by driving road rollers above the same. This process is repeated for the other half of the road. This way, work is completed for 250 metres length and 12 feet width of road per day. Scrap portions of metals are collected from every area at

> the end of the day, filtered for further use and the site is kept tidy at all times. At the end of the work day, everyone participated equally in preparing the boiler, stoves, iron sheets etc. for the next day's work. After the day's work and bath, merriments would start and only around 10'O clock we would spread the mattress for sleep.[8]

Before we discuss the other two types of roads – mechanized black-topped macadam roads and bitumen and concrete roads – we discuss the labour process for the earthen and non-mechanized macadam roads. The labour intensive process of road construction was fertile ground for the exploitative labour process dominated by contractors to emerge and flourish. It is this context that the ULCCS emerged.

THE LABOUR PROCESS UNDER MACADAM ROADS

Thus far we have described the evolution of technology and labour process in road construction mostly in the words of workers themselves in order to highlight their central role in the process. A common characteristic of all the phases has been the relative absence of machinery. For construction of earthen roads there is total reliance on traditional implements such as pick axes, hoes, and baskets and a traditional labour process with no division of labour as all workers were involved in cutting summits, filling valleys, and pulling the roller. This is what Marx called the phase of simple cooperation in the development of capitalism: 'In simple cooperation, there is a juxtaposition of labourers and operations. Numerous labourers work together side by side whether in one and the same process or in different but connected processes.'[9] Marx's

[8] Interview with M.K. Damu, Director, ULCCS, 5 January 2013.
[9] Karl Marx, *Capital*, Vol. 1, London: Penguin books, p. 991.

discussion is based on the evolution of industrial capitalism where existing artisans are gathered in a single workshop for work. But he also cites gigantic constructions of the ancient world, such as the Pyramids, where the colossal effects of simple cooperation can be seen.[10]

In the construction of macadam roads, there is a change in the technique of road construction introducing different layers for foundation, soiling and topping which would result in more durable roads that can withstand heavier loads. New materials such as metals of different sizes and bitumen were also introduced. As a result of these new methods a division of labour for the skill requirements of the various jobs such as mixing bitumen, breaking metals, compacting and levelling emerged. The construction of roads was no longer simple cooperation, but complex cooperation very similar to the phase of manufacturing in industrial evolution.

All these roads have distinct construction processes and can be implemented in one of three ways: directly by the state, indirectly through contractors, or through a cooperative. As we have already noted, the earthen roads were built directly by the state for more than a century before contractors entered the scene. Even today PWD manuals contain provision for direct execution of even complex works by the department in case of urgency or in the absence of competent contractors. With the entry of contractors, the workers were no longer directly employed by the customer, and were now employed by a contractor whose objective is to extract more labour and consequently more surplus value from the workers. In the absence of productivity enhancing machinery, the objective can be achieved only by increasing the absolute exploitation through making workers work longer and harder at a lower

[10] Ibid., Chapter 13.

wage. For this purpose they seek to control and regulate the labour process through harsh measures of supervision or threat of dismissal from the job. This process alienates workers from the labour process while ensuring profits for the contractor. Nevertheless the lack of other job opportunities gave workers little choice but to continue to work on the terms of the contractor.

In contrast, the objective of the labour process in a worker cooperative is not to maximize profits, but to provide quality employment and better benefits to workers. A salient feature of ULCCS has been the keen awareness of the workers of this distinction in the objective of their enterprise. This is evident from the response given by the Cooperative workers to the criticism of over-work that we have quoted at the beginning of the chapter. The workers were aware of the total estimate of the work, the material cost and the profits that accrue after disbursal of their relatively higher wage benefits. The profit did not go into the pocket of any private capitalist but was distributed to the workers themselves or accumulated for future expansion of the firm.

Apart from the higher wages and other benefits there was a perceptible difference in the manner in which labour was regulated. Instead of the traditional foreman or manager who oversee and control every movement of the worker, track every moment of the working hour, and instil fear of punishment for every lapse, best portrayed by Robert Tressell in his classic novel *The Ragged-Trousered Philanthropists*,[11] in a cooperative there is a team leader at the worksite who acts more like a coordinator and worker directors who attempt to rouse worker's class consciousness and motivation. There is no threat of dismissal – except for breaking the clearly defined

[11] Robert Tressell, *The Ragged Trousered Philanthropists*, London: Penguin Books, 2004.

Table 7.1: Person days for 1 km road by type and by activity

	Description	Earthen road	Metalled road	Black topped (old method)	Black topped (with machinery)	bm and bc
1	Earth work	30	30	30	30	8
2	Earth compacting	60				
3	Soling breaking work (60 mm metal)		84	84	35	
4	Metal breaking work (36 mm metal)		350	350	35	140
5	Metal Breaking work (20 mm Metal and down size)			12	12	35
6	Stacking metal		100	100	100	
7	Soling - 60 mm		180	150	150	
8	Metalling - 36 mm		190	160	160	
9	Premixed Chipping carpet				280	220
10	Granular Sub Base (GSB)					40
11	Wet Mix Macadam (WMM)					36
12	Prime & Tack Coat					10
13	Built Up Sprey Grout (BUSG)					64
14	Bituminous Macadam (BM)					24
15	Bituminous Concrete (BC)					12
	Total no. of labours for work	90	934	1166	672	369

Source: Calculated from records of ULCCS.

rules of the Cooperative like working for contractors – and security of continuous work is offered to the members of the Cooperative.

In the absence of machinery sturdier roads with better riding quality resulted in a significant increase in the number of labourers required for construction of a unit length of road. In Table 7.1, we have summarized the labour requirements for constructing 1km of road of 3.6 metres width in the different types of roads. The labour requirement for earthen roads was only 90 person days, it increased to 934 person days for metal roads. The major increase was due to metal breaking and successive rounds of layering. For bitumen topped macadam roads additional labour for topping was necessary and the labour requirement increased to 1,166 person days. Thus, the early development of road technology led to an increase in labour requirements not a decrease.

With the number of workers increasing from 90 for earthen roads to 1,166 for non-mechanized macadam roads, the developments in road construction increased the quality and functionality of the roads as well as the labour requirements (Table 7.1). The rapid increase in the number of labourers needed for road construction coincided with the expansion in the workforce for the construction industry as a whole from the mid-1970s. As we have already discussed in the previous chapter, during the building boom consequent to the increase in the remittances from the Gulf countries, the workforce in the construction sector rapidly expanded. The workforce was becoming increasingly de-skilled due to two processes. On the one hand, there was a process of de-skilling of traditional artisans in building houses and, on the other hand was the entry of large numbers of unskilled workers for new types of work such as concreting. As a result of the growing and changing workforce, the 1970s saw the emergence of a pan-Kerala trade union movement of the traditional artisans as well as a number of construction workers unions.[12] The new construction workers' unions adopted a strategy of closed shop-floor tactics to reduce the competition from new entrants by dividing every locality into small sub-regions where restrictions to entry were imposed. The scarcity of skilled workers due to out-migration to gulf countries and the closed shop-floor tactics of collective bargaining drastically reduced the flexibility in the labour market. Worksites were proving to be unmanageable and wage escalation created a further

[12] Harilal, 'Kerala's Building Industry in Transition', pp.155-160.

challenge. As a result, contractors' profits were threatened and labour saving mechanization became necessary.

The presence of profit-motivated intermediaries in the execution of public works, the rise of militant trade unionism and competitive pressures were important background factors to the entry of labour saving machinery in the industry from the 1980s. The labour process itself did not change dramatically, but certain categories of workers were replaced with mechanization. We now discuss the shift to mechanization and the concomitant drop in labour demand.

MECHANIZED BLACK-TOPPED MACADAM ROADS

There was a plethora of major labour-saving productivity-enhancing machinery that was introduced since the mid-1980s. First, by the end of the 1970s steam road rollers became universal for compacting and levelling roads, replacing the labour intensive hand-pulled rollers. While road rollers had made their appearance decades before, they were mostly owned by the department and provided to contractors for specific periods and the initial compacting continued to be done by hand rollers. The second major mechanical intervention was the entry of metal crushers, replacing the hand crushing of stones. A primary crusher would break boulders into 75 mm metals which would further be broken to required smaller sizes by secondary crushers. The blasting of the rocks continued as in the past, but they were lifted into the tipper lorries by machinery. This single change reduced the labour requirement for preparation of metals from 350 persons to 35 persons. The third major change was the introduction of the excavators which considerably reduced the person-days required for initial land preparation and collecting red soil.

Finally, tipper lorries facilitated the ease of transportation and the tar mixing plants improved the quality of the mixture and also marginally reduced the labour requirement. With mechanization the traditional macadam road construction labour requirement for 1km was reduced from 1,166 to 672.

Similarly, the allied works such as culverts, bridges, and side protection works that were manually done using masonry (laterite stone) in mortar were replaced by concrete for the construction of retaining walls and abutments and also for drainages. Thus, the construction of roads and allied works both experienced dramatic changes in the labour and production processes.

With the competitive environment in the construction industry, ULCCS was also forced to keep pace with the industrial developments. The Society adopted a number of measures such as the policy of aggressively purchasing modern transport and construction equipment from the late 1990s. The shift to mechanized machinery thoroughly transformed the labour process for the Cooperative. Metal breakers – who constituted the largest proportion of workers – rapidly dwindled. There was also a reduction in the number of other categories of manual workers. Nevertheless, while their numbers reduced traditional work categories continue to survive.

In addition, to the reduction in manual workers, they also experienced changes in the rhythm of their work as they had to keep pace with the machinery. For example, once the pace of tar mixing plant was set the work team for cleaning the road, spraying the bitumen and spreading the mixture would have to work at the same pace. Thus, the quickened pace of the mixing plant added pressure on workers, which contractors could exploit to their advantage. While this added pressure could also happen at the Cooperative, the practices of the Cooperative ensured that the work norms evolved through a consultative process. The Cooperative was very clear that entry of machinery into its production process did not alter its primary mandate to create stable and good jobs for its members and thus the difference in the control of the labour process between contractors and the Cooperative remained.

BITUMINOUS MACADAM AND BITUMINOUS CONCRETE ROADS

The process of mechanization took a qualitative leap by the end of 1990s when guidelines as per the Indian Road Congress were adopted in the construction of national highways. The traditional structure of roads (discussed above) consisted of a three layered macadam road with 20 mm topping of chipping carpet. The three layers in the traditional macadam road are replaced by three layers of much stronger and more binding bye-products of the quarry. On the top, instead of 20 mm chipping carpet, a layer of Bituminous Macadam and Bituminous Concrete are laid. Machinery plays a pivotal role in every step of the new construction process which is described below by Anupa, one of the many new generation engineers currently employed by the Cooperative.

> The preparatory earth works are undertaken by the excavators. Given the width of the new road formation, often rocky formations are to be removed through blasting often using chemical method. The difference from the traditional macadam road is that in the new method where earth filling is required, for providing strength for the foundation, quarry waste of required thickness is used. The formation level of the road

is achieved through compaction provided by vibrating road rollers. Over the formation level, a crusher product named Granular Sub-Base (GSB) made of stone aggregates of different sizes mixed in particular proportion with water and dust is laid in required thickness. It is compacted by vibrating rollers. The layer is again covered by another crusher product named Wet Mix Macadam (WMM) which differs from GSB in the proportion of dust and water. It provides required finish for the road. Both these aggregate layers will be mixed at an Optimum Moisture Content (OMC) in a wet mix plant. However, modern crushers have facilities for directly providing the optimal mix aggregates rendering separate wet mix plants redundant. After the road formation has dried, waste dust on the top of the layer is removed by blowing air using air compressor.

After the dust is removed, Emulsion (liquid cold tar) is sprayed using emulsion sprayer as a prime coat. The emulsion will penetrate through the surface of WMM and will strengthen the layer. After the emulsion gets dried properly, hot bitumen is sprayed and 36 mm metal is laid in two layers using a special machine called Motor Grader. Bitumen is also sprayed in between these two layers for bonding them. Each layer is compacted with the vibratory rollers. There may be gaps between this 36 mm metal stones and therefore a layer of 12 mm metal is laid and compacted for filling and locking. These two layers of 36 mm metal and the layer of 12 mm metal constitute the Built-Up Spray Grout (BUSG).

Emulsion is sprayed over BUSG as a tack coat and the next layer of Bituminous Macadam (BM) is laid. Bituminous Macadam layer is constituted of aggregates ranging from 40 mm to 6 mm in size mixed in particular proportion with bitumen in a particular temperature in hot mix plant. It is laid using a special machine called paver finisher. Quality Control engineers are deputed at plant for assuring the correct mix proportion and temperature at the hot mix plant and also the correct temperature at the worksite

Once again, another tack coat of emulsion for bonding is sprayed. Subsequently, a final layer of Bituminous Concrete (BC) consisting of aggregates ranging from 12 mm metal to dust in a specified proportion, mixed in a hot mix plant, is laid. For this purpose a paver finisher with sensor to control the level and alignment is used. The BC layer is rolled to the required compaction using vibratory roller. For the final finishing pneumatic roller is used.

Once the road work is done, then retro-reflectorized, cautionary, mandatory, and informational sign is done. Hot thermoplastic compound is done to do the markings on the road. Also road studs (raised pavement markers) are provided which helps the users at night by reflecting at the light of the vehicle.[13]

With bituminous macadam and bituminous concrete roads, the road making labour process was completely transformed with every activity of the workers integrated to machinery. On the one hand, the number of workers required has drastically reduced from 672 to construct one kilometre black-topped road to 369. On the other hand, the fixed capital per worker increased roughly from Rs 2.40 lakh to Rs 5.60 lakh. The changes also brought changes to the internal membership make-up of the Cooperative as a new group of engineers and technicians entered the Cooperative for supervision of the mechanized road construction projects.

With the computerized mixing unit, the temperature of aggregates, bitumen and mix are precisely controlled and the

[13] Interview with Anupa Sasi, Project Engineer ULCCS, 9 January 2013.

temperature during mixing and laying are also controlled, all of which is very important for ensuring quality. Moreover, scanner controlled pavers and vibrating and pneumatic typed rollers help in laying the mix in required levels and in compacting to the required density for a better surface finish. As a result of these changes, road construction became faster and more quality concerned, which helped in constructing better quality roads and more of them. As the mechanized method of road construction was implemented, the contractors were expected to have the new machinery and quality control laboratory and the capacity to procure the required materials. For participating in the tender process, the contractors are pre-qualified for the work depending upon the qualifications criteria of the particular work. Therefore, in order to compete in the new conditions, the Society had to purchase the advanced machineries and set up a laboratory.

HESITANT ENTRANT INTO BUILDING CONTRACTS

For the most part of its history, ULCCS was largely confined to the construction of roads. It was very hesitant to enter into the building market. One reason for this reluctance was that until 1980s the construction of buildings was a tradition-bound artisan production with masons and carpenters the main artisans involved in the construction process. The head carpenters were the custodians of craft rules related to different types of buildings as enshrined in ancient scripts of science in building construction, known as 'Thachu Sastharam'.[14] As per these ancient rules each building was designed by the head carpenter and the other carpenters followed his instructions. Even for public buildings

[14] Achuthan A. and Balagopal T.S., *Keralathinte Thachu Sasthram*, *Mathrubhumi Weekly*, 5-11 May 1985, pp. 26-31.

the government only provided the overall parameters and it was left to the artisans to construct the building. The Cooperative, however, did not have many traditional artisans in its membership and therefore did not enter the building sector. Artisans who belonged to Viswakarma caste were too entrenched in the traditional customs and practices to join a workers' cooperative of mostly unskilled labourers. Given the skill composition of the membership consisting of largely unskilled workers, the Society focused on road construction and buildings constituted only a very small proportion of the public works.

The only buildings that the Society contracted during the pre-Independence period were the fish curing sheds in the nearby beach area from the Fisheries Department. Fish curing sheds were used for storing dry fish and for housing the fish oil extraction plants. These were simple structures of thatched roofs, bamboo or arecanut rafts, beaten earthen floor and open/half side walls. Their construction did not require a head carpenter's skill and could be built by ordinary labourers and masons. The construction of buildings was reinforced by caste as caste rules, even at the beginning of twentieth century prescribed the size, type and materials used for construction of houses belonging to different castes. The British Collector William Logan noted that only in 1796 that the East India Company,[15] after a century of its existence in Malabar, was allowed to tile their buildings. Up until that time only palaces of the kings and temples could be tiled. The lower castes could use only Kacha materials like cadjan leaves and bamboo/arecanut rafts for the dwellings. The family members themselves constructed the huts with the help of exchange labour of the neighbours. The construction of fish

[15] William Logan, *Malabar District Manual.*

curing sheds did not require any higher skills than the skills employed in the construction of lower caste dwellings.

From 1950s tiled and burnt brick houses rapidly spread and by 1970s constituted nearly 40 per cent of all houses. During this time, terraced buildings also made their appearance in Kerala. During the 1950s and 1960s the ULCCS occasionally undertook construction of smaller government buildings such as school buildings, dispensaries and rural government offices. The construction at that time involved laterite or quarry boulders, foundations, laterite walls and tile-on-timber roofs. The Society had an experienced carpenter, Sankaran Aasari, who coordinated the work of carpenters and masons, many of whom were recruited temporarily on piece rate or subcontracted for certain activities.

The construction boom of the 1980s completely transformed the construction scenario of the state: Reinforced Cement Concrete (RCC) roofs, mosaic/tile floors, cement plaster, painted walls and sanitary and electrical fittings became the norm. With the introduction of concrete beam and pillar technology the walls lost their load bearing function and came to be called 'curtain walls' and as a result the skill requirement of masons was considerably reduced. The new technology also facilitated easier construction of multi-storied buildings. The carpenters were reduced to the skilled work of making windows and doors. Instead of highly skilled traditional artisans, the new methods required modern skilled workers such as electricians, plumbers, mosaic/tile layers, form makers, interior decorators. The new technology also demanded a rapid rise in the number of unskilled labourers for conveying and compacting concrete for roofs, foundations, floors, pillars, and beams. For example, concrete is mixed by skilled workers and then is conveyed to the roof by a long human chain of unskilled workers, put on the form work, and manually compacted and regularly watered for curing. Except for the mixing, the rest of the process requires unskilled workers. The new construction methods challenged caste traditions that limited people's housing options to their caste. The modern house, by contrast, became the status symbol of successful upward social mobility from the caste restricted abode of the past. Yet the new trend in modern houses has been criticized for ostentatious expenditure, environmental unfriendliness, cultural aberration and so on. Alternate technologies that are less wasteful and more environmentally friendly have been proposed, but the new trend in modern houses has only continued to gain momentum.[16] The new trend also brought an important transformation in the organization of building construction through the rapid spread of the contract system.

In the construction of traditional houses, including tiled houses in the post-Independence period, the customer-owner would place his requirements to the head carpenter or specialist designer to prepare a plan of a building. The customer-owner would then hire the artisans and labourers and pay them directly. The artisans maintained control of the labour process and enjoyed a high degree of autonomy. It was only in government buildings that the work was assigned to contractors who hired artisans and workers. However, the ability of the contractor to regulate the labour process and enhance the profits was limited because of the domination of the artisans and due to the fact that detailed plans and estimates were prepared by the department.

It was during the construction boom and the spread of

[16] K.P. Kannan and R.J.S. Spence, *A Social Cost Approach to Choice of Technology in Building Construction – A Study of Some Alternative Technologies in Kerala*, Working Paper No. 30, Centre for Development Studies, Thiruvananthapuram, 1975.

the RCC technique and modern building materials that the ULCCS made significant entry into building construction, but confined its activities to the government sector. During the construction boom the contract system that had dominated the government sector spread to the private sector initially in the non-residential buildings, but then also spread to the residential sector, again bringing a sea-change to the way the private construction sector was organized. Even when customer-owners of small buildings directly undertook the construction project, some of the activities would still be subcontracted. Thus, large contractor firms who were general contractors and smaller contractors who subcontracted from larger firms or contracted smaller buildings from the customer-owners emerged.[17] In addition to these contractors there were specific activity contractors who were mostly skilled and experienced workers such as plumbers, electricians, painters, mosaic layers and the master plan was prepared by architects or design teams who also undertook the role of contract management in order to ensure that the contractor fulfilled the conditions of the contract before payment is made.

It was not automatic that the contract system became universal. This begs the question as to why it became so. First, coordinating a large number of skilled workers for concreting and providing non-traditional construction equipment (such as form work, vibrators, and mixers) could not be undertaken by ordinary customer-owners. Furthermore, given the scarcity of skilled workers hiring and supervising their works was difficult. It was, thus, more efficient to engage a contractor who owned the necessary equipment and understood the labour market so that the adequate number of workers could

[17] Discussion with Shainu P., Assistant Engineer ULCCS, 25 January 2013.

be ensured at a cheaper rate. The contractor would also be in charge of close and constant supervision so that higher productivity is achieved.

Once it entered the building sector, ULCCS started to explore various opportunities, which eventually led it to the current Cyber Park project.

ENTERING A NEW PHASE: ULCCS'S CYBER PARK

ULCCS experienced a steep learning curve in building construction with its involvement in the Cyber Park at Kozhikode.[18] As already discussed, the Cooperative was already undertaking construction of a large scale modern building (4.8 lakh square feet). Up to this time, however, its experience had been limited to much smaller buildings with a maximum of two floors. The new building was ten floors high and also required advanced building techniques (such as post-tensioning slabs), modern amenities (such as centralized air conditioning), and new energy efficient construction materials. The unexpected government decision to set up an IT park and the consequent threat of the large tract of urban land owned by the Cooperative being acquired by government for the IT park forced the Society to take bold decisions. It decided to turn the threat into an opportunity and diversify its activities into IT park services. This was an extremely courageous decision as the Society was wholly unprepared for such activities. A cursory survey of the capabilities of the Cooperative reveals the inadequacy of the technical skill and equipment requirements needed to directly undertake the construction of the Cyber Park.

[18] Discussion with Rajeevan T.P., Assistant Engineer ULCCS, 26 January 2013.

Until this time, ULCCS had never designed a building, as design and drawings were prepared by the PWD architects before estimates were prepared and tenders were called. The Cooperative's responsibility was to strictly follow the design in the construction process and the PWD engineers at the sites ensured full compliance and acted as contract managers. Entering the private sector, however, required that the Society source-in the skills for developing the design and plan. Thus, the preparation of the design and plan of the Cyber Park was the first step for which the Cooperative had to seek external assistance.

Public expression of interest was called for an architect firm to prepare the master plan. M/s Nikken Sekkei, a leading Japanese architectural firm with experience of over twenty thousand projects in forty countries around the world, was selected. Great care and thought were put into the master planning around issues such as traffic density, wind velocity, climatic conditions, environmental impact and also the design perspective. The Chennai based architect M/s CRN, ranked among the top ten architects in India, was selected for preparing the drawing and detailed plan of the building, which is the normal practice to have the same team prepare the master plans and detailed drawings. Usually the architect firm, particularly for smaller projects, also acts as the contract managers who are responsible for certifying the adherence to drawings before the payment is made to the contractors. Given the scale and complexity of the project, it was decided to have a third firm to carry out the functions of contract manager. Accordingly Bangalore based 'Diligent' was appointed to act as the contract manager. Given its vast experience, it is surprising that ULCCS was hesitant to shoulder the responsibility of contract management, which it did not want to do because of the complexity of the construction activities involved. Instead, it assigned the role of general contractor to its subsidiary, ULCCS IT Infrastructure Pvt Ltd.

In the building industry, a general contractor may either directly undertake construction, employing wage labourers or subcontract the work to specialist firms or small-scale activity contractors. All large construction firms normally sub-contract the major activities so that their task is limited to coordination. The coordination involves time phasing of different activities and timely supplies of materials as well as acquiring the necessary machinery so that the building process is completed without time or cost overrun. For this purpose they would have a small salaried staff team consisting of supervisory engineers and overseers, accountants, and store keepers. For example even though most of the activities in UL Cyber Park were subcontracted ULCCS, the general contractor provided the concrete mix and many of the construction materials.

There are subcontractors for every building activity such as earth work, masonry, form work, bar bending, concreting, wood work, laying mosaic and granite, plumbing, painting, and electrification. These activity contractors are mostly skilled and experienced workers or technicians who have a small group of skilled workers and helpers. In the case of certain building activities (such as air conditioning, lift facilities, transformers, generator, chiller, sewage treatment plant, water treatment plant, aluminium composite façade) subcontracting is often undertaken by firms or their franchisees who have access to trademark equipment and technical know-how. The subcontracting firms often further subcontract to smaller activity contract groups.

The activity contractors enable the general contractors to insulate themselves from fluctuations in labour supply and demand and absolve themselves from the responsibility of labour control at the worksite. The competition among the activity contractors in most of the lines ensure that the cost is reduced to the minimum, which is facilitated by the fact that activity contractors are themselves workers and their wage workers are members of closely knit groups, leading them to self-regulate to remain competitive. As a result, subcontracting is an effective method of labour control in the context of general labour scarcity and unionization.

As the general contractor, the ULCCS was in charge of the overall coordination of the worksite including the initial land levelling and marking. The direct construction activities that the Cooperative undertook were limited to earth excavation, levelling of land, roads and compound walls. The excavation process unearthed undulated rock layers far above the level fixed for the foundation, which required a change in the design to isolated footing resting on different levels attained through blasting. Though more time consuming and costly, it was decided to adopt the technique of chemical blasting to reduce the inconvenience to the public. Simultaneously, the construction of the roads, which is the specialization of the Cooperative, was completed in a record time, but because of the delay in excavation the first building could start only after six months.

The main activities in constructing the building structure (namely the pillar and slab and wall masonry) were subcontracted to PMK, an exclusively building construction firm and the largest at this time in Kozhikode. The Cooperative did not have adequate expertise and equipment for timely sequencing of shuttering and reinforcement of a ten storied building. Moreover, the traditional conventional slab method for constructing the floors with which the Cooperative was familiar was not suitable for IT buildings as too many supporting pillars would constrain the use of floor space. IT companies need obstruction free floor space which they customize with wood and glass partitioning as per their space requirements. Thus, slabs of a much longer span that would be further reinforced by tensioning the steel wire ropes after concreting were needed. This technique was seldom used and most construction companies – even the larger ones like PMK – in Kerala did not have the capacity to do it. Therefore a specialist contractor, Ultracon, was engaged for the purpose and another specialist firm was given the subcontract for piling.

While the Cooperative had the competence to directly undertake the masonry work, it had to be given as a package to PMK. But midway through the work, the Cooperative workers were also deployed to complete the masonry work. The utility building and the three storied multi-purpose building outside the gate of the northern wing were directly constructed by the Cooperative. Thus, the Cooperative's direct involvement ranged over a number of activities. Most of the finishing activities connected to the Cyber Park building (such as the centralized air conditioning, elevators for high rise buildings, the glass façade for the exterior, interior decoration and so on) required specialist contractors. Further the building was pre-certified for LEED-GOLD standard by Indian Green Building Council (IGBC), which was achieved by incorporating various strategic methods to minimize the impact on the environment like using natural resources for energy in order to reduce the use of power for lighting and air conditioning. The new techniques, materials, standards and skills were yet to be acquired by the Cooperative, and thus had to be outsourced.

In Table 7.2 we summarize the major activities involved in constructing the first phase of the Cyber Park and the agency executing the activity. The activities directly undertaken by ULCCS constituted 18 per cent of the construction. While this is a relatively low contribution to the construction process, it was the choice of the Cooperative as it did not have all the necessary skills to engage in more of the construction activities. The Cooperative is well aware of this and is in the process of ensuring it acquires more skill within the Cooperative.

CONTRADICTIONS OF SUBCONTRACTING AND THE INTERNAL DYNAMICS OF THE COOPERATIVE

In the construction of UL Cyber Park the Cooperative was functioning like any other general contractor in the industry. Only a very small portion of the building activities was undertaken directly by the Cooperative and the rest were subcontracted. This anomalous situation was an issue that we took up for discussion with the office bearers of the Cooperative. Even though growth and diversification was necessary, the Cooperative faced the threat of degeneration into a capitalist firm. How was this danger to be avoided? The secretary of the Cooperative, Shaju, responded.

> We had no choice other than to go for wide spread subcontracting to complete the first building in the Cyber Park. The construction of the Cyber Park was an opportunity we could not let pass. We are not going to be a general contractor subcontracting the construction to private activity contractors. We are making all efforts to rapidly expand our in-house capabilities for constructing large scale modern buildings. We can never be fully self-sufficient. We will have to depend on outsiders for the

Table 7.2: Distribution of the major activities and agencies involved in the first phase of Cyber Park

	Activities	Agency	Amount (Rs cr)	Cost distribution (%)
1	Levelling the area	ULCCS	6.50	4.78
2	Compound wall	ULCCS	6.90	5.07
3	Road	ULCCS	7.34	5.40
4	Landscape	ULCCS	0.38	0.28
5	Excavation for foundation	ULCCS	3.98	2.93
6	Concrete mix and other material supply	ULCCS	0.17	0.12
7	Steel	ULCP	17.78	13.07
8	Cement	ULCP	5.70	4.19
9	Chemical & others	ULCP	0.95	0.70
10	Piling	PKB Koya	0.20	0.15
11	Pillars, slab	PMK	26.11	19.19
12	Steel reinforcement	PMK	4.28	3.15
13	Post construction wire tensioning	Utracon	2.06	1.51
14	Wall masonry	PMK & ULCCS	2.84	2.09
15	Mechanical, electrical plumbing works	M/s Bluestar	18.43	13.55
16	Transformers	M/s Voltamp	0.44	0.32
17	Diesel generator	M/s Sterling Wilson	4.13	3.04
18	Chiller	M/s Johnson Controls	1.35	0.99
19	Sewage treatment plant	M/s Ion xchange	1.20	0.88
20	Water treatment plant	M/s Thermax	0.09	0.07
21	Façade works	M/s NCGL	11.00	8.09
22	Fire doors	M/s Signum	0.91	0.67
23	Integrated building management system & FAPA	M/s Siemens	1.89	1.39
24	Interiors	M/s Monalisa	6.52	4.79
25	Lifts	M/s Mitsubishi	3.12	2.29
26	HSD Yard	M/s Petromech Eng	0.40	0.29
27	HT cable work	M/s HT & LT	0.50	0.37
28	Truss work	M/s Floreat	0.44	0.32
29	Light fixture	M/S Philips	0.43	0.32
	Total		136.04	100.00

Source: Calculated from the data provided by Anupa Sasi, Project Engineer UL Cyber Park.

> specialized finishing activities like lift, air conditioning, sewage treatment etc. But the main body of work will be undertaken by our own workers. Just as in the case of road construction we shall prove that the cooperative control and supervision of the workers is as efficient as in the private sector, even when the activities are subcontracted.[19]

During the past three years a number of specialized teams have been developed within the Cooperative substantially enhancing its in-house capabilities. Most important among them has been setting up the ULCCS Planning and Design Cell in collaboration with Oficio De Design and Planning LLP (BURO DAP),[20] a planning, architecture and design consultancy firm based in New York, Ahmedabad and Bogotá. ULCCS Planning and Design Cell focuses on project consultancy, capacity building and research work. At present it consists of three architects, two diploma holders and three assistants. By working together creatively from the start of a project, architects and engineers combine their knowledge to devise an integrated design solution so that functional, aesthetics and cultural aspects are achieved. This reflects in each project from site development plans to furniture designs. Within a short period the Cooperative has been able to gain recognition for its design capability so much so that the PWD awarded the construction of three major bridges at an estimated cost of Rs 35 crore to the Cooperative to design and build. Similarly, the new design cell has drawn the designs for a number of landmark buildings such as the Academy of Skill Education (Rs 40 crore) in Kollam, headquarters of the government's cooperative department (Rs 68 crore) in

[19] Interview with Shaju S., secretary ULCCS, 22 January 2013.

[20] MoU with BURO DAP and ULCCS on 12 May 2012. Records of ULCCS.

Table 7.3: Technical teams/cells set up by ULCCS

Type of work	Classification of workers: A class members	C class members	Non-members	Total
Masonry	4	9	10	23
Concrete workers Shuttering/scofolding Reinforcement	31	28	43	102
Plastering	2	9	9	20
Painter		8	4	12
Flooring	3	7	4	14
Carpenter			6	6
Electrical/plumbing	2	12	1	15

Source: Calculated with the date provided by the Project Engineer of UL Cyber Park.

Thiruvananthapuram and EMS Hospital (Rs 12 crore) in Kozhikode.

The other skilled workers related to building construction have been brought together in separate teams and the numbers expanded. Table 7.3 presents the distribution of skilled or technical teams that exist in the Cooperative as of 2013. As already discussed, the Mechanical Engineering and Plumbing (MEP) team is a relatively new skill group whose formation has had a significant impact on the Cooperative. The exterior and interior decoration capability is also in the process of being enhanced.

The Cooperative's experience in developing UL Cyber Park also contributed to significantly modernizing its machinery. For example, the Cooperative acquired a concrete batching plant which is necessary for preparing the accurate mix of aggregates and cement. Similarly, it also acquired a concrete pump for supplying concrete to the higher floors which could avoid delays in the traditional mechanical hoists and scaffolding has also been modernized and expanded so as to undertake multi-floor buildings. The construction of a 23-story apartment building at UL Cyber Park, for which the preparation is already under way, is currently being designed by the Cooperative and will be directly constructed by it. Thus, the Cooperative is quickly scaling up its skill capacity in order to take on more of activities in constructing the UL Cyber Park.

The introduction of advanced machinery has significant implications for the skill structure of the workforce and the labour process. For example, income differences between workers of different skills will widen, their autonomy reduced and the role of engineers and supervisors enhanced. In such a situation will it be possible for the workers to keep their commitment to the ideals of cooperation? What measures are the Cooperative adopting to sustain the feeling of ownership and involvement of the workers? Once again Shaju responded to our questions:

> Yes, we are aware of the problem. The constant technological upgradation is inevitable and there is a danger of workers feeling alienated. To counteract the tendency we attempt to explain to all the workers the totality of the project that all their activities add up to so that they understand what they are doing. In the monthly meetings in which all members are expected to participate all new projects are explained in detail. In the weekly meeting of the team leaders and directors technical aspects are regularly discussed. We have to strengthen the tradition of shop floor meetings.
>
> There is strict discipline at the worksite. But it is not achieved through harassment and threats. This will be clear to anyone who examines the records of crime and punishments in the Cooperative. The involvement of the workers and safety

> measures has been responsible for the low accident rates. Efforts are also being made for the skill enhancement of the workers so that they have occupational mobility. The difference in quality of the workers in the Cooperative we were able to see when our workers had to work side by side with the contract workers that were employed by the specialist firms at the Cyber Park site. It was not the higher wages that made the difference. Even the migrant workers in the workforce of the Cooperative had a sense of belonging.[21]

From this discussion, it is clear that the Cooperative is well aware of the challenges and threats to its functioning. Interestingly, its response is more democracy, more transparency, and more awareness of members as to the goals and mission of the Cooperative.

A perusal of the available information regarding disciplinary actions taken during the last decade supports the secretary's position in the above quote. During the whole period the total number of disciplinary actions is 147 (i.e., less than 15 per annum). As we can see from Table 7.4, 'indiscipline' which includes disobedience to leader and leaving the worksite without permission was the most common offence committed and the second most common offence was the falsification of Daily Labour Report to claim false attendance. This usually happens when someone is working at two neighbouring sites and claims full attendance in both the worksites after working half day each. Rarely is it done in connivance with the leader, and the leader is held responsible if he fails to identify such falsification. Absence without leave, particularly when it is for continuous periods is also seriously taken note of. It is instructive to note that even misbehaviour outside

[21] Interview with P. Rameshan, President ULCCS, 23 January 2013.

Table 7.4: Distribution of disciplinary actions by type and category of employees (2004-05 to 2014-16)

	Dereliction of duty	Indiscipline	Financial irregularity	Falsification of attendance	Misbehaviour at worksite	Misbehaviour outside worksite	Absence without leave	Total
Worker	9	37	17	12	5	4	14	98
Leader	5	6	10	17	2	1	1	42
Tech. Supervisor	4	1	3					8
Driver/Cleaner	5	2	3	7	2	2		21
Director		1			1	3		5
Total	23	47	33	36	10	10	15	174

Source: Calculated from the minutes of Board of Directors meetings from 2004-05 to 2014-16.

Table 7.5: Distribution of punishment by disciplinary actions

	Suspension with metal work	Suspension	Fine	Warning	Removal of leadership	Change in in charge	Total
Dereliction of Duty	13	1		2		1	17
Indiscipline	39	2		2			43
Financial Irregularity	18	2	2				22
Falsification of Attendance	29	1	3				33
Misbehaviour at worksite	4	2			1		7
Misbehaviour outside worksite	5	4			1		10
Absence without leave	15						15
Total	123	12	5	4	2	1	147

Source: Calculated from the Minutes of Board of Directors meeting from 2004-05 to 2014-16.

the worksite which could bring the Cooperative's reputation into disrepute is considered an offense. Thus, members are expected to behave in a manner becoming of the Cooperative at work and beyond.

The most frequent offenders would appear to be the leaders with 42 offenses against them (though the present number of leaders is only 40). Forty-three per cent of offences consist of falsification of daily labour report and their failure to identify the falsification. Any sign of indiscipline, misbehaviour or dereliction of duty on the part of the leaders are dealt very seriously by the board of directors. The board members also adopt very self-critical attitude to offences of their colleagues. Four board members, for example, were suspended for misbehaviour and one member had to resign. This strict self-critical approach of the leadership sets a high standard for emulation at all levels of the Cooperative. The most important conclusion that can be drawn from the data is that there is a very low level of crime and punishment in the Cooperative.

What are the punishments given to offenders? In 83 per cent of the cases members were suspended, but immediately given duty in metal breaking (stone crushing) at the quarries or nearby sites. The income from metal work is much lower than other activities and therefore it is considered a subsistence allowance during the suspension period. After a week or two, the suspension is withdrawn once the offender submits a written apology to the Cooperative. Any suspended leaders get the same treatment and also have to work at the quarry during their suspension period. When they are reinstated they are normally removed from the post and it is very rare for a person to be a repeat offender. Only if direct involvement in financial irregularity is proven, then the board member or leader is immediately removed from the leadership post. Our survey which is presented in great detail in the next chapter found that only 15 per cent of the workers faced disciplinary action during their entire career at the Cooperative.

The objective of disciplinary action is rehabilitative in order to correct the offender rather than to punish. The potential of social disgrace is the most important deterrent for misbehaviour. All the disciplinary actions are reported in detail at the annual general body meeting for ratification. A member can be expelled only with the approval of the general body. Such an instance has occurred in the last one decade.

The Cooperative does not see punishment as the major instrument to enforce discipline, but rather prefers to deepen the awareness of the worker-members regarding the history and goals of the Cooperative, the present strategy and policies and the projects that are taken up. Thus, education about its history, transparency, and information sharing are vital for the Cooperative as its worker-members are its reason for existing and not merely cogs in the wheel. This is achieved through regular meetings in which members, leaders and directors participate. There are a number of different meetings. First, there is the annual general body meeting – sometimes they happen more than once a year – which is a day-long meeting with near full attendance by the worker-members. The report of the secretary is a comprehensive compendium of the activities going on in the Society, the strategy and the vision. Second, there are monthly meetings in which all members have the right to participate, where members can raise grievances and suggestions regarding the implementation of the project. Third, there are half-day weekly meetings where all team leaders, directors, technical staff and selected invitees participate to review the progress of each project, address problems, and fix the targets of the next one month. Fourth,

Table 7.6: Support of workers for modernization and diversification

	Modernization		Diversification		Cyber Park	
	% of workers very much agreement	% of workers in agreement	% of workers very much agreement	% of workers in agreement	% of workers very much agreement	% of workers in agreement
A class member	88.48	10.99	87.43	12.57	95.29	4.71
C class member	85.37	13.95	88.44	10.88	96.94	2.38
Non-member Keralite	77.22	22.78	86.67	12.22	91.11	8.33
Migrant worker	22.55	72.34	31.91	63.83	30.21	54.89
Total	68.00	30.33	73.11	25.33	78.00	17.78

Source: Survey of ULCCS workers, 2014.

there are the daily meetings at the Cooperative's headquarters with team leaders and the board of directors where accounts are settled and day-to-day matters discussed. Fifth, there are daily worksite meetings, which are often informal discussions at lunch time or during leisure hours but can also be a formal meeting called for a specific purpose. This intricate system of regular communication from the board of directors to the worksites and from the worksites to the board of directors is a hallmark of the Cooperative. It is this constant dialogue that gives the workers a sense of participation in running of the Cooperative.

The success of the Cooperative's internal dialogue process is reflected in the level of satisfaction of workers in respect to wage levels, sense of participation, and friendliness of environment, management behaviour, job security and social security (discussed in chapter eight). What is particularly noteworthy is that there is near consensus about the future strategy for growth through modernization, diversification, and the development of the Cyber Park (Table 7.6).

The workers were given three choices to indicate their level of support for modernization, diversification and the establishment of Cyber Park initiatives: 'very much in agreement,' 'in agreement,' and 'disagreement'. Looking at the member responses from Keralites (that is, not including migrant workers), there is near consensus supporting the initiatives. Among A class members, C class members and Keralite non-members there is hardly any dissent. In the case of migrant workers, the proportion of who are 'very much in agreement' is low indicating their lack of enthusiasm for the new directions of the Cooperative which perhaps they fear might affect their employment prospects adversely. It is a misunderstanding that the Cooperative can clarify through dialogue. Despite the migrant workers' relative reluctance, there is a general consensus in the Cooperative regarding the reorganization and redirection of the Cooperative.

The dramatic evolution from earthen roads to highly specialized and complex IT park construction demonstrates the Cooperative's willingness to innovate and take on new challenges, and most importantly to remain relevant to its members. While this new phase of its history certainly brings many challenges and uncertainties, it also provides a fascinating account of modernization and diversification of a worker-owned and worker-controlled Cooperative.

CHAPTER 8

SOCIO-ECONOMIC STATUS AND WORKING CONDITIONS

After agriculture, construction is the largest employment sector in Kerala. There are around a million construction workers in Kerala which accounts for approximately 10 per cent of the total workforce. The rapid expansion of the workforce from the 1980s following the construction boom was also accompanied by an inflow of migrant workers from outside Kerala. We can only hazard a guess of their numbers in the construction sector as there is no data tracking this, but given the trends we would guess about half the workforce is Malayali.

During the boom period, ULCCS also expanded, which brought new demands on its workforce. Until the mid-1970s the number of worker-members was only around 150 (all members), and the Society rarely employed non-members as workers. In order to qualify as an A grade contractor the membership was raised to above 200, but the Cooperative faced difficulties in providing work for all its members.

However, in the latter half of 1990s the scenario changed dramatically when its work orders exceeded the Cooperative's construction capacity. The Cooperative found it difficult to attract new members and was forced to hire temporary non-member workers. This trend reached an unacceptable level in 2001 when non-members constituted more than 80 per cent of the workforce. To address this situation an intensive effort was made to enrol additional A class members and, importantly, a new C class membership category was created for those workers who did not want to become A class members since they did not plan to remain in Kerala long-term. C class members enjoy all the benefits that the A class members were due, other than voting rights.

In this chapter we discuss the socio-economic background of the worker-members, their working conditions, their level of satisfaction, and their aspirations. We begin with the social origin of the workers. The argument we make is fairly well known: construction workers come from socially backward, economically poorer and relatively uneducated backgrounds. Second, we describe the way in which the wage and other benefits from working in the Cooperative have significantly contributed to improving their status. We then discuss workers' increased well-being and satisfaction with the general environment and management of the Society and how this generates a deep sense of commitment and bond with the institution. Finally, we conclude with a brief discussion on the status of migrant workers in the Cooperative and show how they too have deep appreciation for the functioning of the Cooperative.

Our data for this chapter is from a fairly large survey of workers in the Cooperative, covering half of all the workers in the Society calculated during January 2014. The survey was

Table 8.1: Distribution of workers in ULCCS, 2014

	No of workers	%	sample male	sample female	sample total	%
A class member	616	22.1	170	21	191	21.2
C class member	785	28.2	208	86	294	32.7
Non-member Keralite	480	17.2	162	18	180	20.0
Non-member migrant	907	32.5	235	0	235	26.1
Total	2788	100	775	125	900	100

Source: Survey of ULCCS Workers, 2014.

done in the evenings at the worksites in and around Kozhikode. The migrant workers all of whom stay at the worksite and non-member workers who are mostly from the locality have therefore greater representation in the survey. In Table 8.1, column 2 we have also given the distribution of A class members, C class members, non-member Keralite workers and non-member migrant workers for the year 2014. Of the total workforce of 2,788 currently in the Cooperative, 1,401 workers are members and 1,387 are non-members. While Keralite non-member workers are only 480, migrant workers are 907. Thus, in 2014 the non-members constitute 50 per cent and migrant workers are 33 per cent of the workforce.

SOCIO-ECONOMIC BACKGROUND OF WORKERS

Before joining the Cooperative only 13 per cent of the workers were employed in the construction sector and thus were new entrants into the occupation. Nearly half the workers were employed as agricultural workers or other rural wage labourers and a small number was employed in salary work, mostly in the private sector. Cultivation and self-employment played only a marginal role and for one-fifth of the workers, the job in the Society was their first job (Table 8.2).

A deeper understanding of the economic background of

Table 8.2: Distribution of workers by occupation before working in the society

	A class member	C class member	Non-member Keralite	Migrant worker	Total
Agri workers	4.19	4.42	5.56	52.77	17.22
Other wage workers	33.51	40.48	21.11	19.57	29.67
Construction worker	12.57	12.24	16.67	12.34	13.22
Salaried employment	8.38	6.46	13.33	0.00	6.56
Job abroad	0.00	3.06	5.00	0.00	2.00
Agriculture and self-employment	1.57	0.68	0.56	1.28	1.00
Skilled workers	6.28	9.86	11.67	2.98	7.67
Unemployed	31.41	19.73	22.22	9.79	20.11
Others	2.09	3.06	3.89	1.28	2.56
Total	191	294	180	235	900

Source: Survey of ULCCS workers, 2014.

the workers can be drawn from an analysis of the occupational history of parents and grandparents. The most striking feature of their histories is that only for a negligible number of the workers construction work was their traditional occupation (Table 8.3). Only 1.6 per cent of their grandfathers and 5.4 per cent of the fathers were construction workers. The rest of the present workers in the Cooperative are the first generation in their families to be engaged in the field of construction. Agricultural worker families were the single most important source for supply of construction workers to the Cooperative. Forty-eight per cent of the workers had grandfathers who were agricultural labourers and 35 per cent of the workers' fathers were agricultural labourers. Similarly, 33 per cent of the grandmothers and 23 per cent of the mothers were agricultural labourers. Other forms of rural wage labourers were the next important source of labour supply for the Cooperative. Once again, a striking point is that only a negligible proportion of the parents were cultivators. The existence of a large body of landless or marginal landholders not only from the SC caste,

Table 8.3: Distribution of occupation of spouse, parents, grandparents

	Husband/ wife	Father	Mother	Grand-father	Grand-mother
Agri workers	4.00	34.48	23.37	48.07	33.44
Other wage workers	12.59	38.49	10.08	32.90	9.06
Construction worker	1.78	5.38	0.69	1.57	0.31
Salaried employment	2.96	4.24	1.95	2.86	0.78
Self-employment	0.44	3.44	0.00	1.72	0.78
Agriculture	0.15	1.72	0.11	2.00	0.47
Skilled	0.89	1.60	0.23	0.86	0.63
Employment guarantee	7.26	1.15	6.07	0.00	0.00
Unemployed	67.85	5.61	57.39	8.15	54.06
Others	2.07	3.89	0.11	1.86	0.47
Total	675	873	873	699	640
	100.00	100.00	100.00	100.00	100.00

Source: Survey of ULCCS workers, 2014.

but also from the backward caste was an important feature of traditional Malabar society. More than half of the mothers and grandmothers had gainful employment, which looking at the occupational pattern of the spouses of workers continues to be the case today.

The caste origin of the workers fully reflects the traditional occupational patterns of their families. It was the scheduled castes and the backward castes who were fated to work as agricultural and other wage labourers. Seventy-three per cent of the workers in the Cooperative are from these castes with thiyyas the most prominent. In chapter two we discussed that the early members of ULCCS were all from the thiyya caste, and even today this pattern continues with 78 per cent of A class members coming from the thiyyas. Interestingly, the proportion of thiyya caste comes down to 62 per cent among the C class members and further to 52 per cent among the non-members. One explanation for this decline is that as the catchment area of membership moves away from Uralungal, the proportion of thiyya caste declines. Not surprisingly there

Table 8.4: Distribution of workers by caste and category

	SC/ST	Thiyyas	OBC	Forward caste	Others	Total %	Total No.
A class member	6.3	78.0	2.6	9.9	3.1	100	191
C class member	9.1	62.7	9.1	13.0	5.2	100	308
Non-member Keralite	11.0	52.2	8.2	11.0	16.5	100	182
Non-member migrant worker	18.8	0	37.5	12.2	27.3	100	245
Total workers	11.4	46.6	15.7	11.8	12.9	100	926

Source: Survey of ULCCS workers 2014.

is no thiyya caste among the migrants but the backward castes constitute 36 per cent of the migrant workers. Importantly, a section of the forward castes (12 per cent) have entered into the ranks of construction workers. Muslims and Christians are small minorities with 8.1 and 2.9 per cent respectively and more than half of the Muslims belong to the migrants. The migrant workers have a more differentiated caste structure.

The age distribution of workers has a surprising feature given the perceived reluctance of the young generation for construction work. Young workers (age 18-30) who are new entrants to the industry constitute 36 per cent of the member workforce and among the migrant workers 63 per cent are below the age of 30. Even among non-member workers 63 per cent are below 30. This might reflect the conscious policy of the Cooperative to attract younger workers rather than older workers who have been seasoned in the private sector. Member workers have a significantly higher representation of older workers than non-member workers, which suggests that it is still the older generation that are attracted to longer-term commitments to membership.

The educational profile of the workers in the Cooperative is better than the state's pattern, though it is still backward.

Table 8.5: Age distribution of members by worker category

Age	A class member	C class member	Non-Member Keralite	Migrant worker	Total workers
18-30	16.8	20.0	53.3	62.6	36.9
31-40	36.6	17.7	22.2	17.4	22.5
41-50	28.8	27.2	17.8	14.5	22.4
51-60	13.6	26.9	6.7	4.3	14.3
60 >	4.2	8.2	0.0	1.3	4.0
Total	100	100	100	100	100
Total no.	191	305	180	235	911

Source: Survey of ULCCS Workers 2014.

While only 2.3 per cent of the workers in the state as a whole have a degree or higher qualification, the ratio in the Society is 7.1 per cent. Only 23.2 per cent of the workers in the state are matriculates but below degree. Because of the difference in classification we cannot have strictly comparable figures for the Cooperative, but it is likely to be above 30 per cent. Interestingly among the migrant workers in the Cooperative 4 per cent have technical qualifications, three degrees and one post graduate (Table 8.6). As per the 2001 census only 5 per cent of construction workers in Kerala did not have formal education. The higher ratio among the workers in the Cooperative is due to the presence of migrant workers among whom illiteracy is as high as 20 per cent. The educational background of the Cooperative is likely to change significantly with the modernization and diversification process as many of the new jobs being created require specialized and technical skills. Indeed, part of the rationale for embarking on this new phase was to meet the newfangled needs of the next generation of educated young people in Kerala.

Demographic data also shows an interesting difference between Keralites and migrant workers. The average family size of workers is 4.35, but there is significant variation in

Table 8.6: Distribution of workers by education and category

	A class member	C class member	Non-Member Keralite	Non-member migrantworker	Total workers
No formal	1.57	3.93	3.89	20.00	7.57
Primary	3.66	16.07	6.11	17.87	11.96
Upper primary	23.56	24.92	12.22	33.62	24.37
High school	51.31	33.44	32.78	20.85	33.81
Plus 2/Pre-degree	15.71	15.08	26.67	5.96	15.15
Degree	4.19	5.25	17.78	1.28	6.48
P G	0.00	1.31	0.56	0.43	0.66
Total	100.00	100.00	100.00	100.00	100.00
	191	305	180	235	911

Source: Survey of ULCCS workers, 2014.

different categories of workers. Kerala has much smaller family sizes than other states and therefore it is not surprising that the migrant workers have an average family size of 5.5. However, what is interesting, and we have no clear explanation as to why, is that there is a significant difference between the size of families of C class members (3.17) and non-member Keralite workers (4.94). The average number of earning members is also highest among the C class members resulting in a very high ratio of earners (65.77 per cent). The proportion of married members is above 80 per cent while it is only 48 per cent for C class member workers. These differences might be due to the fact that more than half of the non-member workers are below the age of 30.

The demographic characteristics suggest interesting differences among Keralite and migrants from outside Kerala as well as differences between members and non-members. Despite these differences, they do not seem to manifest in hardened cleavages within the Cooperative, suggesting that within the Cooperative there is a fairly strong sense of solidarity and common vision.

Table 8.7: Family size, number of earners, percentage of married and number of children in worker families

Category	Ave. family size	Ave. no. of earning members	% of earners	% of married	Ave. no. of children
A class member	4.23	1.55	36.80	82.20	1.21
C class member	3.17	2.09	65.77	80.33	1.41
Non-member Keralite	4.94	1.89	38.20	48.33	0.79
Non-member migrant worker	5.52	1.85	33.44	53.62	0.94
Total workers	4.35	1.87	43.08	67.51	1.12

Source: Survey of ULCCS workers, 2014.

WORKING CONDITIONS AT THE ULCCS

Cooperatives are unique organizational forms that organize production and profits very differently than typical capitalist companies. They challenge many foundational characteristics of capitalist organizations such as hierarchy, specialization of knowledge, concentration of power, alienation, possessive individualism, and so on that have become synonymous with 'good business.' To join a Cooperative, then, is not an automatic process as it requires a social consciousness in relation to economic activity. The question arises as to why workers joined ULCCS. The survey provided various options that workers had to prioritize. The top priorities are not surprising and are directly related to wages and job security: for 32 per cent of the workers the first priority for joining the Cooperative was 'better wages,' for 21.7 per cent the first priority was 'better working conditions,' and for 19.7 per cent the first priority was 'security of employment.' Taken together these three issues ranked as the top priority for 73 per cent of workers. What is interesting is that 'job security' is ranked by 65 per cent of workers as a first, second, or third priority

Table 8.8: Reasons for joining ULCCS

Reasons	Percentage distribution of priorities expressed by workers		
	1st priority	2nd priority	3rd priority
Better wages	32.2	10.0	11.9
Better working conditions	21.7	23.1	14.4
Efficient management	10.4	18.6	13.2
Friendly atmosphere	2.7	11.1	17.3
Feeling of ownership	11.4	8.2	11.9
Job security	19.8	24.0	21.2
Social security	1.4	4.7	7.3
Others	0.3	0.3	2.7
	100.0	100.0	100.0
Total number of respondents	900	900	900

Source: Survey of ULCCS workers, 2014.

whereas 59 per cent rank 'working conditions' and 54 per cent rank 'better wages' among their top three reasons for joining the Cooperative. While economic reasons ranked as the top priorities for the majority of workers, it is also interesting the relative importance that a significant number of workers (23.5 per cent) gave to non-economic considerations such as labour management practices, friendly environment, and sense of participation. This data suggests that workers' reasons for joining are multifarious and complex and cannot be reduced to economic reasons alone (Table 8.8).

A major incentive for workers to join the Cooperative is the relatively higher wages offered to members. We map the present relative wage structure in Table 8.9, which shows stratification based on skill-level of the job as well as between members and non-members and men and women. Because non-members are recruited for unskilled work, their wages for unskilled jobs is Rs 500 (for women), which is 17 per cent lower than members for the same job. The Cooperative justifies this stratification by making non-members eligible for 20 per cent bonus which they can claim on the basis of their attendance as well as the additional Rs 50 'stay at site allowance' given to all

Table 8.9: Wage structure at the cooperative (Rupees per day)

	Particulars	Members		Non Members	
		Male	Female	Male	Female
1	Directors	1330			
2	A Class leaders	1090			
3	B class leaders	1020			
4	C class leaders	950			
5	Plant operator	1400			
6	Operator(jcb)	1140			
7	Drivers(lorry)	940			
8	Paver operators	1060			
9	*Tar thookkal, kallu chadal*	915	595		
10	Boiler, shovels, spray	1020	620	660	
11	Tar work	900	590	660	
12	Concrete work	900	590	660	
13	Halting	960		720	
14	Labour	840	560	600	500

Source: Wage records of ULCCS.

migrant workers. Metal (stone) crushers earn only around Rs 400 per day, which is not included in the Table 8.9 since they are piece-rate workers.

An unacceptable feature of the wage structure is the discrimination against women members in particular types of work (Table 8.9). The wages of unskilled women workers are 33 per cent lower than that of male workers and women are absent from the better paying, skilled categories altogether. The Cooperative has not been able to overcome the customary social prejudice against equal wages for men and women, especially in the low-skilled jobs.

Over the last thirty years, the basic wage rate for male members has increased dramatically from Rs 17 for the year 1979 to Rs 840 in 2016 and for female workers Rs 9 to Rs 540 during the same period. In Table 8.10 the five year averages of basic wages of the member workers are given. Wages have exhibited robust growth, except for a brief period in the latter

Table 8.10: Trend in average basic wage rates

	Real wages at cost of living index for industrial workers at Kozhikkode (base year 1980-81)					
	Male members (current)	Average annual increase	female members (current)	Average annual increase	Male members (real)	female members (real)
1976-80	18.00	11.76	9.50	11.11	–	–
1981-85	30.00	13.83	15.80	14.11	25.64	13.58
1986-90	41.20	5.51	22.20	5.70	25.59	13.78
1991-95	61.40	10.55	36.00	14.15	25.47	15.00
1996-2000	126.00	14.56	78.00	15.08	35.39	21.91
2001-05	174.00	4.00	107.00	3.16	37.58	23.11
2006-10	268.00	14.24	176.00	15.91	44.74	29.38
2011-14	530.00	14.76	352.50	15.20	61.69	41.03

Source: Collated from the wage records of ULCCS.

half of the 1980s and the first half of the 2000s. Again, one disturbing aspect is the relatively lower basic wages for women workers. In 1980 it was around 50 per cent lower than male wages and while over time the difference has narrowed, female wages continue to be 33 per cent lower.

Membership into the Cooperative is not automatic and workers have to go through a vigorous process before they are granted member status. New entrants into the Cooperative normally have to work as unskilled workers for a period and are subjected to an assessment of their skill and diligence before they are given membership. The average waiting period for members of the Cooperative has declined from five to ten years until the 1970s to around two years for A class members and one year for C class members. Given the significant wage difference between stone crushers, unskilled workers and skilled workers the possibilities of the new entrants to move upwards into higher skill jobs assumes importance. The majority of the present workers joined the Cooperative as unskilled workers where they worked on average for 5.3 years. Twenty-one per cent of them have been able to move into the

Table 8.11: Promotion of stone crushers into higher grades and average no. of employment by grade

	Stone crusher entrants	Average no. of years	Unskilled worker entrants	Average no. of years	Skilled workers entrants	Average no. of years
Stone crushers	176	5.70				
Other unskilled	98	6.93	431	5.34		
Skilled worker	53	5.83	91	6.09	265	5.91
Technician	2	3	4	6.50	6	3
Leader	13	9.55	13	0	10	0

Source: Survey of ULCCS workers, 2014.

skilled worker category where they worked for an average of six years. Thus, the Cooperative provides pathways from unskilled to skilled categories for workers. Stone crushers, the lowest grade entry point into the Cooperative, have sharply come down in importance after deploying crushing machines. Still 176 of the existing workers joined as stone crushers where they have put in on an average of 5.7 years and 56 per cent of them moved into the unskilled category and a further 23 per cent moved into the skilled category. There is also upward mobility for skilled workers who can move into technicians through acquiring the necessary skills or become team leaders (selected by the board of directors). In order to increase the chances for upward mobility the Cooperative is trying to introduce formal skill training programmes and also support worker-members who want to go for technical courses.

Having discussed the structure of relative wages and wage trends, we now examine the non-wage benefits provided to the members. The non-members are considered as temporary workers and therefore are not entitled to any benefit other than the annual bonus. The difference between the earnings of the members and non-members widens further when the non-wage benefits are also taken into consideration (Table 8.12). Seventy-seven per cent of non-members in our survey

Table 8.12: Trend in yearly wage and non-wage benefits of the workers

	1979-80	1981-85	1986-90	1991-95	1996-00	2001-05	2006-10	2011-13	2014-16
Wages (yearly)	4125	6870	9510	14610	30600	42150	66600	126500	129853013
Real wages	–	5871	5907	6062	8596	9104	11119	14726	19477952
PF contribution	495	824	1141	1753	3672	5058	7992	15180	28904620
ESI contribution	0	0	0	0	0	0	827	6009	2446029
Labour welfare fund	0	0	3	6	11	13	15	16	8048
LIC contribution	8	14	19	29	61	84	133	253	9612
Medical aid	10	22	39	60	148	936	2200	1297	3869806
Medical allowance	0	0	0	0	765	1054	1665	3163	4246682
Bonus	825	1374	1902	2922	6120	8430	13320	25300	57089718
Holiday wages	193	321	444	682	1428	1967	3108	5903	7227786
Welfare expense to workers	0	0	0	0	0	297	1557	2168	4559893
Festival allowance	0	0	0	0	0	0	900	1500	4527645
Production incentive	0	0	0	0	0	0	0	1173	0
Total benefit excluding wages	1531	2555	3547	5452	12205	17840	31718	61962	112890015
Total emoluments	5656	9425	13057	20062	42805	59990	98318	188462	132367967
Real emoluments	–	8056	8110	8325	12024	12957	16414	21940	19477952
Percentage of benefits	27.07	27.11	27.17	27.17	28.51	29.74	32.26	32.88	46.51

Source: Collated from the wage register of ULCCS from 1979 to 2016.

expressed interest in joining the Cooperative in order to receive this wider suite of benefits.

The share of non-wage benefits in the total earnings has increased from 27.07 per cent in 1979-80 to 32.88 per cent in 2011-14. The most important component of the non-wage benefit is the annual bonus at 20 per cent of the wage earnings, which has remained unchanged during the last three decades. Previously, the production incentive of 10 per cent of the share capital was given as part of the bonus, but from 2011-12 it has been given under a separate head. In addition, the provident fund contribution is at 12 per cent of the wages. In addition to bonuses and various financial incentives, there are also a number of health benefits. The health support of the Cooperative has four components. In case of accidents on the job, the entire medical expenses are carried by the Cooperative, and during the period of medical leave half the wages are paid. The medical aid as a percentage of earnings increased from 0.17 to 2.23 in 2005-10, but declined to 0.68 per cent in 2011-14. This decline is because of the introduction of Employees State Insurance (ESI) from 2009-10 where all employees earning less than Rs 15,000 per month have their medical expenses met by ESI Corporation. Since 1996, a medical allowance of 2.5 per cent is given to all workers and the Cooperative has insured all workers for accidents and death. As a result the share of health related expenditure in the total benefits to workers has increased from 0.32 per cent in 1979-80 to 0.44 per cent in 1990-95 and then afterwards steadily and rapidly to 5.69 per cent by 2011-14. The rising health expenditure may be a pointer to the increased incidence of accidents and illness. We examine the increased incidence of accidents during the past few years (Table 8.13). With the mechanization as well as the shift to high rise buildings,

Table 8.13: Accident details, 2004 to 2014

Nature of accidents	2004-05	2005-06	2006-07	2007-08	2008-09	2009-10	2010-11	2011-12	2012-13	2013-14
Death due to site accidents	0	0	0	0	0	0	1	1	2	0
Very major accidents	0	0	0	0	1	0	1	3	0	2
Major accidents	4	6	10	15	17	20	20	24	21	30
Total	4	6	10	15	18	20	22	28	23	32
Minor accidents	15	22	30	33	40	50	46	60	58	48
Total	23	34	50	63	76	90	90	116	104	112
Accidents per 100 workers	1.71	2.39	3.67	4.51	4.82	4.91	4.30	5.62	4.99	4.02
Serious accidents per 100 workers	0.30	0.42	0.73	1.07	1.14	1.09	1.05	1.36	1.10	1.15

Source: Sample Survey of ULCCS workers 2014.

bridges of longer span and maintenance work in heavy traffic roads, the accident rate has tended to rise.

The accident rate (accidents per 100 workers) has increased from 1.7 in 2004-05 to a high of 5.62 in 2011-12, which was an exceptionally high incident year, with the accident rate stabilizing below 5 during 2008-09 to 2013-14. The incidence of serious accidents involving death and major accidents is lower, but the trend is similar in that the incidents have increased. The Cooperative has recognized safety as a major issue and adopted a number of precautionary safety measures. The recent annual reports contain a separate paragraph on industrial safety, including the need for workers alertness. Fifty-two per cent of the workers expressed 'full satisfaction' and another 38 per cent 'satisfaction' with the measures adopted in dealing with safety.

An additional non-wage benefit is the meals and accommodation at worksites provided by the Cooperative and which is a special point of pride for the Cooperative. Even when the workers used to sleep in shop verandas in the past, a camp kitchen provided good food and this tradition has continued. The material cost is divided among the workers while the establishment charges like salaries of cooks and charges for fuel, utensils, and so on are borne by the Cooperative. Currently the daily food costs to workers are as low as Rs 20 to Rs 30 per day. In terms of accommodation, either the Cooperative rents or owns houses near the worksite or builds temporary accommodation, and allowances for travel expenses to the worksite is paid once a week. Taken together, these extra forms of support importantly impact on working conditions and frees up wages for other purposes.

LIVING STANDARDS OF THE WORKERS

All the workers that we met were unanimously of the opinion that the steady income provided by the Cooperative had a perceptible impact on their standard of living. Through the survey we collected household income of the workers from all sources and based on the survey data we have also worked out per capita monthly income of workers' families (Table 8.14).

The annual household income is highest for families of A class members (Rs 164,393) while the family income of C class members comes second (Rs 153,016). In terms of household income, the average income of A class members is higher than C class members because the A class members have larger family sizes. The per capita income of A class members is Rs 3,242 and that of C class members is Rs 4,022. The household income as well as the per capita income of the non-member worker families is relatively lower than members and the per capita income of members' families is more than double than that of migrant workers. Thus, income levels of members are significantly better than non-members and migrants.

These achievements are especially impressive when compared to the state poverty line. The below poverty line (BPL) for Kerala in 2013-14 was around Rs 1,000, which means that the per capita income of the member workers are more than three to four times above the poverty line. At the same time, the per capita income of the member workers are significantly below the average per capita income for the Kozhikode district which are around Rs 5,750, reflecting the income inequality in the state.

Another point that is born from the data presented in Table 8.14 is the near total dependency of the worker families on the

Table 8.14: Average annual income of the workers' families

	Wages from society	Other wage income	Salary	Land/ assets	Remit-tances	Others	Total	Per capita monthly income
A class member	151137	4482	6366	1361	1047	0	164393	3242
C class worker	125484	16908	7956	173	1361	1134	153016	4022
Non-member Keralite	130104	2472	4528	1444	0	1511	140060	2361
Migrant worker	103111	2766	426	255	0	0	106558	1608
Total workers	126004	7802	5003	695	675	678	140857	2699

Source: Survey of ULCCS workers 2014.

income from the Cooperative. Wages from the Cooperative contribute 90 per cent of the income of the workers' families and 96 per cent of the income of migrant worker families. The income from the Cooperative depends not only on the wage rate but also on the number of days of employment. One reason for the relatively lower income of the migrant workers is their two to three months annual trip home when they are absent from the worksite. Even the member workers today exhibit a clear preference for leisure to work (which can be a problem for the Cooperative). Every annual report of the Cooperative has an exhortation to the members not to absent themselves but to follow the footsteps of the forefathers who were diligent in their attendance and would work even on holidays and after working hours for the progress of the Cooperative. Table 8.15 presents attendance of the workers for the last decade.

Nearly half the workers' attendance is less than 240 workdays and they have Sunday off and 15 paid holidays. Given the nature of construction activity where work may

Table 8.15: Distribution of labours by the number of days of attendance

	Attendance						Total no.
	0-90	91-150	151-210	211-240	Above 240	Total	of workers
2004-05	29.12	2.11	9.82	15.09	43.86	100.00	285
2005-06	5.03	3.02	13.42	13.42	65.10	100.00	298
2006-07	24.08	3.40	14.92	13.35	44.24	100.00	382
2007-08	5.82	5.61	26.40	22.04	40.12	100.00	481
2008-09	9.52	4.68	13.23	18.71	53.87	100.00	620
2009-10	12.53	12.98	26.85	13.76	33.89	100.00	894
2010-11	18.17	4.50	14.94	18.08	44.31	100.00	1178
2011-12	12.76	5.04	13.35	14.78	54.07	100.00	1191
2012-13	13.76	5.75	16.17	17.88	46.42	100.00	1286
2013-14	14.06	4.81	9.76	14.06	57.32	100.00	1373
2014-15	10.80	6.59	11.52	16.30	54.78	100.00	1380
2015-16	4.60	3.36	13.45	12.97	65.61	100.00	1457

Source: DLR records, ULCCS.

have to be stopped because adverse weather or time required to shift from one worksite to another attendance above 240 days is considered a good record. Nevertheless, there is scope for the average worker to earn more by working more days.

The higher secured income of the workers is reflected in their assets – sixty per cent of workers have their own houses. Only 16 per cent do not have land in their own name (they most likely have land in the name of their parents) and 50 per cent have homesteads of less than 10 cents and 5 per cent more than 50 cents of land. Seventy per cent of the workers built their houses or improved the existing houses after joining the Cooperative. Only 18 per cent of Keralite workers have houses smaller than 500 square feet, while 72 per cent of migrant workers' homes in their home state are smaller than 500 square feet. Eighteen per cent of Keralite workers have houses larger than 1,000 square feet and none of the migrant workers have homes larger than 1,000 square feet. Sixty-eight per cent of the Keralite workers' houses are concrete terraced roofs and 31 per cent have marble tile or mosaic flooring in their homes. Again, the contrast to migrants' homes in their home states is stark as only 10 per cent have concrete terraced roofs and four per cent have marble or mosaic flooring and 60 per cent having bare earthen floors. Ninety-three per cent of Keralite workers have brick walls, while migrants' homes only 30 per cent have brick walls. A class members had superior housing conditions in comparison to the rest of the workers, reflecting their stable employment and relatively good wages. The housing conditions of migrant workers in their home states lies in stark contrast to the houses of the ULCCS worker members.

The Cooperative has a special scheme by which the workers can apply for a housing loan of Rs 1 lakh from Kozhikode District Cooperative Bank on the basis of guarantee from ULCCS without additional security from the workers. By 2012-13, 211 members had received this housing loan. In addition, the Cooperative provides other forms of assistance such as a loan scheme providing an interest free advance up to Rs 1 lakh. In 2012-13 alone Rs 1.7 crore was given through advances to workers. As a result, there are no *kutcha* huts but rather a significant number of *pucca* houses with terrace, superior floor coverings and having more than 750 square feet.

Working in the Cooperative enables members to access institutional loans. As one can see from Table 8.16 the interest free loan from the Cooperative and the loans from financial institutions which are mostly for construction of houses constitutes 75 per cent of workers' liabilities. The indebtedness of workers' households cannot be taken as an indicator of pauperization but rather reflects efforts for asset creation. Interestingly, A class members and non-members have very similar overall indebtedness, though members seem to have

Table 8.16: Indebtedness of worker households (Rs)

	The co-operative	Friends/ relatives	Money-lenders	SHG	Financial institutions	Others	Total
A class member	20754	9267	393	202	48786	1571	80972
C class member	12949	11338	493	2750	30469	357	58356
Non-member							
Keralite	11221	11167	1444	6664	48622	1472	80591
Migrant worker	85	638	574	255	1179	0	2732
Total workers	10901	8070	683	2341	30339	744	53079

Source: Survey of ULCCS workers, 2014.

more access to loans from the Cooperative than non-members who tend to avail the more informal loan avenues such as friends and relatives, money lenders and especially self-help groups (Table 8.16). Looking at consumer durables also reveals that the majority of worker households have consumer durables such as mobile phones and televisions (Table 8.17). The presence of consumer durables is conspicuous among Keralite workers compared to migrant workers. For example, 30 per cent of workers from Kerala have bikes, another 5 per cent have motor vehicles, and 30 per cent have fridges.

Among worker-members' children, there are 16 students who are studying for postgraduate or professional degrees. These numbers imply that some workers are investing in the education of their children in order to increase their social mobility relative to their own generation. Of the currently employed children around 20 per cent are employed in private/government white collar jobs, factories, and jobs abroad.

The high degree of worker satisfaction could be related to economic factors such as wage and non-wage benefits and non-economic factors such as the degree of participation, management practices, and organizational environment. As discussed above, efficiency of cooperative management (10.4 per cent), the sense of ownership (11.4 per cent) and

Table 8.17: Distribution of consumer durables in workers households

	No. of sampled workers	Bike	motor vehicles	Fridge	TV	Washing machine	Mobile	Mixy/ grinder	Households
A class member	191	50	11	54	157	13	180	144	191
C class member	294	80	18	93	241	21	267	215	305
Non-member Keralite	180	60	15	76	139	25	166	125	180
Migrant worker	235	2	0	0	28	0	217	16	235
Total	900	192	44	223	565	59	830	500	911

Source: Survey of ULCCS Workers, 2014.

friendly atmosphere (2.7 per cent) were identified as the primary inducement to join the Cooperative (see Table 8.8 above). An important indicator of the degree of participation would be attendance of workers in meetings. Ninety-five per cent of the workers who participated in the survey attend the annual general body. The monthly meetings – the most important forum where all the member-workers including the C class members come together – also register over 50 per cent attendance. Between 2010 and 2013, there were 38 monthly meetings and all of them formed quorum with over 50 per cent attendance and in six meetings the attendance was more than 90 per cent. This is indeed an unusually high level of sustained participation.

Involvement in the Cooperative also brings workers intangible benefits such as gaining new skills and capacities with 47 per cent of the workers from Kerala agreeing that their experience in the Cooperative helped them very much in this regard and only 6 per cent denied any such improvement. For migrant workers, on the other hand, only 14 per cent reported very significant improvement in their capacity and 12 per cent reported that there was no improvement in their capacity. Similarly 60 per cent of workers from Kerala were very positive regarding contribution of the Cooperative to their self-confidence and only three per cent denied any such positive relationship. In contrast, only 24 per cent of the migrants reported that they felt very significant improvement in their self-confidence after joining the Cooperative and 11 per cent did not feel any change. This data suggests that migrant workers experience the Cooperative in different ways than non-migrant workers. Indeed, the experience of migration itself might colour migrant workers' experiences within the Cooperative.

The high levels of participation in the Cooperative are also seen in activities outside the Cooperative. For example, 28 per cent of members are active in political parties (mainly left parties), and 41 per cent of members are active in clubs, libraries, and cultural organizations. In addition, 18 per cent of members are in youth organizations, 20 per cent are in temple committees and caste organizations, and 18 per cent are active in trade unions. The involvement in trade unions is curious, as there are no recognized or unrecognized trade unions working in the Cooperative. Given the participatory functioning of the Cooperative there is a general agreement among central trade unions that there is no need to organize workers separately.

To further understand the level of satisfaction of the workers in the Cooperative we asked the workers to make a self-assessment of satisfaction regarding seven factors such as wages and other benefits, job security, safety measures, friendship with other workers, behaviour of the management, working conditions and participatory nature of decision making. They were to indicate in a range of five points their assessment namely (1) very satisfied, (2) satisfied (3) somewhat satisfied (4) dissatisfied and (5) very dissatisfied. In Table 8.18 we have given the proportion of the workers who are 'very satisfied' and 'satisfied' in each of the aspects. What is striking about this data is that the scores regarding the level of satisfaction are curiously high. The lowest score of 71 per cent (still extremely high) was for satisfaction with wages and benefits. If 89 per cent of migrants had not expressed satisfaction, the average score would have been nearer to 65 per cent. If we included 'somewhat satisfied' responses then the ratio would rise above 90 per cent.

Some workers raised criticism that the wages were not

revised in 2013-14, and they expect wages to be raised every year. There is another anomalous aspect of the results. It is understandable that migrant workers register a high level satisfaction with their wages and most of the other factors, but it is curious that they also register a high level of satisfaction 'for participation' as they do not participate in the general bodies, monthly meetings or weekly meetings. This is true to a lesser extent for the non-member workers also. The office bearers explained this was due to the fact that these workers might have been referring to their involvement in the deliberations at the worksite. In any case, the data suggests that workers feel part of the Cooperative. Another interesting finding is that the level of satisfaction declines with education. The data presented in Table 8.19 clearly shows that the proportion of educated workers who are 'very satisfied' and 'satisfied' decline in relation to all characteristics except two: with respect to job security and friendly environment everyone, irrespective of education, has high level of satisfaction. The overall general satisfaction among workers is also seen in the industrial relations record of the Cooperative. There has not been a single incidence of industrial dispute let alone any protest action, for which the Cooperative is very proud.

MIGRANT WORKERS IN THE COOPERATIVE

Migrant workers' growing presence in the Cooperative warrants further discussion as their demographic and socio-economic characteristics vary from the Keralite workers. As we have seen the migrant workers are young (63 per cent are below the age of 30), come from backward social background (76 per cent SC/ST, backward caste and minorities), and come from poorer social strata (69 per cent were agricultural

Table 8.18: Percentage of workers who are 'fully satisfied' or 'satisfied' with the selected characteristics of the cooperative

	Total no. of workers	Wages and other benefits	Future job security	Safety measures	Relation to co-workers	Behaviour of management	Working conditions	Participation in decision making
A member worker	191	71	95	84	93	87	93	85
C member worker	294	65	95	91	97	90	94	79
Non-member worker	180	61	95	82	91	92	89	81
Migrant worker	235	89	95	97	97	93	96	71

Source: Sample survey of ULCCS workers, 2014.

Table 8.19: Percentage of workers who are 'fully satisfied' or 'satisfied' with the selected characteristics of the cooperative and level of education of workers

	Total no. of workers	Wages and other benefits	Future job security	Safety measures	Relation to co-workers	Behaviour of management	Working conditions	Participation in decision making
Uneducated	69	68	75	83	88	90	87	74
Primary	108	64	71	84	84	78	76	58
Upper Primary	222	62	76	77	86	76	83	59
High School	307	57	82	77	83	76	79	66
Plus 2/Pre-Degree	137	42	70	59	71	58	56	55
Degree	55	29	62	40	60	56	47	40

Source: Survey of ULCCS Workers, 2014.

Table 8.20: Number of workers by source of information of Kerala and route for recruitment to ULCCS

Source/route	Information	%	Recruitment	%
Labourers working in Kerala	32	13.6		
Friends and relatives	173	73.6	194	82.6
Agents	25	10.6	30	12.8
Newspaper		0.0		
Other sources	5	2.1	11	4.7
Total	235	100	235	100

Source: Survey of ULCCS workers, 2014.

labourers, other wage labourers and marginal farmers). Poverty and unemployment were the main push factors and higher wages and the possible savings the primary pull factors for the inter-state migration to Kerala. Twenty-two per cent of migrants were unemployed in their home states and wage rates were less than half of those in Kerala. The workers confirmed that they send on average Rs 3,500 back to their homes, which constitutes the main source of their household income.

As far as the migrant workers in ULCCS are concerned, labour agents were neither the important source of information regarding Kerala nor the main route for recruitment into the Cooperative. Seventy-four per cent of them came to know about the jobs in Kerala through word of mouth by friends and relatives. Also 83 per cent of the workers were recruited for jobs in the Cooperative through friends and relatives (Table 8.20).

Only 6 per cent of the workers had any experience in construction work in their home states. However, around 40 per cent had worked in the construction sector in Kerala before joining the Cooperative. With the relatively little experience in construction, most migrant workers entered the Cooperative as low-skilled workers. On average they had been in Kerala for the duration of 3.05 years of which 2.23 years they had

Table 8.21: Average years of work in Kerala

Duration (yrs)	No. of workers	Yrs worked in Kerala	No. of workers	Yrs worked at ULCCS
< - 1	94	0.8	158	1.0
2 - 3	73	2.4	42	4.3
4 - 5	39	4.6	24	4.5
6 - <	29	10.1	11	7.3
Total	235	3.05	235	2.23

Source: Survey of ULCCS workers, 2014.

worked in the Cooperative. Though the majority of workers had been in Kerala for only a short duration, 10.1 per cent had worked in Kerala and 7.3 per cent had worked in the Cooperative for more than six years (Table 8.21).

The wages migrant workers received in the private sector was only Rs 374 per day while they receive Rs 554 in the Cooperative. The yearly earnings of the 190 unskilled workers were Rs 100,817, the 40 skilled workers were Rs 111,776, and the five technicians were Rs 120,950, making the average yearly income of a migrant Rs 103,111. The average annual expenditure in Kerala was Rs 21,499 per worker, which allowed for large remittances sent back to their homes The low per capita expenditure is because of the fact that breakfast and lunch (and very often dinner too) was provided by the Cooperative for less than Rs 30 per day. Furthermore, all migrant workers stayed in the houses/rooms provided by the Cooperative. Therefore around 75 to 80 per cent of their income could be saved.

As we have already noted, migrant workers registered high levels of satisfaction in working in the Cooperative. Nevertheless, 20 per cent reported that there was discrimination in wages, 4 per cent were critical of the extra work required, and 2 per cent complained about the management. Sixty-five per cent of the Keralite workers stated that they are very friendly with migrant workers and only 5 per cent were indifferent and 71 per cent had visited the living quarters of migrant workers. However, the migrants indicated that they are dissatisfied with their exclusion from the general social life in Kerala, but 96 per cent of the migrant workers feeling that they belonged to the Cooperative and 76 per cent wanted to become members. P. Ramesan, the President of ULCCS, explained the situation regarding migrants in the Cooperative as follows:

> I think the trend of employing migrant workers is irreversible. Their proportion in the workforce is going to increase. The young Keralites are reluctant to become construction workers. Even if they joined the Cooperative, it would be difficult to ensure the reasonable attendance. We have decided to encourage the migrant workers to take membership in the Cooperative. At present there are only 18 migrant workers who are members. Soon we will be giving membership to an additional 125 migrant workers. Such workers would have to complete two to three years in the Cooperative and prove their skill, discipline and diligence. They would be entitled to all the benefits that any other member enjoys. The challenge would be to generate a sense of involvement and participation among the new members. Literacy is important in this context. From this year we are starting night schools for the migrant workers at the worksites. There would be more community celebrations of North Indian festivals. The objective is to integrate the new members fully into the Cooperative fold.[1]

The wages, working conditions, and worker satisfaction all suggest the Cooperative is significantly improving the quality

[1] Interview with P. Rameshan, President ULCCS, 23 January 2013.

of life of its members and non-members. What is particularly noteworthy is the degree to which workers identify with the Cooperative and feel a sense of community. In this way, the Cooperative has helped to create a different relationship to work than a typical capitalist enterprise.

CHAPTER 9

LESSONS FROM THE EXPERIENCES OF ULCCS

The vital question underlying this book is 'why do worker cooperatives exist?' After all, mainstream economic theory holds that it is in workers' best interest to be employed by profit maximizing and market disciplined capitalists. In order to maximize profit, capitalists are compelled to reduce the cost of production either through squeezing the workers or through increasing their productivity by adopting new technology. Any company that fails to do so will either be out-competed in the market resulting in the failure of the firm or shareholders will replace management. Economists hold that such a process results in the most optimal production decisions, and it is the higher efficiency and consequent cheaper products of capitalist firms that undermine and overtake pre-capitalist forms of enterprises based on community relations and self-employment. According to mainstream economists, a similar fate awaits alternative organizations of production to capitalist firms such as worker cooperatives.

Mainstream economists put forward five main arguments against cooperatives. First, they argue that the lack of capital is the most important barrier to entry for a worker cooperative and thus the difficulties in mobilizing the initial capital needed as well as subsequent credit for working capital and investment for expansion will severely limit the ability of the workers to achieve economies of scale and compete in the market. Second, economists claim that capitalists' single objective of maximizing profit strengthens their competitive edge and the multiple and heterogeneous objectives of workers – such as higher wages, better working conditions, and ideals of egalitarianism – are hard to maintain and can undermine each other and thus are not optimal for production decisions. Third, they argue that worker cooperatives eventually face severe managerial problems as the managers do not have sufficient incentives to supervise the workers who directly or indirectly hire them as managers. The result would be widespread shirking of work, waste and low productivity adversely affecting profits. Fourth, economists maintain that even if the worker cooperative succeeds in generating profits it will have little incentive to accumulate as worker owners cannot lay claim to their share of accumulation at the time of retirement or pass it on as inheritance. Thus, they see individual self-interest to accumulate as much as possible as the key driver for capitalist accumulation and without this a cooperative will be unable to maintain the accumulation patterns necessary for survival. Finally, they argue that even if the cooperative succeeds in accumulation the worker owners will not want to share their accumulated wealth with new workers. Instead they may choose to hire temporary wage workers or resort to subcontracting and hence the cooperative will eventually degenerate into a capitalist firm.

In short, mainstream economists argue that it is very difficult for a worker cooperative to emerge, survive and prosper, and if it does succeed it would soon degenerate into a typical capitalist firm, losing its lofty principles of worker control and worker ownership in creating a more egalitarian world. It is against these arguments that the actual performances of worker cooperatives such as ULCCS stand out as beacons for inspiration and as experiences that can yield valuable lessons for future practice. What are the main lessons to be drawn from ULCCS's experience?

THE GENESIS OF WORKER COOPERATIVES

The emergence of worker cooperatives within capitalism is extremely important in demonstrating that production, ownership and accumulation can happen differently. In Europe there were two broad streams that gave rise to worker cooperatives in the nineteenth century. First, worker cooperatives emerged as instruments of struggle in defensive actions led by workers either during a strike movement or in the periodic recessions that characterized the new era of capitalism. Second, worker cooperatives were motivated by utopian visions of alternatives to capitalism by pioneering socialists such as Robert Owen. The two trends were often engaged in polarising ideological conflicts with more radical working class leaders like Marx and Engels supporting the former trend and criticising the latter as utopian. In the third world, there is a third stream for cooperative emergence: state promoted and supported cooperatives. Here cooperatives are instruments of state policy to help the state provide credit, marketing and other services to people and also to reorganize production in the traditional industries such as handicrafts. In India for example, worker or producer cooperatives have been promoted with substantial state assistance in sectors such as handloom, coir, cottage and, even, small scale industries.

The contrast between the first two streams of worker cooperatives and the third stream is evident: the former are bottom-up processes and the latter is a top-down process. Over the course of its 90 year history, ULCCS has proven that its bottom-up member-driven processes have been vital to both its success and its ability to maintain its values and principles. Based on experiences like ULCCS's, we argue that cooperatives formed by the initiative of workers themselves or ideological motivation from below have greater member control and cohesion and therefore greater chances of success. Cooperatives formed through state-led initiatives of planning from above with fixed targets for the number of cooperatives to be formed or public money to be expended are more likely to result in bureaucratic stranglehold and lack a sense of ownership by the workers and therefore have a higher probability for failure.

In chapters two and three we discussed the circumstances that gave rise to the ULCCS in 1925 and the story of its survival in the subsequent decades during the colonial period. Even though the Cooperative was registered under the Cooperative Act legislated by the British, its formation was clearly an initiative from below. The organizers were motivated by the ideals of the social reform movement promoting egalitarianism initiated by Vagbhatananda. The formation of the Cooperative was a response to the conservative elites in Uralungal and its surroundings who had ostracized the followers of the social reform movement. Its formation was also interwoven with the winds of change that the nationalist movement was bringing through Malabar. The social reform and nationalist movements provided the broad ideological motivation for the pioneers to survive the adverse conditions of the early decades. The high level of idealism, commitment of key organizers, and the sense of ownership of the members kept the Cooperative moving forward until the favourable policy umbrella of the post-Independence period enabled it to enter a phase of expansion.

For much of its early history, the major obstacle to the entry and growth of ULCCS was the lack of capital. The Cooperative was limited by the meagre financial resources it could collect from the worker members and financial support from well-wishers and the credit provided by the District Cooperative Bank was inadequate and uncertain. Indeed, the issue of financial constraints is a recurrent theme in the narratives of founding members for the pre-Independence period as well as the post-Independence period until the end of 1990s. Interestingly, it was government support that proved to be an important factor that enabled ULCCS to overcome its financial difficulties. Here, government did not try to control in a top-down manner, but rather provided crucial financial support to enable the Cooperative to expand. The productive cooperation between government and the Cooperative did not threaten the autonomy of the Cooperative, but rather proved vital to its survival.

Thus, a second lesson that we draw from the experience of ULCCS is the importance of the right type of government support in facilitating a cooperative's success in accessing and competing in competitive markets. Cooperatives face many handicaps by working within the capitalist system, and therefore a special support policy from the government is essential for a level playing field. The role of government is not limited to providing credit, but can also include a range of other supports. For example, the 1957 left government in Kerala introduced a system of preference for government works for labour contract societies and a special scheme for their promotion and regulation. Similarly, the left government's 1996 People's Plan Campaign developed a preferential system for cooperatives and promoted ULCCS as a model for the rest of Kerala and also recognized it as an accredited agency for local government works. These forms of support and recognition proved to be a turning point for ULCCS allowing it to modernize and diversify, which quickened after 2006 when it received another injection of government support. The special support and incentives received from government did not falsely prop up ULCCS, but rather provided it vital strategic support that facilitated its expansion and diversification. From the government's side, these supports were simply a component of its general programme of industrial and infrastructure promotion. The reality is that in normal circumstances the private sector units, particularly the larger ones, are able to wrest concessions from the government and influence policy through myriad of ways. Moreover, government support is not a guarantee for success. Among the hundreds of labour contract societies that have been supported by the state government only a very small proportion succeed. This begs the question of how did ULCCS succeed as an efficient enterprise while maintaining its commitment to its principles and values? What factors contributed to its remarkable double success?

THE DILEMMA OF MEMBER CONTROL AND NEED FOR EFFICIENCY

Once a worker cooperative is established, one problem it immediately will face is the conflicting demands between member control and need for strict coordination and supervision of work. In a capitalist firm the managers and supervisors have full freedom to regulate labour during the working hours in order to extract maximum labour from the workers. The techniques of management science (such as time and motion studies), the threat of disciplinary action, and systems of incentives are employed for this purpose. The capitalist labour process results in workers' alienation from the labour process and attempts to resist capitalist controls render the workplace a contested terrain. In a worker cooperative where workers are the owners, by contrast, such conflicts are minimized. How do cooperatives, then, manage to ensure strict coordination and efficient production without the typical capitalist techniques of discipline and incentives? How do cooperatives ensure that worker ownership does not undermine the powers of the supervisors or lead to laxity and shirking of work resulting in lower productivity? More specifically, how did ULCCS succeed in creating a judicious blend of hierarchy and participation? To answer these questions, we look at ULCCS's experiences in developing a labour process that is both efficient and maintains the participatory process by the workers.

In ULCCS the workers elect the board of directors at the annual general meeting, which also includes a detailed deliberation of the report on the past year's functioning of the Cooperative. The general meeting is not a formality and the re-election of the board of directors is not a foregone conclusion. This was demonstrated in the 1980s when the members changed their president twice in less than one decade until they unanimously settled on the current president, who has been re-elected every year since. Once the board of directors is elected, they are given a high degree of autonomy in procuring contracts, choosing technology, allocating workers to different worksites, and other routine decisions in running the Cooperative. Thus, in effect, the board of directors are the managers of the Cooperative, which means that management is elected by the workers (again the contrast to capitalist corporations where managers are appointed by an unelected leadership could not be starker).

Very importantly, the board of directors selects the leaders and sub-leaders who coordinate, supervise, hire temporary workers, keep attendance, and make payments. The leaders and sub-leaders are chosen from among the best workers with proven managerial ability and who command widespread respect and empathy from their fellow co-workers so that their leadership is seen to be legitimate and deserving. Choosing the right leaders for the day-to-day functioning of the Cooperative is vital to consensual leadership and a harmonious (rather than conflicting) labour process. There is continuous interaction among workers and site leaders regarding the division of labour and procedures at the worksite. For example, everyone – that is, site leaders and all the workers on the site – eats the prepared lunches together and the lunch hour has become a forum for deliberation and discussion about the worksite. While there is a great deal of inclusive deliberation, once a decision is made by the site leader, everyone must abide by it. Disobeying site leaders' instructions, dereliction of duty, financial irregularities and deliberate lapses in performance receive disciplinary action, which is rarely needed. Indeed, perhaps the best testament to this style of running the Cooperative is the relatively infrequent need for disciplinary action. Disciplinary action is also accompanied by social rebuke (all disciplinary actions are publicly reported at the annual general body meeting), which proves to be even more effective in pressuring and monitoring worksites.

Communication and discipline are two-way processes and site leaders and the board of directors are equally bound by the same collective discipline as ordinary members. For example, during the last decade 35 leaders and four members of the board faced disciplinary action for their unbecoming behaviour as leadership and lapses in discipline.[1] In most cases, the leaders and board members were removed from their leadership positions and in extreme cases were dismissed from the Cooperative. Being a site leader or board member does not afford special privileges in terms of disciplinary processes, but rather the same rules impartially apply to everyone. The Cooperative's ability to impartially apply disciplinary rules to everyone has been a crucial element in its success. It has shown itself capable of making hard and uncomfortable decisions when such action is necessary, but unlike capitalist firms, it has done so through a transparent, deliberative, and consensual framework.

Another key to the Cooperative's efficiency is the regular communication among the different levels of the Cooperative. For example, site leaders are in touch with the board of directors in the daily meetings at the Cooperative's head office to review the day's work. For logistical reasons, site leaders from distant worksites attend the meetings once in two or three days. All the site leaders, board members, and technical staff attend the weekly meetings to discuss the status of the worksites. The worker members participate in the monthly meetings where new developments are reported and members can raise criticisms of site leaders or decisions taken by the board of directors. This entire process from daily meetings

[1] In the case of three of the board members, they were all disciplined for 'unbecoming' behaviour outside of the Cooperative, not for behaviour within the Cooperative. And a large proportion of the leaders were disciplined for approving the falsified records without checking them.

on site with workers and site leaders to the monthly general body meetings are direct democracy at work. While engaging in participatory deliberation and holding so many meetings at the various levels – daily site meetings, daily leadership meetings, weekly review meetings, monthly general body meetings, and annual general body meetings – involves a cost in terms of time and energy, it also produces a sense of collective ownership, solidarity, and common mission that contributes to enhancing productivity.

PARTICIPATION AND MARKET COMPETITIVENESS

The major challenge for ULCCS in competing with private contractors is that the Cooperative cannot underbid the private contractors either through curtailing the benefits of workers or through cheating on materials and specifications agreed in the contracts. And since public works projects are notorious for corruption and manipulation, these obstacles prove to be a very serious handicap. The adherence to the contract specifications is a principle that the Cooperative has always considered sacrosanct and has contributed to its stellar reputation in the industry. In its entire history, there have been only two instances of complaints and enquiry regarding the quality of its work. On both occasions, investigations into the complaints revealed that the complaints were deliberate acts by certain vested interests to malign the Cooperative.

The ULCCS's well-known reputation for quality work has led to a steady expansion of work contracts from non-governmental agencies (such as schools and cooperative banks) that do not have to go for public tenders, but have the freedom to negotiate and settle contracts. Another indicator of its success is the rapid increase in its portfolio of centrally sponsored PMGSY road projects. The guidelines of these road projects contain very strict quality specifications and bill payments are paid only after quality tests are conducted by central government agencies. As a result, most private contractors keep away from PMGSY road projects as there is little room for their nefarious activities. By contrast, the Cooperative is often specifically recommended by authorities to participate in the tender for these projects.

The state government gives 10 per cent preference to cooperatives. Nevertheless, this 10 per cent preference is barely sufficient to overcome the handicap from strict adherence to quality norms. Thus, it is not the government's preferential policy that accounts for the Cooperative's ability to compete with private contractors. Rather the Cooperative's competitive edge comes from its high labour productivity, which stems from both the effective use of technology and diligence of workers, including their skill, effort, and commitment. Construction is a labour intensive process and skilled and committed workers are a vital asset. For example, the quality and cost of an ordinary macadam road depend on the thickness of the different layers, the effectiveness of red earth blinding, the evenness in the mixing of the tar, and its timely application on the metal layer. All of these steps require skill, diligence, and commitment from workers. Similarly, in building construction the main body of work is concreting which requires close cooperation of large numbers of workers. The making of the concrete mixture with right proportions of aggregates and water, its timely application on the form work, effective and uniform compacting and sufficient watering of the concrete for curing are dependent on skilled workers coordinating their work efficiently. Thus, the skill and commitment of workers is a major competitive asset of the Cooperative.

The cost of construction is also dependent upon seamless sequencing of the different activities and timely completion of the work. In order to achieve this, the Cooperative must avoid cost over-runs – which are borne by the Cooperative – and locking of scarce working capital in an unfinished project. ULCCS appreciates the importance of these issues and has managed to have timely completion of its work projects nearly all of the time. When time over-runs happen they are very often beyond the control of Cooperative (e.g., the failure to get the worksite in time and weather conditions). While some factors are out of its control, a crucial ingredient to timely completion is the workers themselves. Workers motivated to stick to the time table and avoid the unnecessary waste of resources (such as tar, metals, and cement) are critical to the Cooperative's successful completion of projects on time. Clearly, workers and not simply supervisors or managers are vital to ULCCS's success.

The advent of automatic mixing machines, vibrators, concrete pumps, road laying and levelling machinery sharply reduced the dependency on the skill of the traditional workers in road making and concreting. Nevertheless, even the new machineries are not robotic and require highly skilled workers to operate them, just fewer of them. The lack of experience in some of these equipment and rapid sequencing of the construction activities in multi-story buildings compelled the Cooperative to subcontract the concreting work to a private firm. But the Cooperative used the subcontract experience to learn how to do the work itself. Thus, it turned the entire process of building UL Cyber Park into a learning experience and as a result it has sufficiently enhanced the skill of its workforce to enable the Cooperative to enter into the market for larger buildings. While mechanization requires fewer workers, the Cooperative has managed to grow its workforce by increasing the number of work projects it can undertake at any given time. Thus, there was no opposition to mechanization in the Cooperative because the rapid expansion of turnover translated into an increase in the overall demand for workers. At the same time, the Cooperative's policy of skill enhancement of workers provides avenues for occupational mobility into the new machine based skills.

As the experiences of ULCCS make clear, there is a positive relation between participation and productivity. The greater awareness of workers regarding the overall functioning of the Cooperative and the details of the project they are involved in is complemented by a high level of satisfaction regarding the wages, fringe benefits, working conditions and the general positive environment in the Cooperative. A contented workforce contributes to higher productivity and hence market competitiveness.

THE CONSTRAINTS TO PROFIT MAXIMIZATION?

Cooperatives do not seek to maximize profits and are insulated from the share market compulsions. For mainstream economists this is a criticism levelled against cooperatives. However, for cooperatives this is an important strength in their organizational functioning. The objective of ULCCS is to provide employment with steadily improving wages and good working conditions for its workers as well as quality infrastructure to the customers. Given the fact that much of its work (such as roads and public buildings) is for public consumption, its own members also indirectly benefit from its quality construction as consumers of public goods. For the cooperative to survive, however, it must also generate surplus, which is distinct from profit maximization and increasing share dividends for shareholders.

ULCCS has steadily increased the real wages of its workers. For example, the real wage earnings have risen by 150 per cent between 1981-86 and 2011-14. The various additional benefits enjoyed by the workers have also risen at a faster rate so that their share of the total emoluments has increased from 27 per cent to 32 per cent during the same period. Therefore the overall real emoluments increased by 170 per cent. For example, in 2013-14 the average monthly wage received by worker members is Rs 15,000 and total emoluments Rs 22,594. These rewards are, by any standards, much higher than the prevalent earnings in the private sector. Comparable general contractors employ only a relatively small core team of workers who receive relatively high wages, though still lower than the wages in the Cooperative, and the additional emoluments they receive are much lower. The majority of a private contractor's workforce are wage workers employed by subcontractors and receive much lower wages and hardly any additional emoluments. The inequality in wages in the private sector is also much higher than in the Cooperative, as highly skilled workers receive extra high wages in the private sector and unskilled workers receive especially low wages.

For a brief period in the Cooperative's history it tried to compete by under quoting in the tender process. In order to do this, the board of directors – who is empowered to make decisions about tenders – involved all members in the decision making process regarding tenders that they were under quoting on. Since it does not indulge in petty thieving, the Cooperative could only execute under quoted projects when workers were willing to work longer, harder days and often for low wages. Every time the board faced this situation, it placed the issue on the table at a general body meeting and it was up to the workers to decide to what extent they were willing to concede to the contract. If the workers did not want the contract, the board would not sign the contract. The Cooperative no longer has to under quote on projects for its survival and has shifted its strategy to increase the labour productivity through mechanization so that wages and benefits of the workers are not tampered with in any circumstance.

ULCCS not only uses transparent participatory deliberation to decide on projects, but also provides full financial disclosure at the annual general body meetings. The gross profit margin significantly varies from worksite to worksite depending upon the type, size, and location of the project as well as the rate contracted. The list of all the completed works with the statement of revenue and expenditure is presented in the annual general body meetings. As they understand the different worksites, the workers accept that the profit margin cannot be same at all worksites and therefore they do not link their wages to output. It is the overall gross profit margin of the Cooperative that is important because it incorporates overheads such as establishment charges, interest charges and importantly additional incentives to workers. The resultant net profit is, thus, only a very small percentage of the turnover and the dividend paid to shareholders is even a smaller percentage. At first sight, the 0.3 per cent dividend paid to members who have invested Rs 3 crore in the share capital might look ridiculously small. But added to this is the member incentive of 10 per cent of the shareholding, and thus the Cooperative guarantees a steady return to the capital invested.

THE QUESTION OF ACCUMULATION

Accumulation is a distinctive feature of a capitalist firm. Unlike the pre-capitalist mode of production, the competitive market conditions compel capitalists to accumulate resulting in continuous expansion of capacity, improvement in technology and the reorganization of production. A worker cooperative is constrained to participate in this expanded reproduction cycle for two reasons. First, it does not attempt to maximize profit and to that extent is unable to generate surplus that could be saved and invested. This is true for ULCCS whose net profit and consequently the reserves put aside is meagre in relation to its turnover. Second, a worker cooperative lacks the motivation for accumulation to the extent that it is insulated from pressures generating from commodity and share markets. In the case of ULCCS the question of share market compulsions does not arise as the shares of the worker members are not tradable and cannot be inherited. At the time of retirement, every member is entitled only to the face value of the share owned. The members of the Cooperative do not have a diversified investment portfolio apart from their Rs 3 crore shareholding in the Cooperative – which would constitute a substantial proportion of their savings and therefore would be averse to risk investments.

Yet, a key feature of ULCCS has been its success in modernization and diversification during the past two decades. The Cooperative is on par with its major competitors in Kerala with regards to using and deploying the most advanced automatic machinery available in the state. The value of investment in machinery has increased by thirteen-fold from Rs 2.35 crore to Rs 31 crore during the last decade (2004-05/2013-14). There has also been significant diversification of its activities. The Cooperative is transforming itself from being a mere contractor into a service provider leasing out commercial space in the industrial park and selling residential accommodation space that it has invested in and constructed. The Cooperative is also growing into a total solution provider with its own design team and separate divisions for some of the finishing work such as plumbing, electrification and interior decoration. It has already diversified into sectors not directly connected with construction such as tourism and IT software. Moreover, the ULCCS is not following a conservative strategy of risk aversion which is the expected behaviour from a worker cooperative.

The most important reason for its risk taking is the fact that ULCCS is not insulated from the competitive pressures of the product market, despite the fact that it is insulated from the share market. Indeed, it faces severe competition from private contractors who, as we have already noted, have the competitive advantage of resorting to corrupt practices and petty thieving. In such a situation, contracts can be secured either by squeezing the wages and other labour benefits or through increasing the labour productivity through aggressive modernization. The first option is not acceptable to the Cooperative, and thus the second option of productivity enhancing investment is the only route open. The workers fully understand that modernization is necessary in order to protect their jobs and wage gains. As long as their real wages and benefits steadily improve and relatively higher wage parity with the private sector is maintained, ULCCS workers will continue to support management's strategy of investment for modernization. What is interesting to note is that though the workers do not maximize profit, they also do not attempt to maximize wages, but rather strike a rational balance between the two, taking into account the need for investment in guaranteeing future employment and wages.

The rationale for diversification is even more interesting as it demonstrates the workers' concern for future generations. The present workers cannot hope to reap the benefits from diversification by entering into tourist services and even less the software services. Nevertheless, there is a near consensus among worker members not only for modernization but also for diversification. The workers take an even longer time horizon view in their willingness to invest in diversification. Diversification will improve the employment prospects of their children whose aspirations have moved away from construction and other manual work to high value adding and high paying jobs.

The question arises as to how this expansion could be financed given the low profit margin of the Cooperative. The expansion has largely been credit financed with deposits collected from the public being the most important component, followed by bank credit and own reserves of the Cooperative. The past record of the Cooperative and the prestige it enjoys have been important factors enabling it to source credit from the market. While it has successfully raised credit, the interest burden, which is the first claimant on gross profit, has steadily increased. The delays in government payments for the work completed have forced the Cooperative to borrow heavily to meet its working capital requirements. As a result, the interest burden has continuously risen and claims nearly half the gross profit generated. In this sense, the burden of investing in credit finance is fully borne by the surplus generated by the workers in the Cooperative. It does not affect the earnings and conditions of the workers, which strengthen the autonomy of management decisions. The standard accounting practice by which the capital expenditure is not presented in the profit and loss account, but only as assets in the balance sheet, effectively camouflages the investment.

The high degree of autonomy that the board of directors enjoys was an important factor in fashioning a strategy of modernization and diversification. Again, the board consists of elected worker representatives with proven managerial ability and who enjoy full confidence of the members. The management has remained free from partisan controversies and allegations of corruption. A technically equipped management team consisting of more than 150 engineers and senior administrators assist the board, but do not have decision making authority. Thus, even though modernization and diversification have brought in highly skilled specialists into the Cooperative, it has not changed the worker-led power structure of the Cooperative.

THE DEGENERATION HYPOTHESIS

The standard economic theory argues that the success of a worker cooperative would also be the cause of its downfall – that is, its degeneration into a capitalist firm. As discussed in Chapter 6, as the area operation began to spread away from its home region and the supply of workers willing to travel to distant centres for construction declined, the proportion of temporary non-member workers who were recruited began to sharply rise and reached approximately 81 per cent in 2001. The inherent danger in this trend was quickly realised by the Cooperative, and as result decided to introduce a category of C class membership, who enjoy all the full wage benefits of A class members but do not have voting rights in the annual general body meeting. Currently the proportion of non-members in the workforce has been reduced to below 40 per cent, including workers from within Kerala and migrants from outside the state. Despite its decision to open its membership to migrant workers, the nature of contracts still require that the Cooperative employs at least a small proportion of temporary workers, including highly skilled workers. Nevertheless, the ULCCS is determined to expand its in-house capabilities so that dependency of subcontractors can be minimized. Mechanization has transformed the worksites and many of the existing skilled worker categories are rendered unnecessary or de-skilled. This has led to a new division of labour and the pace of work is linked to the rhythm of the machinery. The changes pose a potential danger in that workers may lose the sense of involvement and bonds of solidarity. The Cooperative is aware of these potential dangers and has responded by deepening democracy in three ways. First, it has deepened its commitment to transparent, open deliberation. For example, a total picture of the project is presented to the workers in the monthly meetings where workers are given a chance to engage the ideas. Second, it has re-prioritized the feedback mechanism from the workers by strengthening the daily and weekly meetings of site leaders and the board. Third, the Cooperative is improving its skills development programmes in order to provide opportunities for occupational mobility through re-skilling and enhancing the skills of workers.

Another lurking danger is the erosion of the spirit and commitment of the pioneer generation among contemporary workers. Until the phase of rapid expansion, the majority of the members were sons or relatives of the pioneering generation, but this has markedly changed with the growth in new workers with little kinship or local ties to the Cooperative. There is a general opinion that the quality of the deliberations at the annual general body meetings has declined and the willingness of workers to do extra work has weakened. There is no easy solution to this trend other than continued education of the workers about the history of the Cooperative, the traditions of commitment and sacrifice, and the principles and values that have made the ULCCS what it is today. Thus, the survival of ULCCS as a genuine cooperative is political. It must generate values of cooperation in a society in which market values dominate.

Clearly, the nature of the local society and politics in which the cooperative is embedded are crucial. The emergence and growth of the radical left culture in Malabar and specifically the home locality of the ULCCS were vital to its emergence and survival over the past 90 years. The working of ULCCS is remarkable for its deep political commitment to egalitarianism, workers' welfare and social progress without ever displaying narrow political party sectarianism. The Cooperative is seen to be a forum of wage workers irrespective of caste, creed, or political affiliation. In this way, the ULCCS could be a harbinger of a new development and political culture that is essential for Kerala today.

GLOSSARY

Amsam: The lowest unit of revenue administration in Malabar, a sub-division within a taluk.

Atmavidya Sangham: An organization founded by Vagbhatananda in 1917 in order to propagate his teachings of mutual understanding, mutual love, peace and cooperation.

avarna: A section of people considered outside the pale of the caste (varna) system, considered 'untouchables'.

benami: Land or property held under a fictitious name or under the name of a third party to circumvent land ceiling and/or other regulations.

brahmaswam: Lit. property of brahmins; land and assets transferred to brahmins.

cadjan leaves: Interwoven coco-palm leaves for thatching.

desam: An administrative unit roughly corresponding to a village.

devaswam: Lit. property of God; land and assets transferred to temples.

ezhava: An intermediate caste in Kerala, largely composed of inferior tenants, agricultural labourers, and toddy tappers.

jenmi: The traditional landed gentry of Kerala.

kanam tenants: Tenants of large tracts of land in Kerala with supreme autonomy over the land till the expiry of the lease-period. This mode of tenancy has now been abolished.

kuri kallyanam: A notice for marriage.

kutcha [huts]: Houses made of natural materials such as mud, grass, bamboo, thatch or sticks.

Manacaudu theru: A street where the families of the saliya community – a traditional weaving community – live.

Mappila: The member of a Muslim community in the northern parts of Kerala.

nair: A dominant caste cluster in Kerala which includes several castes, not all of whom bear the surname 'Nair'.

Namboodiris: Hindu brahmins in Kerala.

orverum pattakkar : Tenants-at-will.

panam payattu: A money gathering game. A popular method in rural areas to collect money for construction of houses, marrying off daughters, sending sons to the Gulf, or meeting other dire financial needs.

panchayat/gram panchayat: The term refers to a democratic body at the village level.

pucca [houses]: Houses made with high quality materials throughout, including the floor, roof, and exterior walls.

tar thookkal: The task of sweeping and cleaning the paths before constructing roads.

kallu chadal: The task of laying stones on the paths as the first step in the construction of roads.

Thachu Sastharam: 'Scripts of science in building construction' – the science of carpentry.

thiyyas: The rough equivalent of the ezhava caste members in Malabar.

uralars: Hereditary temple custodians.

INDEX